D0201123

THE GRAND TOUR

THE
GRAND TOUR

—

ADAM O'FALLON PRICE

DOUBLEDAY

NEW YORK LONDON TORONTO

SYDNEY AUCKLAND

Copyright © 2016 by Adam O'Fallon Price

All rights reserved. Published in the United States by Doubleday, a division of Penguin Random House LLC, New York, and distributed in Canada by Random House of Canada, a division of Penguin Random House Canada Limited, Toronto.

www.doubleday.com

DOUBLEDAY and the portrayal of an anchor with a dolphin are registered trademarks of Penguin Random House LLC.

Grateful acknowledgment is made to the following for permission to reprint previously published material:

Alfred Music: "The Grand Tour," words and music by George Richey, Norris D. Wilson, and Carmol Tayor, copyright © 1974, renewed by Al Gallico Music Corp. and EMI Algee Music Corp. All rights reserved. Reprinted by permission of Alfred Music.

Hal Leonard Corporation: "I Can Help," words and music by Billy Swan, copyright © 1974 by Combine Music Corp., copyright renewed. All rights administered by Sony/ATV Music Publishing LLC. All rights reserved. Reprinted by permission of Hal Leonard Corporation.

Jacket design by Michael J. Windsor
Jacket images: (car) Bill Pugliano/Getty Images; (old man) Jne Valokuvaus/
Shutterstock; (young man) Helder Almeida/Shutterstock; (beer bottles)
Ansis Klucis/Shutterstock; (paper) phloxii/Shutterstock

LIBRARY OF CONGRESS CATALOGING-IN-PUBLICATION DATA
Names: Price, Adam O'Fallon.
Title: The grand tour / by Adam O'Fallon Price
Description: New York : Doubleday, 2016.
Identifiers: LCCN 2015031540l ISBN 9780385540957 (hardcover) |
ISBN 9780385540964 (ebook) |
Classification: LCC PS3616.R497
G73 2016 | DDC 813/.6—DC23
LC record available at https://lccn.loc.gov/2015031540

MANUFACTURED IN THE UNITED STATES OF AMERICA

1 3 5 7 9 10 8 6 4 2

First Edition

For Elizabeth:

first reader, last love

I have nothing here to sell you,
Just some things that I will tell you,
Some things I know will chill you to the bone.

— GEORGE JONES, "THE GRAND TOUR"

THE GRAND TOUR

CHAPTER ONE

———

OCTOBER 2005

ir?"

No.

"Sir!"

Someone shook him awake. A blonde woman blurred into view. He looked up at her, momentarily uncomprehending and depersoned. She was bent close over him, gripping his shoulders with painted fingers, engulfing him in her cloying perfume, a mist of candied strawberry.

"Yes," he said, feigning full consciousness.

"You have to leave."

"Yes."

"You have to leave, sir." The hostile corporate courtesy in that "sir" brought him closer to his senses. She wanted him to leave, but leave what? As his vision cleared, his first clue was provided by the blue tunic she wore, with a winged insignia over the breast. Another clue, quickly following the first, was the rows of seats behind her, telescoping forward to a point where his bad eyes couldn't focus. It all came back to him in roughly the form of a second-person haiku:

Your name is Richard Lazar and
You are on the first stop of your book tour and
You took too much Ambien

"Where is everyone?" he asked, grappling futilely with the thin airplane blanket twisted around his arms like a straitjacket.

"They already disembarked. I've been trying to wake you for a while. I thought you might have, that you were—"

"No, apparently not."

In one violent motion, he wrested the blanket away from himself and rose to his feet, nearly falling sideways into the flight attendant in the process. She stepped back with her hands in front of her, palms up, as though giving plenty of space to a person having some sort of fit. He steadied himself, unwedged his suitcase from the overhead compartment, and lumbered down the aisle, jouncing side to side on dead legs. A friend of his back in Phoenix had given him some pills to take to make the flight easier. Well, they had done that, he thought. Combined with the pint of vodka he'd polished off in the plane's bathroom, they'd made the flight very, very easy—the only problem was actually getting off the plane.

He frankensteined it through the cabin and up the long jet bridge and emerged into the fluorescence of the shabbiest boarding gate he'd ever seen. He hadn't seen many—the result of a lifelong fear of flying coupled with a general disinclination to go anywhere—but this was certainly the shabbiest. Several ceiling panels were half rotten with brown water stains, and one was missing entirely, providing a nice view of the filth-caked girders above. A darkened McDonald's brooded to itself across the empty room.

A tall kid wearing glasses, a backpack, and the faintest ghost of a beard stood alone holding a sign. R M LAZAR, it said in big block letters, each of which seemed to have been laboriously filled in with a Sharpie. He rolled his suitcase up, and the kid held the sign to his chest, as though to protect himself from a blow. His fine brown hair was swept in a delicate fringe across a high, worried forehead. Richard assumed the hairstyle was an attempt on the kid's part to hide what looked like a palimpsest of acne.

"Mr. Lazar?" the kid said.

"Richard. You're Lance?"

"Vance Allerby."

2

Vance lowered the sign and extended his hand with a look of such dignified, grave ceremony that Richard had to fake a coughing spell in order to disguise very real laughter. "Wow," he said. "Excuse me."

As they shook, the kid took a breath and launched into what was clearly a rehearsed speech: how on behalf of the university, how happy they were, how if there was anything they could do, and so on. He concluded, "And as the founding member and president of your regional fan club, the WARL-Aux, I just wanted to say that, on a personal level, this is a real honor for me."

"On behalf of the what?" Richard disengaged his hand.

"The Washington Area Richard Lazar Auxiliary."

It took him a few seconds, with Vance looking at him expectantly, but he finally got it. "The Warlocks. Jesus. How many other Warlocks are there?"

"At present?"

"Yes, at present."

Vance blinked at him. "Well, right now, it's just me. But I'm hoping to expand the operation."

Richard teetered on his rubbery legs, resisting the urge to look around and see if he was being fucked with. He was struck by a feeling that had become common, almost unremarkable, over the last year—that without realizing exactly when or how it had happened, he had been transported to an alternate dimension. This dimension was similar to the one in which he'd lived his whole life, but at certain moments, such as this one, it became transparently outlandish and far-fetched. Recently, for instance, a man who signed his missives *Sgt. Ricky* had obtained Richard's address and begun sending him maps of Vietnam with certain cities crossed out. It was nice to have fans—too bad none of them was sane. Or female.

"Well," he said, "it's an honor to be here. Which way is out?"

"Oh, sorry." The kid grabbed the suitcase handle and led Richard through the ambitiously named Main Concourse, a widish hallway that featured a shuttered newsstand, a shoeshine operation on indefinite break, and a moribund Subway. A lone TSA agent leaned against the wall and mumbled jargon into a walkie-talkie held sideways.

3

"How was your flight," asked Vance over his shoulder.

"I have no idea."

"Have you ever been to Spillman before?"

"Like so many things in my life, somehow it never happened."

Richard gazed fondly at a small bank of rental kiosks they passed, thinking that maybe it wasn't too late to call off the student escort, but they were already pushing outside into chilly damp air, climbing onto a moving sidewalk. Vance walked ahead, but Richard stopped and caught his breath. The overcast sky looked like a dirty sheet pulled over the horizon, the sun a dim flashlight behind it. Everything in the vicinity seemed to be painted gray by the drizzling mist. The sidewalk deposited him in the hourly parking lot, where Vance was already loading a battered Ford Explorer. Its rusty trunk was a patchwork of bumper stickers: KERRY/EDWARDS 2004, of course, but also COEXIST, SUBVERT THE DOMINANT PARADIGM, ESCHEW OBFUSCATION, BLUE-GRASS PLAYERS DO IT CLEANER, and a decal of the USS *Enterprise*. Vance opened the passenger door, and Richard awkwardly hoisted himself up and in. He looked at the hand-lettered sign in the backseat and imagined Vance bent over it, pen in hand and tongue in the corner of his mouth. The image produced in him a surge of unwelcome affection for the kid.

They drove in silence on the highway for several minutes, during which time Richard could feel Vance glancing over at him, working up his nerve to say something. The kid took a deep breath and said, "I love your books."

"Thanks."

"*Without Leave* is probably my favorite, but I've read them all."

"Well, as president of the WARL-Aux, you'd have to, right?"

Vance seemed to be considering the question. "That's true, I guess," he said. Then, after another moment, "I'm a writer, too, you know."

"No. I didn't know that." Maybe, he thought, he could quietly undo his seatbelt, crack the door, and do one of those stunt-rolls down the sloping adjacent hill that overlooked the town. Maybe he'd wind up at his hotel.

"I mean, not like you. I've lived here all my life." Vance gestured out at the landscape, which mostly consisted of aging seventies strip malls interspersed with pine trees. "You've done things. I like stuff that has the force of experience behind it. You can tell." Earnest intensity radiated from the kid like heat off blacktop, and Richard had to resist the urge to disabuse him of all the ways he was wrong. They drove in silence for another quiet minute, during which time he sensed Vance drawing another extraordinarily deep breath. Finally, Vance said, "Actually, I recently finished something. If you have time, maybe you wouldn't mind taking a look at it?"

"Sure," Richard lied, guessing he would probably mind it a lot.

Keeping his eyes on the road, Vance leaned back and felt around on the backseat and produced a copy box from Kinko's, which he laid on Richard's lap. "No rush," he said. "But I'd love to know what you think about it."

"I'll try and take a look soon," he lied again, with deep regret at having said yes to a student escort. Why did he always make the wrong decision? Why on earth had he agreed to this? Why? Well, he allowed, because he'd liked the idea of someone picking him up at an airport with a sign, that was why. Because it sounded like the royal treatment and not a royal pain in the ass. Also because he'd planned on having a few drinks to celebrate his first night on tour and liked the thought of having a driver. Pride, as ever, goeth before a fall. Live and never learn, that was his credo.

The road they were on curved up a hill, and the city, such as it was, stretched out in the valley beneath them. The buildings were meek and low, mostly constructed from beige brick, and the overall effect was a kind of apologia, as though the city fathers had tried to create as close to the impression of a kind of noncity as was possible while still, in fact, having a city. The inoffensiveness of it offended him. Phoenix—enormous, desiccated, crime-ridden, meth-infested, golfing community that it was—at least didn't worry about hurting anyone's feelings.

"That's the college," said Vance, pointing to the left side of the vista, where there were more trees and more beige buildings. "That's where you'll be speaking tonight."

"What is that?"

"Joel Whittaker Auditorium," said Vance, grandly.

"I see."

"Do you want a tour of campus? Or I could show you downtown."

"I heard something about a hotel."

"Oh, yeah. You're staying at a Comfort Suites."

"A Comfort Suites?"

"By Marriott."

———

The room was neither comfortable nor a suite, although according to the sign it was indeed by Marriott. A whiff of sour cologne lingered in the air, the room's memory of a previous occupant. The air conditioner was on full blast, and when Richard briefly turned the dial down to low, the room began to fill with moist, unfresh air that felt as though it were being pumped in from an adjacent men's locker room. The remote control turned on the TV but would not turn up the volume. Over the bed hung a disturbing painting of a small girl clutching a pail, alone on a beach with a shadow looming in the foreground. It seemed intended to be the shadow of a dune or natural outcropping, but the perspective implicated the viewer as a lurking predator. To make matters worse, the child in the painting bore a close resemblance to Richard's daughter, Cindy, when she was young, all blonde ringlets and even wearing the same kind of old-fashioned gingham dress that his ex-wife, Eileen, had liked to dress her in. On the plus side, there was an Andes mint on the pillow.

He put the mint in his mouth and emptied the contents of his pockets on the nightstand: a handful of unwanted change, mostly pennies; a matchbook from a bar at Phoenix Sky Harbor where he'd gulped down two preflight Bloody Marys prepared by a bartender with thinning hair gelled up in a tattered Mohawk, like the dorsal fin of a malnourished shark; his wallet (Velcro); a five-dollar chip from the Apache Nights Casino in Gila Bend; finally, a cell phone that his agent, Stan, had insisted he buy for the trip. He'd never owned one before and had only operated it once, to assure Stan it worked. There was only one number in it: Stan's office in New York. He was to call whenever he got where he was going, since Stan didn't trust him and treated him like a delinquent teenager, which was more or less completely justified. He managed to navigate the two necessary buttons, and Stan's Brighton Beach monotone magically piped in through the ether.

"Richard. Where are you?"

"In Spillman."

"At the airport?"

"The hotel. The English department sent someone over to pick me up."

"Who?"

"Some kid named Lance. A real eager beaver."

"Well, don't give him too hard a time."

"This place is a shithole, by the way."

"Spillman?"

"Well, yeah, but the hotel."

"You're the one who wanted to save the publisher money on lodging. 'I can sleep anywhere,' you said."

"Yeah, yeah."

"Call me tomorrow from Portland. Break a leg tonight."

"Copy that."

Waiting for the shower to warm up, he stripped down to his antique candy-striped boxers and stood wincing in front of the bathroom mirror. Mirrors were a bad idea these days. His cheeks, over the last few years, had ruthlessly annexed the rest of his face; his eyes, chin, and jaw were a Sudetenland reclaimed by these great twin dictators. His belly's wide expanse pushed his arms up on either side, giving him the look of an Oliver Hardyesque gunslinger about to draw in some twenties gag reel. He'd always been fat, but his fatness had lately made the genre leap from comedy to farce. At his once-a-decade checkup, in March, the doctor had frowned at him over the report on the clipboard—an exhaustive detailing of Richard's bad habits and inadequacies—and asked what he thought the life expectancy was for a fifty-three-year-old, one-hundred-pounds-overweight drinker.

"With advances in modern medicine, who can say?"

"Very funny."

Eventually the doctor had badgered an entirely insincere promise from him to change his ways. Why would he do that, he thought, the shabby hotel room framing him in the mirror—they'd gotten him this far, ha-ha-ha. The unjolly fat man in the mirror scowled back at him. At least he'd somehow hung on to his hair. It was his one point of vanity, a still-thick quiff that he pruned back once a month. Greased into an unruly pompadour when he was much younger, it had looked like the hair of a doo-wop castrato; now, almost totally white and silky, it was the hair of the fantasy grandfather he'd never had, all of the men in his family either dying or disappearing as early as possible, like minor characters in a southern novel about female hardship and togetherness. During the seven-year interregnum between his father's departure and hangdog return, he'd often stayed at the farm of his aunt Polly, whose own husband had, at the ripe old age of forty-one, keeled over obligingly in a distant field—a relatively dignified exit.

He took a shower, got out and toweled off, put on fresh boxers, brushed his teeth, made coffee and drank a cup, regretted not bringing any booze to put in it, drank another cup, took a shit, checked the time, and there were still four hours to kill before he had to go speak. For lack of anything better to do, he picked up the kid's manuscript from the desk. Lifting the lid off the box revealed a thin manuscript, three hole punched with a clear cover, entitled *Infinite Galaxies of Sorrow* by Vance Joseph Allerby. Why had he agreed to read any of it? Just reading the title had exhausted him. He sat on the edge of the bed and turned to the first page.

> *I am alone. We all are, children of the universe, all. We come from dead stars and are destined to return to them.*

He carefully put the manuscript back in its coffin, replaced the lid, and ceremoniously interred it in the small trash can beside the table. Peeking through the venetian blinds, he could see Vance sitting out there in his car, his long, serious face inclined toward what Richard assumed was an equally long, serious book. He'd told Richard he'd just wait for him. A weird kid. When he was Vance's age, founding a fan club, let alone chauffeuring some asshole around town, was just about the last thing he would've been doing. When he was Vance's age, he'd been far too busy flunking out of college, getting drafted, and grimly chasing poontang around Knoxville, Tennessee, in constant mortal terror over his impending deployment to Vietnam.

Shivering from the AC, he went ahead and put on his new suit, which he'd bought specially from Men's Wearhouse for the tour. The pants didn't button all the way, and the jacket was a size or two too small. It was a deep shade of forest green and made of a synthetic material that instantly caused him to pour sweat, but it had also been on sale—Drastic Markdown!—for thirty bucks. The amused clerk had thrown in a red polyester tie as a cruel lagniappe. He hadn't worn a suit in decades, since an abortive stint in the early eighties selling appliances at a Sears in Fresno. After being fired on the showroom floor for failure to hard-sell defective washer-dryer combos to poor people, he'd headed directly outside across a blistering blacktop sea toward the fata morgana of a Holiday Inn lounge, where, after several gin gimlets, he swore a blood oath to the bemused bartender and the small audience of regulars that he'd never again wear a tie. Filled with the drama of the moment as well as six ounces of Beefeater, he'd wrenched off his tie and set it on fire in the toilet to the applause of two delighted old rummies. Yet here he was, in a Comfort Suites by Marriott, inexpertly tugging on a half Windsor. Well, you never knew, did you?

No, you never knew. Facing down his image in the mirror for a second time as he straightened the tie, he was again struck by the sense of having entered an alternate dimension. A dimension in which he had written a book people were buying, and reading, and wanted to hear him talk about. *Hello, my name is Richard Lazar. Good evening. Hi. I wrote a book.* He strode to the door, bravely facing up to the obvious fact that he needed a drink, badly.

Vance startled and looked up from his book when Richard tapped on the car window. He rolled it down, looking excited, or as excited as it seemed possible for his long, sad face to look. "Did you change your mind about that tour?"

Richard said, "I did. Let's start with the nearest bar."

"I don't drink."

"That's fine. You can sit in your car reading"—he leaned into the car to see the cover—"*Don Quixote* there, too, if you want."

"I'm not sure this is such a great idea."

"If it would help, don't consider it a request," Richard said.

———

Vance took them to a place called J. T.S' BULLS-EYE—the sign spelled exactly that way. Sitting in a red vinyl booth defaced with knife slits, Richard drank a series of scotches, and Vance bent to the straw in his Coke. A few rough-looking locals played pool and glanced in their direction, and Vance, with his soft hands and pimples and wispy-faun facial hair, seemed nervous, but Richard wasn't worried. He had gotten old enough that no one messed with him anymore, not even rednecks or idiot teenagers. Too old to mess with, he thought—how depressing.

Vance said, "The manuscript I gave you was a first draft. It's really rough."

Richard said, "Look at her."

A young blonde girl carried a couple of beers across the room. She had the type of cutesy elfin face that would be completely gruesome at forty, but she also had a big, swaying ass showcased by jeans at least two sizes too small. Small ridges of fat rode up over her waistband in the back. She walked over to the guys playing pool, who patted and goosed her around in a friendly way, and Richard was reminded of how long it had been since he'd gotten laid. Or, rather, the fact that he couldn't even remember when the last time was. In his twenties, going a month without seemed like inhumane deprivation, a breach of the Geneva Convention. The text of some awful novelty T-shirt he'd seen a long time ago scrolled through his head: 20S: TRI-WEEKLY, 30S: TRY WEEKLY, 40S: TRY, WEAKLY. There wasn't one for *50s*.

"You like that?"

"What?"

"Come on. The girl that just walked by. The behind on her."

"She's all right. But I was wondering if you have any advice you could give me about revising your work. How many drafts do you do?"

"My second wife, Carole, had a behind like that. Bigger, actually. She was built like a tractor, big wheels in the back. Any physical exertion and her face would get splotchy, so it was like riding this big red tractor around when we made love."

Richard turned his glass up and chewed the ice. Vance looked up at the Budweiser clock over the bar and said, "Do you want to go now?"

"No, damn it," Richard said. "There's an hour left."

"We need to leave time to drive and park, for you to meet everyone, get set up."

"Speaking of getting set up." Richard initiated the process of standing and made a circular motion at the bartender.

"You've had four of those already," said Vance.

"Getting limbered out. Up. You really don't drink?"

"No."

"Why not?"

Vance looked back over at the girl as she lined up a pool shot. "People do stupid things when they're drunk."

"Great things, too," said Richard. "Every important moment of my life, there's been alcohol around. Why do you think people get so drunk after weddings?"

"I don't know why people get married at all," Vance said.

"Touché."

Richard got another drink and a Coke refill for Vance. They sat there listening to songs the locals were playing on the jukebox, all of them murkily familiar to Richard, as if he'd heard them once while he was asleep. One was about Mr. Saturday Night Special who puts you six feet in a hole, and in another, the singer shrieked about the jungle over a bunch of shimmery guitar parts that sounded like snakes being beaten into holes in the ground. He hadn't listened to music in years, had completely stopped caring about music around the time of his second divorce. Carole had expensively—and needlessly, in Richard's estimation—had their condo equipped with speakers in every room, even the closets. She was the kind of person who required a sound track at all times; even a trip to the bathroom for a number two had to be accompanied by some squelchy disco tune. When she divorced him, she pointedly kept all the music, a punitive maneuver wasted on Richard, who felt the silence in his new apartment as a Bedouin in his tent might feel a rare, delicious desert breeze.

Vance said, "Like I said, the thing I gave you is rough, but I thought you might have some pointers. It's kind of a memoir, like your book. It's about me and my mother."

"Sounds like a barnburner." The blonde girl walked back to the bar and smiled as she passed them. "She likes you."

A deep crimson blazed from the hollow of Vance's long neck to his jawline and thin cheeks. "I don't think so."

"So you don't drink, and you don't chase tail. What do you do for fun?"

"Fun?"

"Yeah, fun. 'A good time.' Things you do to distract yourself from the pain and terror of being alive."

Vance sat there for a moment, and it occurred to Richard that the kid might really have no idea what he was talking about. Finally, Vance said, "Well, I read."

"Oh boy."

"What? Reading is fun."

"Reading is great, but it's not fun. People don't read at parties."

"I do."

"Jesus Christ. I'm just saying, don't waste your youth being too smart for beer and girls. What else do you do?"

"I write."

"If writing is fun," said Richard, "you're doing it wrong."

———

The smallish auditorium was full and getting fuller. But then, he reasoned, there wasn't much else to do in this piece-of-shit town. He sat in the front row in his hot green suit, sweating and reeking and looking, he knew, like some kind of mentally impaired car-dealership employee at a Christmas Sale-a-Bration. People continued to file in and stare at him all the way to their seats. It was an awkward arrangement, and he was glad he was drunk enough not to care.

Richard looked around. Farther down the row, Vance sat and talked to an older guy with a Sundance Kid mustache and bolo tie. A creative writing professor if he'd ever seen one. Probably poetry—the lowest of the low. Eileen had dragged him to enough faculty parties for him to know. A bunch of worthless, forced eccentrics, he thought, not a wishbone of talent to snap amongst the lot of them. Get cornered at a party by that type and it's all over, forget any hot nooky wandering around.

The director of the English department, a friendly, serene fellow whose name Richard had thus far found completely impossible to remember, approached and patted him on the arm.

"I'm going to go up and say a few words to introduce you, then you're on, okay?"

"And what happens?"

"Normally people read a chapter from their book."

"Okay. That's it?"

"Well, normally people take questions afterward."

"Okay. Then normally what? Normally."

The director gave him a complex, piercing look of amusement and concern, leaned in, and said, "Normally, we go get shitfaced at a restaurant afterward. You've done that part beforehand, though. Then, if you're wondering, normally there's a party at someone's house and my wife takes her shirt off and embarrasses me. Normally."

"Sounds good."

The director patted him again on the arm, then walked to the podium. The crowd applauded loudly. He cleared his throat and spoke, occasionally looking at Richard.

"I'm going to keep this brief. The university is pleased to kick off our fall semester reading series with Richard Lazar. Richard's book *Without Leave*—a memoir about his experience in Vietnam—was published earlier this year to widespread acclaim. It revived the career of a writer the *Chicago Tribune* called 'a forgotten treasure, lost on the seabed of literary detritus, luckily reclaimed.' Dan Rosenbluth from the *New York Times* said of Richard, 'He is, perhaps, the most talented writer overlooked by literary culture in America.' Ladies and gentlemen, Richard Lazar."

Richard walked to the podium, to a welter of violent applause. Looking around the auditorium at people's faces, he was struck by their general look of happy attention and interest. It seemed truly amazing to him that any of them cared what he had written, what he thought about anything. The crowd's smiling indulgence reminded him of Eileen and himself watching two-year-old Cindy climb the stairs. It made him wish he'd brought along the pellet gun he kept at home for shooting coyotes, so he could fire off a few rounds into that unbroken wall of condescension. He suddenly felt very tired and wanted to lie down on the cool, tile floor.

He put the book on the podium. His book. It was a hardback, and the cover featured a picture of him in his army greens, taken by his father after Basic and before shipping out, the only time he could remember the old man being proud of him. His name was embossed across the bottom in a slick typeface. Looking down at the cover, his name, the podium, and the blur of faces in front of him, he momentarily forgot what he was supposed to be doing and just stood there.

"Sorry," he said, shaking his head. There was a murmur of generous laughter as he fumbled the book open and thumbed past the table of contents and dedication page, the deckled edges conveying an authenticity and gravitas about his life that felt richly undeserved. Where was the goddamn chapter? An uncomfortably long silence ensued, but he eventually found the folded page corner, cleared his throat a few times, and began to read.

CHAPTER TWO

I had been AWOL two days by the time I reached the outskirts of Saigon. The last stretch, I spent in the back of an old Datsun truck filled with burlap bags of rice. My lap was heavy with the rucksack that I cradled like a fat, lolling baby. The truck had no shocks, and at first I'd felt every pebble on the Nha Trang Highway as we clattered along. But I was so exhausted by two days of walking and hiding in the bush that I still managed to more or less immediately pass out against the aluminum ridging of the flatbed. Near the city, we hit a bomb crater in the road, and I jerked half awake in malarial sweat, staring at a cloudy sky, reacquainting myself with the unlikely fact that I was in the back of a Vietnamese jalopy hidden amongst rice bags.

The truck stopped near a tin-walled depot. The farmer came around back, lowered the tailgate, and let me out. I thanked him, but he was already hauling bags out of the back as though I wasn't there. I'd paid him twenty dollars for the ride—boo-koo bucks—but I knew it was the sidearm I'd waved that had really bought the ride. I walked away, down a half-paved road lined with a combination of improvised hovels and unreliable-looking, unpainted concrete buildings. It struck me that I didn't even know if this was Saigon.

The farmer had nodded when I asked, but then he would have nodded at anything I said.

Assuming this was Saigon, I had no idea where I was going. I knew what I wanted to find—U.S. Army Command, which I'd heard was located somewhere in the city—but where was it? Had I thought there would be a map somewhere? Perhaps a friendly tour guide? An abundance of English-speaking locals happy to help the dumbass GI stumbling around? I don't remember what I was thinking. What I do remember was the Vietnamese turning as I walked by, the feeling of horrible exposure. In places, the streets did become busier, but the bustle brought no sense of safety—instead, it was more eyes watching me, more heads turning as I passed. I was American, and filthy, dressed in camos and combat boots. Although I'd changed into a Miami Dolphins T-shirt, I looked exactly like what I was, a nineteen-year-old soldier who'd wandered away from his platoon.

I'm sure if I had been more self-possessed, not to mention less shit-scared, I could have stopped someone and asked, and kept asking until I found a local who spoke English and could have pointed me in the right direction. But I felt like the first person I talked to would scream or knife me or ring some silent alarm that would instantly summon ARVN military police. So lacking any better plan, I walked. I walked with my head down, superstitiously turning right whenever I could. I walked past the city limit, a place where grass and dirt visibly gave over to concrete, where the tensed and grasping fingers of the city took hold. I walked past a long, narrow shantytown near the Hue River, in whose churning water old women doing their wash crouched like gargoyles. I walked through an enormous unguarded yard of scavenged cars, past a half-burnt church or school—I couldn't tell which—under a rusted and disused railway trestle that reminded me of where I grew up, in East Tennessee.

As I walked, I sometimes thought about Berlinger. I wished he was with me—Berlinger would have loved the spectacle of a dumb grunt loosed and lost in Saigon. No one enjoyed a clusterfuck more than Mitch Berlinger, and no one had a keener appreciation for the way army organization and superficial polish barely held back lurking, haywire chaos. I imagined his enormous form, the battering V of his crew-cut forehead, like the prow of a battleship, thrown back with wicked merriment at some fuckup or other, someone's misfortune. There was certainly plenty of misfortune here to be merry about. I passed a piebald dog dragging a legless man on a makeshift dolly, the man staring up fixedly at the rising sun as though trying to burn his eyes out and be done for good with knowing what the hell was going on.

Gradually, my circle tightened and I spun back into the neighborhoods, the streets crowded with commerce. A million hunched and blinkered endeavors that didn't even register my presence. Where before I had felt conspicuous, I now felt—not inconspicuous so much as invisible, irrelevant. The swarming, chaotic bustle of late afternoon, half the population trying to get home after a long day at work, and the other half desperately trying to hawk them the last of their wares, quelled my fear of immediate calamity. No one cared about me. I relaxed, and even, at certain moments, found myself enjoying the inadvertent sightseeing. I drifted through downtown Saigon, a morass of long, curving colonial buildings. I walked close beside them in shadows, my head down, peering into storefronts that housed bars and gambling parlors and ad hoc temples and pho shops and God knew what else. The air buzzed jaggedly with the noise of hundreds of scooters and motorcycles, rice-burners. The bikes swarmed everywhere, whining dragonflies ridden by small men in caps: green army, Greek fisherman, Yankees, Giants. I watched them circle the central square in a never-ending loop of pursuit and escape.

All at once, I was completely exhausted. My feet ached horribly, and had I leaned against one of the nearby cement stanchions of the colonnade, I would have fallen asleep standing up. Just then, I heard live music playing from somewhere. The sound issued from the dark innards of a nearby bar—a place called Kosy Klub, if the hand-lettered sign next to the door was to be believed. I entered. The Kosy Klub was a long room, with a wooden bar on one side, and a rock-and-roll band playing loud in the back. The plywood stage was overlit, and you could see too clearly the room's ceiling, which was also plywood. I asked the girl behind the bar for a beer, but she pointed at a line of bottled sodas. I bought a Coke and sat against the far wall, watching the band.

They were all Vietnamese, with two female lead singers in sequined minidresses, and a male backup band in black vests and wide lapels that looked like they'd gotten lost on the way to a gig at the Holiday Inn Albuquerque. They were pretty good, too, jamming on a familiar tune, although with the muddy amplification and the singers' strange inflections, I couldn't quite place it. Then it clicked—the Supremes, "Someday We'll Be Together." The lead singer pulled a Diana Ross and reached out to the small, attentive crowd, holding her hand upside down and delicately pursing her fingers together as she sang, as though she were holding a small hatchling in her palm. She opened her fingers as the chorus ended, and the bird flew away. I've never felt so alone in my life, even decades later, divorced and living out in the desert with no one else miles around. I was completely, utterly bereft. The band launched into a version of "Love Child," and I closed my eyes.

———

Richard stopped reading. His mouth and throat were a barren stretch of hell, his tongue smacking loudly into the mic with every syllable of every word. "Sorry," he said. "Could I get a glass of water up here, or something?" Vance scurried out of the room, and he stood there, looking down at the blurred type, a mass of infuriating black squiggles. He wiped his forehead with a green sleeve and became conscious of the pooled sweat on his back trickling down into the crack of his ass. For an event he'd idly looked forward to his entire life—reading from a successful book to a room full of interested people—it was surprisingly torturous. A beseeching glance at the director yielded a discreetly signaled *ten minutes.* Vance returned with the water, and Richard forged on:

I awoke to someone shaking my shoulder. It was a small man with a large smile, outsize sunglasses crowning a sleek black head of hair. The band had finished playing, the equipment was gone, and the club had emptied out. It was dark outside, and I realized I must have been asleep for hours.

"You GI?" said the man.

"Huh. No."

"Yes, you GI," he told me. "You want a good time?"

I didn't want a good time. I wasn't horny for the first time since I'd turned twelve. "I'm looking for something."

"You look for girl? I find you girl."

"No. I need to find U.S. Army Command."

"Ussami? Camahn?" The man played with the words, trying to arrange them into the plausible name of a familiar whore.

I scanned the dingy club, for someone who could help me. Just an elderly man bent to his broom, and a prostitute glancing over with a look of avid boredom. "Army headquarters," I tried. He looked at me without comprehension, and I was aware at that moment of how stupid I was being, but it seemed that, having started this line of conversation, I was somehow obliged to see it through. "U.S. Army Command," I said slowly, as though he was hard of hearing or stupid, though, of course, I was the stupid one.

He repeated the words again, then smiled and nodded. "Ahmy," he said, pointing at an imaginary row of medals on my chest, then doing a salute, mock serious. He stretched his arms to his sides, doing a credible impression of a large building.

"Yes."

"Okay, come on. You got ten dollar? Need ten dollar." I pulled out my wallet and gave it to him. He examined the bill with a look of surprise that narrowed into mild contempt as he folded it into his pocket. Reading his mind was not hard: You dumb, fucking asshole. He wasn't wrong.

We trudged down the Rue de Gaulle, past a small square writhing with pigeons, so thick with shit that the old stones looked whitewashed. My tour guide walked quickly, and with my forty-pound bag and dead legs, I struggled to keep up. At first, I thought he was trying to rip me off, disappear with my money, but then I realized if he wanted to do that he would already have been gone;

he was simply moving with the efficiency and speed of a man who knew his city, and who had other places to be. At certain moments I had to resist the urge to call out, as his small form turned a corner or rapidly edged into a crowd of people, many of whom were also clad in tan trousers and thin, white cotton shirts. I kept my eyes on his sunglasses, still perched on his head, which marked him out and occasionally glinted with the reflection of a passing streetlight.

As we walked, we seemed to enter a distinct, different neighborhood. The broad streets grew narrower, and electric lanterns hung from storefronts covered in pictograms: a bear, a child, a car, a laughing man—Berlinger. Vendors cooked fish in large pans over open flames; the smell of fish was, in fact, everywhere, and, having spent two days in San Francisco before my flight to Vietnam, it occurred to me that this was Saigon's Chinatown. The streets grew narrower still, like a mountain crevice tapering into nothing, and for a moment I panicked at the thought of being led into a dead-end ambush. Then the street opened up again, and there, improbably, across a large stone plaza overgrown with green weeds, squatted an enormous building. MACV HEADQUARTERS—MILITARY ASSISTANCECOMMAND, VIETNAM—*according to the peeling wooden sign in front of us. I wouldn't have known the place on sight—I didn't know anything then, much as now—but I could read, at least.*

The man smiled and gestured at the building with a grandiose sweep of his arm, like a game-show host presenting a fantastic prize. Then he was gone. The area was eerily silent and devoid of activity— the locals must have known to cut it a wide berth. In the darkness on the far-left edge of the plaza, there was a small, crumbling brick structure, a neglected former supply shed for the main house. I picked my way into the dark ruins. There, behind a diagonal wall of sloping brick, I found a good place to wait and watch.

HQ was located in a formerly grand nineteenth-century three-story French colonial, still impressive, but with an air of decay, of reclamation by time and the local elements. Its façade was painted an unhealthy mustard yellow, cracked and blistered by the heat. A shutter on the second floor hung at an angle off faulty hinges. Two large flagpoles sprouted from an unkempt circular grass disk in front. The U.S. and South Vietnamese flags drooped overhead in the stifling, hot breeze that blew through the city like a close animal's breath. A long, wide bi-level staircase led up into the building—twice as many stairs to the first landing, then a smaller top staircase that led to a first-floor portico and courtyard. Two guards shared a smoke on the landing, their guns propped against their shoulders with such nonchalance that they almost looked unarmed.

I sat there for a long time, obscured by darkness and shadows, watching them. At some point during my vigil, one of them left and was replaced after a minute or two by another soldier, a difference I could tell because the new man was around a foot taller, a hulking goon whose jutting lantern jaw was visible from seventy-five yards. I put my hand inside my field pack and ran my fingers across the smooth pebbling of the grenade. I imagined tossing it, the thing skittering across the wide landing, the moment of horrible recognition, the compression of air, then the blast that would come, the smoke and shouting.

But no. It would have been satisfying, but it wasn't why I was there. I felt around in my field pack for the 9-mm service revolver, grabbed it, brought it out, and held it in my lap. I brought a T-shirt out, rolled it up, and put it between my neck and shoulder. I leaned sideways, propped in the crook of the wall, and dropped into a thin, itchy sleep. In this way I passed the night: jolting awake every now and then, scanning the area, and falling asleep again, waiting for daylight and Lieutenant Christopher Endicott, waiting to shoot him dead.

———

The auditorium rang with applause for what seemed like an absurdly long time, even though he knew it was entirely sincere. He asked the audience if there were any questions. After a few awkward seconds, an older woman in the front row raised her hand, and said, "Do you mostly write at night or in the mornings?"

"Uh. Mornings, I guess. And afternoons. Not at night."

There was another long pause. The director raised his hand. "Yeah," said Richard, still not remembering the man's name. "Go ahead."

The director shifted in his seat to address both Richard and the crowd. He said, "This is your sixth book. You've been at this for three decades, working on the fringe. Now, in your fifties, you have a book getting serious acclaim. Perhaps you could talk a little about what it's like to finally be getting the recognition you might have felt you deserved all along."

"It's pretty strange."

"I imagine so."

Richard stood there for a few moments, during which the director rearranged himself in his seat, propping his elbow on his knee and his head on his hand, in a parody of anticipation. "It's pretty fucking strange," Richard ventured, but this also didn't seem sufficient. "I don't know what to say about it. I wrote a bunch of books no one gave a shit about, and now they finally do. It's nice, but it's a little late. I wish this had happened twenty years ago, when I still had lots of books left in me."

He wiped the sweat from his forehead again and looked forward to the drinks he would have afterward, the way a condemned prisoner might look forward to supping on sweet manna in the promised land. The director turned and asked if there were any more questions, and Vance raised his hand.

"Yeah. Vance."

Vance, again sounding as though he'd rehearsed the words for days, slowly intoned, "Mr. Lazar, what advice would you give young writers trying to get started?"

"My advice would be don't do it. Learn how to fix cars or computers, something worthwhile that people need. Spend as much time on vacation as possible, kiss lots of girls. Thank you."

———

There was no wine at the reception that followed in the English department lounge, but a buffet table loaded with silver banquet dishes of satay skewers and Swedish meatballs and hot-dog mini-croissants attracted enough people from the reading to pack the room. Richard shook hands with an endless parade of faculty and students, all of whom, infuriatingly, had different names. Afterward, the director and his wife—a petite woman who put her hand on his forearm when they talked and looked at him with such a horrible, bright avidity that he felt sure he was forgetting a previous meeting or tryst or possibly a marriage—and a few other professors all took him to dinner. Vance sat at the corner of the table in stony, intimidated silence. The restaurant was an Italian place decorated in high-cheeseball, opulent Florentine-villa style, with fabric billowing from the ceiling and pillars placed randomly throughout, and a brilliantly colored fresco of cavorting cherubim and nymphs over the open kitchen. The food was not very good, but there was a lot of it, and it was free. The waiter seemed to appear every five minutes with a new bottle of wine. Toward the end of the meal, the director pinged his wineglass, said some nice things, and everyone cheered loudly. Richard was relieved no one asked him for a speech, since he was, by this point, more or less completely stupefied by alcohol.

They piled back into their cars and went to the director's nearby home for some superfluous nightcaps. We have ouzo, the director's wife had told Richard at dinner, with great feeling. We have grappa. The house was located at the summit of a large hill that seemed to take fifteen minutes to ascend. Inside, African masks angled down from the walls in gaping disbelief. Someone put on a bebop record with an incendiary saxophone, greatly increasing the room's ambient confusion. A sequence of joints went around. Richard sank into the depths of a voluminous couch, having conversations with people he didn't know, saying things he forgot almost as soon as the words left his mouth. He talked at Vance for a while, feeling like a cartoon character with an empty speech bubble next to his mouth. Then he spent a long time listening—or rather, cunningly, *pretending to listen*—to a fellow wearing a tyrolean hat with an actual feather in it, who had apparently also written a book, or the chapter of a book, or the foreword, or a blurb, or maybe he'd just read a book once; it was hard for Richard to tell, what with the music and drink and also his intense lack of interest. The director's wife walked by and put her hand on his shoulder.

"Can I get you anything?" she asked.

"Your husband said something about you taking off your shirt."

"Oh, yes," she said. "He hates that."

"I bet."

At an indeterminate point later in the evening, her shirt was off, a fact that inexpressibly gratified him. Then it seemed the party was over, and he was being escorted out, out into the cool, quiet night. Insects skronked their own alien jazz in the trees. He didn't know what kind of trees they were. He had, shamefully, gotten to be almost old with virtually no knowledge of the plant kingdom. He couldn't tell the difference between an oak and a poplar, if there was one. Vance maneuvered him into the car. Then they were driving. They dipped under a railroad trestle, festooned with graffiti: PEZ LOVE VALERY in big ornate script, bright red. True love, dangling upside down with a spray-paint can. He forced Vance to stop at a liquor store, where he bought a pint of something brown. Driving again, Vance said, "Did you really mean that stuff you said tonight?"

"What stuff."

"To fix cars instead of writing. That it's worthless."

He sipped the whiskey. It was so delicious. "Yeah, I did."

"Why have you spent your whole life doing it, then?"

"Because it's the only thing I've ever been remotely good at. Believe me, if I could have been a lion tamer, I would have." Vance said nothing, and Richard said, "Listen, it's not just the writing. It's all worthless, everything. Sorry to break the news to you."

"I don't agree."

"Well, I hate to pull rank here, but what do you know?"

Back at the hotel, he got out of the car and nearly listed over like a ship in high seas. He took a few exploratory steps with his feet set wide apart, almost fell, stopped, and sat down on the pavement. He couldn't get up and felt it wouldn't be so bad to make this his new gig. He'd be the parking-lot guy from now on. Then Vance was beside him, pulling him up. Together, they made the door. Then there was the task of getting the key in the lock, yet another gauntlet to run. Ten or so minutes later, the door creaked open, and a blast of cold air escaped. He pushed his way forward and sat on the edge of the bed.

"Are you okay," said Vance, standing in the threshold.

"First-rate. Tip-top."

The kid didn't say anything, just stared into the room.

"Listen, just forget everything I said, okay? Who cares what I think? I'm a pile of shit. Do your thing, you'll be fine." He would have continued in this vein, but Vance wasn't paying attention, was looking past him. He looked where Vance was looking and saw the manuscript, where he'd left it, in the trash. By the time he looked back around, Vance was already slouching out into the dark lot. Richard tried to climb to his feet, but through the window he saw the kid get in his car and pull away. It sped quickly down the hotel's access road and was gone.

The TV, left on all day, now played a nature show featuring falcons, or perhaps they were condors, attacking goatlike creatures that nibbled obliviously on the sparse grass at the edge of a sheer mountain face. The birds swooped down the craggy cliff faces and grabbed the goat things by their legs, then dropped them down hundreds of feet to their deaths. Without volume it was unclear whether this was done for food or fun. He looked again at the painting over the bed, the likeness of his daughter. After a sportive minute of his wrangling with the phone, it began to ring on the other end.

"Hello?" she said. He could hear a TV loud in the background, canned shrieking laughter.

"Cin, hi. It's your father."

"Oh." The TV volume lowered.

"How are you?"

"Fine."

"Listen, they've got me on this book tour." In an effort to sound less drunk, he spoke slowly and overenunciated every syllable like an octogenarian Brit commentating an antiques show.

"Yeah, Mom said."

"Did she?" He was gratified to hear that Eileen had spoken of him, even though it was probably in bad terms. There was silence on the other end, and he found himself already struggling to keep the conversation afloat. "The book's doing really good," he tried.

"Mazel tov."

"How are you?"

"Same as when you asked ten seconds ago."

"Oh, right. What are you doing?"

"Right now? Getting ready for work."

"I forgot you work nights."

"Well, I've only been doing it for eight years."

More silence. Finally, she said, "I've been looking for another job lately."

"Spying on degenerates losing its shine?" She lived in Las Vegas and worked casino surveillance, a job he found both improbable and distasteful. He would rather she'd have become a teacher or professor, like her mother. Or a drug dealer.

"Jesus. What do you want?"

It was a good question: What did he want? What didn't he want? He lay back on the greasy synthetic floral-print comforter and noticed a halfhearted repair job someone had done on the ceiling directly over the bed. Some caulking agent that resembled shaving cream or Cool Whip was smeared over a hole the size of a large serving plate. What might lurk in the crawlspace over the small hotel room did not bear examination. He closed his eyes. "Do you remember when we bought you that bike? I think you were eight?"

She said, "Are you drunk?"

"Don't change the subject. We bought you a white-and-pink Huffy Mongoose from Toys 'R' Us."

"I remember," she said.

"I bought it for you, because Eileen was at a conference that day. I remember walking down the aisles for an hour, trying to pick one out. How do you know the right bike to get a little kid? I guess you just pick one you think's pretty sharp looking, which is what I did. But when we gave it to you, I remember the look on your face surprised me, like you were almost disappointed to get the thing, even though you'd asked for one. Or I think you did, but don't all kids want bikes?"

"Dad."

"And you never learned to ride it."

"You never taught me."

"Yeah, it's probably my fault. But it seemed like you didn't even want the bike, like you were scared of it. Were you scared of it?" On the TV, a bird flashed down through the sunlight like the gleam of an assassin's sword and snatched at the feet of a juvenile goat. He turned the TV off and the whiskey bottle up.

"I don't want to talk to you when you're drunk. Call me when you're in town."

"Did you ever learn how to ride a bike?" he asked. "That's what I want, I want to know if you ever learned to ride a bike, that's why I'm calling." The line was dead.

The whiskey was gone; nothing remained but amber syrup that coated the bottle's crenellated bottom. The birds killed for food, yes, but surely there was also pleasure in it. He found himself staring up at the repaired spot on the ceiling again, and he imagined another kind of wild animal up there, born blind and helpless in the dark, feeding on insects and insulation, and eventually becoming impossibly strong and savage. Having mastered its small domain, it would want out, to hunt in the light.

CHAPTER THREE

A s he pulled through the parking lot, Vance took a last look behind him at the hotel, the light coming from Richard's open
door, and noticed the airport pickup sign crumpled in the backseat, where it had been carelessly tossed. He'd spent two hours on it
the day before, after trashing a first effort because it didn't look spiffy
enough. The second attempt had been completed with a ruler and
pencil first, before being Sharpied within an inch of its life. He reached
back and grabbed it and threw it out the window as he turned onto the
hotel access road. Trees blurred by as he stepped on the gas, as though
he could outrun his own self-loathing.

He was embarrassed by himself, by his expectations over the last
few months, ever since the department had contacted him and asked
if he might like to escort Richard on his tour stop. If he'd like to spend
time with one of his heroes, a man for whom he'd run a fan blog for
two years—why, yes, as it turned out, he would. The intervening time
had been a delirious haze, during which he cranked out two hundred
pages of his manuscript. But what exactly had he expected? Nothing
much, he realized now: just instant friendship, kinship, mentorship—
that was all. Just to have his life changed, that was all.

The specific fantasy he'd been harboring for months—he tightly
clenched the steering wheel to avoid fully summoning it up in
recollection—went something like this: he would write a manuscript
and give it to Richard, who, with a wry and uncontrollably spreading

smile, would read it immediately and pronounce it *very good indeed,* send it on to his agent and editor with a note about the staggering magnitude of talent he'd stumbled across, get the book published, and thereby initiate a durable, decades-long working relationship, capped by Vance writing Richard's biography and executing his estate. Or something like that. And while he hadn't really expected Richard to necessarily take an interest in some kid from the sticks, he also hadn't expected him to toss his novel in the trash and tell him to quit.

He merged onto the empty two-lane that bisected the still heart of downtown Spillman. A couple of leathery women smoked outside a neon-lit sports bar, and one of them turned her face to the sky in soundless, grimacing laughter. A police car crept by, aimless and slow. In perfect concert with Vance's mood, to the right, his old high school appeared: Central County, which sounded and looked like a correctional facility and was run like one, too. As he passed, he caught a glimpse of it, a distant granite goliath where he'd spent four years dreaming about being anywhere else in the world. Now he was free, but to do what? Nothing, as it turned out: take care of his mother, write incoherent nonsense, deliver pizzas, fail out of college, spend whole days in bed uselessly reading and dreaming about himself. His life was a thing he was looking for, waiting to begin, and his heart sometimes ached for it like a beautiful white-tailed buck just visible behind dark trees.

He'd thought about leaving, of course, about just getting in the car and going, but going where? And with what money? Even if he'd had the funds, the idea of successfully moving to a different city, getting an apartment and a job, seemed almost comically difficult. Move to another city? He could barely move across his room. It seemed somehow futile, regardless—himself in another place would still be himself. A deeper change than mere setting was needed, something drastic. But what? To become someone else entirely, he felt, was the real and unfortunate answer. Steering with his knee, he picked up his writing notebook from the center console, flipped to a blank page, and jotted: *Life Improvement Plan: (1) Become different person.*

Past the high school, he entered the long stretch of car dealerships

and brown muddy lots waiting to host car dealerships mordantly referred to in local parlance as the Miracle Mile. He reflexively craned
his head to the right as he went by his place of work. He delivered
pizzas for a local chain called Pizza Boy, the mascot of which was not
a boy holding or eating a pizza, as a reasonable person might imagine,
but a boy *made out of* pizza. Blank pepperoni eyes, mushrooms for
teeth, and the gooey skin of a burn victim. Pizza Boy—the business
and the character—figured prominently in Vance's nightmares. His
manager was a thirty-something burnout named Jarrett, who had long
since surrendered to his destiny. *Hey, the job sucks, but it pays for my
bills, pills, and wheels* went Jarrett's familiar, agonizingly near-rhymed
mantra.

But maybe Jarrett had it right. Maybe that was the trick, he thought,
turning right onto Bell Road. Lower your expectations as far as you
could; even better, have no expectations at all. Why should he, for
example, have expected to learn anything from Richard? Why should
he have been disappointed by Richard not being who he wanted him
to be, by Richard being a loudmouth drunk like his father? Why should
he, for that matter, expect his father, Steve, to be other than what he
was? Why should he expect anything at all? And shouldn't he know
better by now?

As he drove, the orange glow of municipal sodium-vapor street-
lights gave way to the thin yellow of porch lamps, increasingly diffuse
as the space between houses grew. Then empty, overgrown stretches
with no light at all. The ambient darkness grew thicker, and it wasn't
so much that he was driving away from the light of town as he was
driving into something, inside it—a tunnel or a throat. Three miles
down the road, he slowed and turned up the driveway. Black pines
bent overhead, sharers of a secret, conifers conferring. Underneath sat
the house, gray and wraithlike against a dark parcel of state forest. The
place felt poised right on the very edge of town, and in a town like Spillman, where most places felt like the edge of town, it felt more like the
edge of civilization. Vance sometimes lay awake in his bed and looked
out his window at the forest ten feet away as a sailor in ye olden times
might have looked out at the yawning black sea. Here Be Monsters.

The atmosphere inside the house, as always, seemed thicker than the atmosphere outside, as though it were composed of different, heavier elements—molybdenum, francium, cobalt. It was a combination of the smell of cigarette smoke coming from upstairs and the ever-present smell of moldering garbage, the low lighting his mother favored, the yellow nicotine-stained walls, and, most of all, the fat, fog-like silence of long illness. It was hard to breathe at first, but you got used to it. Vance went up the half flight of stairs and paused at the top. Down the hall, light seeped through the frame of his mother's room. He took a heavy breath and entered.

She lay in bed watching the small TV on the dresser in the corner, a thick smoked-yellow glass ashtray on the blanket draped over her wasted frame, Pyramid 120 menthol in hand. A line of faded-orange pill bottles wound its way from the side to around the front of the TV. She said, "Where've you been?"

"I had a college thing."

"What time is it?"

"Midnight, a little after."

"Went late, huh?"

"Yeah." Vance picked up a pile of dirty clothes and dropped them in the hamper. "How are you?"

"Oh, fine, you know. The usual." The usual these days meant she hadn't been out of bed, had spent all day chain-smoking and watching *Law & Order,* maybe mixing in a little reading, some serial killer dreck du jour. It was possible, even probable, she hadn't eaten anything. Her weight fluctuations were an extremely reliable indicator of her mental condition, and right now she was very, very skinny, childish inside a V-neck gray T-shirt. Her skin was translucent from lack of light—it hung from the small bones of her clavicle like a gauzy silk gown off a clothes hanger.

"Have you eaten?" he said.

"I'm fine."

"That wasn't what I asked."

"I ate earlier. When did you become such a serious child?"

"Let me make you something anyway."

"I'm really not hungry." She adjusted the thick glasses on her face and seemed to look at him for the first time. "How's school?"

"Fine," he said, neglecting to mention he'd stopped going a month ago.

In the kitchen, he left the light off to avoid seeing the state it was in, but the smell told him everything he didn't want to know. He vowed to do a thorough cleaning over the weekend—it had been a long time. Even when his mother was in one of her increasingly rare good phases, she was not a natural or fastidious housekeeper. But during the bad spells she couldn't bring herself to clean anything. And left to Vance, who barely had the energy or wherewithal to pull on a pair of socks, the house was constantly in danger of crossing the line from messy to uninhabitable. The toilets furred over, the sink filled with dishes, the counters became shellacked with crust and crud. He assembled a grilled cheese with bread he hoped wasn't moldy and cooked it in a pan he hoped was clean. When he brought it in, his mother looked at it as though he'd set down a shoe or a toaster beside her.

"Thanks," she said.

"Eat it," he said to the side of her face, knowing she was just as likely to shove the sandwich under the bed as she was to consume it. He shut her door behind him and sifted through the pile of unopened mail on the dining room table. He couldn't remember the last time they had eaten at the table; its household function had slowly and inexorably shifted from a place to eat to a place to pile unwanted envelopes. An unpaid gas bill, a love letter from the DMV. Also, the state of the student loans he hadn't yet canceled and grants he'd failed to apply for and letters from the dean of students presumably wondering where he'd been. He still went to his creative writing class every week and helped organize the readings, and that was it. He assumed he'd been kicked out of everything else and was currently being expelled from school, expunged from the system. He wasn't sure because he'd stopped reading emails from the university a month ago and instead filtered them directly into his spam folder. He didn't know how it had all happened; it wasn't as though he'd decided to drop out of school, he just hadn't been able to bring himself to go; and as the weeks went by, instead of deciding to quit or not quit, he'd opted to simply ignore it as long as possible and hope it would go away.

As a matter of course, he looked for a letter from his father, though he knew one wouldn't be there. Not a card for his nineteenth birthday two months previous, not a letter informing them of his whereabouts, and certainly not any of the many thousands in back child support he owed. He'd stopped paying years before, although the small stream of money they were meant to get had, from the outset, come in as a grudging, anemic trickle. When he was sixteen, in a fit of irate curiosity, Vance had spent $29.99 he couldn't afford for a membership on internetsleuth.com, a supremely dodgy website that purported to locate a Steven Marcus Allerby in Queens, New York. Mapquest pinpointed the address in the middle of a neighborhood named Sunnyside. The name, and its ominous cheer, had lodged themselves in Vance's head—he assumed it had to be ironic and imagined his hapless father living in a shuttered tenement that permitted no light whatsoever. The address had lodged itself in his wallet, on a folded slip of paper he kept meaning to throw away.

Through the window behind the table, his car sat in the driveway, gray in the moonlight. During his childhood, a succession of cars had sat where his sat now, usually in various states of repair and disrepair, surrounded by sheets of newspaper on which rested oily bolts and obscure engine segments, like patients at some fly-by-night clinic with their guts out. On the rare occasions when his father found employment, it was as an unlicensed auto mechanic and detailer; he'd escaped, six years ago, in a '68 Ford Falcon he'd spent months with, neglecting his family in favor of restoring it. Vance had helped load up the car, laden with all of Steve's possessions like a pioneer-era dray horse, knock-kneed under saddlebags. This was the swan song in a series of attempts his mother and father had made at reconciliation that went back as far as Vance could remember. As now, his mother had been upstairs in her room.

"Where are you going," he'd asked, setting a lamp shaped like a steam engine on the front seat.

"Anywhere else."

"Why?"

"So I don't kill your mother, and so she doesn't kill me."

"Take me with you."

His father had started the car and looked at him with real tenderness—not a look that very often crossed Steve Allerby's face—and said, "I'll be back real soon, okay?" Then he threw the car into gear and, in his rush to get away, bottomed out at the end of the drive, scraping a trail of sparks. He had not been back, real soon or otherwise.

Vance tossed a few envelopes in the reeking trash, then went downstairs and surveyed his domain. Ever since his brother, John, had joined the army, nearly three years earlier, Vance had had the entire downstairs to himself. Two bedrooms and the larger den area, although it was really all one space and resembled some hayseed branch library gone to hell. There were stacks of books everywhere—on the few shelves but also leaning against the wall in unsteady towers, not to mention strewn everywhere on the floor. There were books in boxes and books in bags and books clustered in piles for which he had long since forgotten the grouping logic, if, in fact, there ever had been any—the cadaverous Irish existentialist balanced on top of Brazilian sci-fi which in turn sat on an obese leather-bound anthology entitled *An Illustrated History of Good Reading.* Over the years, he had spent his meager disposable income on books and not much else. He was a familiar figure at local library sales, estate sales, and Salvation Army giveaway bins across three counties.

That was where, in fact, he'd first found Richard's oeuvre, several duplicate copies of which teetered in a musty stack beside his bed. He'd loved the first, *Skyscraper Blues,* about a young man, not much older than him, who joins a gang of Mohawk Indians working fifty stories off the ground. There was an impossible, bursting freedom in these pages, a palpable yen for adventure and life—the last line existed in Vance's head as a kind of aesthetic beacon: *Bright light rose from the earth far below them, a city still in darkness, but waking before it knew the day had begun.* The other books had less of this sense, but he loved them anyway: the language and the antic comedy, as well as an adolescent self-hatred to which he naturally related. They had made him want to write.

He kicked the tower over. Then he went around the room kicking over the other stacks, and then he kicked the books lying on the floor. He moved to the corner where his laptop was propped on a milk crate, a sock wilted over it. For the last three months, he'd sat in front of it every day, writing his manuscript in a fever dream of possibility. As the page count magically increased, he'd indulged himself in a mounting excitement at the act of creation. And it wasn't just the creation of a narrative—eighty, one hundred fifty, finally two hundred implausible pages—somehow it had seemed like he was creating himself. Now, having seen the pages askew in Richard's wastebasket, the whole thing seemed delusional, the fantasy of a madman or an idiot. He retrieved the file as a coroner might pull out a corpse in its morgue drawer: *Vancenovel/draft18.docx*. He deleted it.

Sweeping some envelopes and clothes off the bed, he lay down in the impression he'd made in the mattress from sleeping in the same spot for so long. At least he'd made an impression somewhere. A book lurked under the knot of blankets at his feet, and he pulled out a bent copy of *Without Leave*. On the cover, a young Richard in his army greens stared back at him, handsome and defiant and stupid, and completely unaware of what would happen to him or who he'd become.

I'd spent most of the flight to Vietnam trying to ignore my neighbor, whose information, ironically, I can still remember today: Lance Corporal Matthew Singleton, from Youngstown, Ohio. Lance Corporal Matthew Singleton from Youngstown, Ohio, had spent what felt like the entire flight, including taxiing on the tarmac in San Francisco, talking about girls he knew back home in intimate and aggressive and slightly nauseating detail—what their cooters, his word, smelled like; what positions they liked best; which ones gave the best head; and so on and so forth. For a while, his monologue had provided a welcome distraction from the flight—the turbulent juddering of the plane and my heart—but it eventually got old. My only defense was

*craning my head away from him to look out the window. For hours,
there had been nothing, just a frayed carpet of clouds on top of the
Pacific's hard floor. Now, our Boeing 707 listed leftward in a slow,
corkscrew approach over Cam Ranh Bay and the surrounding jungle.
The trees and other vegetation below the plane were unbroken and
looked impenetrable—you tried to imagine people down there, going
about their business, living some kind of life, but it was impossible.
A couple of tiny puffs of smoke issued from somewhere, as though
scoffing in response to my line of thought: Shows what you know.*

*"This chick, Teresa Milner," my seatmate was pointing out the
window, "had a carpet on her thick as that shit down there. Had to
grab a machete to make any headway, if you follow."*

"I do."

"Real thick bush, I'm saying."

"Jesus fucking Christ, I get it."

*Stepping out of the plane, you got hit with a type of heat that was
different from any heat you might experience in America. I had gone
through boot camp during the summer at Fort Sill, Oklahoma, hellish
prairie flats that baked steady in August at around 145 degrees,
give or take. But the memory of that was immediately erased by the
January jungle heat of Vietnam. It was like sticking your head inside
a huge creature's mouth and sucking in the rank exhalations, like
crawling into its burning guts.*

*As we trudged across that tarmac to the staging area to await
further transport, the heat descended on us with all the weight of
reality. Until now, the whole thing had seemed like a far-fetched joke.
Even Basic, with its four-thirty reveille trumpet blast, and its forced
runs, and its push-ups and obstacle courses and shitty food, seemed
as much like the YMCA camp I attended for two weeks as a kid as
anything else. It was just a tedious game you had to get through,
and on the other side sat another thin stretch of civilian life before
deployment. But this was real. The heat, the distant sliver of sea, the
less-distant presence of the jungle on the airstrip's perimeter, not to
mention a variety of signage in French and Vietnamese.*

"Welcome to Vietnam, motherfuckers," some rawboned brush-cut

*to my left kept muttering. It was annoying but still beat hearing
any more about Corporal Singleton's girlfriends' pussies. Welcome to
Vietnam, over and over—it felt incantatory, an attempt to ward off
the evil spirits surely lurking in the jungle we'd just been flying over.
It felt like it might work just as well to summon them as ward them
off, though.*

*Within the space of five minutes, clouds coalesced overhead and the
sky dumped rain. As we huddled tight under the overhang of a piece
of tin roofing, our company's CO, Lieutenant Endicott, and two of
his staff sergeants took a headcount making sure no one had deserted
before even getting to base. He cleared his throat, and as he spoke, the
rain behind him intensified to biblical proportions, a solid sheet of
water that looked prearranged as a theatrical backdrop to our arrival
in-country.*

"Gentlemen," he said.

"Hooah," we said.

*"At ease. Here's the deal. At some point today, the USAF will see fit
to send over the choppers we requisitioned a week ago. They will take
us to your new home in Bao Loc. The road to Bao Loc is pretty good,
and normally we'd just drive you in, but there've been heavy mortar
exchanges lately, and command feels ground transport is too risky. So
until then, sit tight with your thumb about halfway up your ass, but
not all the way, and most certainly not up your neighbor's. That's an
order."*

"Hooah."

*We slumped against the tin siding of terminal number 4, Cam
Ranh air base, for minutes, then hours, but the choppers did not
materialize. The rain slacked off, and the sky cleared, but no
choppers. A big kid sitting next to me pulled a piece of wood out of his
pack and began whittling it with a penknife. He shook his head, and
said, "No choppers coming, bullshit bullshit bullshit."*

"Why's that?"

*"Because every goddamn thing in this piece-of-shit war—excuse
me, military intervention—is ass up and clusterfucked. You're new,
right?"*

"Yeah."

"I'm a transfer, just spent four months up near Binh Dinh. Four months is long enough to figure a few things out. No choppers, you'll see."

"I'm Richard Lazar."

"Mitch Berlinger." He stuck his hand out without smiling, and we shook. "No choppers," he said again, with a downward musical lilt, addressing himself back to his woodworking.

———

Berlinger was right. Three hours later, a convoy of olive-drab trucks with camouflage canvas tarps pulled up on the tarmac. The staff sergeant split us up, sixteen men a truck, safeties off and barrels out. I can't speak for anyone else in that truck, but even before we left the air base, passed the guard towers, and began rumbling down that bumpy road into the jungle, I thought I might pass out from fear. It was all happening too fast: sixteen hours earlier, I'd been at SFO, looking at college girls and eating a churro and watching Hare Krishnas sing "Krishna Krishna Hare Hare" and ping their little finger cymbals together. Now I was being driven down a road into enemy territory, a road our CO had just told us was too dangerous to drive down. I shut my eyes and, despite already being an avowed and often annoyingly vocal atheist, I whispered the Lord's Prayer to myself. Just to have something to concentrate on, I told myself, though I knew differently. I was praying as hard as the devoutest Muslim on the road to Mecca.

I guess my prayers were heard and answered, because nothing happened. We drove down a shitty, cratered road for three hours, then hung a left onto an even-shittier, even-more-cratered road for another thirty minutes, until that road petered out into a faint trail of dust, which led us to the front gate of the base. "Gate" is probably a bit grand—the threshold was marked by two large wooden poles on either side of the trail. With the chicken wire and the lazy hills rising up behind the compound, it felt like we'd been shipped in to work on *a ranch in California. But this feeling quickly vanished as we drove farther in, past several mortar positions surrounded by sandbags, past an enormous canvas tent with the Stars and Stripes fluttering nervously overhead, and stopped in front of a row of aluminum Quonset huts.*

We got out and stretched our legs—mine were severely cramped from maintaining a squatting position and a full rectal pucker for most of the afternoon. One of the staff sergeants escorted us to our quarters. It was the last hut, butted up against a dense tree line that ran maybe half a football field to the base of a small mountain or very large hill. Looking up at the hill, I felt my shoulders relax a little with the thought that it would be very near impossible to creep up on us from behind and, further, that we were buffered from the surrounding forest by everything else in the base. It was a little like the feeling you get as a kid, all nice and tucked in, with yards of blanket and pillow keeping the monsters at bay.

"Nowhere to run," someone said, and I turned to see Berlinger shaking his head at the hut.

"What?"

"Any kind of assault on base, we're pinned in here. Retreat would be impossible."

"I was looking at it the other way."

"Glass half full, huh? That'll last about another forty-eight hours here."

We both stared silently up at the mountain for a moment or two, then Berlinger slapped my back, and said, "Well, come on, sweet cheeks. Let's pick our coffins, I mean cots." I followed him into the hut, same on the inside as you would imagine it would be from the outside. Spartan and hot as ever-loving fuck. Twelve cots were laid out, six a side, and I saw that the ones in the corners had already been claimed. I put my pack down next to a cot under a window, and Berlinger sat on the one adjacent. The sergeant told us to get situated, that chow would be at nineteen-hundred, then disappeared. Propped up against two starchy pillows, I pulled out whatever book

I was reading, or trying to read, at the time. Probably Hemingway, predictably enough, and, even more predictably, probably A Farewell to Arms. *I wasn't big on subtlety at nineteen. I'm still not.*

A few other men straggled in and picked a cot, among them the country-faced brush-cut. He looked around at everyone, sitting there in a puddle of their own sweat, and said, "I'm Lester Hawkins."

A few guys grunted their names. I might have. Hawkins grinned broadly. "Welcome to Vietnam, fellas."

"Hey, Lester Hawkins," said Berlinger. "Put a fucking sock in it."

"Hey man," said Hawkins. He put his sack down and sat on a cot near the opposite wall, looking deflated. He had been expecting something else, an experience of instant camaraderie that wasn't transpiring. He pouted like a little kid in time-out. There was something about his face that made me want to punch it, so I tried not looking at him as best I could.

Some other soldier, a dark-haired kid with the deep-set yet bulging eyes of a deepwater fish, said, "Well, I'm Carbone. Tony Carbone." Another chorus of grunts. Carbone sat on his helmet and slouched forward, elbows on knees. "Anybody else from New York?"

"I'm from Manhattan," said Berlinger.

"Oh yeah?"

"Yeah, Kansas."

Carbone looked confused. "Whatever, man. Anybody here from a real place?"

"K-State's in Manhattan, boy. That's as real as it gets. Wildcat Pride."

There were some laughs. Carbone said, "Real country bumpkin, huh?"

"That's right. You got a problem with good country folk?" I glanced over at Berlinger. His face was stone-serious, but his eyes twinkled with comic ire. He was enjoying himself.

"I've got a problem with anywhere you can't get a good slice or an egg cream. That includes this shithole and Manhattan, wherever. Tennessee."

I said, "Let's leave Tennessee out of this."

Berlinger said, "It's Kansas, you ignorant wop."

Carbone made like he was going to get up, but Berlinger had eight inches and a hundred pounds on him, and there was no way anything would happen. "Nothing against Italians, of course," Berlinger added.

"Hayseed. New York City would chew you up and spit you out. We eat punks like you for breakfast."

"You eat your sister's pussy for breakfast!" bellowed Berlinger. This time Carbone did get up and walk across the hut, but a couple of other guys stopped him. Berlinger was cracking up, rolled back on his cot, his feet pedaling in the air like a dog getting his stomach scratched.

"Why don't both of you shut up," a big black dude in the far corner intoned, and everyone did. The silence filled the hut, seeming to fight for space with the choking humidity. It was worse than the arguing; it allowed in all the thoughts you didn't want to be thinking. I got up and went back outside, where the barest trace of a breeze cooled the sweat on my arms. I could hear them inside, going at it again, the rise and fall of voices talking over each other. I walked to the side of the hut, then behind, where the tree line began. The base's chicken-wire fencing, topped with a reassuring whorl of barbed wire, laced around the back of the hut and the adjacent buildings.

A rustling in the trees set my heart jackhammering. I looked up and out, and it stopped. I waited, and it started up again. I looked at the hut, thought of the men inside, and hated them for not running outside to help. The rustling grew louder and I tried to yell, but nothing came out. My God, I thought, it's happening already. I half put my hands up in front of me in a posture of uncertain, preemptive surrender.

The sound resolved itself in the form of a small monkey, elderly looking, with a white mask, that shuffled through a stand of leaves and stopped. It picked insects off a limb, ate, and looked down at me. Its expression was ancient and unknowable, like one of those tormented bearded faces on the side of a Greek urn.

"What the fuck am I doing here," I said, but it didn't respond.

I stood there looking at the monkey and the jungle behind it, and everything was suddenly completely incredible to me, unreal and unbelievable: the monkey; the bluish razor wire pulled through the foliage like ribbon on a birthday present; the nearby voices of other uprooted boys, everyone from somewhere else and now—for reasons it seemed no one fully understood—here; my own outstretched hands palely glowing in the thin jungle light. For the first time since I'd landed, the fear dissolved and was supplanted by a helpless infantile awe. The monkey seemed embarrassed by me, pretended to look over his shoulder as though seeing something important, and scampered away. I walked to the fence and touched the limb where it had just been. I thought about how strange it is that things can be one way then another, how you could wake up in California and fall asleep in Vietnam. The ludicrous mutability of life. I was, as they say, having a moment.

Maybe that's just the ordinary awe of youth, though. Maybe it feels that way for everyone, at war or not. Before everything you do or see is a version of something before it. Before you get older and everything calcifies: your personality and memory and sense of the world. I'm too old now to much remember what it's like to be young, but I still remember looking down at my hands, how they glowed and glowed.

CHAPTER FOUR

—

Richard had gotten the call two years earlier. He'd been pissing in the desert, or trying to. The morning breeze blowing across the Sonoran basin was not yet infernally hot, and it wrapped the mangy bathrobe around his legs with a playful caress. Distant cars tooled by on the John Wayne Parkway, which connected Phoenix, to the north, with Maricopa, to the south. The trailer was located in the Interzone, as he thought of it, a moonscape of sand and rocks and distant, spectral mountains. He heard the phone ring inside the trailer, which was strange, since no one ever called him. For a moment, curiosity did battle with the need to piss, but pissing won, handily. He closed his eyes and waited for his prostate to wake up, and as he did, the phone rang again.

"Coming, goddamn it," he yelled into the desert air.

Inside the trailer, he located the antique, chipped plastic phone, half buried beneath a pile of dirty clothes, which was unsurprising, since everything in the trailer was half buried beneath a pile of dirty clothes.

"Yeah," he wheezed.

"Can I speak to Richard Lazar?"

"Speaking."

"You're a hard man to track down." The voice was mild and pleasant, and more terrifying for that fact. Richard's heart creaked with the

tacit assumption that this could only be someone he didn't want track-
ing him down. Who would track him down that he'd want to talk to?

"Who is this?"

"This is Stan, at Reiner-Goldwell."

"What at where?"

"Stan Rosenburg."

"Why does that name sound familiar?" He sat down on the long
sofa bench that ran half the length of one side of the trailer, propping
his elbows on a small Formica table. In front of him, on the table, sat
the broken typewriter on which he'd written all his novels. Victor, his
dog—a fat bearded collie who had with age, distressingly, become a
dead ringer for his owner—staggered over stiff-legged from sleep and
settled again at Richard's feet.

"Because I'm your agent?"

"Oh, right. Jesus, Stan." The name had been hard to place because
he hadn't heard or seen it in almost two years. Since he'd turned in
the last memoir draft, in fact. Weekly phone calls had become monthly
and then bimonthly, and so on, as reports trickled back that editors
weren't interested in another Vietnam story, or in war stories, period.
In the new millennium, the reading public, it seemed, was all warred
out. Did he have anything with serial killers or lawyers, or serial killer
lawyers? He did not. Finally, having run through his entire list of editors over the course of eighteen months, Stan had stopped calling, and
Richard had assumed he'd never hear from him again.

"Okay, he remembers. Listen, I have good news."

"What?"

"The book. We got a yes."

"What?"

"Listen, I know I said there wasn't anything else I could do, but I
never stopped believing in it. I still passed it around, now and then.
Junior editors and small presses, that kind of thing. Always the same
line, 'No one wants another war story,' right?"

"I have a pretty firm handle on that, yeah."

"But listen, then three months ago we invade Iraq. And I'm not trying to be crass here, but suddenly I'm getting calls."

"What does that have to do with anything?"

He could almost hear Stan shrug on the other end of the line, see the long, sleek face, seal-like with his shimmering pomade helmet. "We're at war. People are interested. So last week, Kathleen Talent at Black Swan calls, says she loves it and wants to put an offer together. And I just found out this morning, she got the green light on it."

"Okay."

"Rich, it's getting published. I waited to tell you until there was real news, didn't want to get your hopes up for no reason. I know this has been a hard stretch. We're still working on the terms of the contract. You need to call her, I have the number right here, do you have a pen? She wants to get you going on a final draft, email you some notes. Do you even have email?"

"RMLazar at AOL dot com."

"Do I get a thank you? There's going to be a check coming your way in a month."

Richard looked around the trailer, to the extent that it was possible to look around a space so comically small. On one end was the dark chamber of his bed and bedding, a gray space half obscured by curtains and dimmed by towels duct-taped over the adjacent windows. On the other end was the sealed-off bathroom, which hadn't worked in weeks. Something to do with the sump pump, his landlord had ventured un-promisingly. His landlord lived a mile away, on the opposite side of the property, and came by twice a month or so to see if anything needed fixing, with no intention of ever fixing anything; Richard suspected the real reason for the pop-ins, as he called them, was just checking to see if his tenant had died yet.

This was where he'd landed, after Eileen, after Carole—after women. And after money. He'd worked construction and roofing until his knees and hips had gotten so shot he could barely climb the lad-der to retile some yuppie nitwit's five-million-dollar Spanish modern; a humane foreman had suggested he move into another line of work and given him a reference at his cousin's bar. Working three shifts a week at the Tamarack had necessitated, as they say, a lifestyle change. He'd had to give up certain luxuries: his crappy studio apartment in

Phoenix, for one, and also things like cable television or ever eating in a restaurant again. He hadn't made money from his writing in years; he'd never really made a living.

"Hello?" said Stan. "Are you crying?"

"No, of course not. I'm just surprised."

"Richard, this is a good thing."

"I know, I know. I'll call what's-her-name."

"Kathleen. I'll email you the details."

After Stan said goodbye, Richard really let loose, cried like a little baby. Like his baby, Cindy, when she was little, tears begetting more tears, his face a hot, smeary mess. Like the baby he was. He took some deep breaths and tried to figure out what he was feeling and why, an exercise he hadn't undertaken in years, since for years he'd always felt roughly the same way—i.e., like shit—and known why, i.e., because everything was horrible.

They weren't tears of happiness, though he was happy. He hadn't realized how much he'd given up, the extent to which he'd surrendered his guns. Out of habit, he still sat down to write every morning, but he hadn't written anything in years, not really. A little thing about desert living for *Harper's,* a brief interview for the *Sun-Times* for an article about local writers, a piece in *LA Weekly* about dogs (he was for them). For the last year, he'd hardly written a word. He just hadn't had the heart, couldn't bear more disappointment, even more confirmation that the world didn't care about what he had to say. Six books in thirty years, the first five all out of print, nothing to show for it except for all the bad stuff—the mess and poverty and waste and wreckage. Message received. It wasn't a decision he'd made—he hadn't thrown his typewriter off a cliff or burned what random pages, yellowing and stained, cluttered his desk. He'd simply stopped working. The scope of his life had narrowed to eking out enough money to feed himself and his dog, keep himself in booze, and pay the power bill. Waking up, going to work, and going to sleep. It was a kind of death.

He blew his nose, and Victor looked up at him quizzically. "That's right, my lad," he said, "our ship has come in."

He hauled the dog up, and they shambled together outside into the

mounting June heat. They used the bathroom in tandem, both looking off to the west and the distant highway. Richard filled Victor's food
bowl, which sat in the shadow of the trailer near the door, then went
back inside and poured himself a triumphant Gilbey's and Sprite in
the cleanest available glass. He drank it and sat around listless, an-
noyed by his desire to share the news with someone that didn't eat
their own poop. He found Eileen's work number written on a torn-off
envelope edge, in a pile of scrap paper contained in the plastic fishbowl
that served as his Rolodex.

"This is Eileen Kline." Her voice sounded the same as ever—
musical amusement softening an essential clipped erudition. Over the
years, the harsh words and unpleasant truths that voice had spoken to
him faded from his memory, but the sound of her voice continued to
remain instantly familiar to him, like the opening chords of a favorite
song.

"Ei, it's Richard." There was a pause on her end, during which he
tried to remember how long it had been since they'd spoken last. Two
years?

"Hi. How are you?"

"I'm good, is this an okay time?"

"It's fine, I'm just getting my lecture together." In the decades since
they'd been together, Eileen had climbed steadily up the academic
ladder and now sat on the top rung surveying her domain. She was
one of the two or three world experts in a field called narratology and
had recently published an apparently seminal monograph entitled *The
Hermeneutics of Implied Authorship,* information he'd gleaned from
periodically googling her name on the library computer. She was also
now a Sward Fellow at NYU, which, so he understood, meant she was
absolved of ever having to do any actual work again.

"This is the one class you have to teach every decade, right?"

"Yes, that's right. What's up?"

Richard sat down on the edge of his shaded bed space, and Victor burrowed behind his feet, hiding from the sunlight encroaching
through the window in a widening frame on the floor. He told her
about the phone call he'd just received.

"Oh, my God, Richard. Well, that's just fantastic."

"Yeah. I thought you'd like to know."

"Of course." After a moment, she said, "Wait, are you calling to let me know the good news, or is this supposed to be kind of an 'I told you so' moment?"

"I don't know. Both, probably."

"Well, listen. I really am happy to hear about it. I'm not sure why you think it's necessary to somehow rub it in or whatever it is you think you're doing."

"I just feel like you never believed in it." He'd begun fooling around with the memoir when they were still together; she'd habitually referred to the project as *The Red Badge of Richard*. "You thought I was a failure."

"No, I didn't, actually. I was always proud of you. I always thought if you just hung in there, the world would come around, and it looks like maybe I was right." He started to point out that it hadn't come out yet, that the world probably still wouldn't come around, but she went on, "I just didn't want to be around your toxic self-hatred, constantly dwelling on disappointment." She sighed. "I'm happy for you, I really am happy. Can't you leave it at that?"

He paused again, uncertain of what to say. She had an ability like no one else to make him feel like the child he was. He loved and hated it about her. He had hated her for it when they were together and loved it about her in memory ever since. Finally he said, "So, how's it going for you?"

"Good. Busy. They have me going to some conference in Frankfurt on Thursday. It never ends."

"That sounds rough."

"Listen, congratulations again, I mean it. I'm going now. Tell Cindy the good news."

The phone went dead, and he looked at it. He would not tell Cindy the good news, because she didn't want to hear good news from him, only occasional reports of minor misfortune—his firings and fuckups and fiascoes, his steady demotion in life since he'd left them twenty years ago. He dropped the phone on the bed and looked at the tiny white hands of the clock on the small stove in the kitchenette: 10:18. The trailer's air had become stifling, as though superheated by his roiling adolescent sense of need. What did he need? To mark the moment, to celebrate, to hear a sincere word of congratulations. For the tree of his present success to not fall silently in the woods of his past failure.

He put on a pair of paint-stained Dickies and a pit-stained T-shirt and went outside again. His car, an unreliable Ford Reliant, sat on the other side of the trailer, its eczematous clear coat peeling off in the sun. The engine turned after only a couple of tries, and he pulled slowly down the long driveway, which led to a longer access road and finally to the John Wayne. His back sweated on the vinyl seat, and the drink sweated between his legs. He finished it before he got to the highway, tossed the glass out the window into the sand, and pulled into the sporadic traffic, Phoenix-bound.

———

The Tamarack was closed at this hour, and as Richard entered and locked the door, a small and complex frisson of pleasure passed through him. He liked being in the place when it was empty. It was the part of the job he liked the best—the only part he liked, in fact. The place was cool and quiet, and the midday sun slanted in through the grime-tinted windows, illuminating the untold billions of ambient dust and silica and ash particles floating in the air, like a sad little cosmos in miniature. In these moments, the bar, despite its state of long-neglected squalor, had a solemn, almost churchlike feel.

He was also inexpressibly gratified at the thought of never having to work there again. He looked around the room: the bathroom door kicked half off its hinges; the low ceiling festooned with profanity-embossed dollar bills (the ones directly overhead reading KASH KREW and SUCK A FUCK DICK); the rows of dusty bottles behind the bar; the wooden bar top with its deep and uncleanable cracks that filled up with syrupy alcohol like tiny feeding troughs for the bar's flies (namesake and mascot of the regulars around whose smokes and beer they crawled); the Megatouch machine in the corner that blooped and bleeped all night as though sympathetically mimicking the idiotic babble of drunks at 1:00 a.m. on a Saturday; the loathsome ersatz-fifties jukebox filled with shitty modern rock the owner thought would bring in a younger crowd. Richard had expected to keep working at this place forever, until it closed or he died—growing old with it like a despised but undivorceable spouse.

A magnum of Moët collected dust in the back of the cooler. It had been there since he'd gotten the job four years earlier. He sprang it from its prison, at first justifying the theft by thinking about what an asshole the owner, Stu—who spent almost all his copious free time golfing on the verdant and manicured courses that gulped the city's scant water supply like sun-sick hounds—was; then by thinking about how the champagne would soon go bad if it wasn't already; then dispensing with the charade altogether. It was there and he wanted it, that was all. He lifted a champagne flute for good measure.

Outside, he locked the door and dropped his key in the mail slot. He straightened in the tall sunlight, feeling like an inmate released from prison on a surprise parole. The book had sold. He realized he hadn't called his editor yet or asked how much money he'd be getting, then he realized it didn't matter: if it was only a hundred dollars, he could take that to Apache Nights and put it all on 27 Red. He drove to the north side of South Mountain and turned up an access road. The road petered out next to a TV antenna station about halfway up the hill, and he parked in the runoff beside a hiking trail, next to a giant NO PARKING sign. He walked slowly up the zigzagging trail, pausing frequently to rest, then left the path and moved through the uneven brush until he found a spot that suited him.

It was a flat patch of sandy scrub, with a huge dark saguaro standing to his left like a terse, disapproving ranch hand watching the town drunk on an epic binge. He looked down the mountain at his adoptive city. From a distance, Phoenix looked like a real place with history and secrets and not the pretend place it was, with everything built five minutes ago, a pastel Disneyland for Republicans and old people and methamphetamine addicts. He uncorked the bottle and turned it up, spilling a frothing mouthful down the front of his shirt. He was embarrassed by his need to commemorate the moment—it suggested there was still a part of him, however small, that remained capable of pride. And, worse, hope. Shouldn't he have known better than that by now?

Yes, but he couldn't help it. Ego and its running buddy Sexual Desire were the nightmare guests at Dignity's party—drunk buffoons that stayed far too late, refused to take polite hints, trashed the place, and insulted their host. The champagne stung his throat as it went down. To hell with it, he thought. To hell with everything. The vast city planing out in front of him didn't begrudge him his frail vanity. It didn't care. And on either side of Phoenix, the empty desert seemed like an absolution. It was why, despite the harsh, alien terrain, and his lack of relatives and family history there, he'd stayed for so long. The desert was unforgiving, yet it forgave. Having no memory, what choice did it have?

On the way home, he stopped at a bar, then another one, then possibly a third. He was there for a while, and everything got foggy and smudged. The day outside had somehow darkened without his notice or assent. He squinted up at the bartender, one of those very fat shornheaded bald guys that grow a goatee in order to create the impression of having an actual face and neck and head rather than just a fleshy head-shaped lump growing out of their collars.

"The book sold," he told the bartender.

The bartender said, "That's the third time you told me. Go the fuck home."

————

As he drove south on the John Wayne Parkway into the desert, the halogen lights of the outer suburbs of Chandler left vapor traces on his stunned retinas. Some kind of animal—a dog or coyote or mountain lion—flashed in his headlights, green eyes ablaze. He jerked the wheel and his head to the right in tandem. There was a tremendous sense of fluid motion, water falling and falling, then hitting bottom with a soft slap.

When he came to, his car was splayed around a concrete overpass piling, the hood buckled and steam escaping with a disgusted sigh. Two cop cars had stopped ahead of him, just past the overpass, their gumballs blinking on and off. In the distance, he heard more sirens. He wanted to tell everyone that he was fine, to go home, not to make a stink about it. He wanted to open the door and jog off into the black maw of the desert. Instead, he sat there with his head on the steering wheel and his nose dripping blood, until something went a-tap-tap-tapping on his window. He looked up to see a penlight and, past that, the face of an unfriendly-looking policeman. The cop tapped the window again, and Richard rolled it down.

The policeman said, "Have you been drinking, sir?"

"The book sold."

———

The first check, when it arrived, was eighteen thousand and change. He stood in front of his trailer and rubbed his finger over the embossed type. There were three more on the way, a very nice contract for eighty-five thousand, gross, less Stan's agent fee. Of course, another chunk would immediately go to taxes, but sixty-five thousand, or however much that left, was still a lot of money. Not enough to never work again. Not enough to move to Europe and live out his life as a grappa-swilling letch. Not quite enough to start his own bar, from which he would ban people like himself on sight. Not enough to do lots of things, but enough to not feel like a complete fool for quitting his job, totaling his car, and getting DUIey-Twoey all in the same day.

It was enough, as it turned out, to buy a nearby house in foreclosure, in a superexurban neighborhood called the Bluffs. There was no bluff visible in the landscape, so perhaps the name referred to the cavalier attitude local banks and homeowners had taken toward the adjustable-rate mortgages that subsequently emptied the neighborhood. It turned out they were giving the things away—all you had to do was show up at auction with a roll of quarters and a ballpoint pen. Richard got the house—a fantastically ugly stucco ranch with a porte-cochere and an ornamental chimney—for twenty thousand down and two hundred a month. It was one of two occupied homes on the street, a lonely cul-de-sac that hung out exposed into the scrubby desert like the caboose wagon in a doomed pioneer convoy. At night the coyotes called and responded across miles of empty land. The desolation of the place seemed a drawback to most buyers, hence the price, but Richard loved it. If only, he thought, the other homeowner on the street would default, it would be perfect.

———

The phone rang in his new living room. Groaning up from the La-Z-Boy, he picked his way across the room, covered with trash, books, and unpacked moving boxes. It was more or less the same amount of garbage and unwanted possessions he'd had in the trailer, just spaced out to fill the larger living area. The white, plastic rotary phone lay on the sofa, next to the sliding glass door that opened to the patio. He sat down and hoisted the heavy receiver, like lifting a small dumbbell.

"Yeah."

"Richard, it's Stan."

"Hey." His attention remained thoroughly commanded by a *Dukes of Hazzard* episode he'd been watching on the TV; or, more specifically, by Catherine Bach; or, even more specifically, by Catherine Bach's ass. An earlier spell hovering motionless over his typewriter had culminated in the bold decision to squander the rest of the day. If he wasn't going to produce anything, it could at least be a choice.

"You there?"

"Oh, yeah." He turned the volume down.

"I assume you haven't checked your email lately?"

"Not in the last few months, no."

"Are you sitting down?"

"Do people actually say that? For future reference, I'm always sitting down."

Daisy Duke bent over the General Lee, and he candidly imagined himself bent over her back. The exertion alone, to say nothing of the excitement, he decided, would kill him within five seconds. Just before the phone rang, he'd been considering self-abuse, a term that became more and more apt with age. "What?"

"I said the book's doing great. The reviews are glowing. It has critical mass."

"I don't know what that means."

"It means everyone's lining up behind it. I've seen it happen before."

"Okay, well. Great."

"You don't understand, it's selling."

"Really." Richard clicked off the TV, and over the next twenty minutes, Stan detailed, in loving and exhaustive fashion, what all of this meant. It meant more money. It meant the other books were going to be reprinted in trade paperback. It meant interviews with NPR, the *TBR,* and a peppering of other acronyms that Richard had never heard of.

"And you know what all this means."

"No," he said.

"Book tour. ASAP. Speaking engagements, some of them paying."

"Which means flying."

"No, I was thinking you could ride a camel around everywhere, like one of the wise men."

"I hate flying."

"So what? Everybody hates flying. Listen, we've been getting calls. There's real interest. Do you know how rare that is? Usually you'd be screaming at three deaf retirees in the Topeka Books-a-Million. Do you hate money, too?"

Richard did hate money, but he hated not having it more. And the amount of money Stan estimated was startling and had a persuasive quality. It would be enough to see him through another couple of years, maybe even pay off his mortgage. Commerce, Stan said, was a cruel taskmaster. He might never have the chance to cash in like this again. Did he want to go back to bartending? Richard imagined talking to the same stiffs, the same horrible bums who came in and bought their beer with quarters they'd dug out from beneath someone else's couch cushions. They got drunk and eventually tipped with the only thing they had that was worth giving: their absence from the bar.

"Okay," he said. "But listen, I drive whenever possible."

"Have you ever heard of Ambien? Get some."

———

He hadn't heard of Ambien, but his foreman friend in Mesa said he could get some, no problem. That they would make flying easy. Over the next month, he became better acquainted with his publicist, Dana, a loud, merry woman he'd had two cursory conversations with months earlier, who suddenly wanted to chat every day. Could he block off three weeks for a tour? He checked his nonexistent calendar, filled with all his nonexistent obligations, and found he could. Great, she said, we'll kick it off at Spillman College, a money gig. And did he want a student escort?

He bought the thirty-dollar suit. He called Eileen again.

"Hello?"

"Hey, it's Richard."

"Hi."

He looked down at the itinerary Dana had sent over. "I'm sorry about that last conversation."

"It's okay."

"No, it's not. But listen, they've got me on a book tour. I'm gonna be in New York on the twenty-seventh. I'm doing a reading and talk at Argosy, then a cocktail party somewhere. I was hoping I could see you, maybe get some dinner."

The intervening pause was almost comically long, but Richard was penitent and silent. He read the names of the western cities on the list—*Spillman, Portland, San Francisco, Los Angeles, Pomona, Las Vegas, Salt Lake City*—over and over to himself, an incantation of sorts, trying to keep his mind clear. He'd learned long ago that the best way to ensure something didn't happen was to consciously hope for it. The only time good things happened in his life was when he hadn't hoped for them to happen (Cindy's conception) or when it was something he'd hoped for, but then it didn't happen for so long that he eventually forgot he'd ever cared (the book). He'd stopped following sports on this basis, finding that any team on which he focused his diseased mojo—the Giants from 1975 to 1982, for example—would immediately get injured en masse or die in a plane crash or at any rate suck in perpetuity until he stopped giving a shit.

Finally, Eileen said, "Yes, that would be nice, I think. Call me when you're close, and we'll firm up plans."

Richard put the leash on Victor, opened the sliding glass door, and walked out into his backyard, as he thought of it, though really it was just the desert. The only rough property demarcation was a small arroyo that began fifty or so feet away. Victor liked to pee in the arroyo and smell the desert wildflowers that bloomed on the edges, and so they went there. Cars were just visible up on the nearby highway, speeding away from Phoenix, and who could blame them? The last stragglers of the rush-hour push to the exurbs, they always seemed sad to him, chasing after something that had already passed by long ago. The empurpled sun clung to its mantle over the desert horizon, and he felt his heart was the same: tired and bruised at a late hour, but still somehow hopeful in its way.

He walked Victor to the end of the gulch, which butted up against the base of the road, the sides rising shoulder high. Motors hummed past. Eileen's face was vivid in his mind. The day before, he had taken the bus into downtown Phoenix to the central library, something he had begun doing to check his email. It was a modern building, described in a placard in the entryway as *a curving copper mesa split by a stainless steel canyon, inspired by Monument Valley*. It looked like a child's toy piano to Richard, carelessly flung down in the scrub and sand. He sat down at one of the free terminals and looked for pictures of his ex-wife and, as always, was surprised by the quantity online.

He was both pleased and disappointed to see that she looked the same as ever. The same as she'd looked the last time he saw her, soon after his second divorce, when she'd stopped through Phoenix to see how he was holding up. Better than ever, really. She looked like she was working out, like maybe she'd had some very subtle and expensive plastic surgery done. In one photo he studied closely, she stood behind a lectern and jabbed at the air with two fingers. Her face still radiated the fierce intelligence and vitality it had always had, but the good looks she'd possessed at thirty had hardened and heightened themselves into a kind of monumentality, a sculptural exemplification of the ethical, intellectual life she'd always prized above everything else. She'd gotten the face she deserved—they both had. He'd been hoping she would look like most fifty-seven-year-old women, i.e., like a fifty-seven-year-old man, but it wasn't the case. She was still beautiful.

He and Victor turned around and walked back, and he watched the red sun fall quickly below the horizon, like a casino chip dropped into a slot machine. Cherry cherry lemon. By the time they regained the backyard, it was evening, and a cooling wind blew from the west, but the day's heat remained trapped in the sand that surrounded him. He could feel it there, almost as though a living thing were breathing underground. It would be well into the night, he knew, before the ground finally acknowledged the day's end and surrendered its heat. He went back inside and began packing his bag.

CHAPTER FIVE

—

He woke in his clothes to the chittering AC, the silent TV on a documentary about insects. A black bug came halfway out of its lair and vibrated furiously, insane. The dim light of dawn leaked under the thin curtains, and he shuddered. The fact that he didn't feel like he was in immediate danger of dying alerted him to the fact that he was still very drunk.

He turned the bedside light on and sat up, and after a few seconds his equilibrium followed suit. His head felt like a balloon on a string bobbing along behind the rest of him. At the bathroom sink, he scrabbled a plastic cup out of its wrap and drank several glasses of tap water. It tasted of punky minerals and the carcasses of small animals long decomposed; he imagined the hotel's piping, never tended to, the rusting circulatory system leaking underground. His own heart rumbled sympathetically in his chest, and a sudden deep swell of dread forced him back to the bed for fear of blacking out, keeling over. He switched off the TV and sat there, trying to organize his thoughts or at the very least not run screaming from the room. He turned to the nightstand to make sure his keys and wallet had made it back with him. They had, which brought him a measure of comfort, however small. A piece of paper jutted from the wallet—a napkin with smudged lipstick on it and a name signed underneath, no number. The signature was executed with the loopy, swooning hand of a teenage girl and seemed like a stage prop; everything in the room did, in fact, and this sense of cardboard unreality made him nauseated. The sheets and even his own cold skin had a waxy artificial feel, and he couldn't shake the sensation of being a figment of someone else's awful imagination.

He closed his eyes, desperate to return to sleep and completely unable to do so. After a few minutes of writhing into his pillow, he got up and went outside. The pressure in his head and his general sense of impending calamity were minutely relieved by fresh air and motion, and so he shuffled barefoot, in widening circles, around the parking lot. The velvet indigo of night was just beginning to disintegrate into gray morning dusk, the unmagic hour. Another impossible day loomed ahead, like an iceberg sighted well in advance yet too late to avoid. Over the scrubby rank of pines to the east of the hotel, the sky was an unhealthy, sallow pink. Sailor take warning. The trees under it, adjacent to the highway, also looked ill, exhausted by exhaust. A sixteen-wheeler lumbered past, its Jacob Marleyish chains clanking, with a picture on the trailer of a mustachioed Italian chef rubbing his fingers together over a table full of toothsome dishes. The entire world, at that moment, truly seemed to him like a gigantic, unadulterated pile of shit.

Of course, it was he who was the pile of shit. He felt, in fact, that he was made of shit. Bullshit, dogshit, horseshit, ratshit, chickenshit. His mental and physical state constituted a sort of Pousse-Café of shit—an elaborate stratification of shit that commingled to create a shitty whole that was much shittier than the sum of its shitty parts. Immediate, automatic remorse was the greasy top layer of shit, which bubbled on top of the churning shit of his hangover, which was generously layered on top of the firmer soil bed of his bad health and drinking and desire for alcohol, which itself sat on top of untold, fossilized geological strata of guilt and fear, decades—a lifetime—of shit.

At the edge of the lot, near the access road and drainage culvert, lay the airport pickup sign, half wadded, with the LAZAR still legible. He bent slowly, allowing his head time to follow his body, and picked it up. The letters had been slide-ruled or something and meticulously colored in. At the base of the Z in his last name, a small slip of the pen had been covered several times with Wite-Out. Jesus Christ. He held the sign and looked at it for quite a while, trying to remember exactly what had happened.

The image of the kid speeding angrily away flashed through his head; it was succeeded by other snatches of the night before in a juddering stop-motion reel. It was a film he'd seen in varying versions hundreds, thousands, of times before, yet it never lost its power to mortify. What an asshole he was, what a joke. Vance's sincerity and desire to do something worthwhile had somehow offended his own sense of self—if you feel your own life is meaningless, naturally everyone else should feel the same way. He was so tired of his own shit and so tired of heaping it on those unfortunate enough to cross his path, and he thought how just once it would be nice to improve rather than worsen another person's life.

Back in the room, he pulled the manuscript from the trash. A phone number and address were printed, heartbreakingly hopeful, on the top of the thing. He dialed the number, got a robot voicemail, and hung up—at a loss for what to say or even why he was calling. He found ESPN on the TV and watched some hockey highlights, if such a thing could be said to exist. Figures glided gracefully to and fro across the white expanse, occasionally punching one another.

He picked up the phone again, and this time, an Indian-accented male voice answered. "Hello, front desk."

"This is room 141."

"Yes?"

"I need a favor from you."

"Yes?"

"I was wondering if you could bring me a beer or two."

"I'm sorry, sir, we don't have room service."

"But could you maybe bring me a couple from somewhere? A convenience store nearby or something?"

"You want me to go to a convenience store at eight in the morning on a Sunday and get you beer."

"I'll pay you forty bucks."

"Hold on." There was a sound of muffled rummaging. "As it turns out, we have a couple in our employee fridge. Room service will bring them right over."

The clerk appeared with two Coors Light cans dangling from a plastic yoke, and Richard handed him two twenties, ignoring the sheepish look on the man's face. Why should the clerk feel guilty? he thought as he drained the first beer. It was the best forty bucks he'd ever spent. Twenty a can? He would have gladly paid a hundred, a thousand.

Becalmed by the beer and a related but distinct sense of purpose, he tried Vance's number again. Again it went right to voicemail, the number he'd dialed repeated back agonizingly slow by the computerized female voice, as though she could somehow sense what an idiot he was. He looked back at the painting, then down at the manuscript in his lap. Though an idiot he was, he was not unaware that his urge to apologize to the kid—to put things right, or rightish, or righter than they were now at any rate—had something to do with the conversation he'd had with Cindy, which he could remember virtually none of, yet was absolutely sure had been bad. This certainty stemmed partly from the fact that he hadn't had a good conversation with her in twenty years but mainly from the feeling he got in his stomach when he thought about the phone call. A lifetime of interrogating himself the morning after, investigating these little shudders and cold spots in his gut, told him it had been very, very bad. Talking to Cindy, of course, was not an option—like Vance, she wouldn't answer the phone—unlike him, she possessed the distinct advantage of living a thousand miles away.

"Vance," he started and stopped, struck by the insufficiency of a rambling, voicemailed apology. "Never mind. I'll see you soon."

Pulling a thin phone book from the nightstand, finding the number for a cab company, he asked himself why it mattered. It didn't, nothing did. Nonetheless, he showered. Nonetheless, he put on fresh clothes. Nonetheless, he stood outside with his bag until the battered green taxi came into view.

———

Twenty minutes later, the cab dropped him in front of a small house set so far back into the nearby woods it looked like it was in the witness protection program. He set his suitcase by the mailbox and trudged up a long, cracked driveway. Finally making the front stoop, he paused for the requisite five minutes or so it took him to catch his breath after engaging in any manner of physical activity, then he rang the doorbell. A black-and-yellow wolf spider duly emerged from its woolen hidey-hole overhead in the space between the wall and drainpipe, but no human answered. He pressed the button again, and the kid appeared, hair askew and cheek striped with sleep lines.

"How did you find me?" said Vance.

He held up the manuscript. "Look, I'm sorry about last night."

"It's fine."

"No, it's not. I was a real asshole. I am a real asshole, I continue to be. I persist in my assholery."

"Okay."

"Tell me what I can do to make it up to you."

Vance shrugged, narrowing his already narrow shoulders, further caving in his sunken chest.

"I'm going to read this. I'll let you know what I think."

"It doesn't matter."

They stood there for a minute. It felt remarkably similar to arguing with one of his ex-wives, the sense that there was some magical combination of words and feigned contrition that would make her unmad at him. The kid took off his glasses and rubbed the side of his face with his palm. Richard said, "It does matter."

"That's not what you were saying last night."

"Hence my apology."

"Say it again."

"What?"

"That it matters. I don't just mean my book—I know it's probably pretty bad. But I'm trying, you know?"

"I know."

"It's not all worthless and it's not all bullshit. Your books matter to me. It matters."

Vance's long face stared ahead, across the yard and tree line past the road. In the sky, the sun sat half mount and recalcitrant red, as though it had just barely been talked into rising and was already reconsidering the wisdom of doing so. Still, it rose. There was a long unknowable day ahead, and Richard felt himself ineffably touched by the kid's hope, even if it wasn't a hope he shared. "Okay, it matters."

Vance seemed to process this, still watching the sunrise. The inside of the house—a split stairway that led up and down both ways into darkness—gloomed out at the dawning day, absorbing the sunlight. Or perhaps it was the day reaching into the depths of the house; for a moment, the kid seemed pitched in a kind of equilibrium between the two. He said, "Good."

"Anything else," said Richard.

"Yeah, let me go with you."

"What?"

"You asked how you can make it up to me. That's how."

CHAPTER SIX

———

Rolling down Interstate 90, they passed through the outer reaches of the town's meager sprawl, then the requisite big-box badlands. Best Buy, IKEA, then Bed Bath &, finally, Beyond—a blessed stretch of pine forest with no visible commerce. Vance had his elbow out the window and an intolerable air of exuberant victory about him, and Richard felt certain that this was a horrible mistake. Why not, he'd thought. He'd let him come along to Portland, and maybe even San Francisco if he wasn't too annoying. He didn't want to have to drive anyway, and at that moment, standing on the kid's porch, the idea of some company did not seem like the worst thing in the world.

But the same little smile kept resurfacing on Vance face, like a cavorting sea mammal periodically coming up for air, and it made Richard want to slap him. He seemed to think he'd won some kind of contest of wills, when, in fact, he'd caught Richard at his lowest point since the DUI, his most vulnerable. A vicious hangover had climbed up on his shoulders and neck, a tireless jungle cat long stalking its prey.

Vance said, "Thanks again, Mr. Lazar."

"Don't thank me again."

"It's just I think I've needed this for a long time and didn't even realize."

"What, to stay at an Econo Lodge with an older man?"

"To get out of here."

Richard reflexively visualized the house, set back in the woods, the door open to a mustiness behind the kid like the groaning maw of some ancient creature. Not entirely unfamiliar with outposts of wretched hermitage, Richard had still been impressed. Yes, he thought, you probably did need this.

As they drove, the sun rose fully and clarified to a brilliant white-yellow, warming the air and bluing the sky, and the morning gathered itself into the kind of rare October day that you want to breathe in and save for the winter. Surrounded on both sides by lush forest, crisp Pine-Sol-fragrant air coming through his window, Richard felt correspondingly worse and worse. The calm of the earlier beers had vanished as his hangover emerged in full, like an evil creature moving up on him through dark underbrush. The pristine surroundings foregrounded his misery; he would have felt better in a condemned hovel, splayed out on a yellowy mattress surrounded by *Hustler*s and dirty underwear and McDonald's wrappers. The kid's smile and the breeze and the golden sunlight coming through the windshield assaulted him, and the inside of his skull pounded like fists on a table, unilaterally rejecting all this pleasure and beauty. He rolled his window down and vomited out a complicated, lengthy rebuke.

It took Vance—still smiling to himself and tapping on the wheel—several seconds to notice what was happening, and by that point the contents of Richard's stomach were streaked down the length of the car. They stopped on the shoulder. An SUV roared by, and someone yelled at them—the entire history of human malevolence seemed embodied in that one shrill, trailing laugh.

"Are you okay?"

"Sorry, yeah," said Richard, still leaning out the window and panting like a dog, though not like his dog. When he took Victor on jaunts, Victor preferred to curl up on the floorboards. Vic was currently housed in a concrete-and-chain-link kennel that resembled nothing so much as Maricopa County jail, which he knew because he'd spent the night there after his last DUI.

They stopped for a car wash at a Citgo a mile down the road. While Vance filled up the tank, Richard went inside and bought a twelver of Busch Light along with a car-wash coupon. Suspecting the kid would give him a hard time about the beer, he skulked around the side of the concrete building, past a fenced-in generator and reeking dumpster, to a concrete break area that featured a Chock full o'Nuts can chock full o'wet cigarette butts and a vista of scraggly underbrush strewn with garbage. He drained two beers in quick, gagging succession and felt the tiger retract its claws from his shoulders and slink back into its fetid jungle lair.

As he worked on a third, he idly tried to describe to himself the sensation of getting drunk, an exercise he undertook with some frequency, probably because he spent so much time describing things and drinking. What was it like? Well, it was like getting drunk, it wasn't like anything else. It heightened all the things you wanted heightened—libido and humor and pleasure in the company of others—and numbed all the things you wanted numbed: everything else, really, but anxiety and sadness especially. That is, until you were actually drunk and not just getting drunk, then the exact opposite was true. All the good stuff died, and maudlin gloom sprang up like an unslayable movie monster, fiercer than ever. Which was to say that, of course, getting drunk and being drunk were two entirely different things.

Back in the car, Vance took the proffered coupon code and nodded at the beer, saying, "Really?"

"Light beer—it's basically Gatorade."

"You think that's a good idea?"

"I think it's a great idea. A stroke of genius."

Vance shook his head and drove them up to the car wash, entered the code, and pulled in. As the brushes rolled over the top and sides of the car, Richard felt cleansed himself. He closed his eyes and momentarily wished he could stay there forever, in the dark and cool, soothed and buffeted by the gentle embrace of mechanical arms in a place with no future and especially no past. But all too soon the car was bright with sunlight again, and Vance was pulling out onto the access road that led back to the highway.

As they drove, the kid compulsively fooled with the radio, trying to find a channel that didn't fuzz out at the bottom of every hill. He finally came to rest on a station playing a band Richard recognized and hated:

the Eagles. The song on the radio, "Desperado," perfectly embodied what he thought of as their signature lyrical perspective, wherein a jaded but wise narrator has some tough advice for the subject of the song and, by extension, the listener. *You might want to be sitting down, you could imagine the singer prefacing the song, I hate to do this, but I'm going to have to disabuse you of some of your most cherished notions.*

He hated them not only for the self-righteous lyrical pap but also or mainly because Carole had loved them, once even forcing him to attend an outlandishly expensive show at the Mesa Civic Center. The only way he'd gotten through watching Don Henley—accompanied by every single person in the arena—sing "Hotel California" was to imagine taking aim with a Browning assault rifle at the disembodied head bobbing behind the drum set, the pleasure of squeezing off a round and watching the pink vapor through the scope. The experience of that concert had made him wonder, and not for the first time, why people ever do anything. Doing things was almost always a mistake.

A succession of lakes passed by the window. First Sprague Lake, then Lake of the Branches, then Varna Lake, hives of strenuous recreational fun that teemed with people in primary-colored swimsuits and life jackets doing things: canoeing, kayaking, Sea-Dooing. He wished he was young again—there was so much he'd never done and never would do. Not that he wanted to kayak or sea-doo or had ever wanted to, but he wouldn't have minded being able to. He remembered fondly being twenty-five and the multitude of things he'd been able to do and hadn't—a paradise of squanderable opportunity. He drank his beer. The nice part about being young wasn't really being young; it was not being old. Like money, the thing time was good for was not having to worry about how much of it you had. The number sixty loomed in his imagination like a titanium wall he was speeding toward, in his smoking Yugo of a body. Sixty, he thought—he should be so lucky.

The forest on both sides of the highway grew thick and dark and he thought of the Tennessee forest of his youth, the trees and cars and girls. He couldn't think about the girls now, it was too much. The monotonous green beauty of the landscape conspired with the beers in his stomach. His head grew heavy and his sight grew dim and he had to stop for the night.

———

The old man's head dropped in several quick increments and came to rest against the window. A nasal, whistling snore reassured Vance he was alive. Richard had pounded back two beers like a man dying of thirst, and those on top of however many he'd had when he'd slunk behind the Citgo. Vance wondered if coming with him had been a mistake. He was like his father, not only in the simple terms of drinking too much but also in the speed with which he cycled through stages of animation, expansiveness, aggression, hostility, depression, and, by the end of the night, a mute stupor. It aroused in Vance an uncontrollable desire to fix something that, he knew, could not be fixed—to avert the next unavertable crisis. Steven Allerby's tenure in his son's life had been characterized by a hectic parade of accidents and misery caused either directly or indirectly by alcohol: the time he'd shot a nail through his hand while attempting to build a doghouse, for instance, or the time he'd slept through the first and only day of a new job despite his son shaking him for an hour. In a general sense, Vance felt he'd spent his whole life around adults who acted like children, who needed constant tending to and worrying over, and a glance at the passenger seat didn't help to dispel the feeling that he might easily take on the same role with Richard.

In sleep, the old man's face lost its perpetual glower and looked younger, with an adolescent expression of mildly devious innocence. The thick shock of hair reinforced the impression that Richard was a prematurely aged teenager. It was hard to believe at that moment that this was a man who'd written a bestselling memoir. Not that it was hard to imagine Richard experiencing what he'd experienced; it was hard to imagine him actually sitting down and writing about it. It was hard to imagine him producing a single paragraph about how he spent his summer vacation, let alone six excellent books. But, somehow, he had. Thinking of the work freshened Vance's gratitude to be where he was, next to Richard, driving the car. Whatever reservations he had about the old man's behavior, being out on tour with him had to beat moldering in his room, and—though the thought filled him with shame—looking after his mother, as well.

He hadn't realized, before Richard had shown up, before the words had escaped his mouth, how much he needed to be anywhere in the entire world but there. He stepped on the gas and gripped the steering wheel a little tighter, and the green piney nothingness that surrounded him, that had always surrounded him since he was born, blurred by. His mother's depression had become his own, and it was like a fog that had enveloped them both, so ubiquitous and thick as to be imperceptible. Only in, however briefly, getting away from it all—his mother, the house, his job, himself—could he see the fog's blurred contours and feel its lingering grasp on his person.

————

When Richard woke up, they were clattering over a bridge into Portland, which lived up to its reputation for being both overcast and silly. They drove through a misting rain, down streets slick with the oily tears of a great clown. At one point, they passed a jug band playing on a street corner, then they got stuck behind a peloton that included a man riding an actual penny-farthing. Finally they made the bookstore, a three-story citadel commanding an entire city block. Vance went off in quest of free parking, leaving Richard in front of the display window. A banner strung across the top advertised his appearance and, below it, there was a stand-up thing with his name on it and a stack of his books. There were other bestselling books in the display window, as well, and they seemed to fall into one of two categories: a book by a woman, named something like *Memories of Feelings* or *Still Sisters,* featuring a picture of a house on the cover, or a book by a man, named something like *The Templar Encryption* or *The Revenge of the Magi,* featuring occult imagery dripping with blood. What was his doing there? It had barely grazed the bottom of the list, true, but still. Maybe the reading public had confused him with someone else; maybe they'd heard his book featured serial killing. It did contain some death and mayhem, so there was that. He called Dana and brought her up to speed, with some obvious omissions.

"You're taking the kid from the college with you?"

"Vance."

"Why?"

"It's just for a stop or two. I needed to make it up to him."

"Mm-hmm, that makes sense. I got an email from the college. Apparently you were in rare form last night."

"I don't know if 'rare' is the word."

Dana sighed, and Richard could almost hear her rubbing her temples. In a pattern that had repeated itself with almost every woman he'd known throughout his life, his publicist's exasperation was somehow deeply pleasing to him; undoubtedly, he knew, it had something to do with a lack of motherly affection, but he just didn't care enough to figure it out. She said, "Look, please just do the reading tonight and go to sleep, okay? I can't worry about you constantly for the next two weeks."

"I'll call from San Francisco, Dana."

Vance slumped across the street. Together, they entered the bookstore, where they were greeted by a tall cat-eyed woman who introduced herself as Anne-Marie. Richard relished the momentary satisfaction of having possession of her name, even as it became enshrouded in the perpetually encroaching fog of his perpetually worsening short-term memory. Her dark hair was held back by a mint-green headband, and she smelled, pleasingly, like cigarettes. He said, "I'm Richard. This is Vance."

"Hi, Vance," she said. Vance had turned and was gawping at the store around him, which was huge and impressive, admittedly. He wandered off like a goggle-eyed yokel in the big city for the first time, which was, more or less, what he was.

"My assistant," said Richard.

She surveyed Richard's condition and said, "Are you all right?"

"Why is everyone asking that lately?"

"Sorry."

"It's okay. Rough night."

"Well, we're very happy you're here, Mr. Lazar."

"Say that again, would you?"

"Why?"

"I've just heard that sentence so rarely in my life. Especially coming from a beautiful woman's mouth."

She laughed. "We're *very* happy you're here, Mr. Lazar," a passable Marilyn imitation. "There's some food and drink in the green room."

The green room, so called, was located in the Employees Only rear of the store, which contained more bookshelves, desks in disarray, special-order forms taped to the concrete walls with no apparent logic, bookstore employees on break, and a card table in the corner on which a carafe of coffee steamed and a tray of cucumber-and-cream-cheese finger sandwiches quietly wilted. A cartoon arrow pointed down at the table, beneath a mordant sign: GREEN ROOM. Despite not liking cucumbers, wilted or otherwise, Richard ate one, determined to enjoy the spoils of success, even if they were spoiled. He poured the coffee, which he also didn't want, into a little Styrofoam cup and drank it with a shaking hand, and by the time what's-her-name came back to tell him he was on, everything was gone.

———

Vance floated around the store in a dissociated fog. As long as he could remember, he'd wanted not only to lose himself in books but to build a physical fortress out of them, a citadel of words to keep the world at bay. And when he was younger, in fact, he'd done just that, building forts from his burgeoning collection. This store felt like an actual adult version of that impulse brought to life. The Russian literature section alone was the size of his bedroom. The nineteenth-century British section was the size of his house. To work at a place like this would be a dream come true—spending entire days here, being entrusted with a key and living here, making camp here at night among the endless, towering rows.

This was a substitute, he knew, for what he really wanted, which was to actually live inside a book. He'd always been a reader, but ever

since his father had left and his mother had gotten sick shortly thereaf-
ter, he'd had a book in front of his face like a shield. It had worked, too,
for better or worse. His brother, John, had spent his high school years
in a constant, simmering rage and put that rage to use in the military
as soon as he legally could. Vance had, instead, locked himself away in
his lair and contented himself with his novels and fantasies.

He made his way through a circular maze of books, one that started
with world history in the outer shelves and, as he walked, slowly
morphed: to English history, then historical fiction, war crimes, true
crime, and finally, in the middle of the shelves, a small alcove filled
with paperback hard-boiled detective novels from the forties and fifties. A young woman sat cross-legged on a bench seat in the alcove,
bent over the sleuthing of Spade or Marlowe, twisting a piece of hair
by her ear. Each twisting pull seemed, in turn, to stab him through
with a sharp, erotic pang. She looked up and registered his presence,
and he hurried away. Back through the conch spiral he went, gathering acceleration until he was shot out into the depopulated environs
of Great Literature.

Frowning, he thumbed through a dog-eared used paperback of *Lo-
lita*. It felt leaden in his hand—not a repository of ideas, the best humanity has to offer, life distilled into words, but like a bunch of brittle
pages glued together inside a cover that featured a jaundiced nymphet
against a sickly pink background the color of raw liver. Dead weight.
He put it back and shuffled on, waiting for something to catch his eye,
but nothing did. As he had in his room the night before, he wondered
if books were the problem. In books, something happens to a character,
and they're never the same. It may be something good or something
bad, but whatever the case, it alters and propels them forward. The
character changes and is unable to go back to their old life. He found
himself idly expecting those moments in his own life—cruxes, hinges,
thresholds, points of equilibrium, moments freighted with such transformative power and import that he might gaze into the darkness and,
with his eyes burning, see himself as he really was.

The problem was, real life wasn't like that. Real life passed without much event, and what event there was provided not epiphany but

narcosis. A slow, deadening acceptance of the encroaching borders of your own existence. He'd watched it happen with his mother over the years. She'd been prone to bouts of silent depression since he could remember, but it was as though when his father left, the illness had moved in permanently to take his place. It had gotten worse over the years despite an endless battery of different medications and despite his best efforts to help. In six years, there had been no turnarounds, no moments of stunning realization—just minor ups and downs, mostly downs, a haze of cigarette smoke, and the constant, faint chatter of the TV. The worst part was not the illness itself; it was her assent to it, her willingness to live in her own shadow. In his manuscript, he had written about her, about living with her, and in this fictionalized version, she pulled out of it. The narrator, a diffident and sensitive young man, watched as she began building a new house in their front yard. Over three years, she poured the foundation, built the frame, and, one by one, laid the bricks. Then together, they destroyed the old house.

"Can I help you find something?" The voice plucked him from his reverie, and he turned to see the same girl from the hard-boiled section. She wore a store name tag, he saw now, although he couldn't read it due to, it really seemed, a sudden attack of eyeball perspiration.

"No." She started away, and he called after her with "Um, D. H. Lawrence?" in a voice so cracking and desperately lame it shocked even him. She stopped and motioned for him to follow. At the end of the aisle, Lawrence's disreputable oeuvre, in many different editions, reclined luxuriously on a long shelf.

"Anything in particular?"

"No, just looking."

"Okay. I have to say, I'm kind of impressed. Not many people read old David Herbert these days."

"He's great."

"I agree." She was not especially attractive, looking up at him with eyes set wide in a pointed, foxy face, but at that moment, Vance would have murdered a thousand men if she'd asked. He couldn't think of anything to say. She said, "Well, enjoy!" and moved away with a bright, brief flash of calf. Somewhere in the distance, a microphone crackled

on, spearing the stale, dusty air with feedback. "Thank you for coming," rumbled Richard's voice, and Vance fought his way back through
the maze, the catacombs of books.

———

The reading went well, or at least undisastrously; Richard took a few
questions from the small but packed room, and then it was over. He
asked Anne-Marie—he had relearned the name, and written the ini-
tials *AM* in tiny script on his palm—if she wanted to get a drink, and
she said sure, that she'd be delighted. He wondered if he'd ever before
occasioned delight in another person. Surely he had delighted Eileen
once or twice during their years together, but that had been a long,
long time ago. He asked Vance if he wanted to join them, but the kid
demurred; predictably, he wondered if it might not be a better idea to
take it easy tonight.

"Make hay while the sun shines."

"The sun's not shining, though."

Vance returned to the hotel—laden with an armful of D. H. Lawrence, of all things—and Anne-Marie took Richard to a place just down
the street that she said was new but that looked old. Waiting an un-
reasonable amount of time to be served at the unbusy bar, he saw it
was a trendy type of faux old, with lots of oak and brass veneers and
vintage mirrors made of smoked glass and a bartender wearing those
arm braces bartenders wear in westerns. Anne-Marie ordered them
both locally distilled artisanal rye whiskey, whatever that was. They sat
in a corner booth, under a speaker that played Sinatra or some similar
wife-beating big-band crooner, a style of music Richard hated. But they
talked about him, which he liked. He got to be all cannily self-effacing
and funny, yet soulful and serious, a routine that he vaguely remembered working with women during the Carter administration. When
she smiled, which she did a lot of, her eyes crinkled a bit around the
edges in a very fetching way, and when he glanced down at her long
legs, he couldn't help but wonder if it was possible he was going to, as
he and his friends used to say decades ago, get some. The last time that
had happened had been three years earlier, with a woman—a regular

at the Tamarack—that the other regulars knew as the Hound. The Hound was called the Hound for many reasons, among them the physiognomy of her face (questingly long and comprehensively jowled), her ability to sniff out a free drink, and the tenacity with which she pursued the men on whom her terrible favor fell. The Hound had taken a liking to him, and one night she had hung out until close, given him a Viagra, and demanded he take her home. He eventually did, and things had happened, terrible things he tried to forget about but couldn't. The possibility that the Hound had provided him his sexual swan song was a thought capable of poleaxing him with regret.

So: Anne-Marie. Despite his lingering hangover and generally wretched condition, he felt compelled to give it a shot. He got a second round, and she drank it; he made jokes, and she laughed. Things were going well—shockingly well—until he leaned over and attempted a kiss.

She pulled away. "Whoa. But."

"Sorry. I," he said.

"I'm. Wow." She stood next to the booth, smoothing down her dress.

"I thought," he said.

"It's just."

"There was."

"I know," she said, pulling her keys out of her purse and pulling a silver necklace with a silver ring dangling from it out of her décolletage. "But I'm married."

"Oh."

"And you're"—she briefly searched the oaken walls of the room, as though what he was was written on them, as though it wasn't obvious— "old."

"You could have left it at you being married," he said. "That worked fine by itself."

"Sorry." She went to the door and looked back. "Good luck."

Good luck. He sat there and drank his drink, thinking how there was no phrase in the English language more devoid of the sentiment it existed to convey. It was probably for the best—he put his odds of having achieved an erection somewhere between one to negative infinity against and none. He stared at the fine grain of the table, the less-fine grain of his own hands. That's that, he thought—women, love, the whole shebang. Goodbye to all that. Who were you kidding?

Back at the hotel, Vance was already asleep, on a cot at the foot of the bed. Richard was touched by the kid's consideration, not to mention the way it reminded him of Victor, who liked to sleep in the same position. He lay on the bed, on top of the covers, not even trying to sleep, just searching for some kind of equilibrium within himself, a state of balance in which he could momentarily stop wanting things. Not finding it, he heaved himself up and made his way down to the lobby, manned by a desk clerk staring intently at his singing phone. Past the front desk lurked an unpromising sports bar called the End Zone. The sign featured a crude painting of Snoopy wearing a football uniform and leather helmet, doing his happy dance after scoring a touchdown. The sign was almost unbearably sad, and he had to look away from it to avoid bursting into tears.

The End Zone was quiet at this hour and probably at every other hour, occupied only by a couple wearing matching Roethlisberger Steelers jerseys and eating cheese fries. The bartender—a dour, mustachioed fellow—emerged from the back with an affect that suggested he'd just been fondly nestling the barrel of a twelve-gauge in his mouth. After Richard's third gimlet and third tip, the man grudgingly asked if he was staying at the hotel.

"Why else would I be here?"

"Good point. What brings you?"

"I'm doing a book tour."

"No shit."

"Nope, no shit."

"What's the book about?"

"Me fucking up over and over."

"Well, looks like you've found the right place."

An hour or so later, Richard was completely alone. He missed Anne-Marie. He missed Victor. He missed the Steelers couple and looked back on their tenure at the End Zone as a sort of golden age of bonhomie. The bartender had vanished again, perhaps having slipped into the back and finished offing himself. The lights overhead had dimmed and made dark yellow spots on the bar, like pools of urine. His drink was gone and he wasn't drunk. Through the window, a car's taillights dwindled, twin red coronas like dying stars. Only two days into the tour and he was completely spent. The rest of the trip, not to mention his life, stretched out before him like one of those bleak country roads that eventually peter into nothingness—like the one he'd recently lived on, in fact. It was strange, after all those years living out in the desert—not happily, but with a certain amount of calm resignation—that two days in civilization had so thoroughly unmanned him. He thought of calling Cindy or Eileen again, but just as quickly banished the notion. Then he pulled the cell phone out and dialed.

"Hello?" came the voice, thick with sleep.

"You asked me the other night, at the thing, what advice I'd give young writers. And I gave you some glib answer, and I feel shitty about that. I probably acted like I think it's all a waste of time, which I do, but still. Everything's a waste of time, but books are better than everything else. There's some kind of dumb honor in it, at least. You know what I mean? At least it's trying, somehow. It admits death. It's not just pressing buttons on some shiny thing. All of this technology, all these bells and whistles, are just distractions from the fact that one day you'll wake up with blood on the sheets, right? No sight in one eye. There's honor in looking into the eye, isn't there?"

He would have continued in this vein indefinitely, had someone not put a hand on his shoulder. Vance stood there, dressed in the same clothes he'd worn that day. He sat next to Richard and said, "She was a little young for you."

"And married."

Richard hung up the phone. They sat there for a little while longer, under the epileptic flicker of a Rolling Rock sign, until Vance finally put his arm on Richard's arm and led him up to bed.

———

The next day, the sky overhead was gray and mottled, a mirror image of the road underneath them. Vance had his elbow out the window, despite the chilliness of the air, and tapped his hand on the side of the car along with a rap song on the radio. Richard wasn't offended by the vulgarity or the constant stream of obscenities or the jittery curlicues of the musical arrangements, but the insistent emotional sameness of it was oppressive. No joy, no despair, no love or humor, just pissed-off boasting, dick jokes, school-yard taunts. On this, as with most things, of course, he knew his opinion was wholly unqualified; yet again, as with most things, he didn't let that stop him from airing it. "You really like this shit?"

"Jay-Z? I don't know, I guess so."

Playing up the ignorant old-timer angle—which, being old and ignorant, was not hard to do—he said, "My jewels, my money, my bitches, my boats."

"My boats?"

"Yachts?"

"It's not all that stuff. You should keep yourself open to new things."

"That's where you're wrong. There's too much stuff in the world, too much crap. You should try to keep yourself closed off to as much of it as possible." Richard reclined fatly in his seat, irritated by the kid's determined innocence and by the length of the pauses he took before he spoke and by his long, mournful face, its look of defeated hope. He said, "Besides, you're one to talk. When was the last time you did something new?"

"I'm doing something new right now."

"What, driving me around?"

"Sure."

"I mean something meaningful. Falling in love. Eating fifty hard-boiled eggs."

In obvious reprisal, Vance changed the channel, cranking the volume on some horrible classic rock station playing a horrible classic rock song. Over a burbling sea of organs and mandolins, the lead singer wailed lyrics that seemed to be, horribly, about chess, admonishing the listener not to surround themselves with themselves. Richard yelled, "So, how long are you going to chauffeur me around, anyway?"

"That's up to you."

"You ever been to San Francisco?"

"I've never been anywhere."

"Why don't we say San Francisco. I'll get a rental there."

"That's only tomorrow. I had kind of hoped—"

"I know, it's really too bad. But let's say San Francisco."

They stopped for lunch at McDonald's, and, waiting in the drive-thru, Vance suggested they take a small highway west and get on the 101. He'd heard the 101 was incredible, he wanted to drive down the coast. It was a travel day, and lacking a good reason to say no, though that was his inclination, Richard grunted an assent into his leathery McDouble with cheese. All along the way, beefy clouds barreled overhead in what looked like time-lapse photography, but when they reached the ridgy shoreline where the highway met the 101, a giant wall of fog hung over the churning water, like some kind of cloud factory that cranked out the cumuli traveling inland.

The craggy splendor of the drive reminded Richard that he had once, decades earlier, taken the PCH from Carmel to Los Angeles. He remembered it being much the same as this: dramatic cliffs, crashing surf, salt-sprayed air, winding roads, old people driving RVs at eight miles an hour. The noncoastal sections of the drive were remote, and the little towns they passed—with their bait shops and flounder shacks and tie-dyed-kite stores and whimsical woodworking concerns—were already abandoned for the off-season. The only person they saw in downtown Waldport was a defiant seagull standing in the middle of the narrow road. When Vance got out of the car, it reluctantly walked away, like a dignified town elder with his hands clasped behind his back. Maybe it was the mayor, thought Richard.

It had been the summer of 1977 when they'd taken the PCH. A stranger had snapped a photo of Eileen (buckskin moccasins, base-ball jersey, pigtails) and him (triangular bellbottoms, vest, shag helmet) smiling next to his old VW on an overlook. This photo had hung to-temically by their front door in no fewer than five different apartments and houses they'd occupied. He had no real feeling about the image captured in the picture, but he had a vivid sense memory of the picture as the last thing he saw before exiting their home. Over the years, its continued presence had made him variously happy, sad, and finally irritated by Eileen's insistence on reminding him of better times. Like an addict—a love junkie—she was always trying to reclaim the high of those early days.

Richard and Vance passed from Oregon into California on a homely little stretch of road, the border parallel with a red-barned gift shop. A new blue-and-yellow sign on the right welcomed them to California, and an old white-and-green one on the left effused OREGON THANKS YOU, COME BACK SOON! No, Richard thought, that was unlikely—he guessed that Oregon had seen the last of him. They drove on, regaining the coast just as the sun was dropping quickly into the sea. In the vicinity of Eureka, they began stopping at hotels, but each one was booked up solid—an infuriating development after having seen no more than a dozen people in nine hours of driving. It turned out every room in the area had been reserved months in advance for something called the Blackberry Arts Festival.

"You want to camp out?" said Vance as they drove away from the fourth place they'd tried.

"No."

"I keep some gear in back. It could be pretty nice."

"No."

The next motel they encountered, ten miles south of town, was a dreary cluster of run-down stand-alone huts called Famous Ray's. Richard assumed the name was in honor of a locally famous murderer who had done his best work on the premises. At the front desk sat an old man bent to the newspaper, pencil in hand, a ragged Jumble with many letters tentatively written in and scratched out pinioned before him on the peeling linoleum.

"Name?"

"We need a room."

"No reservation?"

"No."

"You kidding?" the man scoffed, returning to his work. "It's the Blackberry Arts Festival."

Ten minutes later, they cut off from the 101 and drove alongside the bay, curving around on a spit of land that looked out onto the Pacific and offered spectacular views of a nearby power plant. It was unlit and seemed abandoned, its white-blue domes glowing ghostly in the bright moonlight. Vance stopped the car along the shoulder and retrieved a brightly colored nylon tent from the trunk. Richard got out of the car and followed the kid down a gentle tree-lined slope to a scrubby area twenty or so feet from the water. He gingerly lowered himself onto a large rock just on the dry side of the lapping water and turned toward the land. He liked the sensation of having his back to the ocean, ignoring the majesty, not being humbled.

Vance squatted to pound in the tent pegs with a rubber hammer. Richard said, "This is the kind of place where people get murdered, you know."

"It's beautiful here."

"I'm not saying it's not beautiful. It's just a good murderin' spot. No decent murderer could resist killing someone here."

Vance got the tent pitched and then set himself to building a fire, scurrying around and gathering little sticks and dry leaves. In spite of himself, Richard admired the kid's outdoors facility. Although he'd grown up in East Tennessee, spending much of his life near mountains and otherwise living close to or in the boondocks, he'd never been much for camping or nature. What had he been much for? he wondered sometimes. Drinking, being hungover, chasing skirt, getting in stupid fistfights, arguing with girlfriends and wives, trying to make amends, regretting things, all the while trying to put something meaningful on paper, and usually failing.

After eating rancid Vienna sausages and granola bars procured earlier at a mostly cleaned-out convenience mart, Richard and Vance sat around the quietly crackling fire. Richard pulled out the half-empty pint of Old Grand-Dad that he'd bought from an adjoining liquor store while Vance was using the convenience mart bathroom and couldn't stop him. Vance waved away the proffered bottle.

"Come on, have a drink," said Richard.

"I told you, I don't drink."

"If you can't have a nip of whiskey sitting in front of a fire by the ocean, I don't know what."

"Fine." Vance pressed the bottle to his pursed lips, tipped his head back, and made an unconvincing show of swallowing whiskey that probably never entered his mouth. "That's awful."

"Everything good for you tastes bad."

The water was insistent behind him, like a small child tapping on his back, and he twisted to see what it wanted. Far away, the lights of a fishing boat flashed. Crabbing, most likely, out for forty-eight hours at a time. That should have been his life: out there on all that black water, a world without end—no one to rub up against, hurt, or be hurt by. One wrong move, a towering wave or unsecured mainsail, and you'd be drifting to the ocean floor, completely erased from the world's record. It sounded fine to him, the proper order of things. He'd lived his life far too messily, and even as he'd moved into the desert, thinking it would burn everything down to its simplest essence, it hadn't worked—here he was, in the world again. He needed to push off shore in a leaky rowboat and never look back.

Vance sat cross-legged and was writing in a notebook he'd pulled from his bag. He kept glancing over at Richard as he wrote. Finally Richard said, "You drawing a picture of me or something?"

Vance looked down. "No."

"What then?"

"Just recording the moment."

"You go around taking notes all the time?"

"Don't you? How do you remember things for later?"

The fire danced in front of him, and he was thirteen again, hunting with his father for the first and last time. Scared shitless of killing a deer, and—equally—disappointing his newly returned father. Holding the .22 in his arms like a snake that might bite him—even then he'd had no taste for firearms or shooting things. He liked reading about people shooting things, but that was as far as it went. Silence later around the fire, after a fruitless hunt that had culminated in a clear kill shot he'd refused to take. The deer had bounded away in a graceful, ungainly seesaw. His taciturn father drank something from a bottle like the one he held now, a brown sloshing liquid, probably whiskey, though he didn't know for sure. Unlike him, the old man hadn't seen fit to share—he hadn't earned a drink. Men got a drink. "I have this thing called a memory," he said. "Other than that, mostly I make shit up."

Vance shrugged and continued writing, and Richard scooted closer to the fire. He lay back in the rocky dirt and looked up at the pin-pricked sky. The sky was better than the sea, he thought, infinitely more vast, yet humble—not crashing and clamoring for constant attention. The sky was the real God, fit for worship; the sea was a small god, jealous and mean. He shouldn't have been a sailor—he should have been an astronomer, stationed in Greenland. His mind wandered to the Dutch one, or was he Danish, with the golden nose. What was his name? One of those things that he'd heard as a child and had stuck with him. He feared losing information like this to the ravages of time and alcohol, and so he closed his eyes as he strained to remember. The name was there and then not there in the same instant, an afterimage of itself. He couldn't get it by brute force and began going through the initial letters. Would one light up as he scrolled through? *T* seemed right; it had a soft glow. As he lay there his mind wandered further, an image of the table of Henry VIII, who died from overeating. Was that true? Or poisoned by his own urine, that was someone. Burst stomach either way. Those were the days—maggots festering in the caked-on makeup of courtesans, the writhing painted faces of the ladies of the court. Rampant venereal disease. He'd had VD when the clap was still called the clap. Three horse pills cured it. The good old days—going around with a gold nose on.

When he opened his eyes again, Vance was inside the tent, and the campfire had died down to embers. The kid had covered him with a blanket before going to sleep. He sat up drinking the last of his whiskey and shivering in the wind. Going back to sleep seemed unlikely, given the cold and the strangeness of the surroundings. He watched the dark water, half expecting some terrible, slavering monster to rise out of it.

In the sparse woods to the right of their little campground, something moved. The sound of the ocean did not quite mask the crackling of branches. Before he had a chance to get properly terrified or wake Vance up to see what it was, something ambled out of the woods into the moonlight. In his misty, smoked-glass vision, he could only tell that it had four legs, but that was enough to reassure him they weren't about to be murdered. Likely a deer, of course. Could he shoot it now? he wondered, seeing the doe from his youth—bob-tailed, with walnut spots on the white ruff of her chest—chewing a leaf with a look of nervous distraction. Probably not. He wasn't that different now than he'd been then; so much time and energy spent going nowhere. From inside the tent Vance snored innocently, a soft glottal sigh. Whatever it was out there moved away, grew fainter and fainter, at some point melting back into the smudged darkness of the trees. It had sensed his presence and moved away—embarrassed and unsettled. You are the monster, he thought. It's you.

Tycho Brahe.

CHAPTER SEVEN

They woke with the break of day, as well as an infestation of some kind of sand flea. Swatting themselves like penitent Sufi mystics, they unpitched the tent and clambered back up to the road. Climbing into the car, Richard looked down at his arms, swollen with little red bites. "This is why I never do anything," he said. "Doing something is always a mistake."

Vance scratched his long neck, leaving red trails from ear to collarbone. He U-turned and pointed them south in the gray light, the rising sun still obscured by the eastern forest's edge. Richard burrowed into the crook of seat and door and was just feeling the first welcome tendrils of reclaimed sleep when the car coasted onto the shoulder and stopped. Smoke billowed from the hood in thick, healthy plumes. "Shit," the kid said.

"What happened?"

"Something's wrong."

"Oh really? It's not supposed to be doing that?"

Vance got out and opened the hood, releasing a gust of black smoke directly into his face that bent him double in hacking convulsions. Richard waved at a passing car, which accelerated. But after three more tries, someone with a sufficient shred of conscience, or else nowhere important to be, pulled over. A very fat man—fatter than Richard, an increasingly rare and gratifying occurrence—got out and stood by his car. "You fellas need a lift?"

"Thanks," said Richard. Vance was still bent over the car, as though he might be able to fix what was wrong by sheer force of concentration. "Come on, Vance."

The man dropped them off at a service station a few miles down the road, in a town named Eureka, an unfortunate name for a place that no one would ever be happily surprised to find. It was a gray, dismal village, like a patch of Ohio rustbelt transplanted to the Pacific coast. A surly guy in coveralls gave them the once-over, as though he suspected they were somehow up to no good, then ferried Vance away in his tow truck. Richard waited in a plastic chair in the lobby, soaking in the atmosphere—wood paneling, linoleum, grease, a Samantha Fox calendar on the wall from 1988, two mechanics in terse conversation aggressively ignoring him. Why did all auto mechanics hate non–auto mechanics, he wondered. Hadn't they been nonmechanics first?

The truck reappeared, Explorer in tow. Coveralls told them it was something to do with oil pressure, or maybe something else, and that he could go ahead and fix it, but it wouldn't be cheap.

"What a surprise," Richard said.

"Well, you want me to or not," said Coveralls.

"I don't have much money," offered Vance.

"What a surprise," Richard said. "Yeah, go ahead. We'll take in the sights."

At eight in the morning, Eureka seemed to be mostly inoperative, as though the entire town was sleeping off a miserable hangover, which it probably was. They walked down to a rusting industrial harbor overrun by seagulls. The birds stood together on concrete stanchions out in the water, fluttering their wings in what seemed a lot like anticipatory glee. A small boat called the *Big Sir* bobbed in the unhealthy, greenish tide, its bow very close to the waterline. They turned around.

On the walk back through the middle of town, things improved somewhat. A quaint little strip with candy-colored storefronts featured a row of hopeful businesses that it was hard to imagine succeeding here: a first-edition bookseller, a gourmet wine store. And a small café, just turning its sign to OPEN. They entered, surprising a young waitress who seated them by the window. After waiting for her to stammer out the specials, Richard ordered a black coffee and eggs and bacon and also sausage, and Vance ordered the quiche of the day.

"Real men don't eat quiche," said Richard.

"Sure they do," said the waitress, taking their menus with a fetchingly inadvertent smile that revealed braces. She returned, still smiling, with their drinks, reentered the kitchen, and Richard said, "She likes you."

"Not this again."

"You should ask her out."

"We're leaving town in an hour."

"Ask her if she wants to come with us. She'd probably jump at any opportunity to get out of this dump. I'll ask her for you."

"Don't," said Vance, looking genuinely frightened.

"I'm just kidding, loosen up."

"Why do you care?"

"I don't know." He took a drink of his coffee and thought about it. "I guess it's just you'd be surprised how fast it goes. A pretty girl smiling at you happens like twelve times in your life."

Vance shook his head and addressed himself to his phone. In a few minutes, the waitress returned with food, and Richard appended a Bloody Mary to his order. Mouth full of quiche, Vance said, "It's nine in the morning."

Richard sighed. "Not this again. And nine in the morning is exactly when you're supposed to drink Bloody Marys."

After breakfast and further desultory rambling, they were summoned back to the garage. The comical total was $678.85 for a new oil filter, replacement t-rings, and the towing. Richard retrieved his billfold, un-Velcroed it, and pulled out a personal check. The guy at the register waited until he'd filled it out, then chortled. "No checks."

"That's all I have."

The guy looked backward at one of the mechanics and gestured toward the door, saying, "There's an ATM somewhere down the road, down there."

"I don't want to go somewhere down the road, down there. I'm right here. And I'm pretty sure you're overcharging us by about three hundred dollars, okay? Just take the damn thing." The guy seemed like he was trying to decide between calling the cops, tearing up the check, and vaulting over the counter to beat in Richard's face. "Listen," Richard went on, "it'll cash. I'm famous, look me up."

The guy took the check and grudgingly made his way to an ancient desktop computer in the corner, into which he laboriously pecked Richard's name with one hand while holding the check three inches from his face. He eventually nodded, and they were on their way. In the car, Vance said, "Thanks. I'll pay you back."

"No, you won't," Richard said, again burrowing into the door. "It really doesn't matter."

———

They made San Francisco in the early afternoon. It spread out in front of them, reclined and made up in bright colors like a beautiful but slovenly whore. Vance gaped at it with awe as they crossed the Golden Gate. "Amazing."

"Just wait until you see a hippie taking a shit in the street."

"How long did you live here?"

"Not long. I got here summer of 1971. I had met this guy in Vietnam who was from California and talked nonstop about how great it was here. I thought the second I got across the Bay Bridge, I'd be getting a mescaline-flavored tongue bath from some chick named Rainbow. Talk about disappointing. I spent three months living over a Chinese place in the Tenderloin, walked around smelling like egg foo yong and not getting laid. Closest I came was at a bar on Valencia where I got beaten up and rolled by a drag queen. There's a reason people talk about the summer of 'sixty-seven and not the summer of 'seventy-one. I missed the party."

"That bothered you?"

"Hell yes, it bothered me. I grew up outside of Knoxville on a turd ranch. Maryville, Tennessee."

"I read the book."

"Yeah. In 1967, I was sixteen. Spent my nights drinking RC Cola at the Kiwanis Club, where they had square-dancing, just on the off chance of kissing this bucktoothed redhead who I'd heard was loose."

"That sounds nice, actually."

"It wasn't the Summer of Love, I'll tell you that much. And by the time I got here, it was all junkies and burnouts. I got on with a construction crew in Oakland as soon as I could, did bids all the way down the Central Valley."

Still, Richard couldn't help but feel a wistful pleasure as they drove through the Presidio, as postcardish in real life as it was in his memory—emerald grass and white-bone villas with red-tiled Spanish roofs. He and Eileen had picnicked there twice, on day trips to the city, during the early time in their relationship when he could be convinced or bothered to do things like go on picnics. He thought he could see the exact spot from the car, an old tree—birch? maple?—which stood alone in the middle of a shadowed field. Of course, he knew he was probably imagining it, remembering what he wanted to remember.

They arrived at the Providence, a chichi place in the financial district near the Transamerica Building. Outside, the hotel was a ten-story sheath of dark glass. Inside, it felt as though it had been built five minutes before they arrived, and they were the first people to stay in it. It was a decided improvement on the Comfort Suites and Quality Inn, and Richard made a mental note to thank Stan the next time they talked. The only arena in which it lagged was the absence of an Andes mint on his pillow.

"It really is the little things," he said.

"What," called Vance over the sound of his own pee in the bathroom.

"Nothing."

They lay on the plush beds, and Richard turned on the TV, clicking zestlessly from one channel to the next. Vance was reading a book that it took Richard a minute to recognize as his own.

"I thought you'd already read it," he said.

"I did. I'm rereading it."

"Why?"

"Why do you think? I like it."

"Yeah, but why?"

Vance tented the book on his chest and said, "I don't know. I guess I feel like you used to be like me. You came from nowhere, you didn't know what you were doing. And you made it through, somehow."

"Did I?"

"Yes."

"Says the guy who rescued me from Snoopy's Lounge a night ago."

The kid untented the book and resumed reading, and Richard closed his eyes. Perhaps, he thought, for once in his life, he could stay very still and behave like an adult. His phone buzzed in his pocket, and as it could only be two people, he pulled it out and took a blind guess.

"Stan."

"It's Dana."

"Hi, Dana."

"You make it to San Francisco?"

"Yeah."

"You remember the interview at five?"

"What interview?"

"Public radio." She sighed. "*Cool Breeze,* with Mary Koestler."

"Shit." Dana gave him an address, which, turning on his side, Richard jotted down using the hotel stationery and pen on the nightstand. "I'll cab it down there in a little while."

She perfunctorily scolded him about a couple of things and then signed off. Richard pulled himself up and sighingly thumbed his orthopedic old-man shoes back on. His feet, having become accustomed over the last year to near immobility, were outraged at his recent dynamic lifestyle leap to the realm of mere inactivity. He waved backward to Vance and slumped down the hall to the elevator.

The hotel lounge was a sleek affair, all brushed steel and dim track lights and monochromatic color fields behind the bar. The only other people there were a couple sitting in the corner with hands clasped on top of the table. A slinky, digital bossa nova emanated from invisible speakers. Richard hoisted himself onto a stool. On his own petard. By? The bartender approached, an unsmiling bald man who looked like an

East German villain in a 1980s movie adaptation of a John le Carré novel. Richard ordered a martini, which was delicious and very cold, with a field of ice crystals on top.

"That's twenty-two," said the bartender.

"Jesus Christ. Charge it to room three thirteen. How do people live in this city?"

"You got me. I'm up in Sausalito."

The bartender went into the back, and Richard allowed himself to enjoy or to try to enjoy, for a little while, a feeling of achievement. Here he was, a not-entirely-unknown author on a book tour, put up in a snazzy hotel, drinking an exorbitantly expensive drink. The imagined generic version of this moment had been, for many years, the pulpy grist for his fantasy mill. Of course, in his fantasies, there had been a woman with him (beside him, below him, on top of him), but this was close enough. He wondered, then, why the moment felt so thin and false, why it seemed he could poke his finger through the papier-mâché wall of the hotel, push the entire edifice over like the flimsy scene dressing it was.

He drank his drink and ordered another—not as delicious as the first, though equally expensive. It wasn't only that he felt he didn't deserve success, though he didn't. It was the feeling that it had all happened too late—like his first time around in this city, he'd gotten there after the fact. The party wasn't just over; the party had been over so long that the food left on the table reeked, and the punch bowl crawled with flies, and the hostess was passed out in the corner, her face smeared rosy red with clownish lipstick. What remained were the dregs and remnants of the life he'd always wanted and never had. Getting it now felt, in a way, like cosmic punishment for his bitter, selfish resentment over not getting it the first time around. Of course, he'd already been punished with the loss of his wife and child, but then when has God ever passed up a heavy-handed joke? Maybe he should have just stopped writing altogether. Maybe he should have been a sailor.

"You don't choose your life, Rich, it chooses you." He could still see his father saying that, the morning he'd received his draft notice. Standing there in his boxer shorts on a cold Saturday morning, running his finger over the embossed eagle at the top of the paper. He'd failed out of college and allowed it to happen, thinking it might please the old man, too chickenshit to just enlist. He wasn't sure if his father was right about your life choosing you, but the first part had been spot-on—his entire life had been reaction, fleeting spasms of need, desire, and shame.

Vance slouched through the lobby, hands in pockets, looking fearful of being thrown out for trespassing. He noticed Richard and stopped beside the bar. "I thought you were going to that interview."

"I am."

"After how many of those? You have to do the reading later, remember?"

"Don't worry about it." He pulled out his wallet and handed five twenties to Vance. "Here's some walking-around money. Go check out the city. Make sure you call it 'Frisco,' locals love that. I'll see you back here in the lobby at seven."

Vance looked at the money and said, "What's this for?"

"Just take it. Go have an adventure."

The kid reluctantly took the cash and walked away. He pushed into the wrong side of the hotel's revolving front door and got halfway out, before being repelled back into the lobby by a stampede of Asian businessmen. He glanced abashed over his shoulder, then tilted out the right way and was gone from sight. Richard asked the bartender to call him a cab and ordered one more drink, in the hope that it might reverse the maudlin tide of his mood or, failing that, get him drunk.

———

Vance walked down Sansome Street in no particular direction. The windbreaker he wore failed to break the wind gusting jaggedly up the hill. The clear sky and white, crystalline sun—and the fact that he was in the state of California—had deceived him into thinking the afternoon would be temperate. He debated returning to the hotel to put on a sweater, but he had already walked for ten minutes down the steep grade and decided to tough it out.

He was happy to get away from the hotel, and from Richard. The old man's refusal to take care of himself was infuriating and frustrating; he seemed to sense Vance's aggravation and delight in making it clear how little of a shit he gave. Well, if Richard didn't give a shit, neither did he. He was just along for the ride, anyway, and this was probably the last stop. He didn't know why he ever tried to help anyone—you never could, and he should know better by now, having grown up in the family he'd grown up in. His father and mother both seemed determined, in their own ways, to repeat the same mistakes forever. Thinking of the small picture of the four of them that leaned on the upstairs mantel—Vance and John sitting stupidly in front; their furtive father behind them, craning sideways as though just having noticed the latest woman or bottle or pile of drugs into which he would disappear for the next six months; his mother smiling intently at the camera, as though, through the sheer force and depth of her denial, she might keep his father from bolting out of the frame—his mood darkened further.

He pulled out his cell and dialed. "Hello?"

"It's me," he said.

"Where are you," his mother said.

"I called yesterday. I left a message."

"I haven't checked my messages."

"I had a chance to go on the road with the guy I told you about. I'm driving him, helping out. We're in San Francisco."

She seemed to let that settle in for a moment. "That's great."

"Is it?"

"Of course it is."

"Are you okay?"

"I'm fine." He could see the gray bedsheet, the thin column of cigarette smoke, the cold coffee curdling beside her on the nightstand. "I really am glad for you. Call me soon."

"Mom," he said, but she'd already hung up.

Have an adventure, Richard had said. This sounded like a good idea in theory, but impossible in practice. He was already overwhelmed by the city, and a distressingly large part of him craved the dark sanctuary of home, the brooding silence of his bedroom. In the distance, the water of the bay sparkled, as though it had gold coins scattered across it. He walked toward it for lack of any other destination. Getting closer, he was increasingly surrounded by hordes of tourists, like walking into a hovering globe of gnats. He caromed off the large leader of a large clan of large tracksuited Germans, whose large blond head remained lowered to his tiny phone. When he finally reached the retaining wall by the bay, the water—so beautiful from an elevated distance—was oily and rank with seagull shit and the smell of dead fish. Ersatz shacks set up near the water sold crabmeat sandwiches for fourteen bucks a pop. An authentic black man in sunglasses and a fedora played Mississippi blues through a tiny battery-powered amp for a crowd of overreverent tourists.

When Vance was ten, his father had taken him to Seattle, parking the car by the waterfront. Vance had never been that far away from Spillman before and still vividly remembered his shock at seeing the skyline and buildings and the waves crashing into Puget Sound. He was scandalized by the thought that, while he'd been growing up in the eastern woods, this city had always been a few hours down the road. His excitement was quickly tempered when he realized his father—as was miserably predictable—had no plan and no money. They had loitered around by the waterfront and eventually shuffled hungrily through Pike Place Market, where they were mistaken for a nomadic fishmonger *père et fils* by a family of French Canadian tourists inquiring after *saumon frais*.

Now, he twisted his tall, narrow shoulder to the throng surrounding the man's performance and cut back sideways through the crowd like a parrying fencer. Up on Market, the masses dispersed again; some stubborn cloud seemed to follow suit, and the sun came fully out for the first time since he'd left the hotel. As it warmed his upturned face, he realized how cold he'd been. The upper reaches of the buildings he passed were lit by the sun, their windows aflame as though anointed by celestial truth. Sunlight filtered through the buildings to his left, creating a golden path, which he followed.

As he wandered, guided only by a desire to remain in the shifting grids of warm sunlight, he noticed a girl in front of him. She was consistently about a half block away, a slight person wearing oversize white tennis shoes and a jeans skirt and some kind of zebra-print halter that exposed the top vertebrae of her narrow back. He might not have noticed her if it hadn't been for her hair, which was short and messy and dyed an emphatic red. Not the brick red or magenta punk that daring girls at his high school and college had favored, but a bright, coppery auburn that might have looked natural if it hadn't been for her fawn complexion. She seemed to be walking in the light as well, so Vance just followed the head of bright red hair as it moved along like the cartoon bouncing ball, past Korean delis and pizza shoppes and bar after bar, and here teenagers smoking cigarettes looking mildly dangerous and there a businessman talking into his phone as though it was a walkie-talkie, and he became so fixated on the girl and on following her, and the pleasant yet contradictory sensations of mindless motion and mindful pursuit, engaged somehow in a purpose he didn't yet fully understand, that it took him an extra second to understand what had happened when she was hit by a car.

———

Thirty blocks north and three stories up, Richard had managed to locate San Francisco's NPR affiliate station, in a little room that looked more like an auxiliary storage space than an on-air studio. Cardboard boxes and an array of Cold War–era radio technology and related detritus partially blocked the door. The interviewer was a professional woman in her midforties, wearing business slacks and a tailored jacket, with a serious yet warm demeanor. The interviewee was an unprofessional man, early fifties, wearing polyester leisure slacks, with an unserious yet cold demeanor. Also a half-bombed demeanor, as he'd been unable to resist marking the moment with one more quick drink at the bar beneath the studio. Or "marking the moment," as he'd thought about it, sitting in the bar, with finger quotes around the phrase in his head because, one, what moment was he marking? And two, he marked every moment nowadays. He needed to try not marking a moment—now, that would really make it stand out.

Susan—to the best of his memory, that was the interviewer's name—said, "Today, on *Cool Breeze,* we have Richard M. Lazar. Mr.

Lazar's memoir, entitled *Without Leave,* came out last year and has been receiving a lot of notice. Thank you for coming, Mr. Lazar."

"Thank you, Susan."

"Mary."

"Sorry."

"Okay. So, Richard, without giving anything away, this book describes your experience going AWOL from the army during Vietnam."

"Deserting, actually."

"I'm sorry, what's the difference?"

"AWOL is when you get too drunk on a weekend furlough and miss your plane back. Desertion is more serious and involves intent. Separation versus divorce."

"The title's misleading then."

"Yeah, I think the publisher thought *Deserter* would sound unsympathetic. *Without Leave* is snappier, too, I guess."

"Were you worried at all about publishing this?"

"Why?"

"Well, people finding out you'd deserted, or gone AWOL, for one."

"No, I wasn't worried."

"Did your family know what had happened? Had you told your wife?"

"My wife knew I'd gotten a general discharge halfway through my tour, that there had been a little trouble. She didn't know quite how bad, but I'm not embarrassed about it. At this point, I'm unembarrassable, especially about things that happened four decades ago."

"But you hadn't told her what happened?"

"Not the whole story, anyway."

"Why not?"

"I was probably too embarrassed." The interviewer shifted in her chair, and Richard relaxed into his. He wished he didn't enjoy it so much when people disliked him. If he didn't, he might not be disliked by so many people, which would probably have some advantages. "I guess the honest answer is that I've spent a long time trying to figure out what happened, and I wanted to get it straight with myself before anyone else."

"Without spoiling the book, you also seem to assert war crimes. Was there a concern about libel or the military's response?"

"Well, first of all, the names have all been changed, so no one's getting libeled. Also, I don't know if it's an assertion of war crimes. The army gave Endicott a Bronze Star for distinguished service. It's a moral assertion, maybe, but since when does the military care about that?"

She shuffled her notes and said, "I wonder if you could talk a little bit about it. I mean, obviously the memoir covers your time in Vietnam and a good amount of your childhood as well. Could you describe the path that brought you here?"

"Here where? Here, this studio with you?"

"If you want to think of it that way, sure."

"Okay, I don't know. When I was a little kid, I think we had two books in the house—the Bible and *The Joy of Cooking*. Then my parents split, and my aunt Polly took me in for a while to live with her and her two kids. She'd been a teacher and a librarian, back when libraries were still called lending libraries. Her living room had floor-to-ceiling bookcases, I'd never seen anything like it. She was even trying to write a novel for a while, which for a single southern mother at the time was pretty unusual. I can still remember her after dinner, sitting at the kitchen table in front of an old Remington with a cigarette burning in a saucer. Never wrote anything, I don't think, but still. If I have a literary impulse, that's where it came from. She has a lot to answer for.

"I went to college for a year, dropped out, and my number immediately got called, perfect timing, as always. After the army, I worked construction all over California, taking notes for a book idea I had. Just roamed around, you know, being an asshole moron—excuse me—a dumb kid, in this pair of electric-blue bellbottoms. I wish somebody had been nice enough to tell me not to wear those things, although I should have known. Anyway, I was working on a high-rise in Fresno when I met my wife, my ex-wife. My first ex-wife. She was an assistant professor at Fresno State, and she encouraged me to go back to school. I took night classes and got my degree.

"I was still working high-rises. One day, someone, I never found out who, dropped an eight-pound wrench on me from three stories up, and

I fell three more. When I came to, I was in a half-body cast, two broken legs and a broken pelvis. I started writing seriously during the six months I was on disability. Eileen encouraged me, said she thought I had some talent. I wrote a few chapters while my hipbone was setting. I thought they were pretty good. I sent a couple of them out to agents and publishers and magazines and didn't hear a word back. It was like releasing them from the airlock of a spaceship into outer space.

"But I got the taste for it and kept going after I got healed up and went back to working construction. I wrote a little at night, when I had the time. I finished the first novel that year, 1975, sent it out, and got an agent, and he got it published. It all happened so easily."

"*Skyscraper Blues,* which put you on the map."

"It wasn't a bestseller or anything, but it turned a few heads. Got written up in the *Times* and so on. People were saying, Here's this new kid, Richard Lazar, he might be a real guy. A dude, even. I quit construction for the next year or so, working on the next novel. Eileen was pregnant. This moment when all these wonderful things were about to happen. That was probably the best year of my life."

Mary looked down at a note card. "*The Cassandra Letters* came out in 1978."

"Had you heard of it?"

"Honestly, no."

"No one has. It's been out of print since it got printed. It might have been out of print before it got printed. Talk about anticlimactic. I don't know what I expected when it came out, but it wasn't to go back to rigging elbow joists."

"And then *The Blivet,* in 1981."

"My agent at the time told me it was going to be a hit. It was going to be the one—like, get ready for the big time, put some champagne on ice. Then it came out, and nothing. Just radio silence from the world. I should have known better that time around, but I didn't. That was devastating. And, you know, I wrote two more novels after that. *Tennis in Golgotha* I wrote in the mideighties, when my first marriage was ending, and I was kind of a mess. It's not a great book. Then, uh, *Birdmen of the Antarctic,* which came out in 1993 on a little press. I got three copies of it. That was devastating, too. They were all devastating."

"When did you start work on this book?"

"I'd been screwing around with it forever, little odds and ends, but I never thought I'd do anything serious with it. Then my second marriage ended. She wasn't wild about my work, anyway. It got in the way of us playing golf and rearranging her furniture. I moved out to the desert. Suddenly I had nothing to do but work on it, so that's what I did."

"Why memoir?"

"I don't know. I'd written about it for a long time, little pieces, but never put it all together as one piece of narrative. It felt like something I should do, even though I didn't really want to. I wanted to, you know, drink gin and throw darts down at my local bar. But anyway, I made myself do it and sent it to my agent. I didn't hear from him for two years, during which time I figure I'm done, that's it. Then he calls out of the blue to tell me they're picking it up. Then a year later, it's getting good reviews, it's selling, for some reason."

"And here you are."

"Here I am, yeah. Big success."

She smiled, turned a card, and cocked her head at him, signaling a change of gears. "Do you see your book, at least partially, as a commentary on current events?"

"How so?"

"Well, obviously there's a groundswell of mistrust against the government right now—against the Iraq invasion and the motivations for it and our continued presence there and in Afghanistan, and just a general sense that there's been a failure of moral leadership. In a way, you've come forward at a very opportune time, telling a personal story of questioning the military and opting out, so to speak."

"That makes it sound pretty calculated."

"I don't mean it was calculated, but it clearly has cultural relevance right now. That's part of why it's selling."

"Is it? I don't know why it's selling, to be honest with you."

A young man with a mustache walked by the studio window, carrying three coffees in a cardboard cup holder. Who was that young man, what did he want, who was he in love with? All very valid questions, Richard thought, more valid than the trifling details of his own story, which had already mostly been told. He was struck by an enormous sense of his own irrelevance, and a sense of the interview as an exercise in self-importance, not to mention the need to fill up airtime with something. He said, "But to answer your question, it's not meant to be a commentary on anything. It's just something I wrote in my trailer, out in the desert, to get some things straight for myself. I don't care about current events or politics or what piece-of-shit country we're presently fucking up and dying in for no reason. Current events can go to hell. I wrote this thing for me."

———

The car, a souped-up Honda Accord with a spoiler and tinted windows, stopped in the smoking tracks of its own burnt rubber. It settled with satisfaction back into its haunches like an animal fresh from the kill. The hood was lightly dented from the impact, but it was already comprehensively scarred and dinged. A cracked bumper, a missing side mirror, a paintless gash running the length of one crumpled side like a C-section scar—this was a vehicle with a long history of running into things. It took off down the street and disappeared, to a chorus of outraged yells from the gathered witnesses.

The girl had been thrown to the sidewalk and lay very still; a small crowd of people, Vance among them, clustered around her. There seemed to be no doubt she was dead until her eyes flicked open, and with the aid of a nearby NO PARKING sign, she struggled to her feet. No one spoke—there was a feeling in the air that talking might break the magic, the collective wish that had levitated the girl and now prevented her from collapsing in a pool of blood. She leaned against the pole and moaned lightly. A fresh strawberry swelled on her right jawline, and a trickle of blood ran out of her nose, which she wiped off with the back of a dirty wrist. The man nearest, a fat guy clutching a forgotten backpack, said, "Are you okay?"

She moaned again and then pushed off from the pole, between two plaid-skirted schoolgirls, agog, who parted for her like a pair of saloon doors, and she stumbled away in the same direction as before. People looked at one another, shook their heads, said *Jesus,* shrugged, and moved on—relieved in part that the girl was okay but mostly that they didn't have to do anything or further interrupt their day. Vance alone remained at the spot; he found his own arm supporting him against the same street sign. She was small in the distance now, a block away, turning left. He followed.

———

Not much later, the sun had dipped out of sight and taken any lingering warmth with it. The wind, previously content to gust and flurry, now blew through the streets with mythic force; Vance had to drop his head and slant his long body to meet its wrath. The few people he passed were pitched at the same angle and, like him, clutched insufficient outerwear around their necks. A woman across the street lost her balance and fell over, legs splayed sideways like a dog in repose. For a moment, she sat there, framed by the glowing chartreuse of a Midori ad behind her, seemingly reluctant to get back up and do further battle with the wind.

The girl was only a few feet ahead of him, yet he couldn't bring himself to stop her. She felt her head periodically and spat on the pavement, little pools with ruby-red blood suspended in them. Vance fingered the bills in his pocket; as they'd walked, the surrounding neighborhood had gradually grown seedier, and seedier still. A bearded man crouched on a stoop, his pinwheel eyes spun by the relentless air. Trash skipped gaily past Vance's legs. There weren't any visible restaurants or bars, and what storefronts there were seemed to be either closed or else in the business of selling strange items: one window showcased what looked like bootleg DVDs of pan-ethnic, midriff-baring child stars singing into oversize mics; the next featured mannequins bent in sinister postures over and around wooden wheelchairs and obsolete medical devices. No one was around. It felt as though they had entered a wormhole and emerged in some shattered Eastern European nation during a government-imposed curfew. Without warning, the girl had turned and was facing him in a pugilistic stance, one foot in front of the other.

"What the fuck, man?"

Vance put his hands up in surrender.

She said, "You've been following me."

"No, I haven't."

"Yeah, you have. I've seen you in windows for the last twenty blocks."

"I wanted to make sure you were okay."

She squinted at him and rubbed the lump on the side of her face. "You saw that car hit me?"

"Yes."

"Well, I'm fine. You can fuck off now."

"I can take you to a hospital."

She laughed. "Hold up, let me see if I have my insurance card on me."

Talking to her, he saw that she was younger than he'd thought before—his age, if that. She was thin, with an adult form, but her cheeks seemed to be stubbornly clinging to their baby fat. Her clothes were a size too small and ragged, and she clutched herself against the bitter wind. Her eyes startled him. They were filled with light, and Vance thought it was the light of her seeing him, really seeing him, as a person. Recognition. It wasn't that common to see this light, whether in a fellow student at school or in a teenage runaway, which is what he dimly realized she was.

"How old are you," he said.

"Old enough. How old are you? Who do you think you are?"

"I'm no one."

"What do you really want?"

"Just to help."

"Yeah, sure," she said. She moved closer to him, and he took a step back. He moved sideways, and she followed him into the street. He walked a little faster, crossing the street to a larger road he hoped would lead out of this neighborhood. She fell in line with him, matching his stride, walking with her arms crossed against the cold.

"You want to party?"

"No, no thanks."

"Don't you like to party?"

"No, I don't like to party."

"We could have a good time."

"I don't think so."

"You're cute."

"Thanks," he said. He needed to get away from her and her eyes. Her smell, too: yeasty and fecund, almost unbearably sexual and completely unsexy. He thought he saw the spire of the Transamerica Building or some other tall building downtown, and he crossed the street. She followed.

"I'll suck your dick," she said. "You like getting your dick sucked?"

He had never had his dick sucked, though he'd frequently thought about it and guessed he would like it a lot. "Please go away."

"I can do things," she said. "I can make you happy." He felt the money in his pocket, involuntarily. Partly to make sure it was still there, but partly imagining spending it on her. What would that be like? Where would they go? He felt a sick rush thinking of following her into some dark room, light from a curtained window seeping in, a mattress on the floor, the smell of her corrupt body trapped in the air like the smell of day-old bread in a bakery.

He stopped beside the wooded entrance to a darkening green field, San Ysidro Park, according to the sign overhead, framed in a wrought-iron trellis. The strangeness of the day, the neighborhood, the girl, the wind—all of it cast in the unreal light of dusk—made the park, at this moment, feel like an enchanted place, a garden of unknowable delights and terrors. He said, "Why are you following me?"

"See, not cool is it?" She grinned unpleasantly, baring surprisingly white teeth. The abraded welt on her jaw pulsed in the light, sheeny with lymph. "I do what I want, that's why."

Vance pulled the money out. She said, "I knew it, come on." She nodded back the way they'd come. He handed the money to her. She looked at the cash warily, as though he'd handed her a peanut can she guessed was spring-loaded with snakes. "What's this?"

"Money."

"For what?"

"For nothing. Go to a clinic. Get some food or something."

She flipped the money with her thumb and then grinned again. "You get off on making girls feel like trash, is that it?"

"No."

She studied Vance's face and smiled. "No, I know what it is," she said. "You're a virgin, aren't you?" She pressed the money against the side of Vance's face and kissed him. It was a long, grinding hateful kiss that he hoped would never end, even as he squirmed away from it. Her mouth tasted like cigarettes with an undertone of sweet rot that emanated from the depths of her person. She said, "Call me if you change your mind," then put her mouth to his ear and whispered ten numbers.

For a moment or two, she walked backward away from him, under the trellis and into the wooded shadows of the park, then she turned on her sneakered heel and was gone. He watched her go, repeating the number in his head even as he told himself to forget it. Four one five eight seven three two one nine. He had to resist the urge to follow her, because why would he follow her? But still he stood there for minutes, frozen by indecision, not to mention by the slicing October bay wind. Four one five eight seven seven three two one nine.

———

Sansome Street was so steep that the Providence Hotel seemed to slowly erect itself from nothing, piercing the violet sky with the soft deco glow of its pink-orange floodlights. Inside, Vance spied Richard's bearish form across the lobby, still hunched over the bar, as though he'd never left, which he probably hadn't. Richard looked up as Vance sat down and slurred, "Big day out on the town?"

"It was okay."

"Yeah, it's a nice town besides all the queers, hippies, and China-men."

The bartender cast a slanted look down the length of the bar, then went back to cutting limes. The clear liquid in Richard's conical glass sloshed around in his hand. Vance said, "That's great. Remember that one for the reading."

Richard waved his hand. He said, "I'm kidding. Sit down."

"We need to go. We're late."

"You ever think about having that stick surgically extracted from your ass? Modern medicine can do amazing things." Vance stood. Richard said, "Sorry. Listen, call us a cab. You still have that money I gave you?"

"No."

"Tell me you didn't spend it on some kind of a good time."

"I gave it to someone in need."

"Of course you did. You ever think that maybe you're someone in need?"

———

The reading was sponsored by an online literary site called telescopic .com and took place in the Mission District, in an event space, so called—an open warehouse that looked like the kind of place in movies where someone gets shot in the back of the head by someone they trust. The mic was amplified through speakers jerry-rigged from stacked guitar amps that garbled his voice beyond recognition. One interrogatory klieg light was trained on his face, and the rest of the room—stylishly underlit with a wainscoting of Christmas-tree lights—was more or less invisible. The sound, the lights, and his swimming vision all conspired to make him feel he was shouting into an empty room.

He'd been feeling worse and worse since the interview. This, of course, was difficult to judge considering his wretched normal baseline, but even so he felt especially bad. He'd thought another drink at the hotel bar would help, but it seemed to have locked in a throbbing nausea. The nausea, in turn, seemed to radiate out against his chest, making it hard to breathe. He took insufficient little sips of air as he read, and his distorted voice bounced around the huge room, sounding like a deranged announcer in a third-world train station. Welcome to Garblestan, enjoy your stay. Only five more pages and he could stop, sit down, drink something, die. His gorge yo-yoed, spelunked perilously, up from the cavern of his stomach, down the sheer cliff face of his esophagus. His legs felt weak—not an unusual sensation in itself, but a different kind of weakness than the admixture of age, inactivity, and drunkenness to which he was accustomed. He felt numb all over, in fact, like something dead made briefly and shoddily animate, except for his heart, which pounded in his throat with animal speed and fear.

Skipping to the last page, he managed the final paragraph and a few mumbled thank-yous. The walk backstage was a twenty-foot trail of tears. A battered sofa rewarded these herculean exertions, and someone tactfully killed the lights.

———

When he woke, he was in an unfamiliar room painted light blue. Vance's head floated up into the left side of his peripheral vision like a child's balloon released into the sky.

"He's awake," said Vance to someone else in the room. On the other side, a doctor's head and shoulders appeared. Richard could instantly tell it was a doctor, not only by the white lab coat he wore but also from the general air of disapproval, a response he universally evoked in medical practitioners.

"How are you feeling, Mr. Lazar?"

"What happened?"

"You're in bad shape."

"Well, I guess it just goes to show you can exercise and eat right, and still have problems."

"You appear to have had a cardiac event."

"That sounds festive."

"It's not." The doctor frowned. "It was an episode of transient angina."

"I was joking."

"Transient angina is not an especially funny thing."

"No, I can see that now."

"Your EKG came out okay. The episode seems to have been brought on by a state of severe dehydration, itself likely brought on by sustained

alcohol consumption. You seem to be in the clear, but we'd like to observe you for a day or two, keep you on fluids and bed rest. I'll check
back in later." The doctor flashed a wholly insincere smile in Richard's
direction and left the room.

Vance remained where he was, frowning down. "I found you back
there. I knew something was wrong, you'd gone all white."

Richard said, "Spare me the lecture, if you would."

"Are you trying to kill yourself?"

"No. I don't think so. I don't know."

Vance looked out the open door, at the yellow glow of the long hallway outside. The kid looked down from beneath the fluorescent lights
as he talked, and Richard couldn't really see his face, though his hair
was a delicate wispy crown floating around his head. "I'm going back
now. Thanks for letting me come this far, and thanks for paying to get
the car fixed. Good luck with everything."

Richard propped himself up in bed on his elbows. He said, "Look,
don't go."

"Why?"

"What do you mean why? Because I'd like it if you stuck around."

"Why?" The kid's face was pink and blotchy, blurred with fatigue.

"Jesus, because I need your help, okay? Because I want some company."

"I can't stand around and watch you do this to yourself every night.
Are you going to take better care of yourself?"

Briefly, Richard imagined himself as a trench-coated mobster, tasked
with taking care of himself. No problem, he thought, he'd take care of
that fucking guy. "Like you said earlier, I really don't understand why
you care."

"Do you care why I care?"

"Sure. Yes."

Vance paused for a very long time, long enough to allow in the faint
sounds of the parking lot outside, an unseen delivery truck beeping as
it backed up. "I've never looked forward to anything the way I looked
forward to meeting you. I know it didn't mean anything to you, I know

it probably still doesn't, but that's the truth." Again, he paused. A nurse clicked efficiently toward them down the long hall. "And I guess I hoped you'd be more like you seem from the books."

"The books are the best part of me. Probably the only good part."

Vance sighed, and Richard said, "Listen, I've got a question for you. Do you think you could try to lighten up? Just a little? Maybe have some fun? I'll try to be better if you'll try to be worse, how about it?"

Before the kid could respond, the nurse was entering the room, massaging Richard's forearm, sticking a needle into it. A narcotic wind blew through his mind, and all the trash and junk, previously put in neat little piles, was scattered to and fro. Children's faces floated like exploding stars or paramecia in front of an interstellar, infinitesimal backdrop. Vance seemed to smile and put his hand on Richard's shoulder. The touch, so tender and knowing, dislocated him in time. He was the father and the child, the child and father. The father of the child who was father to the man.

"I'll see you tomorrow," said his father, then he was gone.

———

The doctor reappeared. He sat in a chair in the corner and gave Richard the expected spiel—another day of bed rest, anticoagulants, taking better care of himself. Richard nodded at the appropriate times, awaiting the inevitable alcohol lecture that had to be coming. But the doctor did two surprising things. First, he pulled a can of something out of his pocket that was covered with a large white sticker reading BEER. He cracked it, and Richard took a sip, wondering if he was dreaming or just the subject of a very cruel joke. But no, it was beer—Budweiser, by the particular creamy sweetness of it. The doctor said, "I'm prescribing you two of these a day to prevent withdrawal."

Then clasping hairy hands over his crossed knees, he went on, "You know, I read your book."

"Really." This was probably the best beer he'd ever tasted.

"Pretty good, I thought. Sagged in the middle."

"Fair enough."

"You're on some kind of promotional tour, the boy said?"

"Something like that."

"Do you always drink the way he described, or has it been especially much lately?"

Richard imagined Vance talking to the doctor, like his cousin used to tattle on him—talking quietly to his mother's feet and the yellow-white linoleum of the kitchen—and a small wave of adolescent anger rippled through him. "It's been especially much lately."

"I see." The doctor recrossed his legs the other way and reclasped his hands over them. He said, "Do you think talking about your experiences every night might be playing a role in your behavior?"

"I'm not talking about it."

"Do you mean every night, or with me?"

"Either," Richard said. "Both."

The doctor stood and brushed down his coat. "We're going to taper you off with a couple of these prescription beers for the next forty-eight hours, and I'm prescribing a low dosage of Klonopin to be taken three times a day, which should help with any minor withdrawal effects you might experience. What you do after that is your business, of course, but if I were you I'd think about sources of this behavior, and I hope you'll consider treatment of some kind. The next time it might not just be angina."

Later, the phone, sitting on the counter next to the bed, began vibrating. It was Stan, sounding upset. "The kid, what's-his-name, called me. You had a heart attack?"

"No, not a heart attack, 'a minor cardiac event.' "

"Look, I'm calling Dana and canceling the rest of this thing."

"No, you're not."

"You're not up for it."

"I'm fine. I'm stopping with the drinking."

The length of the ensuing pause as Stan considered this statement seemed inversely proportionate to his faith in it. "Really."

"I can't keep this up. Look, I'm in here for another day. Call Dana, tell her to nix the LA stops and the flight to Vegas. Vance will take me. Get him a room somewhere, too."

Stan sighed. "This is a nightmare."

"No, a nightmare would be if you were being chased by some kind of robot scorpion on wheels with a skull's face. This is just your job."

"I knew sending you out was a mistake," Stan said, finally.

"I tried to stop you, but you wouldn't listen. Call Vance."

———

In the middle of the night, Richard got out of bed and limped over to the window, wanting, uncharacteristically, to be reminded there was a world outside. There was, though what he could see of it was mainly a half-empty parking lot delineated by access roads and, in the distance, a complicated interstate cloverleaf. On it, tiny cars do-si-doed around and around one another in a never-ending square dance. Rain fell: not a cleansing rain—the hard, white, driving rain of redemption; not a cinematic rain, either—you couldn't imagine two lovers joining in the parking lot, clasping each other in the downpour of their own thwarted love; it was a halfhearted, discontent rain, and it pooled everywhere in gummy, black puddles. He was again struck by a sense of the world's cruddiness. He got back in bed and after a minute found himself staring at a pain chart on the wall, a crude line drawing of a child's face in a progression from mild discomfort (one) to agony (ten). In the drawing of ten on the pain scale, big fat tears leaped from the face's wide and frightened eyes. He lay back and looked at the ceiling, the same vacant blue as the rest of the room. His legs ached. His chest ached. He missed Victor, the desert, women, being young. Ten—thought Richard—ten, ten, ten.

CHAPTER EIGHT

H e drank too much, the doctor had informed him. Now this was
big news. From a clinical perspective, he'd drunk too much
since he was a teenager. He'd read the pamphlets, knew the
amount of alcohol prescribed by those scolds at the American Heart
Association: one glass of wine a day, maybe two on rare occasions, like
your wedding night or the death of a parent. As far as Richard was
concerned, the world as outlined in these articles and surveys was an
alternate universe of probity and wise abstention, a wonderland evidently untouched by human worry, frailty, greed, lust, or any of the features of existence that make people drink more than one goddamned
glass of red wine a night.

One doctor, long ago dismissed, had suggested if he was having two
or more drinks a day, he might have a problem. How many did he es-
timate he had a week? Well. Here he utilized a complicated formula,
a version of which all heavy drinkers employ in doctors' offices. Something like $7(a/3) - d$, where a represents the actual number of daily
drinks consumed, and d represents the number of drinks necessary
to subtract from the initial lie to get into a normal-sounding ballpark.
Whatever number he told the doctor, it was still too high. Presumably
doctors have their own counterequations, which they apply to the false
numbers they're constantly given. The doctor edged close to Richard
and in a hushed tone suggested AA, intimating that he himself was a

member, that it had worked wonders for him. In order to get power over the disease, the doctor said, he'd had to accept his own power-lessness.

The problem, Richard decided that night, over a large glass of warm gin, was his lack of powerlessness. If he felt powerless in the face of alcohol, he would have had no choice but to give it up. After all, who wants their life run, and ultimately ruined, by something over which they have no control? The problem was not that he couldn't not drink. The problem was that he didn't want to not drink.

He liked drinking. He always had. It made him feel good. It quelled his anxiety. It made him temporarily interested in other people's lives, and his own. Plus it tasted good. If alcohol had no redeeming qualities, like water, it would be very easy to not drink a lot of it.

Nonetheless, he had quit altogether for two separate stretches in his life. The first time was during a period of chronic unemployment when Cindy was little, two or three years old. He couldn't seem to find any work that summer and wound up Mr. Momming it, making her breakfast in the morning, then lolling around watching cartoons with her, or helping her finger-paint or color in her books, or tak-ing her to the little community park down the road from their apart-ment, watching her stumble around, arms outstretched, in the thick grass, forever toddling after someone's dog. Early on, he discovered that going about this in his usual state of spooked, strobe-lit hang-over was exceedingly unpleasant. For one thing, everything related to childcare—constant vigilance, exposure to loud noises and fast move-ments, anticipating the needs of another person—was antithetical to recovering from a hangover. For another thing, experiencing the pre-cious, fleeting moments of his daughter's childhood as something to be grimly endured made him feel like a complete piece of shit, so he stopped drinking.

It lasted for a few months and was a pretty good time. He didn't say anything about it to Eileen, and she didn't say anything either, in the superstitious manner of someone afraid of dispelling good fortune by acknowledging it. But in September he finally got on another high-rise crew—a group chronically populated by heavy drinkers—and he got back on or fell back off the wagon, however the expression went.

The other noteworthy stretch of sobriety was with Carole. Their life together was anesthetic enough, it seemed at the time. He was barely writing, was trying on the mantle of sober, fiscally responsible, married suburbanite, a mantle that felt very comfortable after years of dissolute, impoverished loneliness in the service of art, or "art." She'd nepotized him into a job as head of landscaping for the property management company she ran. In the evenings, they'd return to her condo, a newly built property in Mesa that looked out over the placid fairways and greens of Casa Blanca Country Club. Sometimes she would pour him a glass of chilled white wine; sometimes she would not. They might sit on her Ethan Allen signature sofa and watch a laserdisc of *Ghost* on her giant TV, and he would swoon in an ecstasy of content despair. For two years of nearly continuous sobriety, during which they got married and honeymooned in Acapulco, he tried to embrace this contentment, which amounted to a kind of meditative acceptance of what felt—deep and also not so deep down—like a reduced state. Paradoxically, in this dreamless, frictionless, numb existence, alcohol seemed not only superfluous but dangerous. It had too much to do with his real self, which he'd kicked into unconsciousness and locked in the condo's basement two years earlier.

His real self, fortunately or unfortunately, eventually kicked down the door and escaped screaming back into the desert night. In his extended second bachelorhood, he'd established a drinking routine that had allowed him to function more or less normally, provided the definition of "normal" included living alone in a desert trailer for five years. Nothing before noon, nothing hard before five, nothing hard after ten. This had served him well enough to work and live, not to mention write the book.

Now, he drank his allotted BEER and looked at the can. It wouldn't be a bad last beer to drink, if there had to be a last one. Anyway, it seemed to be having the desired effect—along with the little pills the nurse brought three times a day, he felt no worse than usual. No tremors, no upset stomach or sweating. Dull and blank, yes, but there was no discomfort. Maybe that was the trick—to embrace that dullness, the real blankness that existed in the heart of every moment and action and thought, the void he'd been running away from as long as he could remember. He finished his last BEER, crushed the can, threw it in the corner, sat there.

CHAPTER NINE

—

We'd been in-country three months without seeing any action. We went on patrol every day, a two-kilometer half-circle sweep around the base of the hill behind us, which we took to calling Mount Neverest. We cleaned our rifles and our living quarters. We ate hearty meals and worked out afterward, jogging around and around the camp (I can still recall the sequence: Quonset huts, mess, armory, heads, clinic, Quonset huts, mess, armory . . .), lifting dumbbells, and doing complicated and difficult variations of push-ups, girding ourselves for what was coming. We scanned the perimeter and sometimes even felt the distant rumble and rumor of mortar explosions, like an earthquake from across the sea, but still there was no action.

We talked about action a lot, all the time, really. What to expect, what it was like. The majority of us were fresh, or nearly fresh, out of training. The guys who'd seen action instantly assumed a semi-mythic status with us, similar to the way seniors in high school appear to freshmen. They'd been through it. Berlinger had seen action in Binh Dinh, but he wouldn't talk about it.

"Come on," I said. A group of us was sitting in the mess after dinner playing dominos.

"Come on what," said Berlinger.

"What happened?"

"When?"

"You know when. Binh Dinh." I didn't know if I was saying it right, rhyming the words in an uncertain singsong.

He put down snake eyes. "I told you before, it was a clusterfuck."

"What does that mean?"

"It means a bunch of idiots in green are shooting guns at these other idiots in green shooting guns back, and there's smoke and fire, and you're running, then at some point you realize whatever was happening is over, and you somehow came out the other side, whoop-de-do. You won, apparently. And if you happened to catch a little shrapnel in the eye or get your dick shot off, some guy comes by while you're zonked on morphine in sick bay, and pins a little Purple Heart pin to your chest. You can trade it in at the VFW back home for half-price Schlitz at the monthly social. Your go, Lazar."

Another one of the combat vets, a black heavy-lidded Texan named Pauls, had fought in the Siege of Hue, during the Tet Offensive in 1968. He'd been honorably discharged following his tour, whored around Houston and Galveston and New Orleans for a year, then gotten bored and reenlisted. We treated him like some kind of warrior monk, our sensei. I remember us sitting around his feet staring up in awe, although surely we were cooler than that in reality.

What's it like, someone might have called out, as guys got drunk sitting around the barracks, tired of the limited entertainments we had on hand to distract us from what we were really there to do, whatever that was. Without putting down whatever jungle-moist Action Comics *or* Playboy *he was reading, Pauls would pronounce something oracular, like "It's what it is, nothing to compare it to" or "Like going deep inside this cave and you walk out the other side different." It sounds like pure bullshit remembering it now, but it sounded pretty badass then.*

The other thing we talked about was pussy. Pussy in its cosmic infinitude of variety. Pussy as the ultimate goal of existence. Pussy as life, pussy as death. Pussy as an almost entirely conceptual entity separated from the women it belonged to. (Once, out on a run, this jug-eared kid next to me said, "Man, my dick's so hard I gotta do handstands to pee. I get back to America, it's all over for pussy. Pussy's gonna rue the day I left Vietnam. Pussy's gonna curse my name.") Women were an entirely different subject, far too depressingly real and scary. In the same sense, we rarely discussed the stone-cold niceties of combat. Tactical considerations, for instance, or emergency triage. Our bullshit sessions about action, in both senses, were limited to the kind of metaphysical Platonism favored by scared young dudes who've never had the real thing.

We didn't look to see action anytime soon, either. Our base was located on the southeastern edge of the central highlands, a relatively uncontested area, what with Cam Ranh and its tactical support within a couple of hours. A similar position on the opposite side of the highlands, near the Ho Chi Minh Trail, would have been looking at daily firefights and the constant threat of mortar attack. Put it this way: if Vietnam was New York City, we were stationed in a toll booth on Staten Island. As far as any of us understood it, which wasn't very far, ours was a safeguard position, making sure Charlie didn't slink down the coast and try to curl around west toward Saigon. That's just a guess, though. No one told us anything, least of all Lieutenant Endicott. He was a narrow-faced, tight-assed New Englander, a descendant of Boston Brahmins with a military pedigree going back to the Battle of Hastings. He had the stink of noblesse oblige about him—there was no other good reason for anyone who could have avoided service to have served. I mean, he certainly wasn't stupid enough to have thought Vietnam was a good idea.

I will say that the area was beautiful. Sometimes, in the purple light of dusk, I would sneak behind the huts and look up at Mount Neverest. With its dark green vegetation interspersed with craggy bluff face, it reminded me of nothing so much as the few areas of California and the West that I'd seen. The surrounding forest was thick, but not overlush, and it was not hard to imagine homesteading there, getting yourself a little local mistress who knew the woods and language, and building a log cabin back in the woods. I'd imagined Vietnam as a fetid jungle, and I knew part of it was, but where we were it was soft-lit and peaceful green, if still hot as hell's half acre.

This backdrop of placid, rugged beauty was the unlikely theater on which we staged our fantasies of action. We imagined scarring the hillsides with zappers, M-32 rounds, calling in air strikes to shear off the rock face. Vast firefights, an Independence Day of tracers and mortar shells, taking it to an invisible enemy that had massed somewhere out there. We imagined leading a charge, using our bayonets. We imagined acts of valor and acts of cowardice in equal measure. Though we were young, most of us were not dumb or naïve enough to pretend we knew how we'd respond in a real battle. That was why we imagined it and talked about it at such great length—we were trying on the clothes of a soldier the way a child tries on his father's suit. We hoped we were up for it and feared we weren't.

I remember in mess, once, Hawkins started talking about what he was going to do when he bagged his first zip, as he put it. "Gonna aim for the stomach, so he goes down but don't die," he said, mouth glistening with fruit syrup.

"Shut up, Lester," someone said.

"No, wait," he said. "Then I'm going to walk up and fucking execute him."

"Jesus," I said.

"I've got a little speech worked out and everything." He grinned, pulling out a piece of paper from his ID wallet.

Berlinger said, "You know they don't speak Dumbfuck, right?"

I don't know where he got his hands on a translation book, but Hawkins looked down and started reading in a halting, cornpone Vietnamese: "Toi muon ban nhin thay khuon mat cua nguoi dan ong da giet chet ban. Doi voi tat ca coi doi doi, linh hon cua ban se thuoc ve toi." He folded the paper back into his wallet with an air of finality, something settled.

"Well," someone said at last, "what's it mean?"

He said, "It means 'I want you to see the face of the man who killed you. For all eternity, your soul will belong to me.'"

"Jesus Christ, Hawkins."

Hawkins may have been a fucking nutcase, but I gave him credit for at least being up for some action. The longer we were there,

*talking about action and seeing none, the more I was convinced
I wasn't. I just couldn't fathom the notion that there were men
somewhere out in the jungle, a whole nation of men, who hated
America and wanted to use their guns and knives and mines to do
away with me. Me! Let alone the idea that I should do the same to
them. I got through my doubts by lying. I teetered around on my
bravado like a pair of stilts. I lied all day, to myself and others, but
at night, in my cot, surrounded by the innocent snoring of my fellow
soldiers, the truth squatted on me like a school-yard bully, pinned
me to the bed and forced me to look it in its bright eyes. The truth, it
said, is you can't do it. Oh, you can fire a rifle and do fifty push-ups
and ten pull-ups. You ran your survival course in respectable time,
finished Basic. You can put on your greens and helmet and field pack,
and look exactly like a soldier. But you are not one.*

*It wasn't from any conscientious objection. I was nineteen—
I wasn't conscientious about anything besides jerking off twice a day.
And I had no conscience to speak of. It was simple fear, yet I knew
most of the men sleeping around me were scared, as well. I knew I was
likely surrounded by a jungle dreamworld full of bloody ambushes,
green malarial death, incompetence, and paralytic impotence in the
face of the enemy. And I also knew none of them felt what I felt, which
was a leaden certainty that I was not going to do this thing everyone,
including me, said I was going to do. What quality separated my
fear from theirs? Was there simply more of it? Maybe so. It flowed
like liquid metal through my veins, made my arms and legs dull and
useless. I only reached sleep each night through the thin comfort of
knowing that in the morning I could keep lying and defer the truth
one more day.*

*When I did dream, I sometimes dreamed about the little strip
of woods behind our quarters, figures weaving their way silently
between the trees. In one memorable nightmare, I was enormous,
towering over the base, looking at myself as I slept. I grabbed the
trees by the tops of their branches, and yanked, and the whole piece
of land came up like a ripped-off Band-Aid. Underneath, thousands*

of tiny Viet Cong writhed in the light, like maggots under a rotten log suddenly exposed to air. I pounded them over and over with my fist, and woke up flailing at the mosquito netting over my cot.

Then, too, there were good dreams—disembarking a Boeing 707, expecting to step out into the choking Indochinese air—only to feel a cool breeze on my face, look at the smiling stewardess at my elbow, and somehow know that I was back in America. But then again, these were also the worst dreams, as terrible as they made waking up, dripping with sweat, under the same mosquito netting, bivouacked in a tin hut somewhere in Vietnam.

———

The one thing that did happen during this stretch didn't happen to me. Berlinger and Tony Carbone had been sent out on morning patrol, probably as punishment by our staff sergeant, Davis Martin, for having to listen to them go back and forth all the time. Berlinger baited Carbone like it was his job. Anything cornily Italian—Dean Martin, Marciano, spaghetti and meatballs, et cetera—was fair game, and Carbone somehow always took the bait.

I was in the yard after exercises, writing a letter back home I knew I wouldn't send, when I heard yelling. Me and two other guys ran to the entrance—Berlinger had Carbone under the arms and was hauling him like one of the giant flour sacks that got dropped off by supply trucks twice a month. He was shouting for help and we ran down the path to where he was, rifles out. Carbone's foot was gone and the meat of the leg was sheared away to the shin, like a chicken leg gnawed to the bone. It trailed in the bloody dirt, left a little divot. The guy to my left, whose name is lost to me, got on his knees and retched. Me and the other guy grabbed his legs, what was left of them, and carried him into base, to sick bay. I remember looking down at the bone sticking out and thinking how odd it was, that it looked in real life the way you would imagine it. That there was no special magic holding our bodies together and no sacred energy unleashed when they were torn apart. Just blood and bone.

That night, sitting sedated, but still ashen and sweating, with his back against the hut's tin wall, Berlinger told me what had happened. Predictably, they'd been going back and forth, and he'd started in about how Sinatra was a fairy and "My Way" was about taking it up the wazoo. Carbone came at him and of course Berlinger, with a foot and eighty pounds advantage, easily fended him off. Too easily—he accidentally pushed Carbone back into a nearby bush, and when Carbone got up, he was covered in shit; apparently some monkey or lemur had eaten a bad oyster and squatted there. Carbone stalked off, furious, momentarily leaving the trail, which, over the last year, had been swept and patrolled into a safe, smooth ring. He disappeared into the woods, and a second later Berlinger's ears compressed and there was smoke and then screaming. Berlinger found him on the outside of a black ring of underbrush, singed and flattened by the mine he'd stepped on.

Carbone was sewed up and shipped home. We saw him off in the back of the green supply truck, got him situated against a couple of those big bags of flour. The morphine he was on dropped his eyes before we could wish him well, and then the truck was pulling out and gone. In the days that followed, recon found no further mines in the area and the consensus was that it was random, possibly a remnant of the French occupation. Just bad luck, shrugged Davis Martin at chow a few days later.

"Bad luck," said Berlinger, looking up from his turkey Alfredo, his tin of stewed apples.

"What else?"

"Stupidity?"

"Yeah, that too."

Other than that, though, we waited. No action, besides the action in our heads. And my growing certainty I wouldn't be able to do it, whatever it was. At a certain point, I even began fantasizing that we would never see action, that my military life would wind up being the same as my civilian life, just a bunch of jerking off and bullshitting, albeit in hundred-degree heat. Then on May 22, 1971, the order finally came down to move out.

———

Vance put the book down and, for the hundredth time in the last thirty minutes, scanned his surroundings for the girl. He sat on a bench beside a small playground at the apex of San Ysidro Park—in the daylight it was not a magic garden, just a city park where people walked their dogs, took their children to play, or, like him, sat reading in patches of sunlight. Below him was a sloping expanse of green, bordered on each side by rows of trees and to the south by a row of interlocking Spanish colonial apartments in pastel colors that reminded him of Easter candy. In the distance, the buildings of downtown pressed up against the horizon; an expanse of gray rainclouds issued from over the skyline. They had a quilted, overstuffed look and provided a sense of three-dimensional depth that prevented the vista from looking like a mediocre landscape painting.

He'd come here today, as he had yesterday, with the dim idea that he might see the girl again—as though, through some primitive magic of repetition, she might be summoned. Now, as yesterday, he felt how silly this was, yet still he'd come. Partly this was owing to a simple need to get out of the hotel in which Stan, who remained seemingly unconvinced of the necessity of this arrangement, had punitively booked him: a place in Oakland called the Jack London Inn—an actual roach motel; every morning, a new one paraded across the stained carpet as though, like mints on the pillow or ballpoint pens, it was compliments of the hotel. He'd hurried out into the bright chill, anxious to escape the room, and his own presence in it—after two days, the hotel room had been contaminated, practically irradiated, by his anxious, futile longing.

Mainly, though, he just wanted to see her again. He pulled out his phone and brought up the number, saved under *Girl.* Four one five eight seven seven three two one nine. He'd brought it up a hundred times before and not called. What would he say? He wasn't looking for a good time; he didn't like to party. Calling her would make something official, transactional, between them, and he didn't want that. But he wanted to see her, he craved the girl. Something inside him he hadn't even known was there before needed her. *You ever think that maybe you're someone in need?* Richard had said. Well, yes, he did think that.

He needed lots of things. He needed the girl and needed her to need him; and if he could provide her the help she so clearly needed, she would need him, help him back. On a certain level, he found this energetic little tautology suspect—in fact, suspected himself of substituting "help" for another four-letter word. Call me if you change your mind, she'd said, the taste of her mouth still fresh in his.

He'd writhed for two days with the memory of that kiss. It wasn't his first kiss—there had been a peck from a mortified blonde, dared by her giggling friends in eighth-grade gym class, and another kiss two years later from one of his brother's girlfriends, who'd gotten drunk one night at their house and laid one on him as he'd lain on the sofa reading *Of Mice and Men*—but it was his first real kiss. Why, at nineteen, was it his first real kiss? The feelings the girl had sparked in him included an uncontrollable, punishing bout of self-analysis, played out in his head and in the hotel room over the last thirty-six hours. The girl had known he was a virgin—it was obvious. This morning, as he'd brushed his teeth and gotten dressed, he'd avoided looking at himself in the mirror, though he knew what was there. A bunch of long bones loosely slung together, a dusting of acne on the back and stooped shoulders, his mother's small eyes peering out over his father's mouth—which could generously be described as "rabbity"—and a schoolboy's cap of flyaway brown hair perched atop it all like a nervous bird waiting to take flight. He was ugly, ungainly, unsure of himself. But then, both of his friends in high school had been ugly, too, and they had still gotten laid somehow. "Somehow" was, he knew, that they went to parties he wouldn't go to and grimly stood against the wall nursing their Steel Reserves. The difference was, then, that they wanted it.

He had wanted it, too, but not with the callow girls in his high school, and not any of the girls he'd met his lone month in college either. He had wanted Emma Bovary and Anna Karenina and Becky Sharp and Jane Eyre and Cathy and even poor, stupid Tess. Since he was a child—since his father left and then his mother started bringing home strange men who condescended to him or who chucked him under the chin or who told him to stop being weird and get the fuck out of the living room or, worst of all, men who simply ignored him entirely—he'd built a fortress around himself made out of books. The thing about books was that they were better than real life. Much better. By the time he was fifteen, he'd fallen in love and had his heart broken countless times, sitting on the couch, watching over the pages as his poor mother went through the real thing. Friday night, she would stand in front of a mirror by the front door of their apartment, clutching her purse in one hand, applying hopeful lipstick with the other and smacking her lips, telling him there was dinner in the oven for him and John, that she might be late. The next day he would find her watching the living room TV in a fog of penitent self-hatred, her face screwed up and her eyes like black pennies. Vance would make them lunch—a can of chicken noodle soup and a peanut butter sandwich, both split in two—and eat his meal at the kitchen table, watching the back of her head across the room while he read, the edge of the plate holding down the pages.

He had gotten taller since then, and read more books, but he hadn't changed. He hadn't wanted to, had never wanted to join that great rush of feeling and calamitous need. And now, he did. The night before, he'd dreamed he was lowering his tiny vessel into an enormous river. The water was black, and the current was horribly strong, but from bank to bank it was choked with other boats of all types and sizes: canoes like his, also yachts, catamarans, speedboats, houseboats, even a regal steamboat with figures in formal dress waltzing on its yellow-lit ballroom deck. Why, he wondered, thinking for the hundredth time about the car hitting her and her small, crumpled body rising as though lifted by invisible wires; the glint in her bright eyes as she'd looked at him; the funny sweet smell or taste, he wasn't sure which, that emanated from her as they'd kissed. Why now, why her? This line of questioning always ended with a shrug, a tug, and a shudder, another damp tissue thrown in the plastic trash under the sink. For better or worse, he thought—and probably for worse—you are joining the human race.

The breeze picked up, gently rustling a nearby palm grove and bringing Vance back to himself. A small child on the roundabout behind him shrieked in a language he couldn't understand. He thought how he'd be picking Richard up in the morning, how he wouldn't see her again, and before he had time to talk himself out of it, he was calling her. He got up and paced, protectively holding the phone away from his ear. It rang and rang, and each ring lasted forever—not an eternity but, say, a year or so. Finally, the voicemail picked up, a monotone male voice saying, *You know what to do.* Vance hung up, embarrassed at himself—the amount of time and energy he'd spent obsessing over a wrong number, probably given as a joke.

The long, complex interlude of recrimination and self-hatred that followed was interrupted by the ringing phone. He dropped it in surprise, and it skittered, vibrating, under the bench. He retrieved it and answered on his knees. "Who is this?" said the girl. Her voice sounded blurry, distracted, like he'd woken her up from sleep, even though she was the one calling him.

"Vance."

"Who's Vance."

"We met the other day. I gave you money, you gave me this number."

There was a pause, as she processed this information. "Oh, yeah."

"The voicemail was a guy, that's why I didn't leave a message."

"Okay, what's up?"

"I don't know."

"You want something?"

"I don't know."

She laughed. "Okay. Where are you, man?"

He tried to describe where he was—the bus route and streets he'd taken, the park and houses opposite. "Oh, yeah," she said. "San Ysidro. I'm pretty close to there."

Ten minutes later, she was in the field below him, unmistakable with her incendiary hair. She wore a black sweater and dirty jeans tucked into black combat boots, and she seemed to be unsteadily looking around, her motion roughly describing an off-balance circle. She gently spiraled in the direction of the westward tree line. Vance walked down the hill and approached her from the side. "Hi," he said.

"Oh, yeah," she said again, looking up at him with unfocused eyes, as though she'd already forgotten who she was meeting, which maybe she had. He didn't know much about drugs, but he knew she was on them. And she was filthy. Not just her clothes—her hair was half matted and sprouting incipient dreadlocks, her arms were smudged with dirt, her fingernails were long and comprehensively grouted with black grime. The welt on the side of her face had scabbed over, but it was red and swollen, with wispy red streaks that reached out toward her ear, her cheek. It was infected—he knew this because his mother had had a similar livid wound on her leg once, which hadn't gotten clean, since she wasn't taking showers at that point.

"That needs disinfecting," he said.

"What?"

"Come on." He held her arm and guided her toward the path, and though she made a face, she followed, oddly compliant. Winding silently with her through the trees, he indulged himself in a third-person perspective of the two of them, a homely little narrative in which the hero finds and saves the girl. He was not unaware of the problems with this point of view, of its triteness and simplicity, but somehow his awareness did nothing to dispel the pleasure of it.

They walked under the iron trellis, braided with ivy, and out of the park. As they crossed the street, a homeless man screaming into a phone booth vaporized the romantic mise-en-scène. The girl began pulling away from him like a bored, petulant child, but after only a minute of further walking, a CVS materialized. Vance told her to wait outside, went in, and grabbed gauze and peroxide and Neosporin and bandages and was standing in the check-out line before realizing he should have brought her in with him, that when he emerged she would almost certainly be gone. But she was still there, seemingly entranced by a white sectional sofa in the neighboring storefront window, or perhaps it was her own image. Like a dog looking into water, wondering at the strange aqua-dog staring up at it, a flicker of recognition passed over her face, then was gone. He led her to a bench and cleaned her wound with the peroxide. The clean place was a full shade lighter than the surrounding dirty skin. He smeared the Neosporin on it, then covered the whole area with gauze and several bandages. She was looking at him with the light in her eyes that he'd seen before.

"You need to keep it clean."

"My hero," she said. He knew it was sarcastic, but his dumb heart swelled regardless.

He put the supplies in the bag, and she took it from him, with a smile of vacant gratitude. She pushed up from the bench and walked unsteadily away, but she looked back twice to see if he would follow. He followed. Her small form was childish at a glance, but her hips swayed along an adult fulcrum. They walked two blocks single file in this manner until she reached an unbused sidewalk café table and sat. He sat down across from her. An older couple sat at the other outside table, talking over their eggs and toast with the luxuriant boredom of the long married. The girl picked up and bit into a half-eaten chocolate scone on the table and poured leftover coffee from a carafe into dirty white cups.

She said, "What's your name again, man?"

"Vance."

"Hi, Vance."

"Hi." He took a sip from the lip-stained cup, despite not liking coffee and being something of a germophobe. She was including him in something conspiratorial and precious. "Where are you from," he said.

"Visalia," she said, and didn't seem to be joking.

"Where's that?"

"Like, halfway between here and LA. Nowhere."

She continued tearing into the remaining food on the table, and Vance realized she was starving, then realized he was starving, too. He hadn't eaten since returning to Oakland yesterday evening, where he'd bought a dinner of jerky and chips from the gas station next to the Jack London Inn. He took a piece of scone from the plate and ate it, then took another. She cleaned the plates, then they drank their cold coffee in silence, as if copying the couple next to them. A waitress wearing a white button-up and black bow tie came out to clear their table; they could see her reenter the café and talk to the vague figure of a tall, bald man who glowered at them through the window. The girl quickly got up and, again, Vance followed, with the sense he was being tested somehow. A block later she cut left onto Vista. Here, she entered a movie theater called the Star Star Cinema. If someone was meant to be taking tickets, they were nowhere to be seen. The lobby was dirty and empty, with peeling wallpaper and handbills strewn everywhere. They pushed into the small, darkened theater and stood in the back.

The room they were in smelled damp and comprehensively bleached. Rustling and shifting sounds close by alerted Vance to the presence of other, unseen people. He felt the back of a seat in front of him, the itchy tweed of theater upholstery. Overhead, the projector whumped on and, to the tune of *Also Sprach Zarathustra,* a man's glistering penis pushed up from the bottom of the screen in ultra slow motion. It kept moving up and up, slowly widening at the base as the shaft grew longer and longer. It reminded Vance of *Star Wars* when the camera pans along the Imperial cruiser for a seeming eternity. He could feel the girl gauging his reaction, and for that reason he stood where he was, watching the screen. It wasn't as though he hadn't seen these things before online, and as his eyes adjusted, he wondered if the handful of men gazing up at the screen, rapt, had ever heard of the Internet. But the few times he'd watched porn before, he'd been depressed by it. Because it was depressing—he didn't see how everyone didn't find it so. Or maybe like his high school buddies going to parties, drinking bad beer, and getting jostled by people dancing to lousy music, they did find it depressing but worth it, nonetheless.

The girl put her hands on the sides of his face and kissed him again, her front teeth scraping against his. As before, it was an act of aggression; as before, it worked regardless. Over her shoulder, the tumid prick still filled the screen, and for an odd moment Vance felt as though there was a camera trained on his own member. She disengaged, and he followed her outside, where it was beginning to rain. A bearded boy sat damp and stubborn, strumming his guitar with an intensity at odds with his ability to correctly finger the chords he stabbed at. In a mangy, wobbling tenor, he sang-spoke in their direction: *Got a wife in Chino, babe, and one in Cherokee, first one said she's got my child, but it don't look like me.*

"All right, man," she said. "Listen, thanks for the money, and thanks for this." She held up the CVS bag. "But tell me what you want, or I'm going to find a cop and tell him you're harassing me."

"I don't know," he said, adjusting himself. He knew describing what he actually wanted—to take her away from the city, clean her up, give her a chance to be the good person he knew she was or had been before and yet could be, perhaps get married in a quiet ceremony at the courthouse of some rustic hamlet where he would build a house for them, board by board—would be met, justifiably, with laughter. "Do you want me to take you home?"

"Home?"

"Visalia, you said."

"Yeah."

"I can drive you."

"Are you serious?"

"Yes."

"No, God." Her face screwed up as she looked away. She couldn't handle kindness—you can get used to so much as long as you aren't ever reminded that alternatives exist. His dank basement, for instance, the moldering press of books, the close light and air in the house, his mother dissipating upstairs in a steady column of cigarette smoke.

"I'm sorry," he said.

"It's okay." They walked slowly down the street, side by side. Heavy drops of cold rain hit the ground around them, one by one. "I don't know, I just don't think I can go back, not after everything that happened. I don't know if they'd take me back."

"I bet they would."

"I don't know. Even if they did, I don't know if it would be a good thing."

"You don't have to go there, but you need to get out of here."

"And you'll take me."

"Yes."

She huddled in close to him as the wind picked up. Frowning at the sky, she said, "It's about to pour. We're right by where I stay; we can wait it out there."

"I don't know," said Vance.

"I want to talk more about it."

As he had in the park, he again saw the two of them from some distance—the girl close to him, a yellow awning covered with faded Chinese symbols overhead, rain pattering on the roofs of cars—and he experienced a wave of amazed gratification. This was really happening: they could ride out of San Francisco, to who knew where. Visalia. Visalia sounded like a pretend town on a postcard—a pastel storybook land with WELCOME TO arching over it like a rainbow. With a little pang, he thought of Richard in the hospital.

"Come on," she said, taking his arm now. They moved in what he now knew was the direction of downtown and the water. They walked past bodegas, taquerias, and flower stores. A dirty fruit stand filled up with plums. The temperature had fallen ten degrees in the last hour, and a rough wind was picking up again. For a moment, he was struck with the insane idea that it was the same wind as the other day, when they'd met—that that wind had gone into hiding in some obscure corner of the city, only to come barreling out again, madder than ever.

She pulled him down a small street and then down an even smaller one. It was as though they were spiraling at right angles, through the labyrinth and into a secret chamber in the heart of the city. She unlocked a door, and they were walking down a ruined hallway, then into a room that was not unlike the one he'd imagined numerous times over the last few days. As in his fantasies, it was small and dark, with the gray light from a single window illuminating a quilted mattress on a box spring. As in his fantasies, there was even a candle burning on a side table, a book whose cover he couldn't make out on the windowsill, and she turned to him with that fierce light still in her eyes. In his fantasies, however, someone did not barge out of the adjacent room and punch him in the side of the head.

The floor came up to meet his face. A foot introduced itself to his side. Pain spread through his abdomen like scalding bathwater, and he went under it. A second or minute or hour later, he opened his eyes. A man stood over him, waiting. No, not a man, a boy, probably younger than he was—underfed skinny, with some sort of neck tattoo or maybe it was a cluster of scabs. He shook Vance's wallet over his face. "Nothing. Piece of shit."

"No."

"So how'd you plan on paying? Think it's free?"

"I wasn't going to do anything."

The boy laughed. Like the girl, his eyes, too, were brightly animate and filled with light. It was the light of atavistic need, Vance now realized, and all it recognized was opportunity, a sucker. He was freshly amazed, as ever, by his own despicable innocence, at how gladly he could get everything wrong if it suited some fleeting fantasy. The boy said, "You got an ATM card in here, man, let's go get some cash." He picked Vance up by the back of his shirt and pushed him through the door. A last-second glance revealed an empty room, no maiden in the tower. The girl was gone, as though she'd never been there, which, in a way, she hadn't.

Outside, it was coming down in gray sheets billowing back and forth like laundry on a line. The water stung his face, reviving him a little. He felt the boy behind him, marching him down the street, right at the corner.

The boy said, "That's my girl back there. My wife basically."

"I wasn't going to do anything," he said again, wondering if it was true.

"I love her."

"Okay."

"I love her, man. She loves me," the boy said.

"I believe you."

The rain fell harder, they stepped out into the road, and Vance was running, flying across the liquid, his feet making a slapping sound, hearing footsteps behind him and a frustrated yell, zaggling across another street to the klaxon of an approaching car, down a larger avenue, his stomach sparking pain with every step, the rain even harder now, other people running too inside now as the sky completely opened up. The horizon was a mottled red with tendrils reaching out to either side, like the wound on the girl's jaw; he ran toward it for something to run toward, but it disappeared, a trick of angle or perspective. He ran and ran, and when he dared to look back, there was nothing, just the underwater city. The boy had disappeared—or, Vance thought, he himself had. He doubled over in the portico of a dilapidated colonial building, vomiting. The rain obligingly diluted the puke and washed the froth away into the street.

He waited for the storm to break, but it didn't. Finally, a bus pulled up at the corner, and he got on it before remembering his wallet was gone. The bus driver, a large, older blonde woman so thoroughly wedged into her seat that it appeared as if the bus had been assembled around her person, looked at him standing there dripping, gaping, wordless with his own misfortune. She sighed and jerked her thumb toward the back of the bus, a gesture of brusque compassion that was at that moment almost unbelievable. He sat alone on the plastic bench in the back. Reports of pain issued from all over his body. Eventually he would find out where he was going and make his way back across the water to the hotel, but for now he closed his eyes and allowed himself to be ferried through the flood.

CHAPTER TEN

———

They plowed down I-5, a thin gash that cut through the belly of the San Joaquin Valley like a cesarean scar; you could imagine the landscape opening, giving birth to the surrounding cities, becoming increasingly barren with each delivery. The valley was as Richard remembered it: a rolling sea of beige offering moments of vivid color—those faraway bluffs of hazy chartreuse! that red-orange crop duster low in the sky!—but more often, scenes of even greater drabness. They passed town after town with economies that were apparently dependent on cowboy-boot wholesaling and Jack in the Box restaurants. In one parcel of drought-stricken ranchland, a black-and-white Holstein calf lay dead on its side, covered by a swarm of flies so thick it was visible, despite Richard's glaucoma, at fifty yards and an average traveling speed of eighty miles an hour. In the distance, the Sierra Nevada lorded over it all with a misty, indistinct haughtiness.

His head felt huge and numb, a grotesque effigy stuffed with discarded T-shirts and dirty rags. The doctor had prescribed him Valium or one of its kissing cousins, and he was on a large dose to stave off presumptive alcoholic withdrawal. He'd told the doctor he wasn't an alcoholic: he just drank way too much all the time. And anyway, wasn't quitting alcohol exactly the kind of thing an alcoholic would do? Was that what the doctor wanted for him? The doctor hadn't smiled as he jotted the illegible prescription on his pad. Richard didn't like the way these pills made him feel, but he had to admit they'd worked so far, abstracting his usual desire for a drink into a fuzzy longing, like nostalgia for an old girlfriend.

Anyway, he was on good behavior for the time being, not wanting to upset Vance. The kid looked like he'd had a rough time and sported a bruise the approximate green-yellow color and shape of overcooked egg yolk on his right cheek. Richard had tried to get it out of him, but Vance's thin lips had remained resolutely drawn. After two hours of not talking, Richard pointed toward the driver's-side window and said, "Fresno's about a hundred miles that way."

"Huh."

"I tell you about when I lived there?" Vance stared grimly down the road, which Richard took as an invitation to carry on.

"Well, since you seem curious, I'll tell you a story about it. This was when Eileen was an assistant professor at Fresno State. She used to drag me to all these faculty events. She was coming up for tenure soon and had to make a good impression. Plus, she likes people. It was every other day for a while—a cocktail party or symposium or reception. Everyone was pretty nice, or nice enough, but there was one guy I couldn't stand. The head of her department, unfortunately, this pompous piece of shit named Grossberg." He scanned his memory for a moment. "Leonard Grossberg, that's right. Every chance he got, he made me look stupid. My first book had just come out, or it was coming out, and I was feeling pretty good about myself, but I couldn't talk out of my ass about deconstructionism. *What do you think of Foucault's new monograph, Richard?* Juvenile shit like that.

"I'm not anti-Semitic—I realize how suspect that claim sounds— but picture the most stereotypically Jewish-looking guy you can think of and then multiply that by ten thousand. Like Woody Allen, this guy, except a real nebbish, you know what I mean? I wanted to kick his ass so bad. Every Tennessee nerve fiber in my body twitched when he talked to me—they were all screaming, *Slap the shit out of this silly clown.* Except I couldn't, of course, because he was Eileen's boss. He knew it, and I knew it, and he knew I knew it.

"And I'm sure he hated me, too. Caught the whiff of redneck on me, the stink of ignorant philistine. And Coors Light—he definitely caught that. I know from his perspective, he couldn't understand what Eileen was doing with me, and to be fair to Grossberg, I'm not sure what she was doing with me either. She was hot stuff. She had great legs—tennis legs. We'd go to one of these cookouts, she'd be in a short skirt and moccasins, getting the stinkeye from every wife there, but she didn't give a shit. She was cool, not to mention smart. Smarter than me and smarter than Leonard Grossberg, too.

"Anyway, we went to this one party that Grossberg and his wife hosted every year. It was the big annual end-of-semester Christmas party. Everyone in the department, all the faculty and grad students and significant others, went to this thing. The house was pretty god-damned nice, set up on this little bluff on about an acre of land, first and second stories with these big balconies that wrap around. And even though it was probably seventy degrees, they decked out the side of the house and the front yard with Christmas lights and a crèche and also a giant inflatable menorah and even what I think was a Kwanzaa scene with ears of corn and some other shit. A joke, right? The campiness of the holiday season. It made me nostalgic for Maryville—my father used to drive us around on Christmas Eve, and we'd look at all the houses lit up. Santas and candy canes and these hand-built Nativity scenes. Poor hicks bankrupting themselves with their electric bills, but it was the only time of year Maryville didn't look like a cornpone turdpatch.

"We walk in, and Grossberg makes a beeline for us and says he wants to give 'us' the grand tour, although it didn't seem like he'd even noticed I was there. We get a walk-through of the loggia, the atrium, the library, the goddamned meditation chamber. That's this circular room with beanbag chairs on the floor and aquariums full of koi lining the walls and some kind of elfin-flute, wood-nymph music going on. This is 1975 or so, right?

"Then we go down to the basement, and he shows us—shows her—the gallery, as he calls it. It's a long white hallway with paintings and prints professionally hung, with those tiny spotlight thingies illuminating each one. Lots of abstract paintings. I don't know much about art—I knew even less at the time than I do now—but I knew Eileen, and I could see her eyes get wide looking at these paintings, recognizing them. There's even a small Mondrian at the end of the hall. Even I could recognize a Mondrian, those colored squares. I get the feeling his wife must have serious family money because there's no way teaching at Fresno State is funding a collection this impressive. Eileen's shooting me glances now and then like *What an asshole,* but with a little light in her eye that she can't hide.

"So later on, we're out in the yard drinking and smoking in this circle of people. Like I said, it's the seventies, I'm sure a joint was going around. And Grossberg comes out and puts his hand on Eileen's waist. Real casual, but bold and where everyone can see, to suggest to everyone they've got this thing going on. She freezes. 'Like a deer' is the cliché, but it works. That's what she looked like—her long thin legs and big eyes. I can still see him standing there, talking about whatever departmental scuttle, smiling at everyone and tapping his hairy little fingers on the top of her hip. Finally, she moves away from him and puts her hand on my arm and squeezes, but the only thing I can do to stop from beating the guy's face in, in front of all his colleagues, is to go back inside. I grabbed a bottle of Tanqueray and roamed fuming around the property.

"I woke up at home in bed with my clothes on. My shoes were even still laced. Eileen was gone, and for a minute it flashed through my head, what if I'd murdered her, or Grossberg, or both of them. I had this feeling I'd done something truly awful, right? Irredeemable. But I go through the house, and the bathtub and toilet aren't overflowing with blood, so I start to relax a little, think maybe I just binked out and Eileen got me home.

"The last place I check is the back of the house, and that's when I see it—the Mondrian. It's leaning against the wall, casual, no big deal, like a dartboard at a yard sale. The canvas is about three by four, and it's these seven interlocking rectangles colored in with red and blue and yellow. Really beautiful, in kind of a dull way."

"What did you do?" Vance had finally turned and looked at him.

"I stared at it for about ten minutes with my mouth open. Then I went inside and ran my head under cold water in the sink, to keep from losing it. Then I checked again to see if it was still there, and it was.

"I called Eileen at work. She said, 'Where the hell did you go last night?'

"I said, 'Oh, you know, got pissed and wandered off.'

"'We looked for you for an hour.'

"'Sorry, sorry.'

"She said, 'This kind of thing is not acceptable, Richard. It makes me look like a flake by association.' Et cetera, et cetera. We'd talk about it when she got home, and so on. Standard angry-woman stuff, but not woman-whose-fiancé-stole-a-million-dollar-painting-from-her-boss angry. I wondered if Grossberg had called the cops, if I'd tripped an alarm system or whatever. I got a beer and went and looked at the painting more. Part of me wanted to keep it—like I deserved it, or deserved it as much as anyone and certainly as much as Leonard Grossberg and his rich wife. You ever feel that way?"

"What way?"

"Like why not you?"

"No," said Vance.

"I don't anymore, but I used to feel that way a lot. So I looked at it for a while, feeling sorry for myself, and then I wrapped it up in a bedsheet and started walking. I walked all the way across Fresno, from the student ghetto where our house was, to the hills where Grossberg lived. Two, three hours I walked. It was lucky I'd stolen it during December, because I remember it was cool and there was this nice breeze blowing. If it'd been summer the paint would have melted right off the canvas, just dripped behind me in a trail the whole way.

"I knocked on his door and he answered it, and I handed him the painting. His little monkey fingers were wrapped around the frame tight like Eileen's waist the night before. We just stared at each other for a few seconds, and then he nodded and closed the door."

"What happened?"

"Nothing happened. I walked back home and slept all day, then Eileen got back and we probably had a fight. She never found out, as far as I know."

"What about that Grossberg guy?"

"What about him?"

"Did he fuck your wife?"

Richard looked at Vance, who had returned to staring straight ahead. The kid's face had a new indefinable hardness to it, the jaw set in a certain way, which seemed to echo the stony angles of the blue mountains in the distance. Richard said, "Not as far as I know."

The shoulder, on both sides of the interstate, was gray dust riven by furrows, as though some desperate fool had tried to plow the ashy soil. A wooden fence followed the freeway, demarcating someone's land, though whose and why? It seemed more likely that God had planted it there in a fit of despairing irony. In a softer tone of voice, Vance said, "That's kind of a lame story, you know."

"How's that?"

"It's unsatisfying. The ending just trails off."

"Most of my books end that way, too."

"Maybe that's why nobody bought them."

"Ouch."

"Maybe you should try figuring out what it means."

"It doesn't mean anything. What it is is what it means."

They drove awhile longer. Finally Vance said, "Okay, but I think that's a cop-out. I think you have to figure out what the point of it is."

"Like a moral? Work hard in the summer, be like the industrious ants and not the lazy grasshopper—that kind of thing?"

"No, not a moral. A point."

"What if there isn't a point? What if that *is* the point?"

"Then why bother telling it in the first place?"

"I guess because you feel like the act of telling *is* the point. That there's not some truth you're trying to get to, but that there's truth in the telling?"

"That's a cop-out," Vance said again.

An adobe rest area loomed, and Richard pointed at it. "Fine, it's a cop-out, Vance. Pull over here and let me take a leak."

They exited, and Richard hobbled into the building, his lower half as stiff and jointless as a piñata. He unzipped and peed, an interminable process that involved coaxing the last pint or so out with his thumb and forefinger, which never failed to disgustingly remind him of the time he was shown how to milk cows on a cousin's farm. When they said youth was wasted on the young, he thought, they didn't mean young people didn't appreciate their opportunities or good looks—what young people didn't appreciate was being able to see things and not having to milk their own dongs. Not to mention not being constantly on the verge of death—that was nice, too. He finished up and got back in the car and said, "How would you end it, then?"

Looking over his shoulder as they pulled back onto I-5, Vance said, "End what?"

"The story. If it's an unsatisfying cop-out, how would you end it?"

Vance thought for about thirty seconds. Richard had never known anyone who actually thought about the things he was going to say before he said them. It was both impressive and irritating, and impressively irritating. And irritatingly impressive. Finally, the kid said, "The problem is it ends too soon. You've set this conflict up with what's-his-name?"

"Grossberg."

"Yeah, and then it's just over."

"It *was* over. Eileen got tenure pretty soon after that, and we got married and had a kid and stopped going to those parties."

"But in the story you should have a fight, something. I mean, he was trying to sleep with your wife."

"Maybe I beat him over the head with the painting?"

"Something has to happen."

"No, it doesn't. It's like life. You bumble along and fuck things up, but maybe manage to avoid fucking up everything. Or not. You don't get most of the things you want or even some of the things you need, despite what Mick Jagger says, but you have your little victories and moments that carry you. Then you wake up and you're getting old, and you think, Well shit. Things happen, but in the end nothing has really happened. Or nothing the way you mean. There's no point."

Vance shook his head. "There is a point, you just haven't found it yet."

Near Bakersfield they got on I-58 to Barstow, then I-15 after that. The sun was just starting to set behind the car, soft-lighting the desert and the mountains of the Mojave Range like an aging actress's face. The sky was dotted with little cruising cumulus clouds; when one would momentarily pass in front of the sun, a shadow hundreds of miles wide would cast itself across the valley. The leading edge of the shadow passing over the car felt like a judgment from God. They made Nevada in bruised twilight, and it was pitch black as they crested the final hill and Las Vegas appeared, a near infinity of kilowatt-hours blasting away the almost-mythological gloom of the desert basin.

Driving down the Strip, Vance tried his best, and failed, to look unimpressed by the casinos, the lights, the hordes of people, the scale of everything. Richard thought about when he and Eileen used to come to Vegas, how they would bring a hundred dollars to gamble with. Even in the nineties, with Carole, you could get by spending around a thousand over a weekend visit. Now you had to mortgage your house. They passed a casino advertising twenty-dollar-a-hand blackjack, as though that was a bargain, which it probably was. The people who ran Vegas, he thought, should install a system at the airport whereby, upon exiting the plane, you would be tranquilized, vacuumed for cash and other valuables, and then immediately dumped back on a departing flight. It would make everything a lot simpler.

Their room was at the MGM Grand, an obsidian megaplex that squatted like a giant, malevolent dog in the middle of the Strip. They parked, traversed a vast, purgatorial parking garage, and trundled their bags into the Boschian chaos: past the smoldering sportsbook; past a street gang of bejeweled, bejowled middle-aged women howling with laughter, enormous plastic tureens of margaritas dangling beneath their overtanned wattles; past a blackjack table crowded by beefy young men, a dense thicket of tattooed biceps (more Chinese characters than a Bruce Lee movie) bulging from the sleeves of ornately filigreed white T-shirts; past a pair of security guards with assault rifles wheeling away a metal lockbox containing the collectivized hourly production of dozens of croupiers, whose alert and expressionless heads dotted the sunken red-carpeted plain of the pit like minor demons working the rim of hell. Richard and Vance walked under a transparent walkway where, above their heads, a lion took a long, steamy piss, an act of entirely justified protest faithfully recorded on a flip phone by the presumptive head of a large clan of hooting Okies. The youngest, and probably smartest, of them peeled off from the group and began walking alongside Vance and Richard. The mother yelled "Darnell!" and the child stopped, looking up at them with mournful eyes that seemed to rue his entire life in advance.

Waiting in line at the front desk, Richard looked up and noticed the ceiling. It recalled the child's eyes, a disquieting robin's-egg blue. Probably scientifically determined as the color that makes people spend the most money, he thought, to remind you of the time right before dawn, when the party's almost over. No doors in the place, no windows, no clocks, just the eerie blue overhead recalling that old big-band number—*Enjoy yourself, enjoy yourself, it's later than you think.*

At the desk, the clerk found their reservation and said, "Mr. Lazar, the management has you in the Presidential Suite."

"That's a mistake, we booked a double."

"No, sir, I have it right here."

"How much is that? I've only got thirty grand in the bank."

The clerk laughed drily to himself. "It's compliments of our executive manager, Mr. Arthur Freedlund."

"Why?"

"I don't know, sir."

"Well, okay. Tell Mr. Arthur Freedlund thanks."

"Yes, sir. Just leave your bags with us, and Milton will show you up."

Milton, a terrifyingly efficient bellhop with cheekbones that could have been used to pry off bottle tops, seemed to appear from out of nowhere. He put their bags on a valet cart, which he wheeled over to a massive elevator bank. In the elevator, Milton used a key dangling from a wrist bracelet to access a row of floor numbers behind a sliding metal panel. He pressed number 30, and they rose with a soft exhalation of air.

"The Presidential Suite, huh?" said Richard. "Is that where presidents stay when they come here?"

"Yes, sir," said Milton.

The elevator doors opened to the room itself, or "room." It was the size of a house—a small one, granted, but still. Milton showed them around with brisk élan. Every visible surface in the room seemed to be made of either gold, Italian marble, lush animal fur, or some combination thereof. Richard ran his hand over the back of a chic sofa—upholstered with the sheeny, lustrous skin of some creature in single-digit endangerment—which sat in a loose cluster of sofas in front of a movie-screen-sized TV. The entire right side of the suite comprised floor-to-ceiling windows that looked down on the gaudy bedlam of the Strip. On the left side, there was a fully stocked bar and a billiards table, a video-game console, and multiple pinball machines. A small, oblong infinity pool murmured to itself in the corner. It was a nice room.

Milton showed them to their individual bedrooms, arranged their bags, and accepted a ten-dollar tip that seemed completely insulting, given the surroundings. There was a note on Richard's bed, handwritten on MGM stationery. It read:

Dear Mr. Lazar,

I heard we have the honor of hosting you during your brief stay in Las Vegas. Your book is an important contribution to our country's dialogue on the always relevant subject of military intervention, with its accompanying rewards and perils. Please accept this room as a show of gratitude, from one serviceman to the other (325th Airborne, '69–'72). Yours, Arthur Freedlund

Richard walked back out to the bar, where he considered pouring himself a quick succession of scotches while Vance was occupied in his bedroom. He hadn't had a drink in four days, besides the two beers a day he'd been prescribed in the hospital to wean him down. There was more liquor here than at the Tamarack, four glittering shelves of it in all its colorful splendor, the entire visible spectrum of booze: red schnapps and pinkish Campari and burgundy sweet vermouth; orange Cointreau, amber bourbon, and yellow cordials; a cool, wooded lake of green and blue gin; vile-looking purple stuff in a bottle shaped like an antique grenade or the head of a royal scepter. Colorless vodka representing the infrared. And a small row of dark, sinister digestifs, for what would come after.

Instead, he grabbed a bottle of "Artesian water from the Alps"—whatever that meant—from the refrigerator and took two of his pills. He scrolled through the names in his phone's contact list, which had, with the addition of Vance and Cindy, swollen to four, and dialed his daughter. The voicemail picked up immediately, confirming his suspicion that she would avoid any potential communication while he was in town. "Hey, Cin." He gazed out the enormous floor-to-ceiling window that constituted one side of the suite and provided a panorama of the blazing city below; she was out there somewhere, living her strange life. "It's your father. I'll be at the Vegas Convention Center tomorrow at one, over there by the Hilton. I'm staying in the Presidential Suite at the MGM, if you can believe that. The view is pretty unbelievable, if you feel like having a look, but you probably don't. You're probably working, you work nights. See, I remembered? Anyway, hope you can make it."

From a distant room, Vance emerged holding a fruit basket.

"I've never even seen some of these before." He picked up a bulbous orange and green fruit shaped like a cross between a banana and a telephone. "What is this?"

"The high point of your life, soak it up."

"Why did they give us this room," said the kid, and Richard handed him the letter. Vance read it and handed it back.

"Spoils of war," said Richard, settling in front of the TV.

————

An hour later, Vance was still roaming the suite, agog. He had taken a dip in the pool, and his hair dripped onto the notebook, in which he cataloged the amenities for future reference (though, he felt, no one would believe it if he told them). His bed, for example: What was larger than king size? Sultanate? Imperial? You could roll six times in either direction without falling off, and when you did, you landed on a plush fur carpet. Richard seemed characteristically impervious to the room and was watching TV, an old movie with Steve McQueen looking cool and unhealthy.

Someone knocked on the door to the suite, and Vance answered it. It was a small, compact man, around Richard's age, with titanium-rimmed glasses balanced on a commanding nose that seemed to enter the room as he stood where he was. The man extended his hand and said, "Arthur Freedlund. Is your father here?"

"He's not my father," said Vance, and pointed to Richard, who was making his way to the door, still holding the remote control. Mr. Freedlund entered, and Vance remained by the door watching as the two men shook hands and spoke, feeling a bit like a valet in one of those BBC versions of Jane Austen that his mother, but mostly he, liked to watch.

"Thank you for sparing me a minute or two of your time," said Freedlund.

"Well, thanks for the room, it's pretty nice."

Freedlund laughed and perched a haunch on the back of the sofa. He had the self-assurance only obtained by people who tell other people what to do all the time. "Well, you read my note. I'm a fan of the book, and I wanted to extend our hospitality to you."

"That's very kind," said Richard.

"I wanted to say that while you might be catching some flak for what you did, I think anyone who was over there could relate to some of the feelings you detail. It was a distressing time, a bad situation. Many of us did things we regret."

"Yes."

"I was also curious, did you happen to know Mike McGrath?"

"No."

"He's a friend of mine, head of security at Harrah's."

"Okay."

"He was infantry, stationed around Bao Loc the same time as you. Camp Meyers."

"Really."

"You don't say exactly in the book, but I assume that's where you were. I showed him the relevant passages, and he swore by it. He would have been there same time as you, early 'seventy-one."

"I mean, a lot of guys came in and out of that camp. Not to mention, I was smoking about a pound of Thai a week at that time."

Freedlund's polite smile mastered the distaste that flashed in the crinkling corners of his eyes. "Yes, well. At any rate, let us know if there's anything we can do to make your stay here more comfortable. This is the number of your personal concierge and assistant, should you need him." He handed Richard a card.

"I don't know. Maybe if you have a spare koala or something."

Freedlund rose from his half-seated position, and walked toward the door, then stopped. "If you don't mind my saying," he said, "it does seem to me you convey a feeling of total regret. That your service had no value."

"It didn't."

"But the experiences you relate, weren't they formative? I mean, surely they were, or you wouldn't have written the book in the first place."

"So what? Maybe I would have worked on a dairy farm, instead. That would have been formative. I could've written about that. Or nothing, that would have been fine, too. I don't think being in Vietnam had some inherent value past what I assign to it."

"And you don't think serving your country has some inherent value?"

Vance noticed that Richard's knuckles had gone white where he clutched the remote control. It was not hard to imagine Richard striking Mr. Arthur Freedlund in the head with it over and over.

"No," he said. "I don't, I'm sorry."

He shook hands with Richard again, and said, "Well, I do. Thank you for it, and enjoy your time with us." He walked out. On the TV, McQueen rode a motorcycle across rolling green farmland, the Alps looming in the background. As black waves of Nazis crested the hills, he gunned his bike back and forth by a barbed-wire fence, like a restless jungle cat pacing in captivity, then he hit a large hill and cleared the fence, framed in a solitary moment against the Panaflex sky.

———

They were situated beside a craps table, and Vance was on a heater like Richard had never seen. The kid had a ritual—he would grab two adjacent dice from the croupier's stick, shake them a few times while mumbling inaudibly to himself, and skip them lightly across the expanse of green felt so they stopped just after touching the opposite wall. He hit seven over and over and over. And after he made eight as the point, he hit that, and the table cheered. The performance had attracted bettors, and now the table buzzed with bonhomie as only a craps table can. Richard had started with a couple of twenty-dollar chips and was now working several hundred. The sparkle-vested cocktail waitress asked Richard for the sixth time if he wanted anything, and for the sixth time, he ordered a Coke for her to forget to bring.

Vance rolled a seven again, then eleven. Even the croupier was grinning as he pushed the chips around. Richard said, "You've really never done this before."

"My dad showed me how," said Vance, and once more he launched the dice.

Richard scooped up the chips pushed toward him and said, "Your dad showed you how to shoot winners at craps?"

"He used to take me to the Indian Casino in Bellhaven when I was little. He said I was good luck."

"I guess he was right."

Vance threw an eleven, a seven, seven, seven, eleven. He established a ten point, then rolled hard four, hard six, hard eight, ten. There was a feeling at the table that it would never end. They would all grow old and wealthy together, a pack of billionaires camped out around the table. He rolled a ten, to a delighted chorus of *Hey shooter, all right shooter!* There is no joy on earth like the joy of free money. Eleven, eleven, seven. A guy wearing a tattered Crimson Tide baseball cap and earbuds approached and put two twenty-five-dollar chips down on the don't-pass line. Vance passed the dice to the guy next to him and collected his chips. He said, "Come on."

"What are you doing," said Richard. "We're killing it here."

Vance walked away, and Richard followed awkwardly, stuffing his chips into his jeans pockets. Vance said, "You see that guy who came up and bet the Don't Pass? He's betting against the table—it'll be dead soon."

"No shit."

"Just watch."

They sat at a nearby lounge—the video poker screens embedded in the bar below their faces purred and chattered, trying to get someone's attention. Over the next five minutes, sure enough, the table they'd been at quieted and began gradually dispersing. Five minutes later, the guy in the Alabama hat was the only one left.

"I'm impressed," Richard said.

"Guys like that are bad luck."

"You don't think I'm a guy like that?"

"No. I don't think you'd bet against the table. You're not an asshole," Vance said, still staring intently at the guy's back.

Richard laughed. "If I'm not an asshole, I don't know what."

"You're an asshole, but not an *asshole*."

"My daughter would probably disagree with you on that." He checked his phone again, but there were no voicemails.

Vance continued staring at the guy and finally got up. Richard watched the kid as he stood directly across from the guy and set three green chips on the pass line. The kid's eyes never moved or wavered, as though he was trying to mentally bore a hole in the guy's forehead. Richard saw the guy look up, make eye contact for a moment, then shoot the dice. They came up snake eyes, and the croupier hooked Vance's chips into the black hole in the middle of the table. Over and over, Vance put his money down and lost it, all the while staring at the guy, who was studiously ignoring him. Finally, the guy pulled out his earbuds and said, "You got a problem?"

Vance didn't say anything, just glared at the guy.

"Past your bedtime, buddy?"

Richard hauled himself up and walked to the table. Vance had one ten-dollar chip left, which he was putting down on the table. "Come on," said Richard.

"I've got one more."

"Save it. You could buy . . ." Richard scanned his mind for something ten dollars could buy in Vegas and came up with absolutely nothing. A key chain? A golf pencil? A side order of ketchup at Cheeburger Cheeburger?

Vance put the chip down on the pass line. The guy looked up again for a moment, shook his head, and rolled a three. The croupier pulled the lone chip away with his curved stick and with a rueful expression walked it across the table and into the hole. "Okay," said Vance, "now we can go."

They drifted away from the pit, through the early morning thrum of the casino. There seemed to be two types of gamblers on the casino floor at that hour: people having the kind of strenuously good time advertised in commercials for Vegas, all barking laughter and goggling disbelief at the fun they were having, and, alternately, people apparently resigned to losing all their money before they could go to sleep. The stone-eyed crones bent over slot machines—with names like Fun City! and Rakin It In and Bonanza Dreamz, and, cruelest of all, Early Retirement!—seemed a different species altogether.

"What the hell was that about?" said Richard as they waited at the gleaming, golden haven of the elevator banks. But the kid said nothing, just looked up at the numbers slowly counting down to one. They got on, and Vance used the key that the bellhop had given him, opening the panel and pressing the 30 button, and they were enveloped in the calm whoosh of the car rising upward. The doors opened to their room; the only thing it lacked was Saint Peter bent over a giant ledger.

"Fuck it," said Richard, waving a hand. "Good night."

Richard hobbled the half mile to his room, the door clicked shut, and Vance stood alone in the giant, dark room. The anger that had overtaken him in the casino now swelled into a kind of defiant elation. Fuck his father, he thought. Again, he remembered standing at the craps table, the edge of which he could barely see over, watching his father throw the dice, taking his turn with them, never understanding why all the other players at the table glared at them and swore under their collective breath. Finally, the gentle old man—gray haired and cardiganned, bent with smiling enmity—who'd explained it: *You're betting against all the other people. For you to win, everyone else has to lose.* Studying his father's face at the table and on the drive home, the little smile and the satisfied cigarettes, realizing he liked it that way.

With a rare sense of his youth as a commodity, not a deficit or deformity, he moved to the bar and poured himself a large tumbler of Macallan 18. He could do whatever the hell he wanted; his mistakes would be his own. He thought about the girl in San Francisco, the winding alleyway with the boot waiting at the end of it, and for the first time since it had happened, he felt no shame. For the first time in his life, he was at the center of his own story. A dumb story, maybe, but better to be the hero of a dumb story than a minor character in some eventless epic. Was this true? He jotted it down in his notebook, his bruised ribs aching in proud accord.

He moved to the window. Thirty floors down, the Strip was still congested and ablaze with frenetic activity at two in the morning. Everyone writing their own novels: lurid romance, frat-boy picaresque, therapeutic hokum, even the odd murder mystery. The liquor tasted like burnt dirt, but he got it down. Toward the bottom of the glass, his reflection in the window mingled with the lights below and became part of one image, as though his essence had somehow left him, spread in the desert wind, superimposed itself over the city. Henceforth art thou the genius of the MGM Grand. He finished the last of his drink and touched his throbbing cheek, and it seemed like his life had begun.

CHAPTER ELEVEN

Alittle before two in the afternoon, Cindy Evergreen Lazar pushed into Conference Room B of the Las Vegas Convention Center. It was a large, semicircular room, perhaps three hundred capacity, and she was surprised to see it full of people waiting to hear her father speak. Some stood in the aisles, and some sat in folding chairs provided by the management for overflow. There were a good number of military types, including two elderly men in those felt-green, sharp-cornered VFW berets that reminded her of the paper hats the cooks wore at In-N-Out. Richard had taken her there, ritually, once a week, until the divorce, one of the few ways he hadn't ever let her down. They would always split a large french fry—eating it first since the fries got soggy and disgusting after three minutes or so—then they would eat their burgers, wrapped in the greasy wax paper, which she would secretly take tiny, illicit bites from while staring out the window at cars going by on Danforth Avenue. She moved to the rear of the conference room, where she hoped she would be obscured by shadows. This spot had the additional virtue of being located five feet from the exit door, which she anticipated pushing through in only a couple of minutes.

She didn't know why she had come. Today was her day off, a day that had begun unpromisingly around noon with the heraldic yapping of her neighbor's dog, an obese beagle she sincerely wanted to murder. Not that she should have minded being woken—her dreams during the night had been a series of vague sketches on the general theme of anxious inadequacy; in one, it was her first day at a new job, but no one had bothered to tell her what her duties were, and so she had wandered around a vast, gray factory floor looking for a supervisor, until she realized no one was there and they had tricked her, whoever *they* were. She got out of bed and put on her tattered sweatpants with the shot elastic waistband, which augmented her feeling of general worthlessness. She washed down a Wellbutrin with a microwaved cup of day-old coffee, added two Vicodin and a Lortab to the mix, and turned on the TV, landing on some reality show that featured rich women being rude to waitstaff and calling one another names. The pills gradually took effect but only served to offset what she'd taken the night before (after her shift, sitting in front of a roulette wheel at the Nugget, avoiding an unavoidable meeting with goddamned Mikhail), and she found herself in a gray and restless shadowland of low serotonin. She got up and took a shower, which did help, at least in terms of giving her something to do, but eventually the water got cold.

She sat down on the edge of her bed, wrapped in a towel, and began plucking hairs out of the crown of her head. This, despite telling herself after her last session—as she thought of them—that that was it, no more. But then, she told herself that after every session. She couldn't remember how or when she'd started doing it—the hair pulling had been a small thing for years, a weird though very occasional habit—but it had gotten worse in the last few months as her money and legal troubles had intensified and was now to the point where she found herself, several times a day, in a glazed stupor with her hand hovering over the top of her head.

The bald spot was the size of a casino chip and almost as perfectly circular. She had allowed herself to see it recently, alone in the beveled fluorescence of a Lord & Taylor dressing room, untying her camouflaging topknot and staring up at it, the cheerful pink of her festering soul. She'd wept. But now, her predatory fingers expertly searched its periphery for the perfect hair to yank. Finding one, she wrapped it three times around her index finger and teased herself with a slight tug, the heavenly feeling of upward pressure on the scalp. She relaxed, then tautened, her grip on the hair many times—as she did, she fell into a delicious whiteout trance; the suffocating anxiety washed gently away from her, and she was like a pier at low tide, temporarily released by the churning sea.

With a pop, she pulled it out.

The following six hairs brought diminishing returns of calm, until she found herself just sitting on her bed, yanking out her hair. She collected the hairs from her bedcovers and dropped them in the trash. She got dressed and rearranged her topknot and, desperately needing to escape her apartment, decided to go for a drive. It was early Saturday afternoon, and the traffic of North Las Vegas had a sluggish feel, as though the heart powering everything could barely bring itself to beat. From her apartment she drove east on Tropical, then south on Commerce, the decrepit buildings of downtown hulking on the horizon. The streets were awash with the usual flotsam of partying yahoos, hustlers, and homeless, though it was hard to tell who was who—the taxonomy of Vegas casualties was indistinct and frighteningly fluid. She'd lived here for eight years now and hardly even noticed these people anymore; like the ubiquitous *plong* and *doink* of the slot machines, you had to tune them out or go crazy. She passed through downtown, took a left on Sahara, and found herself three blocks away from the Convention Center. When she looked up, she saw the marquee and her own last name suspended twenty feet above the parking garage. She admitted it to herself then: she'd known he was coming and was curious. Well, why shouldn't she be?

Now, she watched as her father was introduced and emerged on the stage to enthusiastic applause. It was hard to square her memories of him with a figure people would come to see and applaud for, but there he was. He stood frowning at the podium, waiting for the clapping to die down. She hadn't seen him in several years, and a couple of things were immediately apparent to her.

First, he was fat, much fatter than he'd ever been, and he'd always been fat. Before, the fat had been hard and seemed structural to her, a part of him, like the interior metal girders in the buildings he worked on. Now it seemed extraneous, an add-on. His gut was a soft expanse that, in tandem with his beautiful white coxcomb of hair, created an avuncular bearlike effect that belied what she was sure was still his essentially selfish nature.

Second, surprisingly, he didn't appear to be drunk. As a girl, she'd learned all the signs. His face would always turn an even richer shade of scarlet than usual—in particular, the area on the sides of the bridge of his nose. She had thought of it as his mask. As he'd bent carefully over her to tuck her in, she would imagine pulling it off his face. Even from the back of the room she could tell that the man up on the podium was only averagely red faced. Also, he'd crossed the stage with an insouciant, absentminded trudge. When he was drunk, he walked with the measured, cautious gait of a man moving through a room filled with precariously balanced crystal stemware; when he was sober, he was unapologetically clumsy.

The applause died, and her father gingerly addressed the mic with a shaky left paw. "Thank you," he said. "I'm Richard Lazar." It took him a moment to find his place in the book. He looked up, scanning the crowd, then began to read.

We'd been in camp for almost three months—three months of sitting there with our thumbs up our asses, in some cases literally (a new kid from Idaho named Sanderson was caught in the latrine with three fingers in his bung; he claimed the mess chow had made him so constipated that he was trying to manually extricate a turd, and was nicknamed Brownfinger for the duration of his tour, another two months, as it turned out, at which time he was mortared at Parrot's Beak and sent home without legs or a nickname)—when we got our marching orders.

Sergeant Martin gave them to us after breakfast. They were: a weeklong push to Nha Trang, north of Cam Ranh; pack light on provisions, heavy on ammo; decamping tomorrow oh six hundred; expect engagement. In other words, as usual, no one told us what in the green living shit was going on. We marched all day—our safe little base camp disappearing behind us, through alternating paddies and rain forest—with the question of where the fuck we were going and why going back and forth like a sung call-and-response:

Where in the fuck is Nha Trang?
Why in the fuck are we going there?

*We camped on the edge of a little hamlet that seemed mostly
inhabited by chickens. Occasionally an old lady would peek her head
out of a shack and then disappear again. The chickens didn't seem
to mind us. I didn't honestly mind the march so far. I mean, if you'd
given me a choice I would've stayed at base camp, and I still didn't
think I could fight—still had that dull certainty in my gut—but at
the same time there was a strange relief, almost a physical release, in
finally doing the thing we'd been sent there to do. Getting it the hell
over with.*

*Berlinger, however, was pissed. He stopped Lieutenant Endicott, as
Endicott walked through camp. "What's the mission, Leftenant? I'm
not going any further if I don't know."*

"Yes, you will, Berlinger."

*"I will not. I'm telling you. I'll walk straight back to the brig at
base camp, but I ain't goose chasin' around the fucking mountains
if no one has the good grace to tell me just what I'm doing here.
Common courtesy, sir."*

*"Your staff sergeant told you. Heading to Nha Trang, another five
days or so."*

"Right, why?"

*Endicott looked down at all of us as if deciding something, then he
seemed to shrug into the darkness. "Search and destroy."*

*Search and destroy. The words have a poetic ring. And a Calvinist
logic that suggests if you search hard enough, you'll find something
to destroy. Endicott disappeared into his tent and left us where we'd
collapsed, our gear sprawled out around us like we'd dropped from
the sky through the jungle canopy. Berlinger sat back down and
started carving long strips off a palm frond with his knife. He said,
"Search and destroy. That means a colonel got tired of us sitting in
his pocket, right? Clusterfuck's getting a little unfucked—everyone's
getting shipped home soon, better send us out here to get our asses
shot at while they still got a chance, right?"*

"Shut up, Berlinger," said Davis Martin. He was a surly East Texan, tightly muscled and with all his features bunched up in the central square inch of his face.

"Spread a little napalm around for no reason, something to remember us by, right?"

"I said shut the fuck up."

"Davis Martin, my daddy told me don't trust no one with two first names," barked Berlinger. The guys sitting near us laughed. "Anyway," Berlinger went on, "I don't know what you're getting pissed about. It was in the Reporter, Nixon's drawing down. These aren't state secrets I'm giving away here."

"One more word and you draw point tomorrow, that's a threat and a promise."

"Search and destroy, my ass," Berlinger muttered, but he stopped talking. The thick jungle air hung around us like fine cloth, something you could reach out and grab. I ate my MRE and listened to the night, then dropped into a dead sleep, dreaming of the usual stuff: watching and being watched, pursuit and pursuing, fumbling with a gun in slow motion, a nightmare mist of malarial death.

———

Over the next couple of days, Berlinger went into a livid funk so profound that he couldn't or wouldn't speak. He hadn't been himself since Carbone—he'd mostly stopped with the relentless provocation and bullshit, and it was sorely missed, at least by me. He still played cards with us, even still horsed around some, ribbing Kozinski for being a dumb Polack and that kind of thing, but it somehow felt strained and perfunctory to me, as though he was just keeping up appearances. I know he felt guilty about Carbone. I felt bad about Carbone, too, at least for a little while, but in all honesty the feeling faded pretty quick. It seemed like something I had dreamed, or read about in a book. It hadn't for Berlinger, though. He walked by himself behind everyone, as though he was humping some extra gear, an invisible radio, say, that was pushing him down into the muck. When I waited for him to catch up, he just shook his head at me. I let him be.

*We swamp-assed it through a soggy lowland marsh for two days—
the inside of my thighs chafed red and swollen as a baboon's ass
from the heat and the damp fabric of my combat fatigues—then
the morning of the third we hit higher, drier ground. Pure bliss. We
walked in a steaming line up a wide clay ridge on the side of a hill,
steadily rising out of the grassland. The sun rose as if it was one of
us, up out of its resting place beyond the jungle. Against my will, as
so often happened, I was struck by the beauty of the place, and by the
fact that, given what we were there to do, I was still able to recognize
that beauty. It would have been easier, in a way, if it had been an
uglier country. Easier to keep in mind what you were there to do and
have done to you.*

*We were reminded soon enough. At seven hundred hours, Endicott
sent word around that aerial recon had reported recent VC activity
in this area. A nearby village called Vien Dinh was harboring an
encampment. We held our guns at the ready, hunched down, fanned
out, and slowed up, looking for movement in the treacherous woods,
or the glint of wire strung across our path. We moved this way for two
hours, aching under our field packs and fear, the ridge slowly and
inexorably rising up over the landscape, until we were nearly level
with the tree line. Then five of us—me, Berlinger, Martin, and two
other guys whose names are lost to me—crested the ridge and looked
down at the village of Vien Dinh.*

*It sat a hundred yards below us, innocent, or at least unaware.
Several thatched huts crowded around a central area that had been
cleared of palm trees, with a darkened area that must have been a
communal cooking space. An old person, impossible to identify as a
man or woman from this distance, sat on a wooden bench, stooped
over a plate of food they ate with their fingers. A bare-chested man
appeared on the far edge of the scene, carrying wooden buckets, full
of rice or maybe water. It was strange watching these people go about
their banal chores and duties, the routines they completed daily—
gathering water, cleaning and mending clothes, feeding their meager
livestock, cooking, and washing up—completely unaware of being
watched. It felt indecent.*

*There was no Vietcong presence that I could see. Davis Martin
waved us back off the edge, and we jogged behind him to where
Endicott and the rest of the platoon had stopped. Martin and Endicott
conferred, and then Endicott motioned for us to follow him back
thirty yards or so down the ridge, to a small stone outcropping that
provided shade from the rapidly rising sun. We gathered as close as
we could, and listened as he spoke in a low tone, although there was
no way anyone down there could have heard him talk.*

*"Listen up. We're gonna park it here until the VC make an
appearance. We'll take shifts surveilling. When they do show up,
we're going to get back in formation and blast the hell out of them.
Martin will give firing orders, we clear?"*

*"No, sir." Berlinger stared at Endicott, or past him, as though he
was seeing something out in the dense green foliage.*

"Pardon me?"

"I said, 'No, sir.'" Some of the guys groaned.

*"Berlinger," Endicott began, but Berlinger had unslung his
rifle and handed it to Endicott butt first. The lieutenant took it
uncertainly, for a moment balancing it on its barrel and looking like
an old man with a walking stick.*

*Berlinger said, "Lieutenant, I hereby surrender my weapon and
myself to this platoon as a noncombatant, or an objector, or deserter,
or whatever the fuck the terminology is. I lay down arms." He
pointed to the ridge over the village. "I am not doing this."*

*"You don't have a choice." Endicott tried to hand him back the
gun, but Berlinger wouldn't take it.*

"Respectfully, sir, there's always a choice."

"Pick up your weapon, soldier."

"No."

*Endicott paused, and when he spoke, he spoke slowly. "You
understand you can be court-martialed for this. And you understand
that can mean a dishonorable discharge, maybe years in prison."*

"Yes, sir."

*"Damn." Endicott sighed. "Goddamn it, fine." He handed Martin
the rifle. Martin went over to Berlinger and confiscated his field*

pack. *Standing there empty-handed, Berlinger looked like a little kid who'd shown up late to a playground full of kids playing soldier. He walked away and sat next to a small rock with his hands between his legs. I wanted to go over there and beat his fuckwad prima-donna head in.*

Forty minutes later the guy who'd drawn first watch, a PFC named Tilghman, turned around and gestured wildly. Davis Martin jogged over with his gun in firing position, dropped to his belly, and looked over. He waved at us to follow him, motioning with his palm flat to the ground. We spread out in a predetermined line and moved up the crest of the hill, crab-walking the last ten feet to the edge.

The Vietcong were down there, identifiable by their trademark loose-fitting uniforms, as well as by the rifles slung over their shoulders. They squatted around holding tin cups of something, green tea maybe, carrying on conversations in clusters. We were too far away to hear what they were saying and, of course, we wouldn't have understood it anyway, but the general atmosphere of the scene struck me as one of convivial relaxation after a hard night's work. It was, after all, still morning. One of the Vietcong laughed, a hoarse bark. I was reminded of the time before shipping out that I'd stayed up all night with my buddies in Knoxville, cracking a final beer as the sun came up, relishing the delay of sleep another ten minutes, another five. I reminded myself that if the soldiers below us had pulled an all-nighter, they'd done so creeping through the surrounding forest, the same as they had done in my nightmares over the last three months. Setting claymores and bouncing betties, rigging booby traps with sharpened punji sticks, hoping to wound, maim, impale me—hoping to shear the flesh from my legs.

The tree line across from us was covered with black birds, I didn't know what kind. Were there crows in Vietnam? They perched in their own clusters, occasionally flapping from one frond to another. It looked like the birds were spying on the VC, the same way we were. There was something comic about the situation, a horrible dramatic irony, and a kind of giddiness overtook me—it reminded me of playing hide-and-seek with my cousins all over their big farmhouse.

Looking at their legs through the slats in a closet door. I had to bite on the stiff sleeve of my jacket to keep from giggling out loud.

My attention at that moment landed on someone carrying a sun-faded pink umbrella. From our downward angle, I couldn't see who they were or what they were doing, just a pair of feet now and then. They moved in a circle around the fire pit, now close to the Vietcong. One of the VC looked up and said something, and, seemingly rebuffed, the umbrella floated away. The umbrella and its bright color were fantastic in the middle of all the black and brown and olive green.

The soldier next to me made a fist with his right hand, and I did the same as I looked up the line to my right. At the top, Sergeant Martin held his hand clenched in the air, and if I'd forgotten my field signal training by that point, his meaning when he pointed his M-14 down at the encampment was unambiguous. All the guns pointed down into the little valley, safeties off. One VC got up and wandered behind a lean-to, where he pissed with his hand against a tree. Martin raised his hand again. I sighted my target, a VC wiping out what looked like a large pan with a white rag. Like a party balloon popping in the thick air, a lonely shot sounded, a trigger accidentally pulled by a nervous eighteen-year-old finger from Nebraska or Vermont or Mississippi. The VC stopped talking and looked around. The pink umbrella paused near the tree line.

Then Martin's hand dropped and we were all firing. I shot my VC several times in quick succession, and the last shot pinged off the pan he was holding. The bodies of the men below us flailed as though participating in a lively, impromptu dance. More merriment. The guy taking a piss fell over holding his dick. The people in the lean-tos appeared to sleep through the whole thing. I cannot express to you the pleasure I felt firing my gun, killing those fuckers. After almost an entire year of doubt, of imagining myself running away, or covering my head and pissing myself, there I was, squeezing the trigger over and over, sighting targets and blasting them with casual accuracy the way we'd been shown in Basic. Someone in black ran toward the western tree line and I took the back of his head off with one shot. Then I shot him again to make sure.

With the visible clusters of VC dead or dying on the ground, the field of fire expanded like a hungry blob looking for more things to eat. Someone—probably this guy Harriman who'd played backup QB on his Oklahoma high school football team—pitched an arching grenade the entire distance, an absurdly long throw that blew one of the houses off its supports. The explosion initiated a wave of gunning and fragging that was aimed at the huts and lean-tos. A wounded man limped out carrying something and was shot three times before he hit the dirt. The old person I'd noticed before had fallen next to their bowl of food, carelessly spilled beside them. A snatch of fabric from the pink umbrella, caught in the trees, fluttered as if in surrender.

One thing I remember thinking was how strangely similar it was to scenes in movies when people get shot. If you had asked me before, I might have guessed that there would be some telling difference, however small. It would have to be a small detail, in fact, a key visual detail that Sam Peckinpah or Walter Hill might have imagined wrong, and something that would falsify the corpus of movie mayhem in experienced eyes. But what I saw, two hundred yards away, looked just like something from a film: the noise, the smoke, the dust, bodies jerking and falling, some blood, though not an unrealistic amount. Then eventually silence.

What had happened had taken maybe twenty seconds, probably less. The smoke took another thirty seconds or so to clear, then Sergeant Martin stood and we all followed suit. We walked down the ridge behind him like a line of ducklings following their mother. As we walked slowly among the corpses in the field, everyone had approximately the same look of childish astonishment on his face, disbelief that he could be partly responsible for such a thing. Most of the VC had fallen face-first, but two near me had fallen next to each other on their backs, with their heads nearly touching, as though they were a fond couple sky-gazing, or perhaps two kids making snow angels.

I wonder if the following realization is universal to everyone who's

*just killed someone: that you are now, and always will be, a killer. It
is a very clear line, and once you've crossed it, there's no going back.
You can't unkill someone, no matter how much you'd like to, and you
can't unkiller yourself. For the rest of your life, you have the honor of
being in the select group of human beings who have ended another
human being's life. It is no small thing. I looked at my fellow soldiers
and thought how all of us—Endicott and Martin, and dumbfuck
Lester Hawkins walking around trying not to smile, and even that
zit-faced kid from Illinois or Indiana who'd cried over a picture of his
sister's high school prom, and even me, even me—were killers now.*

*But Berlinger wasn't. I turned and looked, and there he was,
escorted by Endicott. Just visible over the crest of the ridge, shielding
his eyes from the harsh sunlight with his bladed hand, surveying our
work.*

———

Richard thanked the audience and began taking questions. Cindy
pushed through the exit and walked through the entrance hall, past
enormous arching windows providing a grand view of the parking deck
across the street. She was on the verge of crying, a fact that upset her
far more than the chapter she had just heard. Her father hadn't made
her cry since she was fifteen, when she found out he was getting re-
married, to that awful woman whose name Cindy couldn't remember
right at this moment. Carole, with an *e*, a spelling that had always
infuriated her. She'd cried after he'd told her on the phone, locked
herself in her room, and ignored her mother's murmured entreaties
from the hall. But later she felt a powerful wave of relief, secure in the
knowledge that this would be the last time he would wield this power
over her.

Which had been true until just now. The reading had been an unwelcome reminder that he was an actual person, not merely the collection of timeworn seriocomic flaws—the drunk, penniless bungler
from whom she coldly tolerated a biannual phone call—to which she'd
successfully reduced him over the years. She barged into the bathroom

and cupped water onto her face until the wave of childish self-pity subsided. She dried off with paper towels and flashed a false, gruesome smile in the mirror. But she hadn't cried.

She entered the corner stall and sat for a minute, gathering herself. The laminated metal of the door and walls was a pleasing color of dull mustard yellow, and she wouldn't have minded staying in there forever; something about the close space and neutral color made her mind go blank. For a moment she was no longer worried about her life: the money Mikhail was demanding, her job, her debt, her spiraling prescription drug usage, her miserable love life, the impact of the dry desert air on her skin, the funny clunking noise her car was making, her shitty father and his fucking book.

Just one hair, two, and, with a contented sigh, she rose.

She walked out of the bathroom as Richard walked out of the auditorium. He was surrounded by a coterie of older men in a tableau that resembled some ghastly parody of teen idolatry. He saw her and raised his hand, and she involuntarily raised hers. She started to the exit doors, then stopped and sat in one of the iron stairwells that led to the upper rooms, waiting until the crowd dispersed. He walked slowly over, with the strenuous nonchalance of someone trying not to frighten away a small animal.

"Hi, Cin," he said.

"Hey."

A young guy walked up from behind, another fan, Cindy thought, except he didn't say anything to Richard and stood about four feet to the side. A stalker, then, she thought, perversely imagining the guy pulling out a gun and blowing her father's head off. The thought, surprisingly, didn't make her entirely happy.

"This is Vance, my driver," said Richard, pointing backward with his thumb.

"Your driver."

"And valet. Vance, stop being weird and meet my daughter, Cindy."

Vance came forward and stuck out his hand, as though he were presenting her with a piece of questionable fruit for her perusal. She took it. It was large and limp, and as she shook it, she realized she had never fully understood the precise sense-meaning of the word "clammy" until this very moment.

"Nice to meet you," said Vance.

"Uh-huh," she said, taking a better look at the kid. He was younger than she'd originally thought, maybe still a teenager. His high, intelligent forehead was rendered idiotic by the makeshift Prince Valiant perched on top of it. Large hazel eyes swam distorted and fearful and goonishly large inside the twin aquarium tanks of his glasses. His Adam's apple and mouth protruded in tandem, but his lips were curled inward, which gave him a reticent aspect. One cheek was bruised and swollen, and an unluxurious beard pushed through the dusting of acne on his cheeks like industrious weeds in a raspberry patch. He was a fucking mess.

"The thing already happened," said Richard.

"I saw it," Cindy said.

"Oh."

"It was good."

"Thanks. I know you wouldn't say so if you didn't mean it."

She stood. "And it was good to see you. Good luck with the rest of the tour."

"Don't you want to get lunch or something at least?"

"No."

"Come on. Why not?"

"I told you to call, Dad. You said you would call." Her voice sounded childish and repellent in her ears.

"I did call."

"Oh bullshit."

"I called last night. Check your phone. It went straight to voicemail."

Not feeling like explaining that she'd allowed her service to lapse, and not believing him anyway, and furthermore not wanting anything besides to get away, maybe take a Halcion and sleep until it was cool and dark outside, she turned to leave and noticed the parking agent outside ticketing her car. Richard was saying something to her back, but she was already pushing through the hot metal doors, advancing on the small man. His shorts ended indecently high on his bunched thighs, between which he clenched his bicycle while he punched her license-plate number into a handheld ticket machine.

She said, "What are you doing?" closer to a yell than she'd intended. The agent looked back at her, surprised.

"Loading zone, lady."

"Come on. I'm leaving. Please? Please."

He shook his head and continued punching information into the machine. It fed out a little loop of paper, which he tore off, stuck in an envelope he pulled from a fanny pack, and handed to her. She pulled the ticket back out and looked at it. "Two hundred and fifty dollars? You've got to be fucking kidding me."

He got back on his bike and started to pedal away. "Don't ignore me," she yelled—actual yelling now. "Don't ignore me, you motherfucker."

He stopped. "What did you say?"

"Oh, I've got your attention now? Nice job you have."

"You want me to call the cops in on this? Don't park in a loading zone, okay? It's not complicated."

"You know what else isn't complicated? Fuck. You." She kicked the rear tire of the bike, not very hard, but it caused his center of gravity to shift behind him, and he sat on the ground to avoid falling. Before he could get back up, Richard was between them. His bulk was sizable enough that he managed to completely obscure one from the other. He helped up the parking agent and said, "Sorry, sorry. I'll pay the ticket, thanks, sorry about this."

"I could sue that bitch for assault!" the man yelled.

"That bitch is my daughter," said Richard, in a soft tone. "She's having a rough day. Cut her a break, okay?"

The agent felt his back tire, shook his head, and rode away. Cindy stalked to the driver's side, got in, and turned the key. Nothing happened. She turned it again, then a third time, but nothing, not even that shitty clicking noise that usually tells you that you're fucked. She screamed and beat her hands once, hard, against the steering wheel. The horn still worked, at least. At least one thing worked—she did it again and kept doing it. The wheel juddered and the horn honked in dying bleats, and she felt she might have gone on beating it, beating the wheel and the dash and the door, until she was sitting in a pile of rubble, or until her arms were broken and flopping around uselessly, but then her father was holding her still. She tried to pull away, but he held her tighter and tighter, and then—fucking goddamnit shit—she was crying.

CHAPTER TWELVE

———

The first thing Vance noticed when they entered Cindy's apartment was the overpowering smell. He was used to bad-smelling places—besides his own, there was the domicile of his aunt, who lived even farther than Vance and his mother out in the Spillman sticks and who was a crazy cat person that took in strays at the rate of a new one about every three months; the few times he and his mother had visited, the smell of cat piss and shit was so strong that it was like a physical threshold they were crossing—but this was different. It was composed of many different elements—beauty products, cooked food in the dirty kitchen, old marijuana and cigarette smoke, accumulated body odor and sweat, a light and not entirely unpleasant fecal tang—united in a sort of ur-female smell. The odor was magnified by the smallness of the space and the closed windows that looked to have been painted over and never opened. This was a dwelling overwhelmed, overoccupied by its occupant, and the air itself was redolent of an unhappy woman.

There was clutter on every visible surface, and it was difficult to move through the room without stepping on a magazine, a CD, an article of clothing. He and Richard tiptoed across spots of green carpet that appeared sporadically, like rocks in a rushing stream. Cindy collapsed on the sofa and stared at the dead TV, worrying her hands. Her eyes were still red rimmed, but at least she wasn't sobbing anymore. AAA had successfully jumped her car, which Vance had driven over, hoping the mood would magically improve once they got her home, but it hadn't. She seemed to be waiting for something to happen, for one of them to do something.

Richard said, "Glass of water?"

She gestured with her thumb in the direction of the kitchen, the airspace of which was guarded by a pair of fat, territorial flies. Richard returned with three glasses; Vance's was stained with purple lipstick. Cindy continued staring at the TV as though there were a tiny play being staged inside of it for her benefit alone. She opened a little handpainted Oriental box on the coffee table, plucked out a few pills, and washed them all down in one swallow. As he had since being introduced to her, Vance tried to get a handle on what she looked like.

It was difficult. For one thing, she was a blur of nervous fidgets—continually cracking her knuckles and smoothing her overtreated blonde hair back in a lank, high ponytail. For another thing, she was one of those people who looked very different from different angles. From the front, she was striking—gorgeous even—with unusually wide-set eyes that communicated a shimmering intelligence, even though all Vance had seen her do so far was yell at a parking attendant and have a nervous breakdown. But looked at from the side, she had a smushed aspect that reminded him of a dog his father had brought home to appease his mother—an idiot Chow that accidentally strangled itself on its own leash while tied up in the backyard. Vance had come home from school to find it lying on its back, grinning up at the sky, black tongue lolling. He couldn't square the two angles of her face—they didn't seem to belong to the same person.

She said, "You can go now."

Richard sighed and said, "Cindy, I know I'm the last person on earth you want to take any help or advice from, but tell me what's going on."

She opened her mouth to speak, and as she did there was a pounding at the door. She shut her mouth and the pounding stopped, which created the unnerving impression that the sound had come from her mouth. The door opened and a man walked a few steps inside, then stopped. He wore the kind of long, outdated leather jacket that expendable muscle wears in mob movies. But he wasn't muscular, instead was tall and rangy, about Vance's height, and stooped at the neck like a reading lamp. He was either the world's oldest thirty-five-year-old or the world's youngest sixty-year-old; however old he was, the look of unhappy irritation on his face was timeless. Without acknowledging Richard and Vance, he said, "Who are they?"

"My father and his valet."

"Valet?" He pronounced the word slowly with an incredulous rising tone that, paired with the expression on his face as he looked at Richard and Vance, suggested he thought a "valet" might be akin to a catamite or a sexual slave, then he returned to Cindy. "Where were you last night?"

"Something came up."

"Doesn't it always. Look, you can't keep avoiding me, we need to talk."

"I know."

At this, the man sighed and ran his hand through a mortified forelock retreating as quickly as possible from the dour face below. "When then?"

"I get paid tomorrow, I'll come by the Monaco."

He sighed again, and his shoulders drooped. His very person conveyed a world-weariness so profound that it made Vance tired just watching him. He seemed like a man whom life had disappointed beyond all reason and expectation—"long suffering" didn't even come close to capturing the mythic ennui on display. He said, "Can you borrow it from your dad here?"

"I'm sorry, who are you again?" said Richard.

"Mikhail."

"Oh, of course. *Mikhail.* I think my daughter would like you to leave."

"Your daughter would probably like a pony and some ice cream, but that doesn't mean she's getting it."

Richard cocked his head and took an angled, approaching step to the next patch of available floor space, but Cindy waved her hand at him. To Mikhail, she said, "Look, tomorrow, okay? I'll come by."

"This shit is getting old," said Mikhail. "Be an adult, make a payment." He left. They could hear his footsteps pinging cheerfully down the metal stairs.

"Well?" said Richard.

"I owe him some money. He thinks I do."

"Yeah, I got that. What the hell is going on?"

The room again lapsed into silence. She turned on the sofa toward Vance—her strange profile morphing magically into the other face, the beautiful one—and opened her mouth to talk:

———

Her teenage years had been angry and disaffected, full of dubious clothing and bad haircut choices, and silly punk rock played by silly-looking people. Pot figured prominently. She loved math, excelled at it, but hated the smart kids in their AP classes, the way their neat little lives were already chugging down the track to Successville. And though her mother was an accomplished English PhD and a rising star in her field, she could barely get Cindy to read a book. From puberty on, in fact, anything Eileen wanted Cindy to do was anathema. She blamed her uptight, judgmental mother for running off her father and keeping him away; that she hated her father somehow didn't make her resent her mother any less. The six years between twelve and eighteen were a pitched, unceasing battle of wills between mother and daughter with no winner besides their family therapist's bank account. When Cindy graduated high school—barely—she laughed at Eileen's offer to pull some strings and get her into Fresno State. (While she was at it, she said, maybe her mother could pull some other strings and get her into the Special Olympics.) Her best friend, Casey, owned a '66 Mustang that Casey's ex had retooled for her, and they set off on a road trip the week after they'd halfheartedly tossed their rented mortarboards in the air.

They spent the summer down in San Diego working at a fish restaurant on Pacific Beach, wearing tank tops and baseball caps. They were staying with friends of Casey's at the time, a rowdy beach condo full of so many interchangeable frat-surfer types that Cindy never fully pinned down who really lived there. Whoever it was, they didn't mind hosting a couple of good-looking eighteen-year-old girls, even if Cindy did have pink hair and an attitude. Life there was simple—smoke weed all day, hang out on the beach or anywhere, eat something sometimes, work now and then, and party most nights until the sun came up. At the time she was antsy to get back on the road, not realizing (how could she have?) that this would be the happiest she'd ever be.

Eventually summer ended and temperatures plunged into the low seventies. School started up, the apartment cleared out, and their tips at work ebbed away. One night, after their shift, without discussing it but by some form of psychic agreement (or maybe it was just that obvious that it was time to move on), they got in the Mustang and drove north through the night to Los Angeles. They found themselves on the corner of Sunset and Western, a famous-sounding intersection that in real life featured a hot-dog stand next to a seedy motel unimaginatively named the Sunset Suites. For a hundred dollars and a not-inconsiderable amount of corny flirtation, they haggled a double for two nights out of the Persian shift manager. Lying there with the ceaseless Hollywood traffic sounding like it was inches from the window, Cindy couldn't sleep. A dual vision of archetypal LA destinies flickered on her mental movie screen—that is, becoming rich and famous, or getting murdered. Or both—that was the ideal, in a way.

But nothing so exciting happened. Really, LA was kind of dull. She and Casey got a shitty apartment in Little Armenia—the real LA, as the local saying went—that they could still barely afford. Cindy walked through a mile of rank exhaust every day to a job at Rocket Video that the manager often reminded her how lucky she was to have. At night, she drank boxed wine and watched the free movies she brought home; many of them depicted Los Angeles as glamorous and sexy, and she supposed that might be the case if you had the money or inclination to ever leave your apartment. She preferred the seedier versions of LA, the city as a vast and depopulated ghost city, like *Chinatown* or, better yet, *The Killing of a Chinese Bookie*.

When she did go out, she went to bars within walking distance that took her fake ID or else didn't care that she was underage. The places she favored were usually unmarked, besides a neon cocktail

sign, and poooooood of a certain anti Hollywood charm. The regulars—
square-jawed, walnut-faced alcoholic men with marquee heads of hair
booze-glued to their scalps and faded blondes of a certain (very, very
old) age—could have done community service starring in videos to
be shown to any midwestern teen with dreams of stardom. But Cindy
liked these dives. They were dark and quiet and suited her mood;
no one hassled her as she sat in the corner drinking her screwdriver
through a straw and wondering where her life would go next.

Casey started dating an actor/producer/director/model/musician
named Burke and was around the apartment less and less. Cindy got
invitations to a few parties out of the deal at first—mostly held at a
white-walled modern cube in the hills, where she sat by the shimmering pool while everyone did coke somewhere upstairs—but after
a while she realized she was on her own. Casey sometimes didn't re-
appear for weeks. The Mustang, unmoved for street sweeping, gradually accumulated tickets until the windshield vanished under a
snowdrift of white paper.

In June, facing eviction and a sense of utter defeat, Cindy got her
mother to send her eight hundred dollars, promising she'd buy a bus
ticket back to Fresno. And she had sincerely meant to do so, but SAN
FRANCISCO had somehow looked much more appealing on the Grey-
hound departures board than FRESNO. On the ride there, she got in
touch with an old friend from high school, Matthew, who lived in the
Castro and who agreed to put her up temporarily. They had momentarily been boyfriend and girlfriend before Matthew knew he was gay or
was willing to admit it. There had been hot (to her) make-out sessions
in her car, sound-tracked by Operation Ivy and Screeching Weasel,
and even an abortive blow job outside the Mellow Mushroom where he
waited tables. She still had fond feelings for him.

His roommate, an older man named Marco Priminger, apparently
didn't have fond feelings for her; he didn't trust her with a key and
forbade her from touching anything while they were out of the house.
Not that she would have wanted to—the crumbling apartment was
chockablock with seventies kitsch: Partridge Family toys, Sandy Allen
records, Keane paintings, a Skimbleshanks costume from a dinner

theater production of *Cats*. It was like being held prisoner on a John Waters set. Sitting there watching a vacuum tube TV, which supported a glass-enclosed Land of the Lost diorama, she had to come to terms with what she'd felt in Los Angeles: the experiment had been a failure, and it was time to return home and get serious, start taking classes. Apply herself. It sounded like a kind of death, but there it was.

It was one of those moments that didn't seem so pivotal at the time—just depressing—but in retrospect could have changed everything. She was booking another bus ticket, back to Fresno this time, when Casey's number appeared on her flip cell. Burke had dumped her, and she was going to Vegas for the fall, to cocktail waitress at a casino. Did Cindy want to go? She thought of the gray concrete buildings of Fresno Community College, her old bedroom at home decorated with posters of the Ramones, her mother's disapproving presence like a gray fog drifting in and out of the house. Yes, she did.

Up and down the Strip—as they had in San Diego—they applied in tandem, a team. The plan was to rake in the big bucks during peak season, convention time, when the blistering desert cooled down to just unbearably scorching. Then they would take off during the holidays, spend the winter somewhere in the mountains learning to ski. They were young and good-looking and had no trouble getting hired at Harrah's, where they wore incredibly short black leather skirts with sparkly gold tops. They teetered around in heels on the carpet, on endless orbits from the gaming floor to the bar area and back. At their apartment the morning after their shift, they would throw their cash and chips on the bed in a pile as though they'd robbed a bank and cackle over Bloody Marys as they rehashed the night—the losers who had seen *Swingers* and talked about each other being "so money they didn't even know it," the crazy Arab guy who had Casey place a ten-thousand-dollar roulette wager for him, Paul the bartender who slipped them fruity shots in paper cups and wanted to bang both of them and never, ever, ever would.

It was a lark. For a while, they were able to re-create the way it had felt in San Diego—that nothing mattered and everything was fun and would go on being fun forever. But the holidays came and went, then Cassy went again, this time back to Fresno, having gotten tired of screwing around and secretly applied to nursing school. Cindy found herself without a plan, this time not in the good way, and wound up waitressing the rest of the next year in the vague hope that something new would present itself and for a third time prevent her from returning to Fresno in utter defeat. (She imagined writing a memoir—like *The Red Badge of Richard*, as her mother referred to her father's putative war memoir—a slim volume entitled *Returning to Fresno in Utter Defeat*.)

Something new presented itself in the person of a pit boss named Brian, who was eighteen years her elder and twice divorced at thirty-nine. But he was good-looking in a deceptively clean-cut way, and he knew the difference between Burgundy and Beaujolais, and he could improvise plausibly on the lounge piano and wear a suit and Italian loafers the way other men wore cargo shirts and Crocs. She moved into his condo in Henderson, and three months later they got married in a little ceremony attended by their closest friends, mostly other casino employees, that was held in the chapel of the Venetian, which everyone agreed was the nicest of the casino chapels.

It was a good couple of years. Brian called in a couple of favors and got her a job working for the casino surveillance team. It was a nine-to-five gig, mostly spent staring at a cluster of video feeds, piped up to the office from the innumerable black-domed cameras mounted every thirty feet or so on the casino-floor ceiling, like the nests of alien hornets. She looked for any sign of malfeasance—pocketing of chips, collusion between players, card counting, or simple outright theft—and called back down to the pit bosses, who meted out the appropriate punishment, usually lifelong banishment. It was tedious, meticulous work that most people would have hated, but she loved it. She loved the sense of disembodiment, of being a pair of invisible eyes hovering over thousands of unwitting people. It was voyeuristic and exciting. That some of the casino's patrons were, in fact, witting and furthermore despised the unblinking electric eye overhead (at least once an hour, some soused smartass would lift a bird to the camera) meant nothing to her. She liked it, actually: they had no choice; when they set foot in the casino she was their companion—unditchable, unreject-able, undeniable.

It helped that she was good at it, too. In her first eight months on the job, she personally identified thirteen different incidents, all of which were verified after the fact. Her supervisor—an elderly bulldog of a man who seemed to live in the surveillance office—took her aside and told her she had eyes. This was the highest compliment in the business. At the same time her marriage was imploding (inconsider-ation, incompatibility, infidelity), she was being steadily promoted up the ladder. By the time the divorce came through, she was third-shift supervisor, which ran from midnight to eight.

This was considered the most important shift, as it was the time of day when theft and cheating were most likely to occur, and it was, therefore, the best compensated. By twenty-five, she was divorced and making nearly six figures. Her life had a shape now, though an odd one; she was charting her own destiny, free of both of her parents. Eileen still didn't approve, still wanted her to come back home and go to college, but that was a joke. She was making more money than she'd ever imagined making, having fun in Fun City, doing her own thing—why on earth leave? Her plan was to bank most of the money until she was thirty, then travel for a few years, unencumbered.

But over the next few years, the money in her account disappeared like water through a sieve. By the time she was twenty-six, she had only managed to save eight thousand and change. Where had it all gone? Shopping, dinner, drinking, drugs, and, in the last couple of years, gambling. She lived in reverse time from the rest of humanity and needed a form of diversion and relief after getting off her shift in the morning. Slowly, this diversion had taken the form of stopping at Binion's or the Nugget on her way home and playing roulette for an hour or two. She was often kept company by interested—and always uninteresting—men, frat boys on an all-night bender who assumed the chick by herself at the wheel of fortune was looking for company. That was okay; she didn't mind putting them off, watching them fumble their chips uncertainly as they placed what they thought were large bets (*I've never seen a hundred-dollar chip before!*) on their unlucky

lucky numbers, trying and failing to impress her. Eventually they would sulk away and leave her to the cool, relentless clicking of the wheel and the hands of the croupier, first gently releasing the ball, then just as gently passing over her turreted stacks, like a rainstorm over ancient ruins, and sweeping everything into the dark slot of the chip dump.

Sometimes she won, too—once, seven thousand on a two-hundred-dollar thirty-five-to-one shot. But that didn't matter, really. What mattered was the calm that sitting at the table brought her, a sense of completion that let her go home afterward and sleep through the haunted desert day with no dreams whatsoever.

Over the last couple of years, as though via some kind of occult math, her meager savings had multiplied into vast debt. Five different credit cards, the needle buried deep in the red. She didn't know what the exact figure was—she strenuously avoided adding up the numbers—but a ballpark sum floated around in her head like a cloud of noxious gas. A hundred thousand. Around this time, Mikhail had asked her to meet him at the Monaco Club, a dive bar he owned a tiny percentage of. She didn't know why he wanted to meet. They had dated each other, very briefly, but she hadn't seen him in over a year. Mikhail was one of those characters the city seemed to collect like unusual but worthless coins. He had a photographic memory, a computerlike ability to calculate odds, a magician's sleight of hand, and nothing whatsoever to show for it. An inveterate and degenerate gambler and grifter, he'd been banned from almost every casino in town, including hers. In early April, she'd sat down across from him in a booth at the Monaco. Even though it was nearly ninety degrees, he still wore his leather jacket, sweat dotting the upper reaches of his high forehead.

His proposal: If she looked the other way when he and two of his partners were working the floor, they'd cut her in on 20 percent of the take. He said her end would probably be worth at least ten thousand a month, maybe more. He told her it wouldn't involve any actual lawbreaking, just a certain amount of nonvigilance on her part. She told him to get lost. He told her to think about it. Sitting in her apartment later that day, she did, despite herself. It was an obvious no, the kind of plan, with the kind of people, that announced itself as a BAD IDEA in capital letters. No, it wasn't just a bad idea—Mikhail's plan entered the room in a neon clown suit, wearing big, red, floppy shoes, already soaked with seltzer water and banana cream. She sat down and added up her credit card statements, then called him and told him yes.

It worked for three months. Finally, on a Saturday in July, one of the new surveillance hires spotted something in Mikhail's hand. Security took several magnets off him that he was using to rig the craps table along with iron-lined dice. Mikhail and his partner were pinned to the floor and photographed and dragged shouting out of the casino by their collars, a minor brouhaha that made page 3 of the *Las Vegas Sun*. She slept a total of maybe four hours the following week, but no one reported her.

Then came the voicemail from Mikhail saying she owed him ten thousand, that the last payment he'd given her was really an advance payment for the next month and that, since she'd been responsible for keeping them out of trouble, she owed the money back. Plus, he said, he had to hire a good lawyer, and she had a vested interest in making sure the whole thing went away, didn't she? She didn't see the need for the elaborate justification—it was blackmail, of course, pure and simple. They met again at the Monaco, and she told him she had no money, that all of it had gone straight to the kneebreakers at Capital One and Citibank. Stooping to the straw of his tequila sunrise, he told her that she'd better figure something out.

So for the last few months, he'd been intermittently harassing her, and she'd been slowly paying him, in tiny increments. Half of her knew the whole thing was ridiculous and that she could and probably should tell him to fuck off. But the other half—smarter or dumber, she wasn't sure—knew Mikhail could, in fact, make trouble for her. Even if he had no evidence of her involvement, he could talk to her supervisors and implicate her in the whole mess. Tapes could be reviewed that showed Mikhail and his partners skulking into the casino whenever she was working. She could be fired, or worse. It could be bad for her.

But it already was bad for her. She'd had to change her phone number twice to temporarily elude the debt collectors that, for the last year, had been hounding her constantly like a pack of hormonal teenage boys. Her financial problems hadn't stopped her from blowing money constantly; if anything, her spending had accelerated—the week before, she had stopped at a blackjack table at the Sands on a whim and blown a cool thousand on one bet. It felt bracing, like a blast of cold air had swept into the casino from the desert. The next day, she'd tried to buy a sixty-dollar pair of black work flats at Aldo, and her card was declined.

She'd been considering killing herself lately, in the same vague way she'd previously considered visiting Greenland or the ruins at Chapultepec. She was only twenty-eight, but she felt so much older. The years between eighteen and twenty-eight—between sitting down in the passenger seat of Casey's Mustang and where she was now—felt like a wall of bricks she'd painstakingly laid. She'd Amontilladoed herself into her own life.

———

Richard pushed heavily into the Monaco Club. Despite its name, the place was not affiliated with any casinos and at a glance featured no gambling, other than the one you took with your life upon entering. Richard had been in plenty of dive bars in his day, had even worked in one until recently, but he grudgingly admired how the Monaco took the concept of diviness to another level. In one corner of the trapezoidal room, the ceiling had partially collapsed where a pipe had burst. The rusted pipework jutted down like a hernia through a ruptured abdominal lining. The rest of the tiles were sodden and brown and looked ready to go at any second. An incongruous candy machine near the entrance contained what looked like tiny plastic bananas. A grim pair of blondes sipped drinks from plastic cups and smoked by a pay phone next to the bathroom, waiting for a call that would almost certainly not come for them. They were immediately identifiable as prostitutes from their shared bearing, a singular brand of avid hostility. A trio of dodgy-looking men at the bar craned their necks around at him as though he was intruding on a private function. One of them featured a neck tattoo that read STRANGE DAYS in gothic script, with a curlicue extending up over the jawline like the leg of a hidden spider. Richard approached him.

"Is Mikhail here?"

"Who's asking?"

"Richard."

"Who's Richard?"

"I am."

"What do you want."

"Jesus. To talk to Mikhail."

The men looked at one another dubiously. One of them pulled out his phone and sent a text message. Richard waved off the bartender and sat alone at the end of the bar, aware of the trio watching him. He thought how if there was ever a time it seemed reasonable to get a drink, waiting at a bar to confront your daughter's loan shark or blackmailer or whatever the hell he was seemed like the time. But he didn't, he just sat there. That was the trick: you just sat there and didn't do it.

While he sat there not doing anything, he thought about Cindy, sleeping, or unconscious anyway, in the car outside with Vance. She'd been about to speak but nodded off, and they hadn't been able to fully rouse her—some combination, it seemed, of the pills she'd taken plus a more or less complete nervous breakdown. Eventually, they pried her off the couch, to some murmured fussing but no real resistance. On the way down the stairwell, they passed by a man who did the best he could to pretend he wasn't seeing two other men carrying an unconscious woman down the stairs. Not entirely unconscious—she took little shambling steps, helping them move her to Vance's car. Eyes still closed, she scooted into the backseat, where Richard fastened her in place with the seatbelt while Vance went back to retrieve the suitcase he'd hastily thrown clothes into. She lolled as he felt behind her for the strap—her condition oddly reminded him of when they'd gone to Knott's Berry Farm when she was four. As a long day of standing in lines, eating bad concession food, and standing in more lines, all under a vengeful July Central Valley sun, had progressed, so had Cindy progressed through some toddlery version of Maslow's stages of grief:

from excitement to an overstimulated stupor to hot frustration and subsequent sobbing meltdown to an exhaustion so pure as to render her infinitely pliable, holding his hand and trundling toward the car with her eyes closed. The closed lids had fluttered then as they fluttered twenty-four years later, like a butterfly in delicate, momentary equipoise.

Eventually, Mikhail pushed in from outside, in the process letting in a bit of weak sunlight, which seemed to take one look at the inside of the Monaco Club, turn around, and leave immediately. Mikhail sat down next to Richard, exuding fatigue as well as sweat. The bartender, without being asked, set up a tequila sunrise in front of Mikhail and a moment later impaled it with a straw.

"Where's your valet?"

"Outside, in the car. He's also my chauffeur."

Mikhail stared at him blankly. Richard said, "Tell me what's going on."

"She owes me money."

"How much?"

"Ninety-five hundred, give or take."

"For what." Mikhail gave Richard a very abbreviated version explaining for what. Richard said, "I don't believe you. Leave her alone."

Mikhail sucked the straw, further hollowing his already hollow cheeks. "Or what?"

"Or I don't know. Something."

"Something? You're not very good at this." It almost sounded as though he was disappointed.

"I'm a beginner, but I'm willing to learn."

"Okay." Mikhail drummed his fingers on the counter.

Richard had anticipated a tense showdown, but the man's laconic, depressive aura was like a sponge absorbing and nullifying all of Richard's hostility. He tried again. "I don't know, maybe I'll burn this place down."

"Please, you'd be doing me a favor."

"Fine, use your imagination."

Mikhail lit a cigarette. "I have to say, you have a lot of nerve coming in here trying to tell me to forget about ninety-five hundred bucks and acting protective on your daughter's behalf."

"What does that mean?"

"Let's just say World's Greatest Father you weren't." Mikhail sipped from the long straw of his drink, then settled his head in the crook of his bent arm, and said, "She told me about one time you were gone a whole week? Just disappeared. Then came back like nothing had happened."

"I don't remember that."

"I bet. She said it happened a lot."

"I'm not going to discuss this with you."

"She said you were like a dog that kept running away, getting lost, and brought back home."

"I made some mistakes, sure."

"I mean, what do you think that does to a little girl's psyche?"

"Probably screws it up."

"Yeah, probably. Might make her fear abandonment by men and yet be attracted to men who are likely to abandon her." As he spoke, Mikhail's face was finally animated by something other than fatigued displeasure—it was not an improvement. "She told me about another time—you'd already fucked up somehow and were trying to make it up to her—you bought her this big plastic playhouse for the backyard. Only you couldn't figure out how to do it, and you got frustrated and forgot about it. She said the plastic pieces sat in a big pile in the backyard for three days before your wife at the time noticed and put it together. She said she didn't tell her mother about it, because she didn't want to cause another fight."

"Did she tell you about how I used to take her to ballet class when she was five? What about how I used to stay home and paint pictures with her?" The truth was he'd been between construction jobs at the time and had little more to do than sprawl around hungover and daub greens and browns on construction paper, but still. He strained his memory for more exculpating evidence. *I always. I used to. There was this one time when I.* "Anyway, fuck me. Why am I sitting here explaining myself to you?"

Mikhail said, "She told me about one birthday when she was older that you had obviously forgotten about. You showed up at the house to get something you'd left there when you moved out. And you noticed the HAPPY BIRTHDAY banner and half a cake sitting on the counter, and you pretended like you had come for her. And you gave her something from your pocket—was it breath mints?" He guffawed. "Could that be right?"

"It was a Magic Eightball key chain."

Mikhail made a stabbing motion with his cigarette as he bent again toward his drink. "Right. And she told me she held on to it for years anyway. Kept it in her desk. That it reminded her of you and how she hated you and loved you, too, even though she didn't want to. Her words. She might still have it, you should ask her. But anyway, the point is, don't ride into my bar on your high horse about how I'm mistreating your daughter. I'm a piece of shit and so are you."

Richard watched the bartender wipe grime onto highball glasses with a soiled rag and wondered why this assessment of his character made his stomach twist. It wasn't as though he'd ever deluded himself into thinking he'd been a good father. And he regularly thought of and referred to himself as a piece of shit. But there was something about hearing it from this cheesy hustler, sweating in his pleather, that codified it as indisputable, objective truth. This guy—*this fucking guy*—clearly knew from pieces of shit; an abridged family history from Cindy and five minutes around Richard had been all he needed to get it right. Mikhail sucked with a long crackle at the ice in his empty drink, like an enervated spider draining the last bit of life from the husk of his victim.

"All right." Richard sighed. "So explain what happens if you don't get the money."

"I don't know, maybe nothing. Or maybe I email her boss, tell him my side of things."

"Why would they believe you? Why would they even listen?"

"They might not. In this life, there are no guarantees."

"Basically, you're full of shit is the feeling I get here. You're just some grubby dirtbag leaning on my kid. No reason not to, right? It doesn't cost you anything, and if she's dumb enough to pay, you're up ten grand."

Mikhail shook his empty glass in the air. He waited until the new drink had been put in front of him and the bartender had resumed dirtying the glassware before he answered. "That's basically it, yeah. I'm pretty harmless. But the thing you're forgetting, and she's not, is that I know a lot of people who aren't harmless. I'm not saying I want anything to happen to her, because I honestly don't. I like your daughter, she's a tough girl. Really sharp and funny, too. I would genuinely feel terrible if anything did happen to her. . . ." He made a circular motion with his hand as he droned on, like a chess expert going through a tedious explanation of an endgame's foregone conclusion, and finally wrapped up with "Desperate times, desperate measures. Et cetera, et cetera."

"Is that a threat?"

"Yeah, man, of course it is." Mikhail laughed. "See, that's how you threaten someone."

Richard pulled out his overstuffed wallet and found one of the checks he'd brought just in case a situation arose, though he hadn't imagined this particular situation, could never have imagined this particular situation in a thousand years.

"You got a pen?" he said.

Mikhail laughed again. "You've got to be kidding."

"Banks closed an hour ago, and I'm leaving town now."

"Okay. You know what? Fine. If it bounces, it bounces, and she still owes me the money. What's the difference? And I think you do want to help her, even if you don't know what you're doing. Hey, you know what else?" He reached over the bar, felt around, and procured a plastic Bic, which he bounced a couple of times on its end. "I like you. I trust you. You're a lot like me."

"Now you're just being hurtful," said Richard. He took the pen, made out a check for ninety-five hundred dollars, and handed it to Mikhail. He pushed himself up from the bar and stood over the man, imagining, for a moment, plunging the pen down into the bent neck, the exposed ridge of spine. "Listen, If you ever talk to my daughter again, I will kill you. I really do mean that."

Mikhail folded the check into his front shirt pocket. "That's good," he said, looking up and nodding. "Now you're getting the hang of it."

———

Richard doddered through the parking lot, the warm Vegas dusk, and got in the car. Vance sat behind the wheel, jotting something in his notebook. He shut the door quietly and bent backward to look at his sleeping daughter. She moaned in her sleep and turned halfway on her side, her arm unfurling off the edge of the backseat with a languid grace that suggested a hostess at some plantation gala introducing an especially dear and important guest. He nudged her shoulder but to no effect. The limb was unresponsive in its socket, as though unconnected to its owner.

"Okay," he said to Vance. "Let's go."

Very soon, the desert reemerged from under its asphalt and neon camouflage. Squat segments of a rusted industrial chemical storage unit jumbled out into the sand like spilled intestines. A mottled dog limped in their shadows, watching the car long after it had sped past. Various signage on the side of the road desperately advertised LOBSTER! NEW GIRLS, SHOWS NIGHTLY!! WORLD'S LARGEST TRUCK!!! as though the landscape itself was racking its brain, trying to find something to make you turn around and spend more money, in the unlikely event you had any left. As though she sensed a loosening of Sin City's gravitational field, Cindy roused herself. "Where are we? Where are we going?"

Richard said, "Leaving Las Vegas."

"No. No no no."

"Yes. I have to get on to the next stop, and you can't stay there."

"I have a job. And I have to pay off that money."

"I paid him off."

"What?" She pushed herself halfway up in the seat, against the door. "You what?"

"I paid him off."

"How?"

"I wrote him a check."

She laughed incredulously. "A check?"

"They're these little paper rectangles? People used to carry them around to pay for things?"

He waited to hear more objections, then glanced back and saw she was sleeping again. After a few more minutes, they crossed some impalpable line and slipped the very last, flailing grasp of the city: no more billboards, no more industrial chaos or jackpot truck stops or signs of human existence at all, really. He felt himself relax, secure in the certainty that—as with the state of Oregon—this was a place to which he would never return. What was the opposite of *Viva*, he wondered, glancing back once more at his sleeping daughter, and then quickly slipping into his own Bonanza Dreams.

CHAPTER THIRTEEN

———

Later, after the bodies had been searched and robbed, and a kill count radioed in (twenty-six!), and a trench had been dug for them, and quicklime sprinkled, and a recon team sent into the jungle to look for other survivors or other encampments, and dinner had been eaten, and shit had been shot, and someone had said "fucking A" under their breath for the hundredth time, I went and looked for Berlinger. He was sitting with his back up against a little rice palm that waved in the warm breeze. Endicott was evidently not worried about him deserting, which made sense—going out into the jungle without a weapon or map or provisions would have been suicide.

"Hey," I said.

"What's up," he said, without looking at me. He was whittling away on a little piece of wood.

"I thought they took your weapons."

"It's a penknife, Lazar. I'm not going to stage a mutiny with it."

"Why did you do it?"

"I already said why."

"Years in jail. I thought you were smarter than this."

"You thought wrong, I guess." He shrugged and attended to his whittling. It was a little man, rough still, but with clearly discernible legs and big feet splayed out. I was trying to figure out what to say when Davis Martin came up behind us.

"Lazar," he said. "We're moving out soon and Lieutenant wants you to look after Berlinger."

Berlinger said, "What's 'look after' mean? I'm fine, thanks."

Davis Martin didn't even look at him, and I realized that as far as Martin was concerned, when Berlinger refused orders and laid down his gun, he'd ceased to exist. To me, Martin said, "What this means is that you will accompany Berlinger for the rest of this march. You will make sure he doesn't get killed, or get anyone else killed, or run off, is that understood?"

"Yes, sir," I said.

"Good, we're moving soon."

Berlinger arched his back against the tree like a cat stretching, and looked up at me. He grinned. "Got you on MP duty, Lazar. You up for this assignment?"

"Shut up, Mitch."

"You could make your stripes here."

"I said shut up."

He shrugged and went back to whittling his little man. I walked back to where my pack was, through the village. Bloodstains in the dirt around the fire pit were already dry, getting trampled by our soldiers and blown by the wind. It was startling how fast the evidence of what we'd just done was disappearing—soon it would all be gone. I sat on a rock and wrote a letter to my parents that I knew I probably wouldn't send. I never thought I'd personally experience the feeling, but I was suddenly very, very homesick. I told them about the march, about the shitty MREs, about how pretty the mountains were. I even told them how one of the guys surrendered arms, how I was in charge of getting him to base. My dad would like that, I knew. But I didn't tell them about what we'd just done. There wasn't any putting it into words. I'm just now getting to where I can.

———

Cindy looked over at her father, who lay on the other bed watching TV with the volume down. Nick at Nite: *Sanford and Son*, it looked like. His great gray head was cushioned between the stacked pillows behind him and his bulbous neck in front. Richard had protested at first when earlier, on the long drive to Salt Lake City, Cindy had asked for a copy of the book, but relented when he saw her desire was genuine. She'd wanted to read the rest of the chapter he'd read at the Convention Center. She put the book down beside her and said, "It's good."

"Thanks."

"You never told me about any of that. You never told me you'd killed someone."

"I've never told you a lot of things."

"Maybe you should give it a try sometime."

Richard didn't look up. He clicked the channel to a golf tournament. Tiger Woods, flanked by hundreds of people, drove a disappearing ball into the white dome of the upper sky. Two seconds later, the camera swooped up to catch the ball's disorienting reentry as it appeared to arc toward the screen until perspective showed it landing farther away, bounding like a frightened rabbit, and finally coming to rest in a swath of unreal green. Watching it, Cindy felt the nausea she'd been ignoring creep back up her gullet. She'd slept the remaining few hours of the ride, and when she awoke, the pills were starting to wear off. She felt nervous and raw, like her entire body was a scraped knee.

"Listen." He muted the TV and turned toward her. "Why don't you come with us to New York."

"Dad, I really do have to go back."

"No, you don't."

"I have a job. I have a life there."

He snorted. "Yeah, some life."

"How's being a hermit in the desert treating you?"

"I want you to come along to New York, maybe stay with your mother for a little while."

"Have you talked to her?"

"No, but I'm sure when she hears how things are, she'll be happy to put you up."

"How things are. How are things?"

He turned his head and looked at her for a moment. "You really want me to answer that? I'll be honest with you, Cin, they don't seem great."

"I'm going for a swim." She got out of bed on shaky legs, grabbed a towel from the bathroom, and left the room. She was resigned to many things where her father was concerned, but not a lecture on good life choices. Outside the room, the synthetic piling of the blue carpet bristled between her toes; the large hallway stretched out bland and identical in both directions, implying that it didn't matter which way you went.

The night outside was an eerie bliss of desolation broken only by the hum of cars on the distant highway. Despite the parking lot's fullness (a gymnastics tourney, they'd been informed by the somber, garishly necktied desk clerk), the place felt deserted, vacant. It was located ten miles south of Salt Lake, on a rectangle of dust, as though a nomadic team of Sheraton executives had wandered to that spot and seen that it was good. She walked around the pebbled edge of the hotel's patio area. The swimming pool sparkled a beckoning green-white under halogen lights, like a jewel left unguarded to lure a thief, baiting an obscure trap in the surrounding darkness.

The water was tepid, still warmed by the hot exhale of the October desert. She piled up her clothes on the rough concrete that surrounded the pool, though she kept on her underwear. She didn't really care if some car salesman from Provo caught what he might consider a naughty glimpse from his window. That would be his problem, not hers—she was currently at the absolute limit of problems she could have. The needful water clung to her. It was a relief physically, but also mentally, to escape her father's proximity—the radius of his personality that extended around him like a force field—and her own uncontrollable, compulsive desire for his attention and approval.

When she dove beneath the surface, the overchlorinated water assaulted her eyes with a purifying, righteous burn. She let out a few air bubbles and swam to the shallow bottom, which was littered with pennies and a fine dusty residue, the provenance of which was best left unimagined. She was a good swimmer, always had been—a waterbaby, in Eileen's words—though she rarely used her own apartment complex's pool, a dismal square of green water under constant siege by a squadron of intimidating teenagers. She kicked across the bottom to the deeper end, letting the weight of water overhead squeeze the uneasy dope-sick feeling out from under her rib cage. She surfaced with her hands on the cool slick of the tiled lip, then dove again.

———

From the balcony, Richard watched his daughter swim. Or, rather, he watched a blurry form with blonde hair he assumed was his daughter move around in a greenish rectangle he assumed was a pool. Whoever it was was staying underwater for full minutes at a time. He wondered if she'd seen him up there and was, childishly, trying to worry him. The blurriness of her form in his vision allowed him to imagine her as a child again, not the hard, difficult woman she had become. The yellow hair crowned the surface of the water and then disappeared again, and he idly wished he could banish her back to the womb.

He called Eileen. "Hello?"

"Ei, it's Richard."

"Is everything all right?"

"Yeah, fine. I'm with Cindy."

"Really." The musical extension of the long first syllable followed by an octave's drop into the second conveyed an entire marriage's worth of skepticism. "She came to your thing?"

"Yeah. We're in Salt Lake City now."

"She came with you?"

He had planned on telling Eileen everything—the money, the apartment, the pills—but instinctively pulled away from that tack, not wanting to give Cindy one more thing to blame him for. "I guess she felt like catching up. Is that really so shocking?"

"Yes, to be honest."

"Anyway, I was just looking at her, and it made me want to give you a call, for some reason."

"Do I detect a note of nostalgia?"

"No."

"A pining for younger, better days? A sense of loss?"

"Stop it."

"Congratulations on the book again, by the way. It seems as though it's doing incredibly well."

"Couldn't have happened to a nicer guy, right?"

"No, well, obviously it could have, but still."

"Are we on for next week?"

"I think so, call me. I have to go, there's a thing I'm late for. Hi to Cin."

He hung up the phone and returned to the balcony. The blurred green water flickering below, his daughter somewhere beneath it, lost to him. He'd tried, over the years, to re-insinuate himself into her life. Phone calls here and there, a standing invitation for her to visit Phoenix, even an unannounced visit to Vegas, under the pretext of writing some nonexistent travel piece for a nonexistent magazine. But each time, he was rebuffed. Not cruelly or in anger, but with a curt courtesy that was worse for its modulated lack of feeling. The message was clear: thanks but no thanks.

After that Vegas visit—the unsmiling embrace outside the casino, the terse breakfast that followed, and the little wave that dismissed him back to his hotel—he'd written her a letter. He'd never sent it and had forgotten most of its contents, but the upshot was why couldn't she forgive him? Why? He looked at the pale face in the mirror and asked again. What had he done that was so terrible? Divorce her mother? They couldn't stand the sight of each other at the time. Drink too much? It seemed like she should have developed some sympathy for compulsion and addiction. Cheating? He'd never really cheated on Eileen, not when it mattered—toward the end it had all felt like part of the same disaster; who cared if the waiter spilled his drinks, if the piano hurtled into the first mate, when the ship was going down?

He'd left, that was all. She couldn't forgive his not being there, not fighting to be there as much as he could. And the truth was he hadn't wanted to at the time. He'd wanted to be left alone to work on his lousy novels and tile houses and drink and occasionally get laid and always be hungover. She couldn't forgive him those years, and she couldn't

accept his interest, or the possibility that, in some admittedly incre-
mental and insignificant way, he might have changed.

But she couldn't refuse him now. So this was, then, maybe, the second chance he'd been looking for. He didn't deserve it, but he would
take it. He was glad she needed him. He was glad she was fucked up.

———

On the other side of the pool, near the salt barrens at the edge of the
parking lot, Vance stood frozen. He, too, watched Cindy, though he
knew for certain it was her, even at a respectful distance. He'd gone for
a little walk around the hotel, stretching his legs after the eight-hour
drive, when he noticed a blonde woman taking her clothes off. Seeing
her through the metal bars of the pool's fence was like watching a prisoner disrobe. She lowered herself in, went underwater for a long time,
surfaced, dove, surfaced, dove. Her skin was smooth, younger looking
than he'd have imagined.

He hadn't been attracted to her before at all. The intensity of her
demeanor frightened him. And she was both puffy and depleted with
drugs and exhaustion and age. Being close to thirty, she was, of course,
to Vance, a member of that impossibly aged demographic swath that
included everyone older than him. What was it, then, that held his
stare from forty feet away? The consanguinity with a man he admired,
or whose work he admired, was one thing, he supposed. Her breasts,
full and pale under the greenish glow of the sodium lights overhead,
were another thing. Her skin was an innocent white, not what you
would have expected from a longtime desert dweller. Now, the thought
of her in that musty apartment, stalking around like an animal at
the zoo, filling every crevice with her presence, excited him in a way
he couldn't understand. There was no light where Vance stood, and he
knew she couldn't see him, yet he remained stock-still and realized he
was holding his breath.

She dove again. He waited for her to resurface, but this time she
didn't. A breeze came across the desert and rippled the dull-green skin
of the water. His legs tensed in the moment before he would run to

jump the fence, dive in, and pull her out, when she surfaced, gasping, and leaned against the pool's wet lip. Then she pulled herself out, wrapped the towel around her, and exited the pool area. As she did, he saw the bald spot gleaming on the crown of her head. He stared at it, into it, and it was as though a portal to her inner self had momentarily opened. A moment later she was twisting her hair up over it, walking toward the dark stairs, but he had seen it. It was there. He felt privy to an enormous secret, entrusted with something precious by her, even though she didn't know it yet.

He walked once more around the perimeter, collecting himself. The night sky overhead could not have been vaster. Through a strip of patchy grass, he moved onto the concrete of the pool deck. Her wet, fading footprints on the ground were like a bread-crumb trail leading him into the hotel, to the elevators, and up to room 332.

CHAPTER FOURTEEN

I n the morning, Cindy lay in bed with damp sheets stretched to her
chin. This was a compromise position, as she had managed to simultaneously freeze and burn up throughout the interminable night.
Her muscles ached, especially her lower back, which felt like it had
been stood upon for a long time by a very fat person. Vance emerged
from the shower, wearing a towel around his waist, as though to put his
impressive physique on display.

"Good morning," he said to the room, and Cindy responded with
a few quadriplegic blinks. He turned to Richard, on the other bed,
who also didn't say anything, who also had the covers pulled up, in
his own private misery of renewed consciousness. She had inherited
her father's constitutional inability to be friendly or productive until
about three hours after waking. Even at the best of times, when she
wasn't withdrawing from pharmaceuticals, she felt every morning like
her joints were filled with Elmer's glue.

"When's the thing?" Richard asked Vance. "And where?"

"Denver, eight o'clock. We should leave soon."

Cindy groaned. Richard turned to her and said, "You good to go,
champ?"

"No." She got up and went to the bathroom. She ran hot water in
the bathtub, stole two of her father's lorazepam, dry-swallowed them,
and climbed into the water. As she did, she noticed a thin thread of
blood between her legs. She was both irritated at having her period

and relieved; it had been two months since she'd had one, and it also helped explain and excuse how truly horrible she felt. She unwrapped a complimentary soap, tossed the wrapping paper at the adjacent trash basket, and washed herself with the little cream-white seashell. When she got up, a single fresh drop of blood was suspended for a moment in the rusty water, spinning, before it helixed into a pink cloud.

The desk clerk looked mortified when she asked, but nonetheless provided her with gratis sanitary napkins, tampons presumably violating some stricture of Joseph Smith's. In the car, Vance drove, and Richard again rode shotgun. Cindy again sat in the backseat, which suited her fine. Although it made her feel like a child being ferried around against her will, it also absolved her from talking as she glazed out at the land passing by. There was plenty of it to look at—in the open range of southern Wyoming, there was nothing but land to look at—and the air blowing in through the cracked window was cold and refreshing. She was reminded of a family vacation when she was six or so—during an unexpected stretch of relative sobriety and employment, her father had managed to get it together enough to take them down to Mexico. Their ancient Volvo station wagon had lacked air-conditioning, and her six-year-old legs had become almost molecularly fused to the hot vinyl of the backseat, but she'd nonetheless loved every second of the trip. Her parents had bickered their way down I-5, through Orange County, San Diego, and across the border, taking the argument international, but it had seemed distant to her, faint radio chatter as she'd stared out the window.

On I-80, outside of Rock Springs, Wyoming, a dark quilt of clouds was pulled over the enormous white sheet of the sky, and the temperature fell twenty degrees in ten minutes. Huge drops of rain pelted the car, so large they sounded individually on the roof. Vance took the first exit that appeared and pulled into the gravel parking lot of a diner called, cryptically, Pie O'My! Inside, pink neon lights, Frankie Valli, and the smell of rancid grease waged a terrible, pyrrhic battle for sensory dominance. A teenage hostess, chewing gum with her mouth agape, led them wordlessly to a booth by the window. A miniature silver plastic jukebox affixed to the wall next to their table featured tunos like "He's a Rebel" and "Surfin' Safari."

"What is it with people and the sixties?" said Richard. "I remember this stuff. It was already bad the first time around."

"Hmm." Cindy was looking at the menu and intently not listening.

"I don't know why this country always has to enshrine the past. People call baseball the national pastime, but really it's nostalgia. Anything that happened over twenty years ago automatically becomes worthy of a statue. People's memories are way too short. Christ, Richard Nixon got a parade and library. He should have been shot out of a cannon into a brick wall a foot away."

She glanced up. "What are you babbling about?"

"They call it the past for a reason, you know? It doesn't matter."

"Hmm."

Outside, the sky seemed to release all of the water it had been holding at one time, and the car wasn't even visible where it was parked, thirty feet away. Cindy and Vance sat across from him, and for the second time that day, the awful thought occurred to him that something had happened between them. Were they sitting a hair too close? Did Vance's knuckles brush her arm when he reached for a napkin? Did she glance at the boy while looking out the window? And who cared anyway? Obviously, he did—that was the answer, he knew—but the caring came in a reflexive way he recognized as being absurd on its face. He hadn't been there when Cindy had gone on her first date, hadn't provided a single word of advice or warning about the hazards of unprotected sex or the awfulness of teenage boys, couldn't have named any of her boyfriends at any age—was he really going to start now?

"You two stay up late last night?"

"What?" said Cindy.

"You look a little tired today."

Cindy gave him the Hate-Eyed Death Stare, as he thought of it, a terrifying, familiar look of murderous incredulity—familiar because he'd seen Eileen do it a lot over the years. But come to think of it,

Carole had done it as well, so maybe this look was one of those things all women were just born with, like having exquisitely hyperacute emotions and no governing control over them whatsoever. All of the blood in Vance's face seemed to have traveled to his pimple-dusted cheeks, which looked set to erupt with embarrassment. They were rescued by the heavy approach of a waitress with the body of a retired battleship and a name tag reading BECKY FANASTIC. The pad she clutched in her left hand seemed to be just barely preventing her from attacking them with the pen she clutched in her right. "You ready?"

"What kind of pie do you have," asked Richard.

"We don't have pies."

"You ran out?"

"No, we don't carry them."

"But the name of the restaurant."

Becky Fanastic drew several quarts of air into her ample, irritated bosom and said, "It used to be a famous pie shop. Was bought out by the current owners eight years ago. They hung on to the name. You ready?"

She took their order and left, and Vance hobbled away to the bathroom without comment. Richard and Cindy didn't talk until Becky Fanastic returned with their coffees. Stirring in an endless column of sugar, Cindy said, "You just can't resist, can you?"

"Resist what?"

"Being an asshole."

"It's hard for me," Richard said, "try to remember that."

"What's hard for you?"

"Not to be an asshole. It's hard not to be one when you are one."

"Way to let yourself off the hook."

"How does that let me off the hook? I'm putting myself on the hook for being an asshole. I'm putting myself on the asshole hook."

"No, you're copping to being an asshole, which allows you to continue acting like one. It's a preemptive excuse for your behavior, since no one can expect a real asshole not to behave like an asshole. But then people have to give you credit for at least admitting you're an asshole, right? Basically, it lets you off the hook of behaving like a normal person. Normal people act like assholes all the time, but when they do, they feel bad about it and try not to act like assholes in the future. They don't evade responsibility by saying, 'Well, what do you expect, I'm an asshole.'"

"Right," he said, "because they're not assholes."

Drinking his coffee, Richard realized that he felt better than he'd felt in months. Not good—let's not go crazy—but not ostentatiously bad, either. Unwretched. He glanced at his daughter. She looked absently over her shoulder as lashing fingers of rain streaked the window and left behind little scuttling beads. For a moment, everything seemed to be poised in a kind of equilibrium. It was a feeling to which he was unaccustomed; like most drinkers and writers (two circles slightly off-center, a Venn diagram like the coffee-mug stain on his napkin), he was used to experiencing life in binary terms; it was either the World of Shit, in which everything was already predetermined, mitigated, compromised, contingent, and comprehensively fucked, or else it was a numinous paradise of possibility and unknown pleasures. But in between is where most human life exists—small victories, small failures, the hard, slow effort people make, straining blindly upward like green shoots through pavement, easily trampled. He took hold of Cindy's hand across the table.

"What," she said, startled. She tried to pull away, but he held on.

"Listen. I have a proposition for you."

"Oh, God."

"Why don't you come live with me in Arizona for a little while?" She stared at him in silence but didn't lunge at him with her knife or run screaming out of the restaurant, which he took as encouragement. "You don't have to say yes right now. You don't have to say anything— just hear me out."

"Okay."

"I got some money for the book. Not a ton, but enough. I'm set up right now, for the first time in ever. I bought a house. It's ugly and in the middle of nowhere. But it's big and there's a room you could stay in. There's a TV and a fridge you can put food in. I have a dog. He looks like me, unfortunately. But the point is, the place exists, and you could stay there while you got on your feet."

"Richard—"

"Hold on. I'm not going to give you a lecture, but we both know you haven't been doing so hot. I don't need to know the details. I don't want to know the details. But I know you shouldn't go back to where you were. I know you need to regroup and start over somewhere, and Phoenix wouldn't be the worst place for that. I mean, it's a shithole with no water, but there are jobs and people and colleges and so on and so on." She drummed her fingers on the table and again looked over her shoulder out the window, and he could see she was upset, though which particular variety of upset, he couldn't tell. He'd always been bad at that: he would go to his grave without correctly reading a female mood. "I know I haven't been there for you in the past, but I feel like I can be now."

"You could have then, too."

"That's true. But that doesn't mean I can't help you now. Think about it."

She turned to him, seemed about to say something, and stopped, shaking her head. Instead, she rummaged in her pocket and produced two quarters. She dropped them into the jukebox and dialed up "Crocodile Rock."

———

In the bathroom, Vance tried and failed to rearrange his genitalia into some kind of tolerable position. The erection he'd had for the last ten hours was so rigid and insistent that it was like a steel Maglite jammed sideways into his jeans. He was worried about it, having seen warnings in Viagra commercials about prolonged erections potentially causing blood clots. But even imagining a blood clot dislodging from his painful member and killing him was not enough to soften it one micrometer. As he'd driven, he'd tried visualizing other things against the empty screen of the Wyoming badlands, but none of them had worked: his mother, wasted and empty eyed under her sheets like a pile of rotten sticks; his dead grandmother in her faded floral nightgown with the lacy collar; a decomposing bird someone had tossed into his locker in sixth grade. The boner's equanimity through this mental montage made him fear for his sanity. Sitting in the booth next to Cindy, grimly impaling his own stomach for ten minutes, he finally couldn't take it anymore. He'd tuck-and-hunched his way across the parquet floor, and thereupon did he find himself masturbating in a bathroom stall at Pie O'My! outside of Rock Springs, Wyoming.

Someone had scratched the words JEWES LOL into the brown laminate of the stall divider next to him. He closed his eyes and was back in the bed with Cindy. No, he wanted to think about before that, from the beginning. How she'd been lying there in the far bed staring at golf replays on TV with the sound off, the room already filled with a concerto of Richard's wheezing snores. How he'd brushed his teeth and laid a blanket on the floor and turned the light off and how, a minute or two after he'd shut his eyes and was just starting to doze, he felt fingers brush his shoulder. How his heart whipsawed in his rib cage and for a moment he'd kept his eyes shut, not wanting to open them and see the errant edge of the blanket touching his chest. How he'd opened them to see a hand dangling down, her eyes staring over the edge of the bed, pupils barely visible in the flickering dark.

He climbed up into bed with her, hoping she would do everything because he had no idea what came next. It was like deplaning in a foreign land, one for which he had no phrasebook—one in which he didn't even know what the language was. To his relief and disappointment, but mainly relief, she didn't try to initiate sex—however it was you did that—and, instead, she held him against her, burrowed into his thin, broad chest as deeply as she could. She was like a blind, nocturnal creature desperately trying to dig its way underground, and she pressed herself against him so hard that he coughed. The snores issuing from ten feet away momentarily faltered, and Vance went rigid with fear. When they resumed, he relaxed into her.

He put his arms around her waist, tentatively feeling the marble curve of her lower back. The sensation of it under his fingertips was so intense that his leg juddered in response. Even more intense was the dawning reality that she was allowing him to move his hand to her hip, down the long curving line of her thigh and back up. The thought of her entire body, or most of it, anyway, being suddenly available was like having a gift of almost-unimaginable value bestowed on him. It was as though some eccentric billionaire's Edenic preserve, previously fenced off and viewable only at a great distance, had suddenly thrown its gates open to the public.

Over the course of the next hour he roamed the grounds, gradually building to a thorough—perhaps overthorough—investigation of her breasts. She pulled minutely away from him, and he realized he'd been fondling them too long, delaying the next thing. With a sense of urgent, excited dread, he slowly moved his hand down her side, over the soft hard curve of her pelvis and underbelly, to the damp crevice where thigh met crotch. Here, it was warm and dark, and again he felt like a colonial explorer pushing timidly into some uncharted, humid jungle, expecting to be bitten or stung, waiting to die at every moment. Of embarrassment. He didn't know what to do, but there was only one path, and it led down. He moved past the thin elastic of her underwear, through a thatch of surprisingly bristly hair, and was edging toward a soft unknown when she pulled his hand away.

"Not now," she'd whispered, rolling over. "Soon."

He retrieved his wayward hand with disappointed relief and spent the night pressed against her back in a delectable agony. *Soon:* the word echoed softly in his ringing head. The slippery sibilance of the initial *s;* the voluptuous, gratified middle; the gentle moan of the final *n.* Plus what it meant, the actual woman pressed up against the concave mold of his torso. He would fade off for minutes at a time, only to be reawakened by his pounding heart, the movement of her skin against him, and, eventually, the thin light of the desert dawn entering the room. Finally he'd opened his eyes, knowing the night had fully passed; he did the same now, the act completed.

He hunched forward in the stall, shame and relief sprinting neck and neck toward the finish line, but his erection dwindled against his leg, exhausted and unable to continue the race. He wiped off and washed his face in the chipped plastic sink. An inadvertent glance in the mirror shocked him; he had managed to avoid looking in a mirror the last couple of days and therefore occupy his awkward body with less self-consciousness than usual. The night before, he'd been able to imagine himself as an actual man, not the gaping, pustular scarecrow in front of him cowering at its own image. There were no paper towels in the dispenser, so he wiped his wet hands on his jeans and exited back into the restaurant.

Returning to strained silence at the table, Vance could only assume Richard had said something awful, and Cindy had told him to shut the fuck up, or some variation on that general sequence of events. The old man hunched proprietarily over his shit-on-a-shingle, and Cindy stared over her coffee cup out the window, where the rain had slackened to a strafing monsoon. The neon yolk of Vance's eggs had already half coagulated, and he ate them quickly. As he did, her leg brushed against his, and he hardened again.

———

The reading in Denver was at a bar called the Seventeenth Street Tavern. It was packed with the usual motley assortment of veterans, bookish readers, middle-aged women, random spectators, and celebrity seekers eager for proximity to the aura of fame, however minor it might be. Vance watched from a spot in the back of the room, by the bar, drinking free PBR from a pitcher—he was part of Richard's crew, as the amiable and heavily tattooed bartender put it. The bartender had also warned him not to drink too much, saying, "Altitude, bro. You lowlanders can't handle more than about two beers."

Vance had drunk more than about two beers. Hoping to impress Cindy with his devil-may-care attitude, he'd poured himself cup after cup of the rancid stuff. She had countered with her own, more authentic devil-may-care attitude, sitting by herself at a table across the room. At first, he'd gotten into the role of spurned lover drinking at the bar, since, in books, drinking at bars is the kind of thing spurned lovers often do. It gave him a momentary thrill when he realized that a spurned lover was what he actually was, sort of. But he'd drained the pitcher and gotten into another one and now felt more like a victim of head trauma than a spurned lover, like his face was a sucking wound stuffed with cotton and gauze. Nonetheless, he continued pouring beer into his mouthhole, in hopes that eventually it would lift his spirits the way it was supposed to according to advertisements and country songs. So far, it was just making him feel leaden and stupid. It was the first time he'd gotten really drunk, and he vowed never to do so again while pouring himself yet another foaming cup.

Every now and then, through the crowd, he caught a glimpse of Cindy's blonde hair. He thought of the pink scalp underneath, the perfect circle hidden from everyone's view. He already felt he knew her better than anyone had ever known her, though he knew this couldn't be true. No, but he was capable of knowing her better than anyone ever had. She glanced back at him, seemed to shake her head, and returned her attention to the stage. The combination she managed, of tough and doomed and okay with being doomed, yet vulnerable and really in need of help she didn't know she needed, could not have been more intoxicating for Vance if it had been calculated by a team of behavioral scientists.

Onstage, Richard read something, a chapter in which something or other happened. It was all the same, thought Vance. Drinking and death and mistakes and regret and something something something. They march through the jungle and something happens. Something about hope, some kind of chance! Shoots a gun or something. Talks to someone, then something something something, and finally he realizes something.

Vance cupped his hands and shouted, "On the Something Day, the Lord said 'Let there be something,' and there was something and he saw it was really something!"

Richard paused and identified Vance as the heckler. "Take her easy there, Vance."

"You okay?" said the bartender, hoisting his considerable eyebrows.

"No." Vance looked out at the crowd, at all the people with their upturned faces, and silently despised them for blocking his view of Cindy. He poured the last of the pitcher into his cup and drained the warm froth in one swallow. Oh no. If he could press a button, he thought, he would vaporize all of them. He imagined the button on the bar, pantomimed pressing it. He would do anything for her, he thought, and it was a lucky thing, because she needed lots of things done for her. He'd felt her shaking the night before and seen how she was shivering during the drive, though he'd kept the car jungle hot for her benefit. She'd poured sweat during the night, but he thought—hoped—it was the closeness of the room and their physical proximity. Her hand, when he briefly held it while Richard napped, was moist and cold. He wasn't stupid. He knew she was detoxing, probably from the pills he'd seen her take at the apartment.

He also knew she was avoiding him, that she felt uncomfortable about the night before. Richard had probably said something. Fucking Richard. All Vance wanted, at that moment, was a chance to demonstrate his worth to her, his loyalty. He caught a glimpse of the blonde hair again and thought, *Use me*. What sweeter life could there be, than to be put to use by a woman you love?

"Dulce et decorum est pro domina mori," he said to the bartender, and motioned for another pitcher. The bartender took it away from him and shook his head. Vance wagged his finger back, solemn.

He loved her, yes. He knew it was stupid, didn't care. There were worse crimes than being stupid; being stupid was, in fact, not a crime! His heart sang. He felt something real and true for her, and he couldn't—wouldn't—be cynical about it. He rose to go to the bathroom, and the alcohol in his head seemed to be released, like the trapped torrent in a water-park ride, in a noxious flume that roared to his extremities. Whoa, look out, someone said. Timber. When he looked up, the bartender was over him, pulling him up toward the ceiling, walking him to a bench in the back of the bar. People were watching and laughing. "Being stupid is not a crime," he yelled.

"Amen," called a bearded boy, lifting a beefy arm in solidarity.

Cindy craned her head at the commotion in the back of the room, then returned her attention to the stage. Not that she was listening to what Richard read—she couldn't have cared less about that. But she was thinking about his earlier offer to help. A little late, buddy, she thought. She had no intention of enabling this tardy impulse toward fatherhood, now that he was good and ready. Thanks, but no thanks.

Still, help in one form or another was not without its appeal. Las Vegas, she knew now, was no longer an option. Even if she could have gotten her job back after missing two shifts, she wouldn't have wanted to. Her future lay before her like stretches of the Wyoming badlands they'd driven through earlier—a huge, monotonous plain uninterrupted by any points of interest or comfort.

She knew this feeling was at least partly due to the withdrawal she was currently going through. Her father's anxiety meds had provided a brittle shield for most of the drive, but they had worn off. Her back ached and her temperature fluctuated between icy, clattering chills and pinpricks of fire that flared from her groin through her armpits. But the feeling of complete desolation was by far the worst part. She'd gone through pharmaceutical withdrawals before, but was still surprised by the strength and severity with which this detox had bludgeoned her. The night before, she'd held on to Vance like a sailor in a typhoon clinging to the mast: he was approximately as tall and shaped the same way. She knew he liked her, and despite her brain fog had been aware of his adolescent attention trained on her throughout the day, but it had been all she could do not to get sick on herself in front of her father.

The money she still owed loomed in her mind, the Kilimanjaro of debt that would follow her wherever she went next. The top of her head itched, and she could almost visualize the single, naughty hair growing into the empty cavern of her skull, which she would isolate and set free later that night. Perhaps, she thought, you should really kill yourself this time and not just idly think about it.

Unable to sit still, she pushed back through the crowd and stood at the side of the bar. In the back of the room, Vance was slouched unconscious on a bench, his head lolling. She signaled to the bartender, whom she'd immediately identified upon entering the bar as a possible dealer and definite user; he ambled over with a sly smile, and she realized he'd probably identified her as a type, as well.

"I help you," he said.

"I'm not from around here," she said, leaning in. "I was wondering if you have any kind of a hookup."

"What are you looking for?"

"Something to take the edge off."

"I'll make you a drink—that usually does the trick."

"Come on."

"Tell me what it is you're looking for."

"Downers, mostly. Painkillers."

"You're in pain, huh?"

She imagined picking up a beer bottle and smashing the guy in his smug fat face with it, and then when he fell on the ground, kicking him a lot. It would feel very good, might, in fact, be just what she needed in the pain-relief department. "Oh, yeah," she said. "Lots."

———

Vance awoke in confusion, but Richard's voice droning in the front of the room reoriented him. Seeing Cindy talking to the bartender re-oriented him further. But what were they doing? The guy walked out from behind the bar, and she followed him to an adjacent door that they both entered. Vance rose, and his gorge followed. With his left hand on the wall for balance, he lurched to the corner, then turned and made it the twenty or so paces needed to bring him to the door.

The room was a large supply closet that contained cases of beer and kegs, and also the bartender and Cindy snorting something off a shelf up their noses. They turned; Cindy held a rolled-up bill in her hand. The bartender said, "Employees only."

"Leave her alone," said Vance. It was meant to sound tough and serious, but the words rolled out of his mouth in a drawl that sounded equal parts southern and mentally disabled.

The guy laughed. "I didn't force her in here, boss."

"Just leave her alone." No other words came to mind, so he decided to rely on these, the way an inept foreign sightseer relies on a single greeting or expression of politeness to see them through every situation.

The bartender looked at Cindy for help. "Vance," she said, "why don't you go lie back down out there. I'll get you up when we're leaving."

"Leave *it* alone," Vance said experimentally, gesturing at the small pile of crushed-up pill residue on the piece of cardboard behind them.

The bartender sighed. "Come on, bro. Get out of here, what are you going to do?"

It was a good question, and one for which Vance didn't have an answer. He felt like a child interrupting adults in the middle of something he didn't understand, which was more or less exactly what was happening. His childish response was to reach out and swipe at the cardboard—a cloud of white pharmaceutical dust momentarily hovered in the air and then was gone.

"Goddamn it," the guy yelled, and he pushed Vance against the wall. He bounced off and used the momentum to uncork a wild right hook that caught the guy square in the face. Why, then, did Cindy yelp? Why did she drop to the ground? The bartender, completely unscathed, looked down at her. He shook his head and said, "You okay?"

"Fine," she said, holding her jaw.

"I'm sorry," said Vance. "Oh God, I'm sorry . . ."

The bartender pulled her up and said, "Would you please get him the fuck out of here?"

"Come on, Vance," she said, holding him by the shoulder and attempting to maneuver him out the door. The cardboard Coca-Cola box on the rack across from him was stained with its own syrup. One gleaming, viscid drop hovered in the air, suspended on an impossibly fine thread. It's love, he thought, my God, love.

———

They were in the car, driving. Reds and yellows and blues smeared by outside the window, the primary tones of city night. Vance turned to her and said, "I was just trying to help."

"My hero."

"I'm sorry."

Then they were moving through the hotel lobby, leaning in an elevator, entering the room. She put him in bed and turned the TV on. The room spun crazily. She was gathering things from the nightstand, zipping a suitcase shut. She kissed him on the forehead and straightened. "Bye, Vance," she said.

"Wait," he said, managing to prop himself up on his elbows.

"What?"

"Can we talk?"

"About what? I don't think so." But she sat beside him on the edge of the bed, looking away from him toward the TV. He stroked the wisps at the back of her head that had pulled free of her topknot. They floated in the draft of the air-conditioning like the delicate tendrils of some underwater plant, damp toward the roots from the sheen of sweat coating the nape of her neck.

"Where are you going?"

"Nowhere. I'm starting over."

"In Denver? Now?" On the TV there was news footage of tanks rolling through an ancient city of white-orange sand, past blackened husks on the side of the road. The images, a reminder of the greater world outside his fuddled mind here in this dark room, clarified his thoughts and sobered him a little.

"Why not?"

"What about Richard?"

"Tell him I said good luck. I left a note." She pulled away to stand again, but he held her arm. "What," she said again.

"Don't go," he said. "I love you."

She laughed, a note that was mocking but not entirely cruel. "What a sweet weirdo you are. You don't know me."

"I do."

"You don't know anything. I spent years watching people at their worst—guys who probably had wives upstairs sleeping who would hire prostitutes, people with plastic convention tags who'd blow through their family life savings in thirty minutes at the blackjack table. No one knows anything about anyone."

In an impulse he didn't fully understand and regretted as soon as he'd acted upon it, Vance pulled the scrunchie off her topknot; the pink of her scalp was just visible before she whipped her head around, reaching for her hair.

"What in the fuck."

"I know you."

The expression on her face was not what he would have hoped for in response to these intimacies. It was a look of incredulous disgust, an ugly look, close to a sneer but containing less amusement, and it concentrated years' worth of disappointment and anger and various other emotions, none of them good, in its crenellations and divots and furrows.

"I can help you," he said, helplessly. He was reminded of a song by that title that his father used to play all the time when he was very young. *I can help,* the man sang, over a background of horns, mariachi guitars, and breathy female *ahh*s, pleading his usefulness: *If you got a problem, don't care what it is, if you need a hand, I can assure you this—I can help, I got two strong arms, I can help. It would sure do me good, to do you good. Let me help.*

"Oh, fuck you."

"What?" He pushed back on the bed, away from her.

"My father and you, and all your help help help. Who do you think you are? Some knight on a quest? Sir Vancelot?"

"Stop it."

"Here, let me help you."

In one motion, she threw her right leg over him and pulled up her skirt. She scrabbled at his corduroys, and he was pushing against her, but she was pressing down against him with an irresistible, inhuman strength. She got him free of his pants and with a little gasping exhalation forced him inside her. With one hand flat against the headboard, and the other brushing away the protesting tangle of his arms, she ground hard, back and forth. His eyes, he realized, were closed. When he opened them, her face was cast in shadow, and he was glad for that.

He shut them again, submitting to what was happening, which was easy, since he couldn't believe it really was. In the darkness of his mind, he again saw the clogged tributary of boats, felt his own small vessel bob beneath him, buffeted by innumerable wakes. Then with a nearly imperceptible slip, he broke free of the flotilla and picked up speed, pulled along by a great warm current that held the middle of his boat in its grasp. Faster and faster he sped, past the shoreline with its ruffled outline of water grass and cattails, the current and river and his own boat becoming a unified whole, a single vector speeding him toward the water's mouth, a boundless ocean.

A shockwave of fresh disbelief dispelled this vision and lent him the strength to force her off, beside him in the bed. Just in time—he twisted away, shuddering. She got up and grabbed the suitcase, turned the TV off, stood there a moment. He closed his eyes again.

"You're welcome," she said, and she was gone.

———

She took two quick lefts to escape the immediate vicinity of the hotel, then turned onto a tree-lined side street. Suitcase trailing her like a faithful dog, she clicked over a bridge spanning a small river, and on the other side found herself entering a commercial district tailored to the tastes of young, white professionals. Irish pubs and Mexican cantinas fought a vicious land war for retail space. Young men, mostly wearing the same uniform of khakis, oxford shirt, and white hat, clowned past, drunk on a Friday night, happy. And why shouldn't they be? The future, for the moment, was theirs.

The moment was hers, as well. She felt the smooth plastic cover of the checkbook in her pocket. Richard's checkbook, taken from the nightstand. Hers now. She wasn't sure how many checks she would have to write to get on her feet here, to start over and get the debt collectors off her back, but she was pretty sure Richard's ass could cash it. She wouldn't get caught—she thought of the book in her suitcase, with his autograph on the front page. And she was very sure he wouldn't turn her in.

He owed her, after all. The last ten years had been, in various ways she was only just beginning to understand, a response to him. She didn't blame her father directly, but his large presence lurked behind many of the compulsions and tendencies that had conspired to bring her where she was. Her addictiveness, perpetual dissatisfaction, fear of abandonment and desire to be left alone, the hole in the middle of her person that cried out with the forsaken intensity of a supermarket orphan for something or anything to fill it up one more time—it was not hard to see Richard's influence on these traits, and many others, since he had all of them himself. For better or for worse, and mostly worse, she was her father's daughter.

He wanted to be there, he'd said. He wanted to help—fine, he could help. He could help her start a new life, a free life: free from addiction, free from debt, free of bad relationships and broken promises, free of the lifelong resentments and grievances that followed her like the suitcase trailing her now. *You can be there for me,* she'd wanted to say in the diner, *but not on your terms—not when and how it's finally convenient for you, you fucking asshole.*

She pushed into a slavishly Anglophile yuppie gastropub—the kind that featured Arsenal F.C. memorabilia and sold wild-caught fish and organic chips for sixteen bucks—and approached a clutch of businessmen standing around. As was the case with all men in groups, they resembled twelve-year-old boys at a school dance, emanated the same awkward hormonal throb. She assumed their loosened ties were meant to signal that work was done for the week and it was playtime, baby. *In here, it's always happy hour.*

To the youngest and best-looking one, she said, "Buy me a drink."

"Why should I do that?"

"Because it's my birthday."

The men laughed. The guy said, "I'll need to see some ID, of course."

She pulled her ID out of her purse and showed him. He said, "Yesterday."

"Close enough, I'm still celebrating."

He shrugged and said okay and bought her a fruity shot, the taste of which made her hate him even more. She drank it, then left without a word, to the amusement and consternation of the hooting douchebags behind her. Richard had forgotten her birthday again, she considered—maybe that had something to do with all this, too.

The Friday-night crowd swelled around her as she neared downtown—in front of the façade of a large art deco building, a stage was set up on which a bunch of paunchy white dudes mangled "Whipping Post." People pushed past, and she rejoiced in it, becoming part of the throng, the multitude. Faces like the ones she'd watched on camera for so many years moved by her, each one frozen for a moment, pitched back in laughter or anger or dull confusion, and she wondered what someone watching her from above, looking at her face, might think. Would they know anything, be able to divine something about her, her life, or her mistakes? No. No one knows anything about anyone, she thought, and for the second time that day was struck with the feeling that she could start over—that nothing, in fact, would be easier. Denver, why not? She dragged her suitcase into the hot jostle, for the moment immensely pleased.

CHAPTER FIFTEEN

The sea at Nha Trang was that shade of luminous turquoise that only appears in travel agency ads behind a woman in a white bikini. The sand, too, was white and soft—a sand of forgetting that meant escape from the world and from worry, the kind you imagined laying a towel down on and screwing a sweating rum drink into. We were set up in a row of wooden barracks that opened directly onto the beach. It was hard to believe there was a war going on, despite our having marched through the jungle for a week, despite our malaria and jungle rot, despite the peeling white colonnades of the South Vietnamese Air Force administrative headquarters—our temporary station awaiting further orders. Despite planes taking off and landing on the two nearby airstrips night and day. They might have been passenger jets bringing in vacationers.

Probably it was just the easiest secure place for us to decamp for a little while before going on to whatever was next, but it felt like a reward for shooting up the village. Or rather, for eliminating NVA combatants at Vien Dinh. The rest of the platoon seemed to be in high spirits, lounging on the sand and treating the whole thing as a holiday, but when we were off-duty I mostly stayed inside. I'd caught a fever on the march to Nha Trang, and I sat in the barracks during hundred-degree days, as if I could sweat it out of me (the barracks seemed like a Swedish sauna anyway, constructed as they were from untreated lumber with a long bench against the rear wall). The wood

*grain would swim before my eyes, like a river of faces surfacing
and drowning, surfacing and drowning. Eventually I would emerge
for a breath of air, only to feel repulsed by the serene beauty of my
surroundings and go back inside.*

During this time, I developed a twin pair of ideations—obsessions,
it would probably be fair to say. The first was Berlinger. On the
march from Vien Dinh to Nha Trang, Berlinger and I had brought up
the rear, with me positioned behind him. For two days, a thick silence
had been as much a part of the atmosphere we moved through as the
humidity. When I tried to engage him, even in inane conversation
about sports and girls, he ignored me, just whittled away on his
figurine. When I caught glimpses of it, I could see it was becoming
more detailed, with little hands, and features emerging from its blank
face. In response to his silence, I found myself imagining pulling my
rifle up and shooting him in the wet spot between his big shoulder
blades, how easy it would be.

When we first got to Nha Trang, I went to visit him in the brig. The
brig was a small area located in the basement of the administrative
building, past a depressing antechamber full of World War II–era
gray-green file cabinets. I signed in with a young, smiling Vietnamese
sentry and stood in front of Berlinger; he sat on an upturned white
plastic bucket that, according to the label, formerly contained bean
curd. I remember thinking it said bean crud the whole time I was
down there. There was a window on one side of the room and no
bars—the only thing keeping him here, in fact, was the jolly teenage
guard who lit a cigarette and watched us.

"Mitch," I said. He didn't say anything. "Come on, this is
childish."

"Nanny nanny, boo boo," he said.

"It's not going to be so funny when you get court-martialed."

"Go away, Lazar, I got nothing to say to you."

I stewed on it—the arrogant nerve of him, the big silent martyr.
In my fever dreams, I saw his sainted face watching over me from a
shadowed hill, the big wedge of his crew cut like an arrow pointing
down. During this period, I simultaneously became, as a subsequent

psych report would read, "Negatively Fixated on Lester Hawkins."
Negatively fixated—I fucking hated him. I mean, I had never liked
Hawkins, none of us had—he was dumb and loud and always
cruising for approval. But ever since the village, he'd been intolerable.
Like lots of other guys in the unit—myself included—he had been
triumphant after mowing down the NVAs. Unlike most of us, though,
he had continued braying about it throughout our final push to the
coast. Worse, he had taken one of the tan hats—hard topped with a
wide floppy brim—from a dead body, and entertained himself with
periodic and extremely unfunny imitations of Charlie on patrol,
Charlie making fucky-fucky, Charlie eating with phantom chopsticks,
Charlie getting blown away by us. He didn't seem to have any of
the native reservations, the niggling doubts, that eventually caused
most of us to shut our mouths, or write long boring letters home, or
speculate about the Yankees in '71. Or maybe the callous bravado was
his way of dealing with it—that would have been the charitable view.
But watching him in the mess, shoveling food into his face while he
talked, the tan hat just a little big for his head, I somehow found
myself incapable of forming the charitable view.

Instead, I singled Lester Hawkins out for a hatred purer than any
I've known before or since. I believe at the height of it, for the three
weeks we were in Nha Trang, I would have murdered him if I'd had
the opportunity and means. Partly, it was the lack of anything else
we had to do—twice a day, on a rotating basis, four men were sent
out on a two-hour recon sweep up into the nearby foothills. That was
two hours, every other day, in which we were occupied. Otherwise,
we played cards, went swimming, jacked off, worked out, convalesced,
and waited for our next marching orders. Or, in my case, sat alone
in the barracks nursing irrational hatred like a suckling babe at my
swollen tit.

It got to where I blamed Hawkins for everything. Not just the
killing, which we'd all taken part in besides Berlinger, but for
Vietnam, and my deployment there. I saw him as the kind of oblivious
shithead who thought the war was a good thing, who'd vote for Nixon
upon safely returning home—as he inevitably would, because careless

*dolts like him always made it back. I watched him cleaning his M-15
in preparation for patrol, smiling with pleasure like he was in for a
rare treat. I watched him as he swam in the bay, and hoped he'd get
eaten by a shark, if there were sharks here. I watched him do pull-
ups on the side of the canteen and drink beer and make his dumbass
jokes, all the while wearing that goddamn hat.*

I was in the barracks reading—a Time *magazine with Ali McGraw
on the cover in a floral-print dress—when Hawkins poked his head
in. The hat sat back on it at a rakish, relaxed angle. "Lazar?" he
said. His deep Delta accent stretched my last name out to four or five
syllables.*

"What?"

"Some of us guys are getting a poker game together, you want in?"

"Suck my dick, Lester."

*"What?" he said. His bland face registered total shock. In that
instant, I realized two things, closely related. First, I realized that
the animosity that had welled up in me was so fierce, I had assumed
he must have sensed it; more than that, I had assumed he must have
felt that way himself. How could he not have seen it, like stink waves
off a cartoon character? Second, I realized he had no idea. I was just
another grunt to him, one of the crew, a weirdo who mostly kept to
himself. The fact that he had no idea made me hate him even more.*

*I rolled out of bed and walked to where he was standing. The look
on his face changed, from confusion to a slow, wide grin. He figured
I was fucking with him. He was so guileless, so unprepared for
what was coming his way, that he didn't even flinch or move when
I punched him in the face.*

*Now, let me tell you this. I am not much of a fighter, have been
in three fights, in fact, my whole life. If any punches were thrown
in these fights, they were perfunctory, flailing. But this was a real
punch, with real meaning in it. I reached behind me, through the
walls of the barracks, through Nha Trang village, up into the ridge
overlooking the bay, through a hundred miles of jungle, all the way
back to that gulley where the bodies now decomposed in a pit of
quicklime. I clutched those bodies in my hand like a blackjack, and*

I threw the punch with all the force a human body could muster. He fell backward out of the Quonset hut, and landed twitching on sand. The hat flew up in the air and fluttered down several feet away, like a drab bird alighting. I made a beeline to the clinic. I told them I was worried I'd killed Hawkins; I was certain I'd broken my hand—I'd heard the bone snap.

The doctor had just finished examining my hand and gone to find a splint, when Lieutenant Endicott pushed through the light blue dividing curtain. He sat down by the bed on which I lay, in my camos and Donald Duck T-shirt.

"You proud of yourself?"

"Yes."

Endicott shook his remarkable head and continued to look at me. He was hatchet faced, in the sense that his face was shaped like an ax—it was narrow even at the ears, and the cheekbones angled in to the long blade of his nose, on which you could have sliced tomatoes. His lips were thin at the best of times; the displeased grimace they were now set in had virtually caused them to vanish. His branch of the family was from a small town in Massachusetts called Endurance, and he looked like what he was, one of those severe New England types with icy bloodlines running back to Cotton Mather. I picture him now on a lonely, scenic mountain homestead, performing some impossible pioneer chore like building a well, looking exactly the same as he did then, since he already looked sixty in 1971.

"Normally, we let you idiots punch each other and take care of things yourselves, but Hawkins has a severe concussion. Throwing up and seeing double, thinks Eisenhower is president. How's your hand?"

I looked down at the Christmas ham in my lap and said, "Fine."

"Doctor said it's broken in three different places, if I understood him properly. Joe Frazier puts on gloves first, you know. They wear them to protect their hands, not the other guy's face. Why'd you do it?"

"I don't like Hawkins."

"I don't like green beans," said Endicott, "but you don't see me

beating the shit out of them. I've never given green beans severe head trauma." I didn't say anything, so he went on, "I don't want to see you disciplined over this, but it's out of my hands. I'm going to talk to him on your behalf, but if Hawkins decides to make a stink, it's all on record."

"Yes, sir."

"For what it's worth, between the two of us, Lester Hawkins is a grubby little booger-eater, and I didn't too much mind seeing him in that bed, looking like a raccoon. But I've still got to brig you up for this."

"Yes, sir."

"One more thing." Endicott looked down at his hands. "While you're there, maybe you can talk to Berlinger on my behalf."

"I tried. He's not talking to me."

"Well, try again," said Endicott. "He's putting me in a bad position here. I'm trying to get him to take a Section Eight discharge, and he won't do it. Psychiatric discharge—it's not ideal, it'll follow him around, but it's not the end of the world. It's not dishonorable, and it sure as hell isn't prison. The stubborn son of a bitch is going to force me to bring him in for a court-martial, and I don't want to do that. But I can't do nothing."

"Why not?"

Endicott looked at me for a moment, as though I was an idiot. I was, in fact, an idiot, but what I had just said didn't feel idiotic. "Lazar, he refused to participate in a military action under direct orders from his commanding officer. And he did so in front of twenty fellow soldiers."

"I know what he did."

"A military court might consider that aid and comfort. They might consider it treason and let him hang."

"Couldn't it be 'conscientious objection'?"

"If he was still stateside, sure."

"Couldn't you just forget it? He's got maybe six weeks before his tour is up."

"Not in this political climate. Not with that mess at Kent State last month. Not with hippies burning Nixon in effigy. A Section Eight is the best I've got. Go and talk to him."

Berlinger couldn't help but smile when the MP escorted me in, looking up from his whittling, the little soldier now almost complete in his hand: face, combat boots, tiny rifle at attention behind a tiny shoulder. I said, "I punched Hawkins."

"I heard," he said. "I heard you just about killed him."

"You heard?"

"Word travels."

I sank to the ground, back against the hot wall, holding my throbbing hand. In spite of everything, my main feeling was a sense of relief that Berlinger was speaking to me again. "So, how much longer until they drag you in front of a tribunal?"

"Martin came by, said tomorrow."

"You think about pleading insanity?"

"Not for one second."

"You want martyr of the year, or something? Why don't you just take the Section Eight?"

He stood and I hunched away from him, surprised, as always, by how goddamned big he was. "Endicott tell you to talk to me?"

"Yeah, so what?"

He laughed. "You realize what a joke that is? I should plead insanity, when I was the only sane one there."

"How's that?"

"It was a massacre, Lazar, you dumb fuck. That's how."

"A massacre. They were VC."

He snorted. "Oh yeah. That old woman was VC for sure. The kid with the umbrella."

I could see the pink umbrella spinning around the village before, the torn fabric after. My vision seemed to darken at the edges, and my ears filled with hot water. "They were working with them, the whole village was. Command said, I heard Endicott on the radio."

"Oh, bullshit. Bullshit, bullshit, bullshit."

I wiped my face, clearing away the image of the smoldering village. "Do you really want to go to prison over this?"

He crouched and leaned in toward me. Our faces were close *as he*
talked quietly. "No, I don't. I want to provide honest testimony before
a judge and God. I want Endicott to go to prison. Endicott, fucking
Westmoreland. Lyndon Baines Cocksucking Johnson."

"Good luck with that."

"Gee, thanks." He backed off a little.

I said, "Look, I don't know, maybe you're right. Maybe it was
fucked up, maybe it was a bad call. But orders are orders, all the
way down. Take a Section Eight, you'll be back in Kansas in a week.
Endicott's trying to help you here—he doesn't want to see you court-
martialed."

"Is that what he said? You know why Endicott wants to Section
Eight me? He doesn't want me testifying at a trial. Not that the army
will do anything, but he doesn't want my testimony on record. The
word 'massacre' might jump out at some bored correspondent reading
a transcript."

"It wasn't a massacre," I said. For a few moments we looked at
each other in silence. My mind felt like a car with its back tires
caught in the mud. "And what about Carbone?"

"What about him?"

"You forget his leg? One of those VC might've planted that mine."

Berlinger laughed again, right in my face, and I felt myself turn
red with the knowledge of how far I was reaching. He said, "One
might have. All of them didn't. The village didn't. And who gives a
fuck, anyway? Did you give a fuck about Carbone? I didn't."

Outside the window, some jungle bird cycled through an endless
three-note song. "Okay, fine. I tried. So what's your defense gonna be
at the court-martial then?"

He picked up the wooden figurine by the tips of its feet and head,
and spun it around and around in his huge hands. "Lazar, I ever tell
you about my father?"

"No."

"He was a real piece of work. Got fired from every job he ever
had, drank all the time, had an affair with just about every woman
in Manhattan. He made my mother miserable, and he was a shitty

father to me and my sister. He didn't hit us or anything, just wasn't ever there and could have given a shit, you know? I fucking hated him."

"Yeah, I have a father, too."

"Listen, so one night after dinner, I must have been around fifteen, I waited up for him to come home from wherever he was. Around midnight, he came in drunk as usual, and I let him have it. Told him what I thought of him. You know, 'You've never been there for us,' and blah blah. I said he'd never given me a single piece of fatherly advice I could use. He laughed and said, 'That's the best advice I could ever have given you, Mitch. Figure things out for yourself, and don't listen to what anybody tells you. Nobody knows a goddamned thing, at least I don't walk around pretending I do.' Berlinger moved to the window and set the figurine down on the sill and for a moment they both looked outside, at the beach and sea in what he must have realized was an absurdly dramatic pose, because he quickly shook his head and returned to the middle of the room, sitting again on the bucket of bean crud. "And he was right, you know? Rip those stripes off Endicott's sleeve, he doesn't know a goddamned thing. Nobody knows a thing all the way up the line, bunch of dipshits and yes-men and cowards and hacks, all the way to whoever at command sent down that fucking kill order. And I'll be goddamned if anyone is going to tell me to take part in a massacre. You wanted to know what my defense is going to be, there it is."

The next day, Berlinger was led out by the MPs. He nodded back at me and was gone. I noticed that wooden soldier was still where he'd left it, standing on the windowsill, looking out. I had the strange sense, that whole day, that he'd left it as a sort of totem, a miniature version of himself standing guard—although whether over me, or the outside world, I couldn't tell.

————

Two days after that—two days of the most intense boredom and dread I've felt in my life, short of waiting to see the Eagles on the Hell Freezes Over tour—the Vietnamese MP waved me out. Davis Martin was there, said Hawkins was conscious and wanted to talk. If I was smart, he said, with a look suggesting he thought I probably wasn't, I would apologize, grovel if need be. I went over to sick bay, a cinder-block cube on the edge of base, and found Hawkins on a metal bed in the corner. He really did look like a raccoon.

"Lazar," he said. "I just wanted to tell you I'm not pushing for a court-martial."

"Thanks."

"Why'd you hit me?"

"It was the hat, I think."

He seemed to consider this, then said, "Here's the thing. The doctor said it looks like when I fell, this little itty piece of my skull chipped off inside. Says it's fine, no big deal, 'cept I can't be out in combat, that a mortar concussion or something like that could cause it to kill me. They're sending me home in a week, you believe that?"

"No."

"So I called you in here to say thanks. I've had these nightmares ever since I've been in-country, slept like an hour every night for three months. Thought about shooting off my own toe, turns out all I had to do was wear that gook's lid, and your dumb fucking ass took care of the rest."

"I'm glad to hear it."

He said, "I bet you are. Hey, one more thing. You hear about your buddy Berlinger?" I guess the blank stare on my face informed him I hadn't. "He got zapped on the way down to MACV for his tribunal. Tough shit, huh? No good deed, huh?"

"You're lying."

"Unh-uh." He rearranged himself on his bed with a look of satisfaction, like a man who'd just eaten a little more than he should have. "Ask around. He got ambushed on that same convoy line we rode in on when we first got here."

His big rubbery lips were assembling themselves into the formation of a smile as I retreated from the room. "Poor old Berlinger. I guess maybe it don't matter much how smart you are." He turned, grinning horribly now. "Hey, Lazar. I hope you get shot just like your buddy."

I couldn't get out before hearing him say, "I hope some gook sniper draws a bead on your fat head. Brains for monkey dinner. You hear me? I hope you get cut wide open, you fucking son of a bitch."

———

Davis Martin confirmed the rumor at an impromptu meeting in the mess hall during lunch and told us, matter of fact, that Berlinger had been killed in transport to army headquarters in Saigon. An insurgent mortar attack, the wreckage discovered by the supply truck fifteen minutes behind it. Endicott had gone to Saigon, too, to testify at the trial, but he'd been choppered in. Martin told everyone to shut up and observe a moment of silence, bowed his fireplug head, then left the room to its questions, its inane chatter, its guilty feelings of relief that it hadn't been them, its turkey potpies. No one seemed that bothered, and it occurred to me that most of the guys considered him a traitor.

I walked outside. It was a gorgeous clear day. I went back to the barracks, polished off the warm dregs of a bottle of brandy, and vomited. I sat there for a very long time, sweating, watching the river of faces on the wall, watching Berlinger surface and resurface, live and drown, over and over again. I watched as the other guys came in chattering, laughing, lying down, snoring. I watched in the dark. I didn't get up in the morning, and I didn't get up when someone was in the door talking, surrounded by a rectangle of harsh, white light. I didn't say anything and they went away, and then I was alone again, with the same thoughts circling in my head: It had been a massacre, Endicott had given the order, I had followed it, Berlinger hadn't, he'd been right, and he'd died for it.

That evening, I approached Martin in the canteen. A ceiling fan overhead seemed to beat in slow motion, and I could see the helicopter touching down, Endicott crouching under the spinning blades, getting the news from some crew-cut hack. I could see his long face, touched with sadness, and with relief at being spared the trial. Martin was drinking a beer and thumbing through a Whole Earth Catalog someone stateside must have sent him.

"Look who it is." He didn't look up, kept thumbing through the pages.

"Sir, can I ask you a question?"

"You already did. Just ask."

"I was wondering if there was any more news about Berlinger."

"What other news could there be?"

"I mean, is there any word about what happened?"

"Just that the truck got hit."

"Did they recover the bodies?"

He put down the catalog and gave me a look, his eyebrows screwed up. "How the fuck would I know, Lazar? And why does it matter? Either the mortar got them, or Charlie got them after. What happened to their bodies I don't know, and I don't want to know."

"Is Endicott still in Saigon?"

"Lieutenant will be back next week. Until then, I'm your CO." He went back to the catalog. "And I don't give a fuck what kind of miserable state you're in, Jack, you better be up and on duty tomorrow. Ten-hut."

Ten-hut. Back at barracks, I loaded my field pack with clothes, water, provisions, sidearm, and a grenade; I ate an MRE and brushed my teeth; I lay in bed and pretended to sleep, and later I walked off base.

———

Deserting was surprisingly easy. I waited until the barracks were filled with the rattle and hiss of several dozen sleeping men, opened the door, and walked out. The beach side of the base was dark—no one was worried about a surprise attack by the famous NVA Navy— but the moon and the photoluminescence of the water provided enough light to see. I scurried around the edge of the base, almost to the eastern gate and its guard post, and I waited. There wasn't really much to it—when guard shift changed over, there was usually a little lag as the guy on duty grabbed his sleeping replacement. It wasn't how things were supposed to work, but not much here worked how it was supposed to. I waited until the guard walked over to

the barracks, then ducked through the gate and into the shadows
by the perimeter wall. The spotlight swept the road in front of the
base, and when it passed, I ran. In what seemed like only a few
seconds, I'd dashed across the road, through the open, weedy strip
that buffered base from village, past the village itself—a sprawling,
chaotic Tinkertown of concrete structures, colonial houses, thatched
huts, and lean-tos; everyone, even a mottled terrier sleeping near a
crumbling stone wall, dead asleep at three in the morning—and up
a steep and sparsely wooded hummock. In a small clearing, I caught
my breath and took a last look toward the sea. Spotlights on each side
of the base scanned the road and moved up into the middle dark; the
airstrip and distant conning tower were lit yellow and orange and
red, and the whole thing glowed glamorously in the night like a movie
marquee. As I climbed farther, it was the last of this light that led me
to the distant, indistinct scar curving through waist-high elephant
grass, up the hill, and into the jungle. It was the dirt road we'd
walked in on, that Berlinger had been killed on—the road to Saigon.

CHAPTER SIXTEEN

O utside the small, oblong airplane window, the midwestern landscape unspooled in agreeable uniformity, a drab flatness in perfect concert with his mental state, as though the entire world
below was one endless five-mile loop. The only sign of real movement
was the occasional clouds that sailed past and underneath the plane, a
regatta of schooners and clippers and yachts and little sailboats bound
for nowhere in particular. In the distance, another airplane shouldered
bravely through the blue waves of the midwestern sky. The sky was the
real God, but I should have been a sailor.

He pressed the call button on his seat again. The man next to him
read *Business Weekly* or *Weekly Business* or some other deadening
money rag with ads every other page for gold investment and studiously avoided acknowledging Richard's sodden presence. This was a
task, as he was nearly as large as Richard, and it was all they could do
not to merge amoebically together over the armrest.

While he waited for the flight attendant to come out of hiding, he
attempted to piece together the events of the previous twenty-four
hours. This was also a task: his consciousness during this time was like
a drowning man, briefly coming up for air and catching a momentary,
frozen glimpse of the world—the surrounding ocean and a snatch of
blue sky, perhaps dotted with a lone gull—before going under again.
It didn't help that he was still incredibly drunk, although less drunk

than he had been, a fact manifest in his serial memory of getting on the airplane, falling into his seatmate, and annoying the stewardess. Somewhere in there, he'd vomited into a vintage barf bag with jet-set typography, which had, in turn, instantly voided its contents onto his lap. Earlier events, however, floated on their own, suspended in amber, and he closed his eyes with the effort of ordering them, at the same time wondering what difference it made. None, was probably the answer, he knew, but when you give up on making sense of anything, you've given up on life—he was close, but not quite there yet. So:

———

Lying beneath a giant hamburger. No, before that.

———

Someone opening the door, bathing the room in fluorescent light. He stood there, a dark figure in the threshold. Other men lay in the room, snoring, moaning, talking to themselves, palsied hands waving through air humid with urine.

"Get up," the person said. It was Vance.

"Where am I," Richard croaked.

"Jail. The drunk tank. I was out looking for you all night."

"Where's Cindy?"

"She's gone, don't you remember?"

Out of a lifetime spent waking up in strange places and not knowing where he was, this was the most disoriented he had ever been. The light in the room refracted crazily off fragments of his own story. He couldn't shake the notion that the kid that stood before the bed was in the army. Home from. When Johnny comes. Tie a yellow.

"I'm done with this," the soldier said.

"Negatory to that," he mumbled. "AWOL will land you five years. Do your duty, son. One more tour."

The kid came over and helped him upright. "There's no more tour, it's over."

"I'll run it up the CoC tomorrow. We can still make New York."

The kid sighed. "Come on."

"Copy that," said Richard, and together they moved toward the shining door.

———

Before that. Driving through Kansas, the remorseless prairie scrub whipping past. Drinking from a half-empty bottle, which he'd hidden in his bag under a pile of unfresh T-shirts and socks and boxers. Stowed away, for emergencies. Well, if this wasn't an emergency, he'd thought, unscrewing the top and bringing the bottle to his lips, he didn't know what was. Life was an emergency.

Vance looking over at him. "I thought you weren't drinking anymore."

"I wasn't. Now I am."

"Why don't you wait until after the reading?"

"Because I want it now. Because I want. Because, because, because, because, because." Singing off-key with the Kansas grassland dancing in all directions. When they stopped for gas, he climbed into the backseat and positioned himself where the kid couldn't watch him, and he sat for the remainder of the drive with the whiskey sloshing against his lips. Give baby his bottle! There was something gratifying, freeing, about completely giving up any pretense of control—really, he should have done it years before.

———

Standing in front of a university, an imposing gothic building that resembled an enormous sea monster bearing down, maw agape, on the unsuspecting green quad. Shaking hands with people, and these people leading him into an elevator and up to a room where he shook other people's hands. Sitting for a while in a burgundy leather chair, the impressive kind embroidered with iron nails, and they—whoever they were—diligently approached him, with an air of mild, gracious irony, like savvy villagers paying respect to a cut-rate viceroy. Despite Vance's vigilant chaperoning, he managed to get one young girl to sneak him a glass of wine. Then they were in some sort of backstage area, which he was able to deduce from the red velvet trembling in front of him.

The kid was holding his arm. "Let's go. I'll tell them you weren't feeling well."

"I feel fine."

"You're not fine."

The audience applauded on the other side of the curtain. He wrested away from Vance and attempted to push through it, but became caught in its voluminous folds. He felt a hand on his arm again, but again he twisted free. For a moment his person was fully contained inside the heavy, red sway. Why was the entire world against him? Finally, he'd picked up the curtain's weighted bottom edge and pulled it over himself, or himself under, to a room full of laughter. *You like me, you really like me.*

———

Staring out at the audience staring back at him with a massed expression of amused dismay. Vance looked on grimly from the side of the stage, arms hanging limp at his sides. The auditorium's silence was broken by a cough, which brought him back to the task at hand. He looked down at the book and tried to figure out where he'd left off. What the hell was he reading? It seemed like nonsense to him— unfollowable, hieroglyphic.

"Sorry," he said, uselessly flipping the pages. The problem was the lights. They were instruments of torture, designed to confuse and blind him. He needed water, craved it as he never had. His tongue was a fat snake stuck in the dirt hole of his mouth. He picked the book up and held it about four inches from his squinting eyes. His face was a crumpled wad of paper. Finding a paragraph that looked familiar, he resumed reading, though it was more like running some kind of horrible obstacle course in which every word, every syllable, was a barrier to be surmounted, defeated, climbed over. In the middle of the thing, he kept forgetting who the characters were or what they were talking about. It was not an unfamiliar sensation or mode of reading, although typically it happened right before he went to sleep, and not in front of an audience of three hundred people.

Somehow he got to the end of the chapter. He turned the page, just to make sure, and discovered that it went on! Ah, wretched life! Ferdinand Magellan himself could not have been more anguished to see the limitless Pacific stretch out before him after navigating the straits that—like Richard's book—cruelly bore his own name. He continued for a moment, but finally stopped again in the middle of a sentence and peered out into the audience. Some blonde woman whom he momentarily thought was his daughter pushed out of the room and loudly slammed the door behind her. But Cindy was gone, he remembered. Vance swayed on the side of the stage. The whole room swayed in unison, underwater plants doing a gentle, sinister hula.

"I'm sorry," he said again, shutting the book. "My daughter hates me."

———

An endless series of hallways, lost in the guts of the beast. Emerging into an expansive atrium, its walls bedecked with portraits of similar-looking old white men. He got lost trying to leave, twice entering the same lecture hall, the second time to sarcastic applause, before finally pushing outside into the dim, merciful chill. As he lurched directionlessly down a brick-lined path, the men in the paintings seemed to stare at him from the ether of the early purple dusk. They were rich men, obviously, viciously sober and responsible men; men who had dedicated their long lives to making money and building things; things that bore their names in etched stone; stone that exemplified their belief in themselves and God, in life's inherent value and design and purpose. If they could see him, what would he look like to men like that? Nothing, of course. Just a ridge of shit, a russet smudge under the waterline of a dirty toilet.

He shuddered across the campus in a kind of time lapse: a building would appear in the distance, and then he would be careening past it; a remote cluster of girls chatting among themselves seemed to teleport to his right flank, where they pointed and whispered. He hadn't expected, or meant, to get quite this drunk. The problem, of course, was that he hadn't been drinking—he wouldn't make that mistake again. Once more feeling the intense need to escape—from the campus, from public view and comment, and, ideally, though impossibly, from himself—he aimed toward a distant wall of trees.

———

Scurrying through the woods. To his right, red and blue lights flashed horribly. What had he done? All he wanted to do was get away. But you couldn't do it—you couldn't get away, you just couldn't. He tripped over a rotting tree stump, got up, tripped again, felt something in his ankle buckle. It hurt, everything hurt. Ten ten ten. He paused, panting next to a large tree. A used condom hung off one of its lower branches, like an offering to the gods. He pressed on, past strange shapes hanging in the trees, nightmare fruit, people watching him, faces looking down: leering strangers, the judge at his DUI trial, old lovers turned to crones, his daughter's, his own. Why couldn't he get away?

Without warning the woods opened up. He was thrashing through grabby underbrush, stumbling up the grass strip beside someone's house. Through the blurred rheum of his own twinned vision and thick patio glass, a large TV glowed blue and cast in shadow the two people on the couch in front of it. A wall of books, a table and chairs, gas grill on the patio. It looked simple, perfect. Why do other people's lives always look so much more appealing than our own? Eileen had told him once that his problem wasn't that he didn't count his blessings; he just also counted everyone else's. Standing before a window, a child sleeping, a little boy with a brown swirl of hair and delicate half-moon eyelids lit by the dull-orange glow of a night-light. A look of uncorruptible peace that suggested an absolute faith in his security, in the adults in the other room. Had Cindy ever looked like that? Then the child's eyes were open, locked through the window on Richard's, and the look was gone, replaced by the opposite. The mouth in a black O, screaming at the monster from the deep, the murdering ogre in the night.

———

Lost again, sitting at the end of a cul-de-sac, watching the squaddie pull in. Its squawking siren and flashing lights—his unwitting accomplice in the ruination of childish sleep. Another car pulled in behind, prettily bathing the dark lawns in red and blue. A cop got out, mumbled something into his staticky shoulder, graciously opened the rear door of the car, and Richard obligingly tumbled in.

———

Riding in the cool dark, lying down on that cool seat, oh never never never let it end.

———

He'd fully regained his senses—an unfortunate development—in the back of another car: Vance's. Outside a place that served hamburgers, apparently, judging from the giant plastic patty melt on its mammoth concrete plinth. It hovered upside down in Richard's vision like an invading UFO. The spray-painted green of iceberg lettuce and the floppy red edge of a beefsteak tomato floated merrily overhead. Vance returned with a grease-stained bag from which he pulled a small bouquet of wilted french fries.

"Where are we going?" said Richard.

"The airport."

"Why?"

"So you can fly back home."

"The tour's not over."

Vance started the car. "The tour's definitely over."

They arrived at the airport. KANSAS CITY, the sign said. DEPARTURES, the sign said. Large midwestern people pulled large midwestern bags from large midwestern SUVs. The kid set his battered Samsonite on the sidewalk and waited for him to clamber out. Richard steadied himself on the suitcase handle, and for a moment they stood there looking at each other. Vance offered a solemn hand, as he had when they first met—but how different he seemed now.

Richard said, "I'm still going to do the New York stop. Come on. It'll be fun."

"You think this has been fun?"

"Yeah, some of it."

"I thought you were dead last night."

"I thought I was, too. Look, I'm sorry, okay? Come on. Don't you want to find out how this all winds up?"

"What?"

"This trip. Remember how you said my story was a cop-out? How I needed to figure out the ending?"

"Yes."

"Well, you head west on that interstate, you're copping out. It's not a real ending."

"And you think there will be a real one in New York?"

"Yeah, I do," Richard said. "Come on."

An airport police car approached and honked three times. The cop motioned out the window for them to wrap it up. "Sorry," Vance said. "Good luck."

———

He bought an exorbitantly expensive same-day ticket to New York, then, after somehow making it through security, bought an exorbitantly expensive Bloody Mary at a place called Tiki's Jungle Lounge. He sat in a dark corner table under a mounted, hopefully fake, tiger's head, its mouth open in what was probably meant to be a snarl but seemed closer to a grimace, the default expression of everyone in the establishment. Plastic palm fronds scraped his arm as he drank and quietly retched away the three hours before boarding. An unpleasant and debasing phone call to Dana, marked with many apologies and as many false promises, reestablished the New York stop. But it wasn't really that hard of a sell in the end—after all, she wanted him to make the appearance. It wasn't ever that hard to convince people of something they already wanted to believe.

"And you think you can tone it down for the next few days?"

"Oh, yeah," he said, stirring his third or was it fourth drink. "Absolutely."

Then the boarding, the shambling entrance, the barf bag, and now the flight attendant, unsmiling, nixing his request for a timid glass of rosé before he'd even asked. He leaned away from his hateful double, steeling himself for what would come, the blue, serene ozone a millimeter from his hot face.

———

In a sweating dream, he was pursued through a giant indoor mall by a man wearing a bear suit. The man waved his arms and growled unfrighteningly, and Richard felt sorry for him and therefore compelled by civility to feign terror and keep jogging past stores filled with exactly one item each: a toaster, a hair dryer, a book of stamps. He stopped at a shop that contained some sort of parchment or scroll, and when he had the scroll in his hands, the man in the bear suit entered, and he saw that it was, of course, himself. He and himself in the bear suit stood looking at each other in mutual embarrassment, for a long time.

The bear began speaking, some alien language that, as he woke, morphed into a garbled announcement from the captain. Seat backs, tray tables, laptops, twenty minutes. His temple remained pressed against the cool window, night falling on the turbid marshlands below. Manhattan bristled into view. He'd been to New York three times in his life, twice after his army discharge and once with Carole. They'd ridden doltishly around Central Park in a hansom cab, but he'd drawn the line at reenacting the "Chopsticks" scene from *Big,* which had caused a tense moment at FAO Schwarz. He'd never known what to think of the place—its immensity and persistent growth in the face of all reason or common sense said something grand and tiring that he didn't feel like figuring out but that struck him as essentially human, in the best and worst ways. Equal parts indestructible hope and unconquerable stupidity, or something like that.

He caught a taxi and slept most of the way to his hotel, the strangely named Best Western Hell's Kitchen. His legs were leaden with fatigue, not to mention with the hangover he'd had since Kansas City, a hangover he suspected he would have for the rest of his life. Standing in line at the front desk, he momentarily turned to talk to Vance before remembering he'd gone home. Not that Richard blamed him. He didn't blame anyone for getting tired of dealing with him. On the other hand, he couldn't feel too sorry for Vance or anyone else on that count, either—he'd been dealing with himself for over fifty years.

In the lobby, a white-haired black man slept in one of the armchairs, his head tilted back and mouth wide open, agape at whatever outlandish dreamworld he inhabited. The walls of the hotel were some kind of textured faux-adobe that made Richard's eyes swim. He got the key and rode the grease-smeared elevator up to the third floor. Door locked and blinds drawn, he called FreshDirect, ordered up a pallet of beer and three days' worth of imperishable foodstuffs, and hunkered down for the next seventy-two hours.

CHAPTER SEVENTEEN

———

Vance pulled away from the curb. In the rearview, Richard struggled heroically into the airport, counterbalanced by the suitcase he dragged wheels up, but Vance didn't watch. He sped down the airport exit ramp, coasted out onto I-435, and was free. The junction with I-70 approached in ten miles. He'd looked up the route while waiting for the station clerk to process Richard's paperwork. Back the way they'd come, I-70 to Denver, I-25 to Cheyenne, I-80 to Salt Lake, 15 North all the way to Butte, and then good old 90 east, back home to Spillman.

He turned on the radio in an attempt to dispel the twinge of doubt he felt about this return journey. Accompanied by reverb-soaked guitar and anodyne fiddle, a country singer effused in a yodelly hiccup about the bygone pleasures of rural puberty: fishin' 'n' dreamin' 'n' kissin'. Vance tapped his fingers on the steering wheel along with the music, batting away one by one the uneasy thoughts that kept popping into his head. Pizza Boy. The dining room table and its snowbank of bills. Particularly insistent was a vision of his bedroom, the dark ossuary of his own adolescence, with its cairns of books, like markers for each year he'd spent down there, gladly entombed. He thought guiltily of his mother, and he hoped she'd eaten something in the last week. A week: it felt like he'd been gone for six months. He didn't want to go back.

He turned off the radio and said it out loud: You can't go back. To go back and be happy, he would have to unexperience everything: one billion Las Vegas lights winking in unconscious concert, Richard gray faced in the hospital bed, the howling insanity of the San Francisco wind. Cindy grinding down on top of him, her face in shadows—he still didn't know what to make of that, and he wasn't sure he ever would. He wasn't sure what any of it meant, but that was okay. The meaning had been in the doing, and in the doing he was different now. Not an adult, maybe, but he was no longer pupal—no longer content to bur-row into the comfortable darkness of his own lonely inertia—and no longer a pupil, either, of other people's fictions. He was writing his own now, for better or worse.

Which, perhaps, was why what Richard had said niggled at him: *Don't you want to find out how this all winds up?* Characteristically, Richard had meant himself and the tour—his own story—but he wasn't wrong. Vance did want to see how it all turned out. It was only in abort-ing the trip, only in the prospect of not continuing on to New York, that he realized how much he'd been looking forward to seeing his father. "Looking forward to" wasn't exactly right—you didn't look forward to going to the dentist after five years, but you knew you should. You looked forward to getting it out of the way. And his father—or not so much his father as the father-shaped outline in his mind, the fact of his father's perfect absence—was in Vance's way, had been for as long as he could remember.

Merging right onto the 70 exit, there was only a single mile until the east-west split. He worked his wallet out of his back pocket and pulled out the sheet of lined notebook paper: *35 Greenpoint Ave., New York, New York.* Three years of friction had nearly worn the printing away. Nearly, but not quite, not enough. He put the sheet on the dash, his foot on the gas, and stayed left, Saint Louis bound, barreling past the exit west toward Topeka and home. A yellow traffic sign in the crook of the split featured two black arrows pointing toward each road—there was something soothing about the simple graphic representation of this decision: you did one thing, or the other, and at any rate, you'd made a choice. He settled back into his seat, rolled down his window, and yawned with pleasure at the open rolling vista yawning back at him, the road endlessly unscrolling, the black arrow that bore him along.

———

Like a magic trick, New York appeared and disappeared as gray dawn broke over the New Jersey marshlands. It was there for a moment, and then the road would dip and turn, and it would vanish like an image from some fever dream. Under a bridge, the road curved up to the right, and there it was again, aggressively real. The I-495 entrance ramp to the Lincoln Tunnel sustained the sleight of hand, first allowing an extended panorama of Manhattan before curving coyly and vanishing the glittering rabbit behind its back in exchange for a scrubby bluff dotted with an array of drab seventies apartment complexes and Toyotathon billboards, a panorama that would have felt anonymous and bleak in Spillman. One more quick flash of the city before the ramp slipped him into the tunnel and under the river. The dripping water and ghostly orange lights were a waking dream prefatory to the moment of bottoming, at which point the car rose with a sick sense of heavy, mounting speed before being released onto Fortieth in an alarmed flurry of pigeons and mourning doves.

The map he'd bought at a Jersey Citgo directed him into a gap between two proximate enormous buildings dwarfed by a phalanx of much more enormous Midtown skyscrapers in the near distance. This brought him to a roundabout and a cyclone of traffic that prevented him from exiting. He turned right, almost hit a taxi, braked hard, was almost hit himself by a honking delivery truck with birds raised from both windows, and careened toward an irate traffic cop blowing her whistle at him well after he shuddered to a stop.

In a cruel pantomime of helpfulness, she elaborately extended her arm in the direction of the road as the light turned green. Vance pulled into a parking lot on the right, cursing, vowing never to drive in this city again. He got out of the car, shouldered his duffel bag, handed the attendant his keys, and accepted the ticket with a grateful, shaky hand. After a deep-breathing session in the shadow of the neighboring building, he surveyed his options. He pulled out the map and located himself, roughly. He traced the route to 35 Greenpoint Avenue, where his father, or at least someone named Steven M. Allerby, lived. It would be a very long walk from where he was, but a long walk sounded perfect—despite only catching two hours of itchy sleep the night before at an Ohio rest stop, he felt enormously charged up, like a prizefighter bouncing in his corner, waiting on an unseen challenger to appear. If he was ever going to sleep again, he would need to discharge the electricity that hummed in his chest and crackled in his joints.

He got as far as two blocks east before coming to a stop in front of a Blimpie. His image cowered furtively next to a window ad for an unappealing bagel; he was intensely unready to go to Sunnyside. "Frightened," that was the word. He tried to picture his father and came up with memorized details (short, pugnacious, small featured) that failed to coalesce into a full image. The thought of seeing the man after six years filled him with an anxiety that started at the very base of his spine, like the buzzing of a phantom tail tucked between his legs. It had been one thing to decide, in Kansas City, to make this journey; it turned out those first twelve hundred miles were no problem—the last three were the hard part.

As a delaying tactic, he bought a root beer in the sub shop and decided to just enjoy the city, to wander for a little while. He did so, in mounting disbelief that New York, seen in person, looked the way it looked in pictures and film—in other words, exactly like New York. He'd always figured cameras must gigantize the island, the way an actress's face in close-up sometimes took on an emotionally all-consuming aspect. But no, it was even more ludicrously huge than he'd thought.

He zigzagged around the West Side in a stunned ramble. As he'd come up out of the birth canal of the Lincoln Tunnel, he'd imagined the density of people and buildings and the crush of commerce would be overwhelming; instead, the overload had a numbing effect. There was so much to be aware of, your mind gave up trying. He seemed to float along the sidewalks on someone else's feet, letting the trivializing superabundance of the city surge past. The haphazardness of the chaos was somehow pleasing: someone in a blue-and-red dashiki yelled into the doorway of a cell-phone store; a mannish blonde walked a Weimaraner that sniffed at Vance's legs; a Con Ed truck with its crane extended blocked an incensed clot of traffic.

A double-decker tour bus roared past him, and the guide's amplified gibbering —*Here we see the Chancellor Towers built by the infa-mous Thomas Van Wyck in 1887 better known for his role in Tammany Hall*—broke his train of thought. He looked up at a street sign that read W 47 ST, retrieved the damp map from his back pocket, and resituated himself. East several city blocks, then north to Central Park and Fifty-Ninth Street, crossing the Queensboro Bridge into Queens. He forced himself to walk, thinking, what are you afraid of? As he started east, clouds swung in the same direction overhead, their shadows spread-ing like spilled liquid across the buildings and the streets all around. It created an atmosphere, a novelistic feeling, of tension and drama, and he saw himself move, invigorated and purposeful, foregrounded amongst the insignificant crowds, the minor players who scurried like rats in every direction, scared of a little rain. He had been scared at the thought of finally seeing his father again, but he now felt no fear at all. Assuming he had the right address—a pretty big assumption in the first place—he would say hello, catch up a little, stay the night, and be on his way. It had to happen for him to move on to the next thing, whatever that might be. Follow the black arrow.

There were so many places he wanted to stop along the way—the New York Public Library with its handsome marble lions; marquees on Broadway that advertised actors he'd actually heard of in plays he'd ac-tually heard of, performed in grand buildings that looked like Broadway theaters as represented in the movies because they actually were; the green edge of Central Park and its clean, peppery smell of horseshit—but he kept moving. The pedestrian footpath on the bridge bustled with tourists taking pictures of the river and of the island below it. Who lived there? He moved on.

By the time he arrived at 35 Greenpoint Avenue, it was early af-ternoon, but he was fading quickly, the manic energy of the last two days having burned away on the trek. The apartment was located in a four-story building, over a storefront that sold and tuned pianos, called PIANO. The building was redbrick and in relatively good repair, with newly painted white shutters. The area itself had surprised Vance. Ex-pecting a loud, claustrophobic, garbage-strewn shitscape, he'd instead been met with a modest, friendly neighborhood. The buildings were smaller here, and there seemed to be more air, more sky. He was both relieved and disappointed that his father hadn't continued or completed his slide into a state of abject poverty.

He rang the buzzer, and as he did, two related thoughts occurred to him almost simultaneously: first, how very unlikely it was that www .internetsleuth.com had led him to the right apartment, and, second, that for several years he'd unwaveringly believed it would. A third train of thought quickly followed, the common refrain that he needed to stop living in a fantasy world, but it was cut short by an unfamiliar voice, distorted by static, that he instantly recognized as his father's saying, "Yeah?"

"Hi. It's Vance."

There was no response from the other end for a good ten seconds or so. Vance was about to ring the buzzer again when the call box crackled on, but no one spoke. Through the crackling static, the ambient sound of a room emerged: a faint rumor of music and a distant, ghostly voice speaking unintelligibly. "Hold on," said the voice, finally. Ten seconds later, the door opened and his father emerged.

Vance looked down at him from an acute angle. Steve Allerby was five feet seven inches on a very good day, and this was not a very good day. The last time they had seen each other, six years earlier, Vance was already helplessly shooting up past him. Steve had always worn his thick hair longish and gelled up in a rockabilly helmet to make up ground—a precious extra half inch—and he still did; though the hair had gone a bit grayer, it was no less thick, and from Vance's vantage the lustrous whorl on the crown looked like a Doppler 5000 hurricane image.

They looked nothing alike. It was not, as they say, like looking in a mirror. Even facially, there were no similarities—where Vance was long, angular, Ichabodian, Steve had the bunched-up, pug features of a child star. It was the kind of face that people had found hard to resist punching a lot over the years, which had lent it some much-needed character and asymmetry. His nose had been broken in two places in a bar fight that Vance dimly remembered, in the context of being left alone in the house while his mother, phone to her ear, ran yelling out to the car. The crooked nose twitched up at him, wrinkling at the brow. Vance had spent more time than he wanted to admit looking at pictures of his father and trying to find similarities—the curve of an eye, the coiled muscle along the jawline—and finding nothing; still, he had never for a moment considered the possibility that Steve Allerby wasn't his father. After all, what woman in her right mind (and Vance's mother, for all her problems and depression and general helplessness, was very much in her right mind) would pretend that he was the father of her child when he wasn't? It wasn't as though anyone had ever looked at his father and seen dollar signs or the possibility of some kind of support or assistance, financial, emotional, or otherwise.

Looking down at the man, Vance had the curious feeling of returning to a mythologized childhood home and being shocked at the humble dimensions of the place, the drab, peeling wallpaper and the weird smell and general cruddiness. "So." His father picked at a broken bit of plastic on the call box. "How'd you find me?"

"The Internet."

"Oh, right. Huh." His father glanced up and down the street as though scanning for a prank-show camera crew or maybe wishing an initiate gang member from some rough adjacent neighborhood would drive by and shoot them both dead. He leaned against the doorway and crossed his arms, the casual tough teetering on a pair of silver-strapped motorcycle boots. A de rigueur dragon peekabooed shyly around the forearm. His father smiled unpleasantly, a reflexive and defensive baring of his small, perfectly white and straight teeth. Vance found himself looking at the teeth and wondering if they were dentures. As his father spoke, they seemed to move up and down independently of the mouth, lending him the look of a chattering ventriloquist's dummy.

"So what, you came all this way from Washington just to drop in?"

"I've been driving this guy around on a book tour. New York's the last stop."

"A book tour." His father processed this unlikely information with obvious displeasure at the number of questions and amount of conversation it prompted, then his face cleared as he settled on the superior option of ignoring it altogether. "Well, how are things?"

"Good. Can we go inside?"

"Look, Vance, you've kind of caught me off guard here."

"Well, I would've emailed or called, if I could have."

"Right. I know."

"And I was hoping I could stay here tonight." He realized, saying this, that the duffel bag he'd carried for hours had cut a deep welt into his shoulder, and he put the bag at his feet. His father looked down at it.

"What about the guy? The writer? Don't you have a hotel?"

"Not really."

"This just isn't a great time."

"One night." He heard his voice ascend into a higher, childish register, as though attempting with a half-octave leap to deny five long years of puberty and his recent deflowering.

His father sighed. "The thing is, I've got a pretty good deal going. I'm engaged to this woman, Liselle. She's got a daughter. I kind of decided to start over when I moved here, make a clean break. I care about you and your brother, and Patsy, but that was a whole 'nother life for me. One I'm not superproud of, you know? I mean, the way I used to be."

"You don't seem that different to me."

"I am." And now Steve's voice had an almost-pleading note in it. "I've got a good job, restoring old cars. That's mine over there." He pointed across the street, at some car from the fifties or sixties that looked like it had done time ferrying cuff-jeaned, brush-cut boys and poodle-skirted girls to sock hops and soda fountains. It sat there, contented and fat, new cream-and-white paint job gleaming under sodium-vapor lights that had clicked on in the twilight. "I've settled down. I go to PTA meetings, for Christ's sake."

"So what you're saying is they don't know about us."

"Well, no, not exactly. It was just so much easier to start over, you know? Start fresh."

"So I can't stay here."

"Well. No." A woman wearing large headphones walked by with her dog, a swaybacked German shepherd, which turned to look at Vance and Steve, as though detecting the curious tension between them, then snapped its head forward again, embarrassed and pretending not to have seen anything.

Vance said, "I need to use the bathroom."

"What?"

"I've got to use the bathroom before I leave."

"Oh." Steve awkwardly opened the door and said, "Look, I'm really sorry about this, but would you mind if I said you were from work? From the garage?"

"Sure." Vance followed him up the long, rackety stairway to an apartment on the fourth floor down a short hall. He knew, in a sense, what he was doing was juvenile. He didn't need to use the bathroom—in fact, all of the fluid felt as though it had been drained from his body, and he was made of sawdust, filings, cigarette butts. But he did want to see the apartment, and, more important, he wanted to make Steve Allerby squirm. He dropped his duffel bag outside, by a small pile of wooden molding next to the door, and they entered.

"This is Vance," announced Steve, too loud. "He works with me at Paulson's."

A large dark woman with long hair in tiny multicolored braids looked over at them from the open kitchen, where she stirred something on the stovetop. The apartment was small and completely suffused by the cooking odor—something rich and spicy that Vance felt sure he'd never smelled or eaten before. She said, "You hungry, Lance?"

He had eaten a limp hot dog hours ago, and at this point his stomach had cramped up like a poisoned spider, clutching itself. Nonetheless, the look on Steve's face was enough to formulate his response for him. "No," he said, "I just need to use the bathroom, if that's okay?"

"Oh, sure. Right down the hall there."

He walked a few paces across the room to the first door in the hall, and as he did, he was passed by his half stepsister, or whatever she was. He guessed it didn't matter, since they would never know each other. She was around twelve, with pretty dark eyes staring confused at his mumbled apology and abashed profile slipping into the bathroom. He heard her ask who that was and receive some kind of response from his father, her father. He sat on the toilet with his pants on, head in hands, but the sawdust man couldn't cry. A circular piece of embroidery on the wall next to the cramped shower read BLESS THIS HOME AND ALL THOSE WHO ENTER IT. He knew it came from a kit—some little prefab thing you buy at Michaels or Walmart—because his mother had made a similar one that still hung in the upstairs hall. He tried to remember what it was, word for word: THIS IS THE DAY THAT THE LORD HAS MADE; LET US REJOICE AND BE GLAD IN IT! It was easy to remember the quote because of the horrible comic dissonance that always occurred seeing her withered form in bed seconds later.

Rejoice and be glad, he thought. He got up, flushed the empty toilet, and splashed water on his face. Back in the living room he took in the tableau for posterity: the living and dining room all one space, demarcated by a worn green runner that extended from the door to the middle of the room; Liselle in the kitchen to his right, humming to herself; the nameless girl splayed on a floral-print sofa reading a Harry Potter hardback, studiously ignoring his presence; Steve Allerby seated in a wooden dining room chair, his legs crossed and hands knitted in a worried arabesque on the table. Vance considered announcing to Liselle and the girl who he was, but the urge passed as soon as it arrived. Why upset them, why introduce doubt into their lives? He didn't know what they thought Steve had been in his younger years—a trucker or deep-sea fisherman, a rodeo clown or astronaut—but why disabuse them? To get at his father, of course, but that wasn't good enough, and it wouldn't satisfy him anyway, he knew. "Thanks," he said. "See you tomorrow."

"What?" said Steve.

"At work. Nice to meet you all." Then he was grabbing his bag, moving down the stairs and back out onto the street. He hailed a cab, told the driver where to, and rested his head on the greasy black vinyl. He was more tired than he could remember ever being, far too tired to walk back. And where the city's life before had felt transformative, it was now merely assaultive. Here, a gaggle of teenage girls in sequined jeans; there, a man with a blaring boom box taped to the handlebars of his Schwinn—everywhere, the incessant noise and color and motion of the city blurred past his window. There was too much desire elbowing for space in the narrow storefronts, too many stories in the anorexic apartments stacked higher and higher. His stomach spasmed, queasy with its own hunger, and he closed his eyes for the rest of the journey in a half-sleep, listening to the tinny chitter of the driver's Bluetooth, the insectile ticking of the meter.

———

Earlier that afternoon, Richard sat at a bar table in the Four Seasons lounge, waiting for his wife to arrive. His ex-wife. For the first time in his adult life, he'd ordered "Just a water." An unrestrained ripple of loathing lapped across the broad lake of the bartender's face, and Richard didn't blame him. He hated people who drank water. But he hadn't seen Eileen in nearly a decade and didn't intend to confirm all of her correct assumptions about him.

He wasn't sure why she'd chosen the Four Seasons. Perhaps it was close to where she lived now, though he'd thought she was living in Brooklyn. Maybe she liked the view—through the tall rectangular windows, a tiny jade slice of Central Park's southeastern edge was visible. It couldn't have been that she liked the bar, a cavernous space decorated in an anonymous pseudo-deco style more Sheraton lounge than Algonquin Hotel. Tall puce vases against the far wall contained enormous plastic palm fronds, an unnatural green that nonetheless provided a visual break from the rectilinear earth tones. Two or three of the other tables were occupied, by businessmen and businesswomen with a distinct conventioneer air about them, all false bonhomie and strained laughter. The room's corporate blandness might have prevented him from having thoughts of romance, if he'd had thoughts like that, which he didn't. He wasn't sure what he really thought, or even how he felt, about the meeting, but the hot sweat luxuriously bathing his armpits provided a clue.

He looked down at the menu, and then someone was standing next to him—a woman. Her. "Hi, Richard," Eileen said, draping her coat over the back of the chair.

"Hey. It's good to see you."

"It's good to see you, too."

Her face didn't convey the sense that it was good to see him, exactly. Interesting to see him, possibly, or amusing or strange. Good, no. She half smiled as he awkwardly rose and embraced her across the back of his chair. She went to the bar and returned with a sweating glass of white wine. He now wished that, instead of just a water, he'd ordered a real drink—say, an octuple Manhattan served in an ale tankard. She nodded at the menu in front of him. "Anything look good?"

He read from the menu in the most facetious voice he could muster. "Oh, everything. I'm trying to *choose from an assortment of delectable light fare such as Kobe beef sliders and tuna sashimi.*"

"How are you," she said.

"I don't know," he said, putting down the menu. "Terrible, I guess. How are you?"

"Good," she said, and this time the word seemed sincere. She wore a gray pencil skirt and a thin, black cashmere sweater with a small string of pearls strung across the open V of her expressive throat. It was tanned and freckled and taut, and if there had been work done to it, it had been good work. Her lipstick matched the vases behind her. Again, he found himself thinking how radically differently time had treated them. Time was like a whimsically cruel father that had lavished gifts upon his daughter and taken his despised son behind the woodshed for daily beatings.

"I know," he said. "I'm fat now."

"You were always fat."

"Not like this. I don't know what happened. Well, besides sitting on my ass and eating garbage for a decade. Anyway, you look beautiful. How are things?"

"Good. Things are good. I mean, there's the usual departmental squabbles and politicking, but work's good. I'm publishing a new book next year." She sipped her wine. "And Molly and I are engaged."

The expectant air was unmistakable, and he obliged. "Excuse me?"

"Molly, my partner."

"Your partner? Are you ranch hands?" Eileen stared at him. "She's a woman?"

"Last I checked, yes."

"What. When did this happen?"

"When did what happen? When did I become a lesbian? I'm not."

"You're getting married to a woman, but you're not a lesbian."

"It's not an unusual position these days, Richard. A lot of people find those cultural boxes stifling."

"It sounds like you don't find her cultural box too stifling."

She began to push up from the table, but he put his hand on her hand and she sat, warily. "Sorry, I'm sorry. This is just surprising. Cut me a break." The table of business folk were looking over and talking under their collective breath. "How long have you been with her?"

"Eight years."

"Wow. I didn't know."

"Why would you know? It's none of your business."

"You're right," he said, and slowly withdrew his hand from hers; swollen by food and booze and age, it looked like a catcher's mitt next to the thin lines of her fingers, the fine, dignified ridges of her knuckles. Eight years. They had been together for ten—at the time of their divorce, it had been almost a full third of his life, the main portion of his adulthood. At this point, he'd already lived in the desert for eight. It was funny—though not at all humorous—how as you had increasingly less time remaining, your sense of time expanded; it seemed like it should be the other way, that increasing proximity to death should heighten your sense of urgency, but it didn't work like that. You became lulled by the unscrolling of your own life. "Congratulations."

"Thanks. Why am I here?" she said. She twisted the stem of her wineglass between her fingers and seemed poised to spring from her chair at any moment.

"I'm sorry," he said, with more conviction this time, simultaneously realizing it was really true and feeling surprised by that fact. The feeling of not meaning the words as he said them was much more familiar. "Have you heard from Cindy?"

"She called me yesterday."

"Really?"

"Yes, from Denver. She sounded happier than she has in years. I don't know exactly what you said to her, or what happened, but whatever it was really seems to have helped. She said she's making a fresh start."

"Yeah, I guess she is." He pulled Cindy's goodbye letter out of his jacket pocket and smoothed the Hampton Inn stationery on the table. Eileen leaned forward and read it and looked up.

"Wow."

He'd decided beforehand against telling her about the money. It would only worry her, and he'd done enough of that over the years. He said, "I wasn't sure why I wanted to meet, when I called you months ago. But I guess this is why, basically. I know we're twenty years past that, and it's completely meaningless at this point, but I am sorry. I'm sorry for how things went with us, and I'm sorry I didn't do better."

She looked at him, clearly unsure of what she was meant to say. He knew she wanted to say it was okay, but he also knew it wasn't and she couldn't say so. She looked past his shoulder, and he looked where she was looking, at the thin green wedge of Central Park. A blindered horse cantered around in a circle, the cop on its back talking to another mountie. "Well," she said, "it was a long time ago, and we both made mistakes."

"It wasn't that long ago. And you didn't."

"Of course I did. I dropped every ball in the book with Cindy. I still can't believe I couldn't get her to go to college, it's disgraceful. I make things up when my colleagues talk about their little Rhodes scholars."

"You were there, though."

Eileen looked away from the window, at him, at his quivering bulk, at his fat cartoon hands, vibrating in his lap, clutching an ethereal drink. "Yes, that's true. I was there." She glanced again at the letter and exhaled. "But still, this is a little much."

"I disagree."

"What happened between the two of you?"

"Had enough of me, I guess. A little goes a long way." This was an old line between them, and he hated himself for recycling it, but he was just about out of new ones. He would have to make do with the old chestnuts, like the *really* old guy who used to shamble into the Tamarack, order a Jack and Coke, and tell the same story every time, about how he used to own a little cabin up in Caugerties, New York, right next to Big Pink, and how he one time saw Dylan walking around in his tighty-whities. *Must have gotten locked out*—Richard would grimly deliver the punch line along with him.

But Eileen was gracious and smiled, cocking her head to the side as she did, and the full vision of her as she'd been when they met returned to him in an instant and with surprising force. She was beautiful now, yes, but my God, he thought, she had been incomparable. Long legs tapering into the thinnest ankles, like a fawn standing doubtful in a clearing, though she'd never been in doubt a moment of her life. In his mind, the image of her vibrated with the nervous shiver of youth and potential. He could see her, some forgotten Sunday afternoon, lying on their sofa with a book, and the sunlight through their small apartment windows gleaming so bright off her copper hair, it was as though it radiated from her person. The bartender rattled ice in a shaker, and that time was all gone. But even after the emotional impact dissipated, a ghostly afterimage seemed to remain, an aura that surrounded her.

"Richard," she said, and this time put her hand on his. He dumped the silverware out of a cloth napkin and pressed it for a moment to his face. Then he was clambering to his feet, bumping the table, sloshing wine over the lip of the glass, slipping his meathook from her grasp. How he'd missed her.

"Hold on," she said.

"I'm sorry," he said, his voice gone soft and froggy. "I'm late for a thing. Maybe I'll see you tomorrow."

She was saying something else behind him, but he was already in midscuttle, moving out of the misty, smudged room, down the red center line of the gray carpeting that led past a bank of elevators and into the domed lobby. As he passed through, a concierge with linebacker shoulder pads swiveled at his station with a bemused expression, like a robot attempting to fathom human emotion. Richard pushed through heavy doors out into heavy city twilight. The surrounding buildings seemed to huddle together and whisper as they looked down appraisingly at the frail figure escaping from the hotel.

He felt simultaneously both very old and very young. He knew almost nothing, but he knew almost everything he was ever going to know. *Why does baby cry? Baby is too old to cry!* He raised his hand for a cab, for the moment the entire weight of all his unappeasable desire trained on getting the hell away from East Fifty-Seventh Street.

———

He sat in the hotel drinking and watching TV. Alcohol and TV: in times of need it was good to have these staunch, reliable companions, stalwart allies who would never lead him astray. Someone knocked on the door. He opened it, and Vance stood there.

"Okay," said Richard, finally. "I'll bite. What are you doing here?"

"I decided to look up my dad."

"How did you find me?"

"I had your itinerary in my email. Can I come in? Do you mind if I stay tonight? I'm driving back tomorrow."

"Of course."

For some reason, this answer provoked a quiet fit of sobbing. Vance collapsed on the edge of the bed, and his shoulders slumped forward even farther, something Richard wouldn't have thought anatomically possible. He muted the TV and sat beside the boy, experimentally putting his arm around him, then stopped doing that. He took a long draw of whatever the rotgut was he'd gotten from the liquor store down the block, manned by a babushkaed babushka who spoke nary a word of English and who furthermore didn't even seem to understand Pointingese. In the end, he'd wound up gratefully accepting whatever the plastic bottle was her pink, wavering hand eventually settled on. He said, "I tell you about when I was a kid, what my first job was?"

"No."

"It was tarring roads around Maryville. These country roads would get torn up, or else some rich redneck retiree would get sick of driving down gravel, scratching up his Corvette, and bribe a buddy on the zoning board. Anyway, it would be eight hours of walking behind this truck that sprayed smoking hot tar out of its asshole, spreading it around nice and even, throwing hay on top of it to cool it down faster. You ever seen *Cool Hand Luke*? Don't say no."

"No."

"Well, anyway, there's a scene in that movie where a prison gang tars a road, and it's as bad as they make it look. Maybe worse. And the foreman was this fucking prick named Vallon Faire—I'll never forget that name as long as I live. Vallon Faire. He was this skinny guy with big cheekbones and bulging eyes, like something in his face was trying to get out. No matter how hard or fast we worked, it wasn't fast enough. He'd walk alongside us yelling, checking for lumps and bubbles in the tar, criticizing our technique. This is in the middle of summer—this was the summer vacation my father had planned for me.

"So one day, I was on lunch break. We'd been working alongside this ridge that sloped down into a meadow. The meadow was filled with all these summer wildflowers I don't know the names of, but these little yellow and blue flowers. And past that, there was this little stream. The whole thing looked like a postcard, and there we were, the crew, sitting alongside this reeking stretch of hell, eating our bologna sandwiches. I kept looking at this field down below us, and before I knew it, I was scooting down into it sideways, walking through the flowers.

"I hadn't realized just how bad the tar smelled, or how hot it was, until I got away from it. The wind picked up now and then and brought the smell of tar wafting into the meadow as a reminder. I lay down in that beautiful field, and all I could think about was how much I didn't want to go back. I fell asleep. Then I heard Vallon Faire yelling, 'Break time is over, you lazy son of a bitch.' So I started up the incline, to where this carpet of white flowers thinned out. The smell of tar hit me full-force just as Vallon became visible over the ridge, his face bulging down at me. So I turned right around and walked back into the meadow. I expected him to be yelling, but there was no sound; the crew had already moved off down the road. I went and followed the stream for a while and found this spot deep enough to take my clothes off and sit in, cool off.

"Later, when I got home, my father whipped my ass for quitting, but it was worth it. It would have been worth ten whippings. I've regretted lots of things in my life, but I never once regretted walking away from that job. I guess my point is never forget that quitting is an option. Quitting is underrated."

Receiving no response, he turned to find Vance sitting asleep. His long chin was tucked into his collar, and a filament of drool extended from his upper lip all the way down to a tiny dark spot on his corduroyed knee. "Right," Richard said, "that's the spirit."

He gently leaned the kid back, put a thin pillow under his head, and covered him from either side with the comforter on which he lay. The kid's feet remained planted at the foot of the bed, but Richard didn't want to wake him. He put on his old Carhartt jacket, grabbed his brown paper bag, and slipped out of the room, inching the door closed until the latch slotted with an almost-imperceptible snick. In the lobby, the same old man as when he'd arrived sat fast asleep, reclined and snoring quietly in one of the lobby's worn cream armchairs. Richard envied him, whoever he was—he seemed to float outside time, outside worry and strife, in a river of his own happy oblivion.

The night outside was either warmer than Richard had thought it would be or he was drunker than he thought he was, or both, and he took off the jacket, tucking it under his arm. But he felt clearheaded as he bobbed along—more clearheaded than he'd felt the entire tour or, for that matter, for years. With a peaceable, numb equanimity, he took in his surroundings as he walked. Hell's Kitchen sounded like an intriguing area, but it didn't live up to the name. The hotel was located next to a deserted glass building that advertised AMENITY-RICH LUXURY RENTALS! The several blocks on either side described a bland zone of warehouse space, green glass, and tasteful beige apartment towers, enlivened by the occasional Duane Reade drugstore. Skyscrapers in the distance confirmed that he was located somewhere in the vast cityscape, but the immediate area could have been anywhere else in the world.

He moved slowly through the convention-center-centric, parking-deck-bedecked, warehouse-housing limbo of west Manhattan. Two older men, around his age, walked by holding hands, and he not only had nothing shitty and knee-jerk to say about them in his head but found himself obscurely moved. The grayer of the two limped and leaned against the other. They were dressed up, maybe returning from a play or party, and bescarved against the chill. The chill—Richard felt it now, as they drew near—a thin wind slicing off the Hudson. The younger man nodded at him as they passed. This world, he thought, how fine it is, how lovely, let it go on and on and on; then he thought that if he needed a sign of his impending dotage, being moved right to the verge of tears by a pair of old queens would probably do the trick.

Farther west, the wind blew harder, oily and lugubrious. He put his jacket back on. This was life: you were too hot and took your jacket off, then you were too cold and put it back on. Past Twelfth Avenue's retaining wall, small ships bobbed in the water. As he watched them, he realized he had decided to end things.

He continued walking north, the black rushing void of the river a cataract in his left eye. A small park appeared unexpectedly at the end of the block, catty-corner across a narrow cobblestoned street. He tripped twice crossing the road but persevered, strangely drawn to this little plot of green shadows. The path into the park was lined with streetlamps, solicitously curved at the top, as though in polite deference to his arrival. In the distance, a strange figure that he couldn't make out interposed itself on the path. As he moved closer, he saw it was a man, a man standing stock-still and brandishing something at him. A knife? A gun? Richard moved toward the man, unafraid, thinking maybe this is it. It.

It wasn't It. It was—according to its plaque—a bronze statue of the jazz legend Bix Beiderbecke. Bix wielded his trumpet like a weapon, holding it upside down, pointing the reproachful mouthpiece out at the city that adopted then killed him. Richard sat for a while on Bix's cement plinth, pulling from his brown bag and resting his legs before the return journey to the hotel. No such luck, he thought—no one's going to do this for you.

CHAPTER EIGHTEEN

I sat behind that wall, in the shadows, until the first light of dawn lit the plaza like a gray pail of dirty water thrown into the street. The rising sun was obscured behind the army building, still hidden behind its gated sprawl. I kept thinking about Berlinger, whether he would approve of what I was doing. On that subject, what was I doing? Had I really planned on finding Endicott and killing him? The whole thing seemed ludicrous, like the plot from a film I'd seen long ago and copied, this climactic act of dumb valor that would bring order to things. But seen in daylight, it was impossible.

I put the gun back in my pack, stood, and stretched, every muscle in my body twanging with fatigue. My mind was completely blank— what to do next was utterly unfathomable. Turning myself in to the guards was the obvious and easiest choice, but some part of me resisted. It would be too easy, and everything would be for nothing. Fueled by a few dim embers of righteous anger, and by a very real need for food and water, I crept through the rear of the ruined building.

Doglegging right down the nearest street, I immediately saw the mistake I'd made. The street curved inward toward the army building, and driving directly toward me down the cobblestones was a jeep. I scanned for side streets, for any kind of cover, but there was nothing, nothing to do but keep walking, head up. Just a soldier out on forty-eight hours' furlough—a bit dirty, true, disheveled after a

long night, but otherwise unremarkable. The jeep stopped alongside
the building, and the passenger door opened. Endicott got out.

For a second, we stared at each other in a kind of pure, primal
embarrassment. He took in my appearance: the Dolphins shirt, the
dirt and muck on me, wild white eyes blinking in the light. He said,
"Lazar?"

"Hello, sir," I said. I could feel the corners of my mouth draw back
in a grinning rictus of shit-eating guilt. "I came looking for you."

"Okay, well. You found me." He glanced at the guy driving the jeep,
then over at the distant MACV guards. "Why don't you come inside
with us?"

"Where?"

"Into admin. We'll get you set up."

The jeep's driver watched us with a curious expression. He
wore a white cotton shirt, and sweat beaded his fat face like tiny,
ornamental jewels. In one motion, I slung my bag sidewise across my
chest and stuck my hand into the opening.

"I came to see you, sir. I have something for you, sir."

"Drop it." He fumbled for his sidearm, but it was too late. The look
on his face was, I only realized in that instant, the look I'd come here
for: fear, yes, but not just fear—his face seemed to sag inward as he
capitulated to the fact of his own death and, furthermore, the strange
truth that I would be the one who killed him.

I pulled out Berlinger's wooden figurine and held it in front of
me. Endicott's pistol was halfway drawn, and he held it at his waist
in a pose of uncertain violence. For a moment, I saw him raise it
regardless, pull the trigger, a flash of light, nothing. The other man
got out of the car and said, "Chris? What is this?"

"Go around front and get a guard, would you?" he said.

The fat man disappeared around the front of the building. I still
held the trembling figurine in both hands. With bashful hesitation,
Endicott took it from me. He turned it over a couple of times and
looked up. "I don't understand."

Without looking, I turned and ran. I ran back into the corkscrew
maze through which I'd come the night before. Looking back once,

I saw what might have been Endicott and one of the guards, their mouths open in hoarse pursuit. Taxis hurtled by. Two young girls— out far too early or far too late—stood in an alcove sharing a cupped cigarette. Distant voices called, American in their flat, drawling vowels, but the sound faded to nothing as I zagged randomly down every side street I could take. A thin crowd surrounded me, the last stragglers of a red-light district in the horrible white glare of day. I ducked into the closest place that seemed open, a tin-sided warehouse that still bustled with voices and transactional chaos.

The place was crowded near the bar, but it was empty where the tables were. I ordered a small bottle of Suntory cognac, the only zip liquor whose name I knew, from an exhausted-looking waitress. She brought me the bottle, and I sank into the chair, black plastic covered in condensation. On the wall to the side of me, an old print of The Wild One *flickered and jumped. The projector was powered by a generator with an alternating putter and roar, like one of the old British motorcycles on-screen. The film itself was silent. Marlon Brando pulled into frame and stared wistfully in the direction of the exit, as though he wanted to get the hell out of there. I couldn't blame him. It was already getting hot outside, and it was hotter inside, thanks to the lack of air circulation and air-conditioning, and the combined body heat of the thirty or so hookers and johns going about their business at the bar in the rear of the place. Every inch of my body was slick with sweat, including parts of my body I never knew had sweat glands: the soles of my feet, my elbows, teeth, eyeballs. I nodded off and woke up minutes, hours, later. It hadn't been that long—Brando was still up there, brooding hugely. I sat there and drank and gradually noticed a voice coming from over my left shoulder. I realized I'd been hearing it for a while without registering it. The voice seemed to have followed me out of sleep. It was faint but familiar, and I strained to hear it over the shouts of the johns and the whirring clack of the projector.*

It was Berlinger. At first I thought he was at the bar, talking loudly to the bartender, probably fucking with him, but when I turned he wasn't there. When I turned back to the movie, his voice became

louder, and after this happened a couple of times, I realized that it
was like with those floater things that you can't look at directly or
they disappear. He was there in the periphery, in a space in between
here and somewhere else. When I turned halfway with my head just
so, I could see him sitting there behind me, elbows on knees, big
shoulders hunched in anticipation of vicious fun waiting to be had.
I turned back and watched the movie, and his voice behind me got
louder and louder.

"What the fuck are you doing here," he said.

"Watching a movie."

"Don't be cute, Lazar."

"I'm not. It's The Wild One." *The close-up of Brando's face was*
geological. You half expected a tiny eagle to go flying past the twin
orbits of his eyes, the lunar caverns of his cheekbones.

"You're fucking up is what you're doing. How'd you find me?"

"You found me."

"Same difference."

"I don't know what to do."

"You think I did?"

"Did?"

"I'm dead, you know that."

"I'm sorry. What's it like?"

"Not that bad. You think it's going to hurt, but by the time you
realize what's happened, it's over. You just have to lie there for a little
while and cry, boo-hoo. Easy-peasy."

"What happened?"

"Some NVA irregular shot the truck with a homemade mortar from
three hundred feet. Lucky fucking shot. I went all the way from the
back through the windshield, stung like a son of a bitch. One time
in Manhattan when I was a kid, I climbed up this cedar tree by my
elementary school and accidentally pulled down a hornets' nest. Like
that, but not as bad, really."

"What do I do now?"

"I'll tell you what you don't do, don't fucking desert and hitchhike
all the way to Saigon to ambush your CO, and then hand him a

fucking figurine." He laughed, that barrelly laugh I remembered from when we first got to base camp in Bao Loc. He laughed and laughed, and laughed more. *"Oh my God."* He sighed, finally, with pleasure. *"That was a good one."*

I was crying. He said, *"Hey, Lazar. Come on, take it easy. What's the matter?"*

"I'm sorry."

"What for?"

"I should have killed him."

"Why, to prove a point? Look where that got me."

On the wall beside me, Brando swung at a cop; from the back of the room, by the bar, a bottle shattered with a pop, and someone yelled. It was as though the spirit world was invading the real one, or vice versa. *"I think I'm going crazy."*

"You think?"

"I'm sorry," I said again.

"Stop apologizing to me, Goddamn it. Do you even know what you're sorry for? You think you got me killed? I got myself killed, dummy." In my peripheral vision, I saw the corners of his mouth turn up in a cruel smile. *"You're not responsible for that, you Tennessee shit donkey. You'll be lucky if you're ever responsible for anything your whole life."*

I turned the bottle up until the bottom was dry and clear against the light of the movie screen. *"I don't know what to do."*

"I tell you what to do, that's why I'm here. You listening?"

"Yeah."

"Go back and tell them exactly what happened. Tell them you got drafted and were afraid for your life. Tell them you ambushed some VC and some villagers, too. Tell them you held me prisoner. Tell them how I died and you felt guilty as hell and ran away to Saigon and wound up hiding outside army headquarters, and how you gave Endicott a wooden soldier. Tell them you got chased and wound up in a brothel bar talking to my ghost and that I sent you back. Tell them exactly that. It's perfect, don't change a thing."

———

The memoir closed in Vance's hands with a little puff that emulated the sigh of content melancholy he felt upon finishing a book he liked. Ideally, he thought, the pleasure of completion should be exactly equaled by the pain of parting company with someone whose company you enjoyed. Another kind of pain, the real kind, coursed through his sprawled body—after nearly twenty-four hours of sleep, his joints felt like they'd been arc-welded together. He put the book down on the nightstand and moved stiffly to the window, where he braced himself and arched his wooden back, staring down five floors at the city street. It was time to go to the reading, but he didn't want to go back out there.

He called his mother. "Hello?"

"Hi, Mom."

"Where are you?"

"New York."

"Wow. Are you having fun?" She sounded incredibly distant, like she was talking into a satellite phone on the deck of some weather-blasted explorer ship in the Arctic.

"I went and saw Dad yesterday."

"What? How?"

"I found him online. It wasn't hard."

There was a pause on the other end. "And?"

"He's fine."

"What's he doing?"

"Nothing. Restoring old cars. Seems good."

"Are you staying with him?"

"No, I already had a hotel. Just wanted to see how he was doing."

"And he seemed like he was doing good?"

"Yeah." He stared out the window, thinking about which direction was east, thinking about his father's hair, the whorl in it like weather. The woman had seemed very nice. *Bless this home and all who enter it. This is the day that the Lord has made.* "He seems really good. He says hello. I have to go, Mom, there's a thing in thirty minutes."

He hung up and got dressed. The young Richard on the book's cover peered stupidly up at him, and for the thousandth time he tried and failed to square the boy with the man. But it was impossible—too many years, and too much damage, had come between. What unrecognizable version of himself lurked in his own future? Catching a glimpse of himself in the mirror, the idea of someday being a completely different person wasn't the worst thought.

———

The reading area at Argosy Booksellers was on the third story, a newly renovated room with polished hardwood floors and a small podium set in the corner in front of rows of leather-bound volumes of—at a glance—Thackeray, Austen, Stendhal, Diderot, Cervantes, both Jameses. It was hard to tell if this was for ironic effect or not, since an upcoming events placard featured a celebrity chef and a NASCAR driver who'd written a children's book. For the last hour, Richard had been standing at Stan's side, near the stage, shaking hands with various fans and well-wishers. He stood there and said things, and whoever was standing in front of him laughed and nodded. Fortified by the drinks he'd had earlier in the dark little bar next door, he felt better or at least capable of functioning more or less as he was expected to; the panic that had been nipping at his heels all day had been beaten back and sat snarling at a safe distance.

He'd finally met Dana, his publicist, even larger and more voluble in person. When they shook hands, she'd taken a quick whiff of his breath. Also his editor, Kathleen: a very nice, very thin woman in a black pencil skirt, who embraced him like a long-lost relative. She said how happy she was for him, how well the book was doing, how proud everyone at Black Swan was. She said they were starting a promotional push for various awards, two of which he'd heard of. It was all very nice indeed, and he really did wish his attention wasn't mostly focused on the window behind her and his intense urge to jump through it.

She brought him out of his daze by asking, "What are you going to read?"

"What do you think?"

"You should do the ambush scene."

"I thought maybe a short story."

"No, you have to read from the memoir. No question."

Then the bookstore functionary he'd been introduced to was at the mic, making a gushy, overlong introduction, and then everyone was looking at him, and Kathleen patted his arm, and he shouldered his way through the crowd to the stage. It was standing room only, and as he reached the podium, the crowd in front of him looked like one organism, a creature with a hundred heads. He pulled the novel out of its Kinko's box, set it on the podium, cleared his throat, and read:

I am alone. We all are, children of the universe, all. We come from dead stars and are destined to return to them . . .

He read Vance's novel for ten long minutes, despite the increasingly loud murmur of dissent that filled the room. When he was finished, to a smattering of confused applause, he put the pages down and stared out at the crowd, which stared back at him. He picked out Eileen in the back of the room, her brow furrowed and lips pursed in an effort not to laugh. A voice rang out in the middle of the crowd.

"Why don't you read your own book?" Although Richard couldn't see the acne-ridden forehead or the Adam's apple bobbing up and down like a fishing lure, he recognized the grinding, adenoidal tone.

"Hey, Vance," he said into the microphone. A relieved chuckle went through the crowd: this was clearly some sort of inside joke. "I like yours better than mine, that's why. I read the whole thing last night. It's not perfect, but it's real, at least." A cardboard stand-up of his book's cover wobbled flimsily by the entryway.

No one spoke. He pointed to the stand-up and said, "What I'm saying is, none of it happened. It's bullshit."

The words surprised him as he spoke them. How true they were and how momentarily unburdened he felt saying them. He realized just how much time and energy he'd spent telling himself that it wasn't bullshit at all or that there was enough mitigating truth in it to make it not entirely bullshit or that, if it was bullshit, it was a type of bullshit that was truer than simple truth and lots of other similar bullshit. He realized he'd spent as much time and energy, probably more, simply not thinking about it.

He was also surprised to learn that a hush falling over a crowd actually sounded that way. It was as though a physical thing—an invisible layer of some kind of heavy silt—had been dropped from the ceiling on everyone. Everyone looked at him. They were, he realized, searching for a sign in his face that it was a joke or waiting for a mitigating statement. He reflexively located Eileen again, now shaking her bent head with an incredulous look he'd seen a lot of over the years. *Just when I thought you couldn't sink any lower.* He put the manuscript back in its box and walked out into the crowd, which parted for him. He handed it to Vance and looked around at the newly individuated faces—Vance, Stan, Kathleen, an older man wearing a bomber jacket with insignias from places he'd served—then walked through them. Eileen reached for his sleeve on the way out, but he had momentum working for him, along with an intense desire to fuck right off. He spiraled down an iron staircase, ducked out the front door, and immediately doglegged back under the sidewalk scaffolding into the stygian darkness of a neighboring shithole.

"Back so soon," said the woman behind the bar without looking up from the sink full of glasses she was washing. She'd been washing them when he was there before as well—the apparent endlessness of her labor in the painted black of the room created the impression that this was a sort of purgatorial space. Maybe by the end of the night he would be chained to the bar with an eagle tearing out his liver. But no, he thought, that wasn't purgatory, and, anyway, he could do a perfectly decent job of tearing out his liver himself.

He peeled off several twenties and fanned them out in front of him. "Set me up with a bottle of Bushmills and a glass, if you would."

She wiped her hands on the rag that dangled from her front jeans pocket and bent over the bar on tattooed forearms—the left a harp and the right a bow and arrow. "What does this look like to you, the Wild West?"

She poured a glass of whiskey neat, set it in front of him, and relieved him of a bill. From the cash register, as she made change, she gestured to the outside world—the still light of late afternoon—and said, "Little early to be throwing the top away, don't you think?"

"There's nothing for me out there."

"There's nothing for you in here, either."

He drank. "At least here, there's no pretending."

"There's nothing here but pretending."

He sat there for a while pretending not to pretend. Then the door opened, and Vance stood beside him, hands on the bar, looking straight ahead in a way that, again, reminded Richard of Carole; she would sit right next to him and stare off silently, as though he couldn't have sensed her displeasure from farther than three feet away.

"You okay?" Richard said, finally.

Vance shook his head and said, "I believed in you."

"Well, there's your first mistake."

"Was it all made up?"

"No." He sipped his drink and thought about his words carefully—he didn't think he'd say it again, and he wanted to say it right. "I was drafted, and I went to Vietnam. I drove a supply truck for a few months. We mostly delivered stuff that got airlifted into Cam Ranh Bay around to smaller bases. Bao Loc was one. Food, bottled water, beer, medical supplies, ammo, maps, foot lockers, flares, radios. Canteen supplies—pots and pans and ladles, knives, colanders, potato peelers. Boxes of books for little private libraries in the officers' clubs: lots of Zane Grey and Louis L'Amour. Michener and Hemingway, maybe a little sci-fi—Heinlein was a biggie. And we sometimes delivered mail when the Army Postal Service got too busy.

"I got a general discharge in July 1971, same as in the book. But mine was for being drunk and erratic, imagine that. Unsuitable for further duty. Threw a punch at an officer in the canteen, that was the last straw. My CO liked me, or felt sorry for me, and he put me in for a general, just to get me the fuck out of there. Same as in the book, too."

The kid stared at him, waiting. He went on, "So that part of it's true, I guess. Fucking up, and not knowing if I could do the thing they were asking me to do. I was scared to death driving that truck, every time we went on delivery. I know what the fear is like. We got pretty close to being zapped one time, too, a mortar went off in the road a hundred yards in front of us. I don't know if someone was aiming for us or if it was just a random shell or if a monkey jumped on a landmine. Whatever the case, I shit my pants. Literally shit them, drove the rest of the way with shit in my pants."

"But you never fought. You weren't infantry. You didn't go to Saigon."

"No."

Vance shook his head, as if trying to clear it out, make room for a concept that was too big to fit, even though there wasn't really anything to understand. "I just don't get it."

The whiskey tasted metallic and greasy, and he signaled for another. "I'd thought about doing a memoir forever, played around with stuff. When my second marriage was breaking up, when I moved out to the desert, it felt like the right time to really dig in, tell my story. I started writing about my time there, and you know what I realized? Nothing. When I thought back to it, nothing really happened, nothing that dramatic or interesting, and what I remembered was just me. Same as always. My dumb thoughts, my little postage stamp of awareness. Nothing anyone would be interested in. Hell, I wasn't interested in it. I guess, looking back, I wished that there had been a real story, you know? Something that mattered.

"So just for fun, I started writing the version where something big, something real, did happen, like it did to lots of guys over there. Like Berlinger—he was a guy I knew from Bao Loc, this big, funny asshole, like in the book. He saw some bad shit on patrol, freaked out, and deserted. Got captured in Saigon three months later, strung out on dope, living in the back of an evangelical church. He did five years. Another guy I knew got his leg blown off. I wrote their stories. I wrote other stories I'd heard about—guys who went nuts, guys who lost friends, lost their minds, guys who had to make half-second decisions that changed their lives forever. And I got into it enough that it started feeling like it was mine, you know? When I sent it out, people assumed it was a memoir. I didn't even have to lie, I just kept my mouth shut, let them believe it happened to me."

"But it didn't."

"No," Richard said. "The only thing that ever happened to me was me."

The kid turned and walked out of the bar, into a rectangle of softening afternoon light. He paused outside for a moment, framed in the window, a still rock in the rush of people streaming by. He seemed to be making his mind up about something, or maybe he was just trying to orient himself before he started walking. Then he turned left and was gone.

The bartender came over with the bottle and put it in front of him. "Here," she said, collecting several of the bills fanned in front of him. She poured them both a shot, knocked hers back, and raised the empty glass. "To your health."

CHAPTER NINETEEN

———

You can't sleep here."

The voice was male and not particularly friendly sounding. The statement itself was demonstrably false, as Richard had been sleeping undisturbed in the back booth of the bar for what felt like a long time. Obviously you could sleep here—that someone didn't want him sleeping there was an entirely different issue. He began formulating a response to that effect, when he felt rough hands grabbing his green sports jacket, hauling him up from the bench. Anyone strong enough to lift him from a prone position would have to be terrifyingly enormous; he opened his eyes and verified this fact.

The bouncer, a bearded leviathan encased in jeans and a black Zildjian T-shirt, deposited him with gentle condescension on the sidewalk in front of the bar. Before closing the door, the man clapped his hands together as though dusting them off, a bit of gratuitous cruelty that drew a laugh from somewhere inside. Inside where? The bar had no sign, just a giant, ornate letter M stenciled on the window that Richard could barely make out in the dark. Of course, not knowing the name of the bar was the least of his concerns. He also didn't know where he was, past knowing he was somewhere in, or near, New York City. A man in a charcoal business suit with a phone to his ear skirted balletically around him without a downward glance. Richard slowly pulled himself to his feet and looked around, bleary. There were no skyscrapers here, no identifiable landmarks. A gust of wind blew a sheet of newspaper past a row of storage units next to where he stood. He imagined picking up the paper and discovering, *Twilight Zone*–style, that it was some impossibly distant date in the future.

What had happened? He wasn't sure. It felt like his brain had been replaced by a urinal cake—he was having difficulty remembering anything that happened longer than about ten seconds before. His ejection from the M Bar already had a reported quality, as though it was someone else's anecdote. Vaguer still was an earlier memory—more of a ghostly afterimage—of walking down the street drinking from a paper bag, singing, babbling to himself, getting pushed over by someone. He was just sober enough now to have a sense of how incredibly drunk he'd been, and how unbearable sobering up the rest of the way would be, if he let it come to that.

He moved slowly down the sidewalk, toward the black shard of water visible between buildings, just to have something to move toward. Like life, he thought, immediately hating himself for always having the same thoughts; his mental landscape was like the background in one of those cheap Hanna-Barbera cartoons he'd watched with Cindy when she was young and he was unemployed, in which the same five background frames—a house, a rock, a bird, a car, a dog—cycle past again and again, although in his case: pointlessness, deception, regret, and so on. The shimmering, sinister glass of a storefront momentarily reflected his image, and he thought how incredibly tired he was of this guy, this scuttling lump.

He wasn't so much tired of his defects—they were so old and familiar that, like a tattered quilt, they brought with them a certain shabby comfort—as he was tired of the splinter of his consciousness that recognized these defects yet refused to do anything about them. This, in fact, was the truly defective part, the part that knew better but didn't care, or didn't care enough, or had just given up a long time ago. The derelict mansion of his life had been built from bricks of fear and weakness, but wholesale surrender to his own worst instincts undergirded the whole rotten edifice.

The sidewalk petered out into cobblestones and a sort of open-air plaza near the river. Stumbling through it, he was dimly aware of other people doing things: walking their dogs, talking, laughing, playing music too loud, eating, drinking, sleeping. *Dimly Aware of Other People:* now there was an epitaph. A gray concrete retaining wall impeded his progress, separating him from what, despite his brain fog, he recognized as the East River. It had to be, because Manhattan glowed behind it, a smeared stadium of light. Somewhere in Brooklyn, then. The interior of a taxi flashed in his mind, but his motives for coming here were lost to him. Movement for its own sake. Escape. He threw one leg up on the wall, then leaned forward and leveraged the considerable remainder of his person up. Though he could have simply lunged or rolled his way over the side, some ridiculous part of his ego—as though there was an unridiculous part—commanded him to stand and enter the water like a man. This took some doing, but he eventually was looking down at his own feet, then farther down to the greedy froth churning at the base of the concrete wall below, garishly lit by the streetlamp overhead: plastic bottles, beer cans, used condoms, candy wrappers, dead pigeons, mud, and other stuff floated in the water, topped by a sparkling blue bacterial foam. A whirlpool of junk, like your own life.

Someone yelled, and he jumped.

CHAPTER TWENTY

———

The subway car emerged from its tunnel with an operatic shriek and slid to a halt at the platform. Wet-looking mosaic on the wall read: BLISS STREET. Bliss Street, Sunnyside. He got the joke but wasn't in the mood. He'd gotten increasingly lost on the subway over the last two hours, until he'd finally asked an off-duty MTA employee who seemed to intuit the magnitude of the mental breakdown he was about to have and personally escorted him to the correct platform. From there, he'd only gotten lost once more, before backtracking and taking the correct 7 train to Queens.

Instead of mitigating his anger, the Odyssean journey had somehow concentrated and ratified it. Bouncing around somewhere on the Lower East Side or perhaps Harlem, watching a junkie contort himself in a gymnastic display of balance, bent backward on the nod, Vance felt the righteousness of the task before him in his bones. The task was this: he was going to find his father, and he was going to fuck him up. He wasn't sure exactly how, but he figured he'd figure it out when he got to Sunnyside. The important thing was getting there, and getting there with this cold, purifying rage unmelted in his gut. He exited the train and bounded up the station's concrete steps, accompanied by a blast of warm air, like a junior demon released from hell on his first assignment in the world.

He was soon lost again. He'd thought he was walking north, and it took him five blocks to figure out the cross-street numbers were going down, not up. He pivoted and nearly knocked over a small woman carrying two armfuls of groceries but did not apologize because he was through apologizing. Behind him, he faintly heard imprecations, spat out in some closed-mouth Asian tongue. He didn't care—fuck her, fuck everybody. FUCK THE WORLD, as per his brother John's tattoo, rendered on his bicep in cheery cartoon script.

Fuck his father: though this phrase had crossed his mind at various points throughout his young life, he'd never really meant it (his brother had often said it out loud, and meant it wholeheartedly). In the back of his mind, he'd always appended a *Yes, but* . . . to any perfectly justified anger at his father's failings. Fuck his father: yes, but he was a drunk and not entirely responsible for himself; yes, but Steven's own father— Vance's long-dead grandfather—had been a famous tyrant, next to whom even Steve looked kind and circumspect; yes, but he was doing his best; yes, but his best was just not very good. As recently as yesterday he'd done it, excusing the worthless asshole for pretending he was just some kid from work. Thinking about it now—standing in that living room, dumbly nodding, playing along, as he always had, wholly complicit in his own abandonment—made him livid, made him walk a little faster past brick row houses, past a bodega advertising ten-buck burners, past three little girls in a postcard-sized patch of green playing some obscure little-girl game. He had spent his entire childhood apologizing for adults who behaved like children, bearing their inadequacy and failure as his own due. Richard's deceit and general crumminess, while not directed at him, had somehow been the last straw. He was done playing the fool.

The fourth-floor, corner apartment of the PIANO building was brightly lit, a false lighthouse in the Sea of Queens. He jammed the button for 4C and waited, but there was no response. He jammed it again, this time holding it in for ten seconds and listening for a sound from upstairs. Still nothing. He could imagine his father—itinerant handyman that he was—unscrewing the front of the buzzer box and detaching the relevant wire. It would be easy. Just for while he was in town, no more surprise drop-ins.

The stoop and façade of the adjacent apartment complex were

under construction. A passel of building supplies—rebar, some two-by-fours, and several boxes—had been left inside the gate behind the cordon. He entered the gate, ducked under the tape, and grabbed a handful of roofing shingles. One after another, he sailed them up, up, at his father's apartment. At first, they uselessly bounced off the wall or boomeranged backward into the tree behind him, but after the first few, he got the hang of it. They Frisbeed easily through the air and hit the window with a satisfying clatter. A teenage couple walked by, murmuring with trepid amusement. He felt other passersby watching him as he threw, but couldn't see them because his head was craned back. After the third or fourth hit, a window opened, and a pomaded head gleamed in the high shadows.

Twenty seconds later, Steve Allerby, wearing black track pants and a white V-neck T-shirt, slammed through the door. He didn't say anything, simply lunged forward and swiped the shingles away, scattering them against the wall with both hands. "I tried to be nice about it before," he said, "but since you can't take a hint—get the fuck out of here and don't come back."

Vance turned around and walked to where the car was parked, its cream-and-white coat gleaming like voluptuous fur. The thing sat on its whitewall tires with an air of contented self-regard, like a jungle cat licking its paws after a big meal. He climbed up on the hood, and for a moment just stood there, as shocked as his father at this development. He hadn't had any plan other than to confront Steve with the uncomfortable fact of his fatherhood, since he had spared him the night before. But this felt good, this felt right. With exploratory hesitance, he did a little impromptu jig, feeling the paint scuff and scratch under his feet. He danced more, leaping into the salty air once, twice, gratified by the look of amazed horror on his father's face. He kicked the windshield hard and was again shocked as it shattered beneath his heel. It took him a moment to free his foot from the steering wheel, and Steve was grabbing at his legs, but he extricated himself and danced away. Steve got ahold of his ankle, and Vance kicked again. His father fell backward, fresh blood lining the pursed O of his mouth like the slapdash lipstick of a little girl playing dress-up. He gazed up childishly from the sidewalk at his son. Vance danced his way up onto the roof of the car, jumped up and down a few times, and felt the metal buckle a little. He stomped on the rear window, breaking it out whole with a satisfying pop.

Through the clogged mist of his rage, he became aware a crowd had gathered, and of several people holding their phones in the air. His awareness of being photographed lent a performative quality to the destruction and a tidal urge to destroy bigger and more. He ran back to the building site, grabbed a piece of rebar, and again advanced on the car. The thing looked wrinkled and baggy, like a drunk the morning after an especially hairy night. Steve had gotten to his feet and assumed a defensive position next to the car, and he was shouting something, but Vance's ears seemed to have filled up with blood, and all he could hear was a dim echoing sound, like yelling heard from under the surface of a pool. And when his father saw the look on his face—or perhaps it was the piece of metal pipe in his hand—he reassumed his previous position on the sidewalk. In the back of the crowd stood Liselle, her hand over her mouth. Over the next two minutes, they all watched as Vance systematically beat the car to pieces. The windows, the headlights, the taillights, the side mirrors—even the radio antenna, which he bent to the ground. Having done as much damage as he could do to the exterior, he climbed back onto the hood and drove the rebar into the refurbished control panel, using it as a lever and prying out the speedometer and odometer. He was just uselessly banging the pipe off the top of the car, like a child with a tin drum, when the cops arrived. The crowd cheered. He did exactly as they said—got off the car and got down on the ground—but still the one yelled at him, still the heavy knee in his back, still they dragged him away and threw him in the car.

———

The backseat was dark, the vinyl smooth and cool. An ammoniac whiff, now and then, the stale piss of previous occupants, but it was otherwise surprisingly comfortable, and all things considered, he was enjoying the ride. The handcuffs were a bit tight, true, and his ears still rang, but it was fading and the sounds of the world—the police scanner in front, the hum of the engine—began returning.

The cop in the passenger seat, the one who had cuffed him, half turned and said, "Jesus, kid, did you ever do a number on that car. Do you know what that was?"

"No."

"Fucking 'fifty-seven Bel Air."

The cop driving said, "Oh, shut up, Jesse."

The cop looked at the cop driving and said, "Man, you know what a classic that thing is? Was."

"Eh, they're all the same to me."

"Not to me." He turned again to Vance. "Hey, next time you decide to take out some aggression, do it on a fucking K-car, huh? Do it on a Ford Escort, not a mint Bel Air, you dumb shit."

"Sorry."

He wasn't sorry—in fact, he felt very good about how the whole thing had gone and knew he would relish the memory of his father's bloody face looking up at him in terrified awe for years to come, probably forever. His feeling of self-satisfaction dwindled a bit, however, as the squad car pulled up in front of a hulking, gray institutional building. QUEENS CRIMINAL COURT AND CENTRAL BOOKING read the words embedded in the stonework by the front door, through which he was roughly escorted.

It occurred to him, at that moment, that he hadn't entirely thought through the consequences of his actions. He'd dimly known he was risking arrest and hadn't cared; that consideration had been dwarfed by the furious Goliath striding beside him. Now, as he was photographed and fingerprinted, the fury had absented itself and was replaced by fear and a large dose of regret. Not regret for destroying the car—he would never regret that. He regretted not running away from the scene of the crime when he could have. It had seemed important at the time to pry out the dashboard. As the enormity of his situation dawned on him, he also began to regret not thrashing his father with the pipe, really getting his money's worth.

His possessions were inventoried and baggied, and he was led into a holding cell, half full of the kinds of people you would expect to find in a New York City holding cell. Some obviously homeless, some probably homeless, some possible gang members, some random teenagers, most drunk and/or high on something. A couple of confused, normal-looking types that were probably DUI charges. A few of them looked up and registered the new arrival, but most didn't. He found a spot by himself in the far-right corner.

Sporadic conversations erupted in the silence, often in languages or patois or tones of voice that Vance couldn't understand. A man catty-corner to him—dreadlocked, with pitted scars on his face and eyes like smoked glass—was the most animated, periodically railing about the police, his lying bitch of a girlfriend, the condition of the cell, his mother's cooking. He was also clearly the most fucked up, and Vance willed the man not to notice him, arms between his knees, trembling in the corner. His fear, of course, attracted the man's attention in short order.

"And this one over here," he shouted to no one. "What are you in for, robbing a library?" A few cackles rang out, spurring him on. "They're gonna eat your skinny ass up in Rikers. Probably cut you into three pieces, have you for breakfast, lunch, and dinner. You hear me? I'm talking to you, scarecrow motherfucker."

Vance remained silent, head down, but his deference seemed to enrage the man. He bounded out of his seat toward Vance, fist cocked. Vance threw his hands up in an involuntary motion, and the man stopped.

"Damn," he said. "All right, all right."

Vance didn't understand, then he looked at his hands. He hadn't noticed them since being arrested. They were swollen, like miniature boxing gloves, covered in dried and half-dried blood risen from a crosshatching of small cuts and abrasions. It was the piece of rebar, he realized, from unloading on the car. His grisly hands throbbed in front of him, and the man nodded with an air of respect. He reclaimed his spot on the bench, where he grew mostly silent, occasionally muttering to himself, his chin down against his chest, as if he was speaking to something in the middle of his person.

After eighteen hours—a thousand or so minutes spent dozing in the cold corner, jerking awake in terror, then drowsing painfully back into tortured nonsleep—Vance's name was called. He was led down many halls into a cold courtroom, where he sat with some of the other men with whom he'd shared the cell. He was asked if he wanted a court-appointed attorney and he said yes. A frazzled bald man in an ill-fitting suit, clutching a clipboard like an aegis, talked to him for thirty seconds and advised him to plead not guilty. It was another two hours before the judge—a small woman with a much-more-frightening demeanor than the man in the holding cell—called his name. After watching dozens of men called before him, he knew where to stand.

"Is your name Vance Joseph Allerby?"

The experience of standing in a courtroom, in handcuffs, being asked these questions by a judge wearing a big black robe was wholly unreal. He'd only ever seen the inside of a court, and this kind of proceeding, on television and in movies; the cognitive dissonance that this could really be happening to him was so intense it made him feel distant and faint, although that may have been the nearly twenty-four hours he'd gone without food.

"Yes," he croaked out.

"Mr. Allerby, you're being charged with three counts of disturbing the peace, criminal mischief, and felony destruction of property. Mr. Carney," she turned to the public defender at Vance's side, "how does your client plead?"

"Not guilty, Your Honor."

"Bail is set at ten thousand dollars."

The bailiff wordlessly led him to an area with pay phones. He stood dumb in front of it. The situation both magnified and particularized his panicked sense of utter disorientation and helplessness. The majority of his fellow prisoners conducted themselves with the confidence and lazy efficiency of men at a job they'd held for years, decades. There was a lot of familiar banter between the jailed and jailers, and if you took the guns and uniforms away from the guards, it would have been difficult to tell the difference. The guard behind him sighed and motioned vigorously at the phone. Not knowing what else to do, Vance picked it up.

"Operator," said a female voice he was surprised to hear.

"I, uh. Hello?"

"Yes, operator," the woman said again, unmistakable irritation pulsing through the distance and static.

"I. Um, can I place a collect call?"

"Number?"

What was his mother's cell number? He didn't know. He didn't know any numbers offhand besides the old house line that he'd had to memorize as a child, so he told her that one. The line rang—miraculously, it seemed to be working. He imagined the phone, sitting on the floor by the old hutch in the living room, half buried under an avalanche of magazines. After six rings the line clicked off. He desperately attempted to remember another number, any number, but the guard was already yelling at him to put the receiver down and move on.

He was led with a group of men into another holding cell, this one without a clock on the wall. Some very long amount of time later, the door opened, and everyone in the room was put in two lines. Two guards holding guns watched as a third went down the line and shackled each man to the one next to him with handcuffs, hand and foot. He was cuffed to a small Mexican with gelled hair and delicate, pretty features. The man was nearly a foot shorter than Vance, and as they were marched down the hall, he had to hunch and walk with tiny, mincing steps to avoid jerking the man off the ground like a doll. Several times, in spite of trying not to, he yanked the little man's ankle and wrist, which elicited a muttered torrent of Spanish invective—he understood *pinche* and *culo,* but he didn't know what *joto* meant.

They shuffled outside, into the gray afternoon, where a bus waited for them in a parking lot surrounded by a fence topped with coiled barbed wire. Vance and the little man instinctively turned toward each other and edged up sideways, one foot at a time, successfully boarding the bus. They maintained this close posture—like old dance partners preparing to clasp or spring apart into synchronized ballet leaps—all the way to an empty seat. The wordless cooperation lasted until Vance was situated on the plastic bench and began to weep. His seatmate made a puffing sound and averted his gaze, staring out the window in disgust.

A swell of conversational volume on the bus roused Vance just in time for him to read the white sign they passed at the intersection. RIKERS ISLAND, with subscript that announced, oddly, HOME OF NEW YORK'S BOLDEST. He hadn't believed they'd really be going to Rikers Island, a place he'd heard used solely as a byword for terrifying and inhumane incarceration. The bus bounced over a grooved metal seam and up onto a long bridge. Gray water crashed against the retaining walls on either side. Gradually, the indistinct shape in the distance resolved itself as a cluster of parking lots, gray buildings, guard towers, all surrounded by and topped with the ever-present whorl of razor wire.

They were taken off the bus and led into the main building, unlocked from each other, and ushered single file into one of the large central cells just past the guard station. This cell was bigger than the last, but there were also more men. On the edge of the room sat a toilet that looked as though it had literally never been cleaned. It was streaked with shit and clogged in useless protest with rotting food that writhed with maggots. He swallowed the vomit that rose in his esophagus and sat against the wall on the filthy floor, careful to keep his bloody hands on full display.

Most of the men slumped exhausted on the wooden benches or on the floor. The ones who didn't were in the grip of some kind of drug withdrawal—fetal, vomiting—or in the grip of some kind of drug, scratching, pacing in tight, hostile circles. After an hour or so, a guard brought in a plastic bin filled with trays of food. The smell may have been unappealing on its own, but here it was a rare perfume that temporarily masked the stench of shit and piss and BO. Vance waited until most of the men had grabbed a tray, then took one and ate. He would previously have considered the beef stew completely—definitionally—inedible, but as he swallowed the mush and gristle, he considered how flexible a word "inedible" really was. Almost anything was edible, given lack of options. The trick was not chewing.

The stew was seawater salty, but they were given no water. Many more hours later, several guards came in and escorted the prisoners out of the intake cell into a large tiled room, where they were told to undress. The showers were turned on, spumes of freezing water that rapidly warmed up to just regular cold. Despite the temperature, Vance stood under a showerhead and drank the water, choosing not to care or think about the condition of the pipes and spigot it was traveling through. Most of the men had the same idea—although the most drugged out or drug sick hunched hydrophobic in the corners—but unlike Vance, they cupped the water in their hands to drink it. He kept his hands away from the water as best as he could, desperate for them to remain bloody.

They were strip-searched, given ill-fitting orange DOC clown pants and tunics to put on, and divided into several groups—housing units A, B, C, and D. Vance was D. An older guard with a feathery blond mustache, who looked like a gym teacher, led them to an interzone between buildings, toward what looked like an airplane hangar with a giant D on the side. They moved past a guard station to a chained-off area inside the building, where they were again searched and then gave their names to another guard carrying a clipboard. Vance's name was checked off the list, and he was ushered through a door, into the jail area proper.

It was a two-level building with a large common area on the lower level, which mostly seemed to be used for clustering in suspicious groups, wandering around in menacing circles, or doing push-ups, or just shouting incoherently. There was one main staircase, lined with green railings; from both sides muscular, shirtless men did implausible numbers of pull-ups, dangling for minutes at a time like overripe fruit. The second floor was invisible from the first. Vance asked the blond guard which cell was his—the guard laughed and said in a passable British accent, "We have you in room fifteen, sir. When would you like your supper to be served?"

At the far side of the common area, there were two telephones. Vance moved hesitantly toward them, but there was a long line against the wall. Two men toward the rear got into a minor scuffle over who had gotten there first. Lacking any better plan, Vance climbed the stairs to the second floor. At first glance, it seemed preferable, in that less of the population was upstairs, and the overall volume level was much lower. On the other hand, the still silence of the prisoners here, lolling half hidden in their cells, somehow conveyed more menace than the yelling and carrying on downstairs. Individual voices coalesced into a soft, generalized moan, a murmur that expanded and contracted like breathing. Vance walked around the large circle until he found a cell that only had one man in it, a small white man in a knit cap, taking careful notes in the margin of a book.

Vance said, "Can I stay here?"

Without looking up, the man said, "You set foot in here, I'll kill you."

Farther around the block, he found a room housing a man who seemed terribly ill, gibbering and sweating on a stained gray cot. Though the concrete floor was spattered with yellow bile, which probably explained the absence of other cellmates, Vance entered and lay down, and immediately fell asleep.

———

The next day, late in the evening, he got to use the phone. His roommate, Danny, a friendly young junkie from Staten Island, explained the process to him between bouts of dry heaving into (also at, around, and near) the disgusting stainless-steel toilet. You could make two phone calls a day, provided the phones were available. You charged the calls to your commissary account. When Vance told him he didn't have a commissary account, Danny frowned with worry, a troubling look to be receiving from a guy with crusted vomit all over the front of his shirt.

"No one knows you're in here?"

"Not yet. That's why I need to make the calls."

"Oh, man. Okay, wow."

Whimpering with sickness, lying on his side with his arms crossing his stomach, Danny told him to just use his account. His parents put money in it, he said, it wasn't even his money, he didn't deserve it. He repeated the eight-digit code several times.

"Thanks," said Vance. "Can I get you something?"

"Nah. I just gotta wait this thing out, nothing else for it. Hey, buy yourself a candy bar or something, too."

Vance made his way downstairs and took a place in the line, which didn't seem to have moved at all in twenty-four hours. And after an hour of standing in it, it still didn't seem to have moved. By the institutional white clock up on the wall, it took three and a half hours before he was in front of the guard booth, giving them Danny's commissary number. He held the phone to his ear, and his breath, after giving the operator his mother's number. This time, a man answered.

"Vance? This is your uncle Joe. What's going on?" Uncle Joe was a dubious personage who lived in Idaho and operated some sort of heavy machinery, whom they had last visited when Vance was thirteen. He remembered a fat, floridly pink-faced guy wedged into an armchair in front of the TV, so inert as to seem helpless, paralyzed by the spectacle of the World's Strongest Man competition.

"What are you doing there? I'm in jail."

"Yeah, the operator said. The fuck."

"Put Mom on."

"What the hell's going?"

"I fucked up. I'm in jail. Put Mom on."

"Vance, she's in the hospital."

"What?"

"We've been trying to get ahold of you, but your phone was off." An image flashed through his mind of the dead phone, cocooned in a plastic evidence Baggie in a bureaucratic mausoleum of former possessions.

"Is she okay?"

"No. She's having heart problems. Not enough potassium or something. They said she was severely malnourished."

"Malnourished?"

"I guess she hasn't eaten in a month or something, weighs like ninety pounds. She's hooked up to machines, under observation. Critical condition." His uncle sighed, and Vance could very clearly see him standing there in the filthy kitchen, feeling nothing at the moment besides put out. "Well, anyway, sorry. What do you want me to do for you?"

"I don't know. Post bail. They set it at ten thousand."

"Jesus H. What did you do, rob, uh, Carnegie Hall?"

"I beat a car up with a pipe."

There was a pause as Joe considered this information. "We don't have ten thousand dollars, you know that."

"I don't think you have to pay that much, just call down here and give them my name."

"How long they got you in for?"

"I don't know, I could be in here months before they even have the trial."

"I mean, maybe it would be good for you, you think of that? You can't just go around fucking cars up with a pipe."

"Tell Mom. Is she awake?"

There was another long silence at the other end. He suddenly desperately wanted to get off the phone—Danny's gracious company seemed like a tropical paradise compared with the prospect of continuing this conversation. Joe said, "I'll see what I can do," and the phone clicked off. Vance hung up the greasy chipped plastic receiver and headed back upstairs to his cell.

CHAPTER TWENTY-ONE

———

The water felt and tasted even worse than it had looked and smelled when he'd been standing far above and peering down at it. His mouth and nose were filled with a thick putrescence, bitter chemical rot, that seemed to contain every horrible thing mankind was doing to the planet. He gagged underwater, swallowed more of it, and came to the surface flailing for purchase against the concrete wall beside him. He had changed his mind, he wanted out. But there was too much accumulated slime on the wall to get a grip. Cans, cigarette packs, rotten food, sodden cardboard, and an interstitial green foam created a solid layer of scum that he disturbed with his thrashing. He went under again and came back up, his face barely breaking the surface of the water. His loathsome leather shoes, the orthopedic clodhoppers he'd bought for the tour, were like concrete blocks on his feet. He went under again and couldn't make it back up but continued to thrash ineffectively, while some corner of his mind waited impatiently for the peace and acceptance everyone said comes to drowning victims. It didn't seem to be happening—where was this goddamned fucking peace he'd heard so much about? Where was it? All he felt was an angry and terrified desire to live more and remorse at the life he'd lived, which was, thankfully, not flashing before his eyes.

Something did flash above him, however: red light and a barrage of muffled noise. It was the world—he wished it away. Having depleted his already depleted reserves of energy, he floated down into the verdant murk of the water. He seemed to watch himself there, arms and legs splayed forward in a semicircle, like some giant, mutant prawn. It was quiet now. His white hair waved back and forth in the water, and he suddenly felt an intense, fond sadness for himself. Goodbye me, I'll miss me. It surprised him that he felt this way.

———

When he woke up there was no sound, and he seemed to still be underwater. There was a woman, some kind of frantic commotion. No need to make a stink about it, he wanted to say. Someone stuck something in his arm. To his right, he thought he saw Eileen, but that couldn't be. Then the dark rolled in again, like a summer storm rushing in overhead.

———

Everything in the room was white—white bare walls, white ceiling, white sheets on the white bed on which he lay. White light streamed in from a distant skylight, which framed a small patch of white cloud. For a few moments, he couldn't shake the certainty that he'd been wrong his entire life: there was, in fact, a heaven, and moreover, heaven had taken him in. How embarrassing to discover all of those dumb Christians he'd always mocked had been completely right. And, of course, he'd been wrong about it—why should the afterlife be any different than anything else?

But slowly small, human details of the room emerged. A picture of children on the bedside table. The faint sound of music issuing from somewhere. A door to the immediate left of the bed, through which he could see a toilet and the red rubber of a plunger. These details didn't, in themselves, preclude the possibility that this was the afterlife, but taken together they imparted a much more terrestrial feel to the room.

"Hello," he shouted, but his voice was reedy and weak, and there was no reply. He lay there for another few minutes, already exhausted by consciousness, but curiosity finally got the better of fatigue. Pulling himself upright against the iron bars of the headboard, he managed to throw his left leg over the side of the bed, but he was tangled in the sheets and couldn't get the right one over. He managed to get the sheets off and saw, around his abdomen, the unmistakable puff and pucker of a diaper. This knowledge sapped whatever remaining will he might have possessed. He curled back into himself and pulled the sheets up and sank back into the snowy white of the mattress, the prison, the crib.

———

When he woke again, the room was mostly dark. The skylight was an indigo stamp on the high ceiling. He was hungry and terribly thirsty, and his diaper felt wet against his skin. Again he shouted, but this time his voice came out in a rough whisper. Again, he pulled back the covers, and spent a tremendous amount of energy getting his legs over the edge. He leveraged himself up woozily, then stood, which was a mistake. It wasn't that bad actually: the wood floor smelled of lemon polish and felt cool against the side of his face. He crawled to the door.

Outside was a small landing with a staircase leading down. "Hello," he whispered again, uselessly, and to no reply. The staircase was walled on both sides, with a door to the right at the very bottom, so it was impossible to see what waited below. Holding on to the wooden banister with both hands, he swiveled around on his ass and began working his way down, step by step. He would achieve a stair, pause and catch his breath, and attempt to summon the will to conquer the next one. He remembered the time he and Eileen watched two-year-old Cindy climb the three stairs leading up to their apartment in Fresno. Much the same as this, it had been long and arduous, a real nail-biter. Halfway down, his arms began to quiver. Two-thirds of the way down, his arms gave out and could no longer support his weight. Unable to go down or up, he straightened himself out and slid down the remaining stairs, coming to a rest at the base of the stairs in a sprawl.

When his heart had calmed to a mere hammering, he turned over and crawled through the door into an empty living room. Some kind of percussive, fluty number jazzed its way out of two tall wooden speakers that stood on opposite sides of the room like sentinels. The Oriental rugs he crawled over looked and felt as though they were from the actual Orient, and not just a store with "Oriental" in the name. With the last bit of energy at his disposal, he managed to pull himself most of the way up onto a crushed-leather sofa, on which someone had been thoughtful enough to leave a tartan wool blanket out for him. He wrapped it around himself and promptly passed out again.

————

A large person stood over him, and he was a small person, obscurely ashamed. He'd done something—it was his mother. No, it was his wife. No, that was a long time ago. The vaporous figure of Eileen finished coalescing in front of him, smoke made flesh in a tailored houndstooth blazer and black jeans. "Back from the dead. How are you feeling?"

"I need to go to the bathroom."

"I bet you already have."

"You're enjoying this."

"Oh God, no, not at all."

It took a great deal of time and energy, but she managed to get him to the bathroom, and he managed to get his diaper down and lower himself onto the toilet, which he pissed into for another long stretch of time. Drained, in all senses, he hobbled with her the ten feet or so back to the sofa. She sat down beside him and covered him back up with the afghan. He said, "What the fuck happened?"

"You fell into the East River and got pulled out by someone nearby. They said you were dead for a couple of minutes, but the paramedics revived you. It made the evening news; a friend told me what had happened. You were in New York Methodist ICU in a coma for four days, then you woke up, but they kept you asleep with drugs, so you could heal faster, I guess. That went on for a few more days, and they moved you to a regular bed, at which time I pulled some strings and got you released to home care. Some paramedics carried you up to the guest room. They'd wanted to keep you there for another week of observation, but I figured at seven thousand a day you'd prefer to stay here. I'm only charging you five."

"Thanks," he croaked.

"Were you trying to kill yourself?"

"No. Yeah, I guess. I don't know."

"Oh, Richard."

He lay back and looked up at her, feeling for all the world like a wayward child awaiting parental judgment. She stroked his plastered hair back from his forehead.

"How did all this happen?"

"I don't know." He was going to elaborate on this, then realized there was no further elaboration possible, although it was certainly necessary. He didn't know—that would have to work for now.

She thought about that for a minute, then sighed and pressed up from the sofa. "I can't get you back upstairs by myself. Maybe Molly can help me. You'll have to stay on the couch for now."

"Thanks," he said again.

"Sleep," she said, and he did.

———

The next day, with the help of the estimable Molly, a rotund person with an orotund voice, whom he immediately feared upsetting, he was reinstalled in the guest room. He slept more. Later, Eileen stood over him holding a Formica tray that supported a bowl containing canned chicken noodle soup and a stack of soda crackers, plus a small plastic pill container. She set it beside him on the bed and regarded him, then nodded at the food. "You haven't had anything solid in almost two weeks. You should eat, if you can."

"I'm not hungry."

"That doesn't matter. Here, take these and then get a little food in your stomach." She took the pillbox from the tray and emptied the contents of a compartment marked MONDAY—two large speckled horse pills and three smaller ones—into his palm. He washed them down with a swig of orange juice. She said, "I'll be back for the tray later. We're going to a movie. Don't come back downstairs, okay? Stay put."

"Okay."

She left. He ate the soup and stared at the whiteness of the wall. He was reminded of staying home from school sick when he was a kid.

His mother had always forced him to stay in bed, reasoning if he was too sick to go to school, he was too sick to walk around. She would even confiscate his books, saying he needed to rest, not read. It was a clever strategy and one that prevented him from feigning illness in all but the most dire moments of paper incompletion or test unreadiness. For a person whose being craved stimulation and distraction at almost all moments, staying in bed with nothing to do was a real kind of torture. He needed entertainment, food, TV, and alcohol. Alcohol—despite everything that had happened, the dull craving for it persisted somewhere between his spine and stomach. It was like the abusive boyfriend he kept crawling back to—*He loves me, he really does, he didn't mean to push me into the East River, you just don't see all the times he's nice to me.*

He finished the soup, lay back, and let his various cravings clamor like traders on the stock exchange floor. Gradually they quieted, and he was just lying in bed looking at dark city air through the skylight. Maybe the trick was to just allow yourself to want things. To accept the wanting without attempting to gratify it. Fighting the want did no good, because it was impossible to make yourself not want things. Furthermore, fighting the want somehow promoted it, legitimized it, made the desire for booze or women or whatever else terribly strong and potent.

He'd spent his whole life looking for consolation and had wound up unconsoled, inconsolable. Drink, food, women, TV, and sometimes writing had succeeded in distracting him, but from what, and why? The what was easy—life. The great, gentle backdrop of minor feeling and small event and day-to-day effort, victory, and failure. Why he needed relief from that, he didn't know. Because life was boring, because his brain chemistry was all wrong, because his father had been the same way he was. Because life reminded him too much of death. That was a big part of it. For decades, going back to the war—before the war—one of his main goals had been ignoring the fact of his own mortality; if it required anesthetizing himself, so much the better. And after a while, the damage he'd done to achieve this primary goal had to be ignored in its own right, which of course required more consolation, more evasions, more anesthesia. And so on.

An easier way to put it is that you're a coward.

He sprawled out on the bed, staring down at the snow-covered land-scape of his own body under the sheet. The hill of his paunch, the parallel ridgelines of his legs, the valley in between. He felt old, weak— and he didn't feel himself getting any better. Those two minutes in the poisoned water had changed him, aged him, sapped his hideous vital-ity. And maybe that was a good thing. In an increasingly thick Demerol drowse, he imagined a child tramping joyously across the snowy field in front of him. An undisturbed vista of white, every footprint a new footprint. *You can make no more footprints, for now you are the field.*

———

Molly stomped from the office to the kitchen and answered the cord-less, which was ringing for the fifteenth time this morning. Richard muted the TV as she charged into the living room, wielding the phone like a blackjack. He cringed in half-anticipation of a bludgeoning. She had tolerated his presence well enough to this point—she had been, as they say, a good sport—but after two weeks in the apartment, the strain of his presence was beginning to show in the small muscles of her jawline, bunched up with the skin pulled taut and shiny over them.

"Make it stop," she said, covering the receiver. "Talk to them, okay?" It had become clear in recent days that the press had somehow figured out where Richard was and gotten the landline number, but it was the number Molly used for her dog-care business, so turning the ringer off wasn't an option. They had agreed it would be best for him to ignore the interview requests, but they hadn't anticipated the callers' persis-tence or the journalistic interest in the story. He had made page 8 of the *Times* and page 1 of *USA Today* and the *New York Post*. Nobody really knew who he was, since nobody read anymore, but the spectacle of a quasi-known writer discrediting himself before jumping into the East River had a lurid interest disproportionate to his celebrity or lack thereof. Molly extended the phone to him. "And answer it yourself next time."

"I can't."

"Are you crippled?"

"Yeah, kind of." The physical therapist who made a house call two days ago had urged him to move around as much as possible, saying that the episode had damaged his already damaged heart and possibly also some neuromotor functions of his brain. Heart and brain damaged, he said—yes, that sounded about right; that sounded like him. Walking to the bathroom, to say nothing of actually using it, left him panting for a full minute.

"This is Richard."

"It's Stan."

"Oh."

"Who did you think it was?"

"I don't know. Someone from the *National Enquirer* or something. I was about to yell 'Fuck off.'"

"That's my line."

"I know, I know. Listen, I'm sorry about all this. I was going to call."

"Were you?"

"I almost died, maybe you heard."

"You didn't quite kill yourself, but you finished off your career. I'm calling to say good luck. Maybe someone else will be stupid enough to touch you, take advantage of the little bit of publicity. But that's not me."

"I'm done anyway. There's nothing left."

"You made me look like a fool, Richard."

"I know. I'm sorry." That was all he did these days, apologize. "Hello?"

The line was dead, and that was that.

————

The phone rang, and he answered it. Over the last few days, he had been talking to anyone who called—reporters, wire agencies, random lunatics—having decided it was better to give them a boring story that would quickly be superseded by something more interesting (literally anything else) than to continue holing up and stoking curiosity. Yes, he had misrepresented his war experience. No, he hadn't really meant to. Yes, he felt bad about it. Yes, he wanted to apologize to the infantrymen from his division. No, he hadn't meant to jump; it had been an accident. That was at least partially true. He still wasn't sure if he'd jumped or fallen, or some combination of the two. In a passing moment, you could make a decision without deciding anything, your choice made for you by the intuitive twitch of a rogue muscle or synapse. Especially after drinking for ten hours. Regardless, even if it qualified as a decision, it was one he'd regretted the instant he'd hit the water. His commitment to suicide, it turned out, had been as steadfast as his commitment to anything else in his life.

"Hello?" he said.

The voice on the other end, a bored female one, said, "Collect call from Rikers Island, do you accept?"

"Who what."

"Do you accept?"

"Uh. Sure."

There was a click, and the quality of the background static on the other end changed, from a snowy distance, to a closer thrum. A voice said, "Hello?"

"Vance?"

"Yeah." There was a muffled shout from the other end, and then the kid returned. "I'm in jail."

"You're in Rikers Island."

"Yeah. I tracked down your agent, and he gave me this number."

"What in the fuck, Vance?"

Vance told him what in the fuck. Like a car driven to empty, he finally lurched his way to a stop and finished by saying, "I didn't want to call you. But my family's not helping me. My mom's been in the hospital, and she's pretty out of it, I guess. My uncle said he'd look into it, but he hasn't done anything. I guess they don't have the money, and I figured I would try to just make it until my court date, but . . ." From somewhere on the distant end, a man yelled clearly, his voice filled with all the force and freedom of insanity.

"Why didn't you get ahold of me sooner?"

"I was mad. I'm still mad."

"You can keep being mad once your bail is posted, too, you dumb shit." Vance didn't say anything to this. Richard said, "Okay. Hold tight, I'm coming to get you. Don't go anywhere."

———

Richard and Eileen sat in the visiting room of Rikers Island. They had been sitting there for going on five hours, and due to some outraged lumbar nerve gone rogue, Richard's entire lower body was numb. He wished the same was true of his mental awareness, but his daily course of pain pills and sedatives had done little to alleviate the experience of being there. Visiting was located next to intake. It shared common air with the other room's muffled shouting, the not-so-muffled smells, a fine floating residue of grief, the ambience of human anguish on an almost-molecular level.

The bail bondsman had called around three, saying the bail had been processed and delivered, and the prisoner might be released within the hour. They had hurried into Eileen's car, not wanting to make Vance wait a second longer than necessary; he looked back on the two of them then with an attitude of fond indulgence. How foolish they were this afternoon. They might have learned their lesson from the previous twenty-four hours they'd spent waiting in the various antechambers of New York's labyrinthine justice system: precinct, bondsman, central booking, bondsman again, and finally the jail. The whole thing seemed designed to be as punitive as possible to all parties involved—not just the felon but the families and friends of the felon and even the guards and cops and lawyers and judges.

Eileen read a paper she'd brought with her, something called "Monadic Nomads: Wittgenstein and the Instantiation of Third-Party Inelectives." She was bent to it, legs crossed, somehow able to tune out their surroundings, and, in doing so, becoming a small island of sanity in a place where none existed. At the moment, she was the only thing preventing him from running outside and doing a gainer back into the cold scum of the East River. She had been a saint through the whole process, helping him at every turn, taking the day off work and driving him around and, most important, imparting a feeling of calm by the simple virtue of her adult presence.

He pointed at the paper in her lap, and said, "Little late in the year for light summer reading, isn't it?"

"Funny."

"Looks like a page-turner."

"Potentially revolutionary hermeneutics." She smiled faintly without taking her eyes off the page. It was an old joke of theirs, something she'd said seriously once and for which he'd relentlessly mocked her, without, of course, knowing what it meant. Thirty years ago, at this point. He was searching his memory for the appropriate retort in this time-worn little skit, when Vance emerged from a nearby corridor. He was wearing what he'd been wearing the last time Richard saw him—jeans and a striped button-up—and the lack of orange prison jumpsuit created a momentary cognitive dissonance, as though the kid had just happened to walk into the same room as them, on Rikers Island.

But a longer look dispelled this impression. His eyes were black hollows. He was even gaunter than he had been before. He looked like an effigy with the stuffing beaten out of it, just a pair of pants and a shirt fluttering in the breeze. His sparse facial hair had grown out into a field of even sparser wisps, completing the meth-addict Halloween ensemble. "Are you ready to go, or do you want to hang out here a little longer," Richard said.

Vance's face dissolved, and his entire being seemed on the verge of melting away into the cracks and ruts of the concrete slab floor. Richard climbed unsteadily to his feet, his back protesting, and he hugged the kid, whose arms hung limply at his sides. Together, he and Eileen managed to maneuver Vance out through the long metal corridor, past an unsmiling checkpoint guard, and into the comparatively fresh air outside. They got to Eileen's Audi and she got the kid inside. A sneaker still dangled outside the car, and Richard gently pushed it in with the rubber tip of his cane. They drove through the fences and gates and soon were surrounded by the water and its relentless lapping. The smell of the river brought Richard back to the time he'd spent drowning in it. He rolled his window up. Manhattan to the right and Queens ahead exploded with light, festivals of human activity, proof of life in this dark place. Vance sat in the dark of the backseat, quietly weeping and reeking all the way back to Park Slope.

———

They installed Vance in the guest room. Over the next two days, while Molly and Eileen were at work, Richard would make the kid food in the kitchen and yell up to him, and Vance would come silently downstairs, retrieve the tray, and vanish again. Richard's culinary talents lay mostly in opening cans and putting the contents in the microwave, but if Vance had any complaints, he didn't voice them. He didn't voice anything—he barely seemed capable of stringing five words together, and any effort at communication seemed to leave him completely drained. He gangled like a half-crushed spider, dragging its innards around as it waited for an abrupt, enormous thumb to come out of the sky and finish it off. Richard worried that something traumatic had happened at Rikers, beyond the inherent trauma of being at Rikers.

He mentioned this to Eileen, and she said, "I think probably he just needs some space. He's had very little of that for weeks."

Molly said, "I know that feeling, too."

Richard also knew that feeling. Despite moments of intense depression over his infirmity, not to mention a natural predisposition to avoid doing things, he finally became so bored and stir-crazy that he attempted a solo walk. Cane in hand, he exited the duplex, boldly humped into the elevator area, and rested for ten exhausted minutes on a decorative settee. In the lobby, he leaned against a row of golden mailboxes as a woman in yoga pants approached from the outside. She unlocked the door, an impossibly heavy oak-and-brass-filigreed portal, and nodded gravely at him as he shuffled through, out into the surprising cold of late November. Retrieving Vance was the only other time he'd been outside in the last month. The building's long burgundy awning stretched out over the sidewalk, and for a minute or two, he stood under it, like a long-distance runner awaiting the starting gun's report. He moved west on Garfield, then north on Seventh Avenue—past a drugstore that called itself a chemist, a grocery store that called itself an urban green market, a liquor store that sold artisanal spirits, and an eye shoppe. It was no wonder people hate the rich, he thought. Even their words for things have to be nicer. Turning the corner and heading east on Carroll Street, he walked past a limousine waiting silently at the curb like a well-trained dog in front of its master—a white building that took up half the block. The delicate black bars on the first-floor windows imprisoned the entire outside world and protected the precious freedom inside. Doormen moodily loomed. As he crutched south again on Eighth, his face was slick with freezing sweat. His poor legs vibrated as he lurched along, and by the time he made the burgundy awning's finish line, he was completely spent, just a shell of his former self. Old, he thought, you're old now. He was still bent over his cane minutes later, when the door opened and, awkwardly enough, the same woman emerged. She sighed and held the door, and he entered, vowing never again.

———

But like most of the vows he'd made during his life, he didn't keep it. He began going on walks around the block two or three times a day, then over to the park and once even all the way down to Midtown. It wasn't exactly that he was getting stronger—his entire body felt the way a clenched fist feels in the morning, ghostly and drained. But though his strength was gone, in its place he found he could get by with a makeshift combination of stupid vanity and sheer plodding force of will.

During these slow rambles, he couldn't decide what he thought about New York, whether it was a place suitable for human existence. The bad aspects of city life were obvious and included things like muggings and subway suicides and diapers filled with shit lying on the sidewalk and emboldened sewer rats that went about their business in broad daylight as though they were just another part of the city's vast citizenry, which, in a way, they were. The good parts were less obvious, but they were there. The life, of course, and the strange beauty of the city. Also, the way the multitudinousness of the population and the population's collective personality pressed on all sides against his own personality and made him smaller. Twenty years ago—ten or even five years ago—this would have struck him as an unequivocally bad thing. Now it felt healthy. The vast space of the desert, far from humbling him, had allowed him the space for his personality to grow unchecked. His ego, his grudges, his desires, lacking any counterbalancing force or presence, had stretched out over the empty landscape like Phoenix's exurban sprawl.

He missed it, too: he missed himself. The hardest habit to break was the habit of selfishness, and he wondered if it was even possible. *Don't surround yourself with yourself,* as the man sang. But did anyone really not do that, really not surround themselves with themselves? Or was the point more that everyone was inclined to crawl up their own assholes, but good people at least made the effort not to, and that effort was what mattered? He wanted to be good, or better, at least. When he'd had similar thoughts before in his life, which hadn't been very often, it had been more that he wanted to want it; he'd felt the lack of moral desire as a void deep inside of himself, in which thoughts of doing good echoed around and quickly dispersed. This intermittent desire to desire unselfishness was, of course, in itself entirely selfish.

But now he really felt different. This difference was small, perhaps, but it was something. He worried about Vance, for instance. He'd expected Vance to pull out of it, but very quickly the kid transitioned from emotional illness to actual illness. He spiked a fever of 103 degrees, and his glands stood out on the sides of his throat like Frankenstein's neck bolts. A doctor came by—the surest sign Richard had yet seen of Eileen's towering personal prestige—diagnosed a pernicious bacterial infection, and couriered over a prescription bottle of enormous white horse pills. Over the next few days, Richard climbed the stairs, dripping sweat onto endless trays of food and water.

The upside to all of this exercise after nearly dying was that he was the thinnest he'd been in at least ten years. His belly had deflated like an air mattress with the stopper out. In the bathroom mirror, his real face—the face he envisioned himself having—emerged from the mask of jowly fat that had covered it for so long. There was even a hint of his teenage self in there somewhere, and it reminded him of being young and looking in the mirror, wondering what his grown-up self would look like. If it was true that you got the face you deserved, he thought, he should have just retained the face of himself at eighteen: evasive, spooked, and ignorant.

———

One day, he returned from a walk to find Vance sitting on the couch, seemingly intent on the black screen of the TV. He stood as Richard caned his way in. "I've been waiting for you to get back before I left."

"Where are you going?"

"Back to Spillman." Vance stuck his hand out for Richard to shake it. "Getting my car out of impound and driving back. I wanted to thank you for helping me out."

"What are you going to do in Spillman?"

"Nothing. What am I doing here?" He lowered his unshook hand.

"At least you're doing nothing in New York City. That's something."

"I have to move back in with my mom."

"No, you don't," he said, a bit more emphatically than he'd expected, and the kid looked surprised. "Your mother is a grown woman. She should be able to take care of herself."

"But she can't, obviously. She needs me. And anyway, you're one to talk."

"And what about your court date?"

"That's not until March. I'll come back for it. Or I'll miss it and just never come back. What's the difference, anyway?"

"The difference is you're in New York now. Okay, so you spent a little time in Rikers Island. So what? Everyone who comes to New York eventually goes to Rikers. But here you are, nineteen—"

"Twenty."

"Twenty, out on bail in the greatest city in the world." He spread his arms as if delineating the contours of a glorious vista, though they were just standing in the smallish living room. "You want to be a writer? Here you are!"

"I'm not going to be a writer. I'm going to see if Pizza Boy will let me have my old job back."

"Jesus Christ, Vance. Take a look out that window. Anything you want out there could be yours. Find a job and a crummy apartment. Get out there and live your life."

"I already tried that. I got beaten up, I got sexually assaulted, and thrown in jail. I've had enough of living my life, thanks. I want to go back to not living my life, it was better that way."

Vance picked up the small plastic bag that contained whatever valuables he possessed. He moved past Richard, then stopped and seemed to be considering a wall outlet for a long moment. "You know, while I was in there, seeing all this horrible stuff—watching my cellmate go through withdrawal, watching guys get beat up and trying not to get beaten up myself, and listening to the crying and yelling all through the night—I kept thinking about something you said when we first met. How everything is bullshit, you remember? I kept thinking about that, and, honestly, it really helped. Goodbye, thanks for everything."

CHAPTER TWENTY-TWO

———

So it was that on a bright late-fall day, unseasonably warm—what he remembered calling Indian summer when he was a boy, although it was probably now known as Native American summer, if anything—Richard set out in the city. He wasn't exactly nimble, but he was proud of how he navigated the turnstiles and stairs, the shuddering subway trains, the packed sidewalks smeared with dog crap, the blaring taxis and blurred cyclists, the ceaseless impedimenta of urban life.

First, the bank. He sat at a Wells Fargo on West Thirty-Third, explaining to the balding, furrowed forehead of the skeptical associate that he wanted to open a second checking account. And close the first? No. The man pointed at the computer screen, noting that four checks had been cashed in Denver over the last month, to the tune of twenty-two thousand. Might his account have been compromised? Not really, he said. Did he want them to investigate? No, he said, never mind, he just wanted a new account. Move the balance to the second one, but leave twenty-eight in the first. Fifty thousand should be enough, he thought, at least for now. He signed two sheets of paper, and that was that.

Then, he talked to realtors. He wore his freshly dry-cleaned green sports jacket with a straight face. (Having almost drowned in it, he now had sentimental feelings about the jacket, fool that he was.) After six hours and three appointments all over Brooklyn, none of which had borne fruit, he limped out of the Nostrand stop. The neighborhood was only on the other side of the park, but it felt about as far removed from Park Slope as you could get. Several blocks east, a brown bantam chicken crossed the sidewalk in front of Richard, huffily flapping its wings, chased by two kids shrieking with laughter. Music seemed to come at him from all directions; after a few minutes of moving through the streets, it started to feel like part of the essential atmosphere of the place, along with the briny smell of cooked meat in the air and the rich layer of grime on the buildings.

The realtor, a brisk and efficient blonde woman who radiated visible annoyance at his sluggish movements, showed him the place, a newly renovated one-bedroom. The apartment was completely empty yet still felt tiny. He couldn't imagine it with furniture. Maybe one carpet in the middle of the room, with a chair on it. A small one. On the other hand, it was clean and didn't seem like the kind of place where someone would off himself in the bathtub.

"It's modest, of course, but livable. Do you need a lot of storage?"

"It's not for me."

"Oh. Your child?"

He looked out the window at the exploding street, the high sun firing off all the windows at once. "Yeah, my son."

"College?"

"Mm-hmm."

"That's nice. You're setting him up."

"Trying to."

"Mine is in high school. A sophomore, but we're already looking at brochures." She shook her head. "It's such a cliché, but they do grow up fast."

"No shit. They sure do."

He signed the lease and wrote out an appallingly large check, shook hands with the realtor, and it was done. As he walked back to the subway, he thought about furnishing the place. A cot, a table, a typewriter on the table. It was all the kid really needed—anything more would be a distraction. A cot, a table, a chair, a fridge full of cold cuts. A nice rug, too. He wanted to make it nice. And he could, still had some money left, despite Black Swan dumping the book and pulping the remaining copies. He hadn't been able to think about any of that yet, though the formal mass apologia he owed Kathleen and Dana and everyone at Black Swan, and lots of other people besides, floated horribly in the back of his mind on the long ride—the jolt, jerk, and jumble—back to Park Slope.

If he did ever write another book, *I'm Sorry, Richard* would really not be a bad title. Or *Richard Lazar: Sorry 'bout That.* But then, no, he was done with books. He was now a full-time—a professional—apologist. Having done none of it the first five decades of his life, he was now condemned to get through his quota in the sixth.

Climbing the stairs at the Ninth Street exit, his legs and lower back felt all six of those decades. A young Sikh wearing a blue silk turban bent and asked him if he needed assistance, but he waved the guy away, too breathless to thank him. Finally having surmounted the stairs, he moved past an Eastern Orthodox church topped with its own swirling turban, and a squadron of middle-school kids all wearing identical T-shirts the neon yellow of highlighter pens. As he walked, he mentally composed the letter he would write. Something about how he'd been wrong. How it wasn't meaningless, or that even if it had been for him, it didn't have to be that way for Vance. That there was an apartment and there was money, some anyway, for now. Enough for at least a year, and a lot can happen in a year, especially when you're nineteen. Twenty now. Get things straight with your mother and come back. I'll probably be staying at the place, sprucing it up. I'll give you the key when you get here. Let me do this.

Sorry, Richard.

He'd been thinking a lot, lately, about his aunt and what she'd done for him as a child. Taking him in, yes, and taking care of him. Teaching him to love books. But mainly, sitting in front of that typewriter every night, trying. Despite having no real hope of being published, she'd sat there with her cigarette burning an oily, yellow furrow in its dish, intent on the white page fluttering in front of her. Because she wanted to, because it felt good to care about something. To give a shit—she'd shown him what it was to give a shit. So after spending half a life trying his best not to, he could think of no better amends now than to give a shit. Lots of it. He would give an endless amount of shit, as much as it took.

Turning the corner left and north toward Eileen's apartment, he found himself a block from Prospect Park. Despite his aching legs, as well as generally disliking parks (on the basis of other people visiting them to have fun), a foolish autumnal nostalgia pulled him toward the green and gold-brown, the soft oranges of the dying year. He entered by the Lafayette monument, the bronzed general gazing at a fixed point in the distance while some poor sucker tended to his horse. He tottered past quiet baseball fields, a lake, into a narrow warren of wooded aisles called the Ravine, and back out onto a large street, down which he plodded along like a blinkered Clydesdale, eyes on the ground, pulling a carriage filled with his entire life. He sat and rested for a bit on a wooden bench, watching people walk past, watching them watch him, content to play the part of the frail, older gentleman cooling his tired heels, since that was exactly what he was.

Growing chilly in the shade of the oaks and poplars that lined the street, he pushed himself up and moved toward a vast neighboring field. A sign on the edge told him it was called THE NETHERMEAD. Every neighborhood, building, avenue, street, road, roundabout, park, green space, and patch of dirt in the city was named, as if to inoculate by proxy the nameless millions from anonymity.

The field was a bright and unlikely emerald bathed in the last hour or so of daylight before the sun would dip below the western tree line. It was filled with people self-consciously, strenuously, enjoying what might very well be the last nice day of the year, and the area was enlivened by a feeling of happy desperation. Richard walked through it all: past an underdressed, laughing couple wrapped shivering in their blanket; through an absurdly circumferous Frisbee circle; by a group of young bearded men in sweatshirts and blazers drinking beer from plastic cups; near two young women of unfair, infuriating beauty; alongside a dreadlocked man in a serape walking a large gray poodle; and finally into a small, unoccupied patch of brownish grass in the middle of the meadow. He lowered himself. The sky was blue, but white clouds edged in over the park's southern and eastern borders, peering down like adults crowding curiously around a newborn's bassinet. *Is baby happy? What does baby want?* He still wanted so much, but just for the moment he tried to forget himself and become part of the overwhelming life that surrounded him. For the moment, it was enough.